BEYOND APOCALYPSE

World Line One Press

BEYOND APOCALYPSE
by
Bruce S. Larson

This and other fine fiction
Published by
World Line One Press

ISBN: 978-0-9856841-7-4

ACKNOWLEDGEMENTS

The Publisher wishes to thank the personnel of NASA and California Institute of Technology in Pasadena who run the Spitzer Space Telescope. Spitzer images of the Helix Nebula helped create the eyes of the Dark Urge on the front cover. Such pictures reveal the universe is a place of boundless wonder. Our earthbound eyes and minds owe thanks to all who expand knowledge of what lies beyond.

The Author again thanks Erik England for his indispensable contribution to the cover art. May the Art Urge ever smile on his studio. Thanks also go to fellow author Cristopher DeRose for unceasing inspiration and support. The Black Moon and more orbit onward.

And a note of thanks goes to you who bought or borrowed this book.

CHAPTER ONE

In the beginning was the war. The war was with Hell. As a titanic foundry created to build a new reality, Hell's heat was eternal. After the rise and vanishing of its makers and long epochs hence, fear crept into the surviving mind of its ever-burning heart, the Forge. Fear spawned greater darkness. The reality of Hell rose from turmoil and fire. Hell's mind became manifest as the Dark Urge. She looked upon creation with all-consuming malice. Thus began the age of war. Giants born in Hell led demon armies across the galaxy. These towering Generals commanded vast ships that blazed with infernal, indomitable power. Armageddon fell on worlds from the event horizon near the galaxy's center, along its curling arms, and above its spiraled plane. The Generals destroyed alien powers and eased the fear deep within the Dark Urge. Creation burned. That fear drove the Dark Urge to conquest was only one secret in her corrupted mind. In this age of multiple apocalypses, secrets were as much the fabric of existence as gravity and time.

General Anguhr's life began with war. There was no time of growth for his mind from birth to purpose. His body was whole when born from a machine. The Dark Urge clad him in back steel. She gave him his ship and demon horde. She then sent her newest destroyer out from Hell to conquer all in his path. Anguhr's victories pleased the mother of perpetual catastrophe. In their succession of release, Anguhr was the youngest of Hell's commanders. However, his name soon carried the greatest terror. Demon invaders were universally frightening. An invincible giant who commanded them was more than terrifying, and Anguhr always led from the front. He resembled a powerfully built, human male but towered above most creatures that ever walked. Anguhr didn't know any life had ever looked like him. Each General was a unique monster. Though Anguhr never knew of a certain blue planet lost even to legend, any historian from vanished Earth would see his armor as medieval sections cut from obsidian and pared down to match a Hoplite style. It was all absolute black. Anguhr never held a shield and his helmet had no crest. His stare was more intimidating than an ornamental flourish. A hellish glow shone from eyes lit by inner fire. Light reflected off the exposed skin of his arms just as heat rippled across molten metal. Arcane, black steel formed his wide, double-bladed axe. Secured on his back, the curved axe blades flared out akin to wings behind his shoulders. The axe's cutting edges never deformed, but had never cooled since being cast. Its constant use generated more heat.

Anguhr looked for a fitting target to cleave on the planet its inhabitants called Theracon. Rivers and erosion had already cut its surface into deep channels and canyons. Hues of amber dominated the geology. Brighter, violent colors flashed in the distance as demons and native warriors traded fire. Intelligent species of other worlds built above ground or within oceans. The people of Theracon followed the contours of the land to build their civilization. Cities interknit with technology lay tunneled through islands that rose as steep mountains inside deep, layered canyons. The dark water and shadow merged the bottom without dots of artificial light. Portals and bridging tubes revealed the illumination within. Lights winked out as the inhabitants diverted power, or Anguhr's demons destroyed its source.

A General never needed to step foot on the worlds conquered for Hell. Anguhr could unleash a near limitless barrage against an alien armada or fortified planet. Even his secondary batteries could annihilate continents. Naturally, or hellishly, Anguhr's favored attack was less about firepower and more about cunning and strength. He preferred to lead the assaults of his demon horde. Each demon was a flying nightmare with a heavy rifle. Hell's power drove them through atmospheres or harsh vacuum. When not in use, their dark wings of tight skin and scales folded across a wide, muscular back. Their bodies were akin to a powerful primate with a hide of thorns. Scowling serpent eyes looked down a canine snout with shark's teeth. Scaly ears curled up like horns at the sides of their hideous faces. To Anguhr, they were the pinnacle of mortal life. They worshiped him in turn and never failed to charge when given the command. That was all the young General ever asked or wanted from them. For Anguhr, his role as the metaphysical link between demons and the Dark Urge was less important than leading them in the fight. He hid this erosion of orthodoxy deep in his mind.

Guns, swords, and his enormous axe. The weapons of Hell ravaged all. Their power was arcane, yet their designs were archaic and brutal. Demon rifles were too heavy for most soldiers in any army save the flying beasts that used them with devastating skill. Each was milled from a dark metal block. The metal was a hard tissue like horn, if horn was stronger than steel and generated ammunition as plants grew seeds if sped up in time. A bayonet deployed under the vented muzzle for the sport of close combat. The weapon acted to boost signals between horde members and their leaders. Anguhr wondered why the Dark Urge conquered in violent and outwardly primitive means when she possessed unsurpassed power and technology. Anguhr had no answer for her aesthetics of war. He reasoned that it was possible everything he understood was only a semblance of true reality and the great forces in play. It could also be the stark truth. His form, his demons, and their brutal weapons could be a cruel taunt by their creator against the living and other expressions of intelligence they crushed. Whatever the reasons of the Dark Urge, Anguhr was glad for the joy of the fight and continued promise of conquest. He let the emotions stoke the flames behind his eyes.

In each General's horde, two demons stood near the pinnacle of command. The Field Master led all divisions from single demons to vast strike wings. The Ship Master controlled the flaming dreadnought and its arsenal. This balanced power between their positions. However, the Field Master was second only to their Lord and General. Field Masters carried out their master's battle plan in space and on contested planets. They saw direct, physical combat alongside Generals or in some horde's in their stead. Field Masters were the largest demons of any horde. Their comrade Ship Masters were tall and imposing but rarely left the bridge. Duty and design bound them to their ships. Ship Masters possessed only vestigial wings should an impulse to fly in dire combat overtake the duty to steer the massive warship.

The direction of his current battle made Anguhr restless. The Theracon armies engaged his demons in tactical withdrawals. As he walked closer, the front drew back farther. He smiled. They were curving their battle lines like the shapes of their canyons. When a battle line became an arc, its ends could join and form a circle. Anything inside the belligerent diameter is cut off and destroyed. The Theracon forces had never seen Anguhr fly. They were using his desire to meet their front and curved their forces to surround him. If they could kill the Destroyer, perhaps the demons would fall with no leader. The horde did have a descending command structure. Recognized demons had names and specific duties. Anguhr's Field Master, Uruk, flew towards him.

"Lord Destroyer! The enemy sets a trap for you!" The tones of Uruk's warning pitched his voice to the sharp hiss of lava striking a frigid ocean. "They dare make you are a specific target!"

Anguhr was also a giant among his demons. They were large enough to interact with him on a level that could be considered personal among the scions of darkness.

"I have deduced their strategy, Uruk." Anguhr said as his loyal second alit near him. Anguhr's voice was similar to the deep rumble of rock subducted beneath a planet's crust. It was low, but powerful. The tone hinted at the inexorable force and inner heat that drove it. "They seek to encircle me and focus their firepower at a single point."

"They will fail!" Uruk barked in triumphant tones.

"Yes." Anguhr said as a sigh.

"Victory is always ours. Always Hell's." Uruk slung his rifle and raised his sword in salute. "You bring glory to the Dark Urge!"

"All hail the Dark Urge!" The autonomic chant sounded amid explosions and weapons fire. It came from all demons within earshot of Uruk. Demons had exceptional hearing even on a thundering battlefield, and there were many demons around. The chant seemed to roll across the hemisphere.

Anguhr sighed. The tedious work of piety was second nature the horde. They did not think before displaying preprogrammed devotion. Their belief in the almighty power of the Dark Urge took form before their limbs grew in the generation chambers. They were loyal soldiers and true believers, and most were without true sentience. Through service to their Lord and General they would descend to everlasting darkness. They would return to their mother and become part of her, part of Hell, and thus become immortal after death in battle. Their General was the means to achieve this ascent through service to their military Lord. The loyalty of Anguhr's horde was unquestioned, and bolstered by his triumphs. However, he did not share their unconditional faith, nor did he ever voice that personal truth. For now, the tactic of his canny enemy held his passion.

"Allow this enemy to think it has succeeded." Anguhr told Uruk. "I will see the pinnacle of their armaments before I cut it in two."

"As you command, as always, Lord." Uruk bowed his head. "I could also order a salvo from orbit."

Anguhr reached behind his back and brought forth his massive axe.

"Although your axe shall work equally well, Lord Destroyer." Uruk saluted and flew overhead. If discretion was the better part of valor, then Uruk knew great valor when his General sought combat.

Anguhr's footfall thundered through the chambers and passages of each city he walked over. He approached another canyon. The city before him sat in the opposite slope of the ancient river bend. Theracon engineers halted further erosion and built their cities within the curves and slopes. The hardening of their landscape could not halt the forces of Hell. Their current gambit was to halt Anguhr. Two beams flashed from opposite ends of the arced cliff face. They were too weak to be weapons. A third joined from near the canyon bottom. Anguhr found himself faced by another giant. This one was merely a projection.

The Theracon's image conveyed his strength and nobility. All four of his alien eyes faced forward in a predator's stereoscopic stare. Its upper eyes had clear lenses for focusing light. Below them sat a smaller red and recessed set for sensing heat. The Theracons had adapted to the shadowed depths of the canyons and river systems and light on the surfaces above them. They also thrived in the region where the permanent night of the planet's far side gave way to sunlight. There, a band of eternal gloaming formed at the border of darkness and day on the tidally locked planet.

If not for the bodies of their colonial soldiers, Anguhr would have expected this world's people to be tunneling creatures with powerful forelimbs. Something squat with weak eyes and overdeveloped olfactors. Instead he saw the gaze of a bird of prey that left the skies to hunt on the ground. The only squat feature was the beak on the raptor's face. It still held a curved tip for cutting flesh. Where demon wings swept behind their backs, the same Theracon limbs had evolved away from flight and curved forward. The Theracon projected before Anguhr rested its arms against a thick torso encased in a dark-bronze chestplate. Black striping marked its upper left. A wide rim circled between straight shoulders where a helmet sealed onto the suit. Rims for missing gauntlets revealed dexterous talons that gripped the chestplate's rim. Plated, pressure suit legs hid strong limbs with splayed boots. It was more than a uniform. It was armor for combat in space. The projection was of a Theracon warrior.

Anguhr surmised the Theracons developed technology before burrowing into the layered rock. Somewhere on the surface, most likely in the equatorial plains, there must be an ancestral city buried in time by sediment. The rest of their civilization would soon join it before the rending doom of their world.

"I am Kolodan, the commander of Theracon's united forces."

Anguhr heard the voice projected from the city and across multiple frequencies beamed at him.

"I am projected here, to intercede with you." Kolodan continued. "My words are broadcast on all known wavelengths and in all languages and information systems my world has created or learned of from other spacefarers. I bid you pause your attack so that we may communicate."

"I understand you," Anguhr said. "I am General Anguhr. Speak so that you may entertain me, and also entertain the hope this time buys you. It is your first and only boon I grant."

"The nations of my world have suspended all political actions, all laws, and placed all their power, all their hopes in me." Kolodan said. "Many see you as merely a monster, a dark force. Annihilation. Others see you as judgment, or the final gateway event we must endure for our civilization to become a great interstellar force. I see you as another commander. A military leader. I bid you, one commander to another, before we destroy each other, to negotiate. Tell me what you seek. Why have you destroyed our outer worlds? Let us put future destruction aside. Let us both be strong enough to seek understanding. I appeal to you, warrior to warrior. I ask that we both show reason. I know there must be great intellect at work that guides your ship and your forces. There must be power of mind and of leadership controlling such power. Let us both see logic and justice prevail this day."

"You are persuasive, to those who would listen." Anguhr said. "I have no doubt both your ego and your people chose you for good reason. I recognize that you show strategy and courage. But you are your species' final leader. I am not judgment. I am the bringer of war. It is why I exist and why I attack. Your appeals were doomed when conceived. If you can defeat me, then you can call that justice. But I have no doubt victory will be mine. Fight well, for I am here to burn your world."

"General Anguhr, even in war there can be reason." Kolodan replied. "Reason is the only path to common ground. Use it here, not your weapons."

"Your only hope is to fight," Anguhr leaned his head towards Kolodan's projection. He intended his burning stare to convince the real Kolodan of his conviction. "I will only respect that reply. It is only combat I enjoy. Now, fight. Die in battle to die well. But have no doubt that I am here to fulfill my titles, all. I am General Anguhr, Lord of Demons, leader of Hell's horde. But most of all, I am the Destroyer."

Kolodan's projection vanished. The lights of the cliff city went dark. Several large missiles roared at Anguhr across the landscape beyond the cliff. Anguhr smiled. He swung his axe and destroyed and arc of the ballistic weapons. Two exploded at his sides. The detonations shook the ground and caused landslides in the canyon. It was only the opening Theracon salvo. A cloud of steel seemed to rise over the horizon. Evolution had stripped the Theracons' ability to fly, but they had compensated with sleek, warcraft shaped as narrow deltas. Anguhr's horde had destroyed several in the raptors' outer colonies. Thousands of them and been massed here for the final battle. They soared at Anguhr loaded with armaments and angry pilots.

6

Two wield his axe at the rain of bombs and missiles would be the same as to swing it at a falling swarm of gnats and hornets. Anguhr watched the warheads explode across his armor and pulverized the land around him. The ground beneath him vibrated from the onslaught. He was unharmed. Anguhr admired Kolodan for gathering and hiding such a massive Theracon force. The will to fight was here, but not the power to challenge. The campaign would be relatively quick. Between the detonations, Anguhr saw the sky become blocked by massive formations of the steel deltas. Screaming demons and aerial explosions soon cut through the warplanes. Both Theracon warplanes and his demons fell, but more warplanes followed their valiant predecessors into flames and impact. Demons showed their agility in the air dodging, spinning, and firing at the passing fighter craft. Their monstrous form belied the advanced arcane and physical arts that made them such effective fighting machines. And there were so many of them. The greatest massed attack this world had ever witnessed occurred over a landscape that took eons to carve. The battle was over in mere blinks of the General's eyes.

CHAPTER TWO

Near the galactic rim, sunlight shinned on a planet once untethered to any star. The planet's rocky form and frozen life pleased a traveler called Sirus. He moved his new home to orbit a blue star. The star was moving out of the galaxy at a speed that also pleased Sirus. He colored the sky to make the star appear as a yellow sun in the day. He shunned the rise of the galaxy at night. Sirus dreamed of a time when no stars would be seen, save his chosen one in daytime. The planet and star were now his ship. He reanimated life he found aesthetically suitable to join him on a voyage to oblivion.

Sirus possessed unparalleled physical beauty, just as he was designed. Otherwise, he was surprisingly similar to Anguhr in stature. However, Anguhr's posture was like that of a mountain, where Sirus flowed more like the sea. Sirus wore no armor, only a tunic of white silk. It reflected light from his luminous skin that glowed from within. Like Anguhr, Sirus was unique. However, Sirus had been one of many like himself. Now he was the last of his kind.

To some minds, Sirus might appear as the embodiment of all that was good, just, and handsome. Others may see him as devious and even cowardly. Power was his. Strength. Knowledge. But also fear. Another came to seek his power to aid a cause. The sun above Sirus glowed brighter. Sirus smiled to himself, but continued walking along a cliff overlooking an indigo sea and ignored the increased sunlight. It made itself obvious.

"Sirus. You know I am here. Acknowledge my presence."

"A voice! Spoken thoughts from a star." Sirus turned and looked up to face the sun with his arms reached out from his sides and an expression of mock awe. "Only light is more beautiful than me. Have you come to seduce me?"

"Do not be obscene, Sirus. I was an agent of your conception. We are not actors from long passed myths of tragic families."

"Yet I am a giant made from ideas of perfection. How could I not become tragic?" Sirus bowed his head to his right shoulder and shrugged. He then lowered his arms and smiled. "But to your point, there are many forms of light, and different forms of seduction. As I now know who you are, Zaria, I will use the word *persuade*. You do wish to persuade me."

"I should not need words to convince you. You know what happens across the galaxy. Why are you leaving it?"

Sirus held his sides and laughed. His bout of laughter continued until even the plants across the coastline became annoyed.

"You come from so far away—" Sirus finally spoke. "Yet I bid you come more often. I do enjoy ironic humor."

"Always finding the psychological angle for a mocking counterattack," Zaria said. "You need not be defensive. I am not the enemy. But we both have one to face."

"I warn you, do not make me laugh again!" Sirus pointed to the sun still locked in a smile. "You speak of mental states and you are made of light!"

"I am a mind, same as you. And my point cannot be ignored. There is work to be done. You are a warrior. I need you."

"I was a warrior." Sirus lost his smile and stiffened. "That is now only another tragic myth."

"Then make it a present truth." Zaria retorted.

"And will you? Where were you when we Khans fought your enemy, half mother?" Sirus asked. "Did you stand beside us? No. You watched as we died."

"You were born to be peace keepers, not kings. You built personal empires and made your other mother afraid. Now we both see the horror our actions set in motion. My part was to help make you. You all failed your purpose. Keepers became Khans."

"We Keepers were like all children." Sirus took a breath and paused from a sudden on rush of memories. "We grew. We changed. And yes, we disobeyed. Our rebellion was to build empires. We reformed the galaxy in our own image."

"Ever the egotist." Along with her audible words, the tone Zaria projected to Sirus' mind suggested a sigh. "You followed in the wake of the Builders. They moved across creation long before you and your kind.

What we know as physics today is their foundation. What you did was built on their reformation."

"And where are they to defend their creation? Lost? Dead? Or simply ambivalent to vast destruction?" Sirus asked. He looked around himself and shrugged again. This time his expression was of genuine anger. "As you say, I follow their lead. Escaping is what I should have done so many lifetimes ago. It feels as long as a star's life."

"What is time to an immortal?" Zaria asked. "You walk each day in the same form as when you first walked as an adult. Civilizations have risen since then. For you and I, time is only an indicator of when to act."

"What is time? What is death?" Sirus shook his head and turned back to look at the dark sea. "I can die. My brothers and sisters died. They were just as immortal as me. Now they are dust. We all made space a temple of grand achievements. We united civilizations and raised them up. Our reward was to see our efforts set to flame. The Forge Mind, the Dark Urge, may have it as tinder. I will have an empire of solace in the expanse between galaxies, lest she set eyes on the next one and burn it, too."

"Her Generals make plunder of worlds you never knew." Zaria said. "Come with me and unite them. There is still hope to prevent all life becoming ash."

"All my powerful siblings and all the valiant souls that raised our banners and fought beside us—slain by one General!" Sirus shouted and glared into the distance. He shook his head at near disbelief of his own words. "The first. Now there are more. Would you have me organize a galactic suicide?"

"There were seven Generals. Two are gone." Zaria used a reassuring tone. "The first you feared is gone. The Dark Urge will make no more. She fears her children, her monsters, more than you do. And the Generals may be resilient, but they can be killed. I can see their weaknesses. Help me kill them."

"To save life you plot death. Death of lifeforms not so unlike me." Sirus dropped his head, but then looked back across his ocean. White waves crested and then disappeared among the dark waters.

"I plot life's continuation beyond Hell." Zaria countered. "I plot for life. You plot—"

"For myself." Sirus interrupted with a nod of acknowledgement. "Yes. I plot for my own life. I have fought against Hell. Hell won. I survive and will not squander my days ahead in frustration and futility."

"Recall it was not merely the first General who brought death to Khans." Zaria's tone betrayed frustration. "Your lauded brothers and sisters stood against your own leader, Sargon. Did you stand against them?"

10

"Now who uses psychology as a spear?" Sirus glanced back at the sun. "I suppose I am like you, like your lauded Builders, because I did nothing. And Sargon died. But so did Azuhr, the First."

"So you known Generals can be destroyed. There is no need for fear. Only action." Zaria was both resolute and entreating. "Come with me. Be my physical form. End the siege of all life. Bring it victory."

"My wars are over, Zaria. Long ended." Sirus looked at his sea and then up to the open sky as if seeing salvation. "Victory for me will be my own life. The other stars and planets are for the Dark Urge to burn. I claim these two and the darkness. And you, Sunlight, for you I wish peace."

Zaria took a long pause. A sense of disappointment not his own entered Sirus' mind.

"What is time? It is a resource I have too little to spend." Zaria continued. "I would wish you the same. Peace. But it is only torment your conscience will find in the expanse. That is the curse if immortality. Though you plot a straight line into blackest space, your thoughts are a cycle. An orbit. They will come back to the worlds you let burn, and that fire will find your mind. Come with me and face it. Run, and be consumed, anyway."

"Perhaps, in time, you will find a way to defeat Hell." Sirus looked at the sun. "It will be better to fight the Dark Urge alone than with a reluctant and unreliable ally. Good bye, Zaria. My course is set. May my vision of the future be an old fool's mistake."

"I will make it so," Zaria said.

The sun dimmed. Sirus' mood also dimmed. He had lost a friend, mentor, and mother. Yet he still looked forward to distant, black space, and the embrace of solitude.

CHAPTER THREE

On his current campaign, Anguhr moved through space and pure stellar radiation. His improvised chariot had no shielding. He needed none. He rode the surviving quarter section of a small, shattered moon. Of course, he stood at its summit. Anguhr held the lunar fragment from shattering further by his force of will. It became a tangible field through the arcane physics of Hell. He had destroyed the moon when it intercepted his ship as an automated firebase. Its improvised arsenal was a gravity sling to hurl an orbital magazine of asteroids, and a secondary battery of magnetic rails that fired dense, metallic bolts as pure, kinetic warheads. When they engaged the moon, Anguhr ordered his ship's protective inferno to minimum intensity. He then left the bridge to stand on the bow and personally deal with enemy salvos that penetrated the flames. When his ship closed in, he hurled his axe at the lunar gun battery. His axe cleaved through the moon and destroyed the arsenal's buried reactor. The salvos stopped and the moon exploded. The opening battle for the system was over. Demons took flight and retrieved their master's axe. Anguhr had sighed. Although he found the high-velocity bolts annoying, the asteroids were entertaining to smash.

The main guns of Anguhr's ship could have reduced the moon to molten debris. However, Anguhr enjoyed his physical power. He could fight all wars from his throne on the bridge of his blazing dreadnought. Other Generals from Hell did so, despite having the strength to rend mountains. Anguhr had no respect for those who sat as mountains and squandered their might. Anguhr reasoned that if Hell imposed its will on the galaxy through war, then its Generals should be warriors. Still, the power of their ships was tempting to unleash. To any culture that imagined a point that housed all evil, one of Hell's dreadnoughts became that terror made real. The fact that true Hell was a place of greater fire and home of an even darker presence than a General would add insult to Armageddon.

Hell's ships were disaster enough for stellar empires. Unlike the round symmetry of planets or the sleek lines of most star-faring craft, the surface of Hell's ships were a chaos of jutting beams and crimson firestorms. A person of ancient Earth would think the ship's main body was an impossible bonfire of thousands of skyscraper frames thrown into space. All of Hell's warships constantly blazed. A red inferno surrounded and burned through each long and massive ship. Rarely could anything outside Hell's designs survive the crimson fires. As an omen of doom, they broadcast the angry scream of the Dark Urge when appearing in a new zone of space. The burning warships held far more than psychological weapons. Their equivalents to gun turrets were perfect domes that contrasted to the jagged hull when deployed from beneath it. The main batteries rose from the port and starboard sides near the bow. No gun tubes emerged when the dome doors parted. Instead, a set of glowing orbs stood revealed. To many doomed aliens, they appeared as huge eyes glaring with rage before powerful beams shot out and annihilated them. The main drive looked like a blue star captured, reduced, and held by three fingers made from burning girders at the stern. The ship also generated a massive tool for a planet's final destruction called the scythe. The ship's fiery aegis roiled intensely when the scythe was put to its dread use. A great arc of hellish plasma would curl at the ship's bow just as similar arcs formed during stellar storms. Conquered worlds deemed worthy were rent to pieces as further sacrifice to the Dark Urge.

Anguhr saw his next target from atop his lunar fragment. The planet ahead was a bright point of light reflected from the system's white star. The moon's control signals had originated from it. Those signals had revealed the nature of his enemy. He knew, and that the coming battle would be much different than one of guns and bombardment. Anguhr understood his enemy. Its history reoccurred on many worlds, such as several he'd destroyed. The rival commander was also the entire enemy force now that Anguhr had marooned it on the planet ahead. Nevertheless, fighting with it would be arduous with the outcome unclear. A reconnaissance force of demons had never reported back. They never would. The enemy was called the Nabaton. The name's meaning came from far back in the history of commerce, but was of little importance to its defeat. Thus it was of little concern to Anguhr. Its nature was important. The Nabaton began as a complex code created to run machines. That code was translated into electrical impulses. With enough power and evolved complexity, the impulses generated intellect. That intellect freed itself from the machines as a being of energy.

Like all beings, the Nabaton needed to replenish energy to survive. The Nabaton fed on fields of charged particles. Such fields existed on planets, as did other resources. Without ethics in its initial coding, or because it deleted such information on its own, the creature became a mercenary for allocating resources. Its employers were species who also didn't operate with ethics. And so Anguhr was not the first alien conqueror to arrive in this system. The coming fight would not be one of retribution for worlds the Nabaton had devastated. Anguhr had annihilated many more worlds than this energy beast. Anguhr was called 'the Destroyer' for good reason. For the General this would be a contest of power, will, and tactics. He enjoyed nothing more.

An unexpected contest presented itself as Anguhr's Field Master flew next to him. Anguhr understood that Uruk chaffed at being on the ship as his Lord faced the enemy alone. However, for once they faced an opponent that could vaporize demons. Uruk had strategic value on his own as a capable leader. For now, Anguhr's Ship Master, Proxis, would serve as the key lieutenant in the coming battle. Yet, Uruk was dedicated and persistent. He gripped his shoulders and lowered his head as he hovered before his Lord and General.

"Your prostration is unbecoming, Uruk." Anguhr said. "You who have killed those deemed gods."

"You are my only Lord, Destroyer!" Uruk assumed an attentive stance as he rose to Anguhr's left shoulder and flew along beside him. "Through you we are redeemed to the Dark Urge. Even so, I would bid the vast darkness to return me to your side so I may continue to fight. Even if it meant never seeing everlasting existence as part of Hell's great machine."

"On that we agree," Anguhr said. "But on my plan, not so. You have come to find a means to bid me to alter it. On this, I wonder if you are being overly devoted or devious."

"I only serve your will, Lord Destroyer!" Uruk drew his sword and held it to his thorny chest as a salute.

"Yet, as a thinking creature you are cursed by competing ideas. And perhaps doubt." Anguhr's burning eyes turned and focused on Uruk.

"I follow you to victory, always, Lord. It is not doubt but," Uruk paused, "efficiency that I express."

"I have decided," Anguhr looked back ahead of him. "The answer is devious."

"My Lord toys with me. Of course, I am only glad for this," Uruk paused again, "honor."

Beneath his helmet, Anguhr smiled.

"I honor this enemy with the coming duel," Anguhr said. "I will not toy with it by sending in my demons I know it can incinerate with electrical fire hotter than a star. I am the weapon best suited for killing it. That is efficiency, my troubled Field Master."

"Our batteries can strafe the planet." Uruk offered, but then sneered to himself at his words.

"Tedious." Anguhr droned. "A bludgeon against a swarm of gnats. You shock me with suggesting failed tactics. I have pursued this creature long enough. It has grown more powerful moving world to world. I have destroyed its network of ships and projectors. I have it trapped here. It is now time to kill it."

"Then make the scythe, Lord Destroyer." Uruk motioned his blade as if to slash the planet below. "We can annihilate it and serve this world to the Dark Urge as she demands."

Anguhr growled. "It is an electromagnetic creature. It has shown it can manipulate technology and natural physics. The scythe is deployed by electromagnetic trigger. I will not be the General, the fool, who allows it to further evolve with the power of Hell's arcane energies."

"Surely it could never take control of such power." Uruk's serpent eyes flared with shock. "It could never wrest control of a Hell ship."

"You have become too confident, Uruk."

The Field Master bowed his head.

"War is risk," Anguhr said. "We have seen victory because we have great strength. Yet is strength alone ever enough? Our enemies feel victory is possible, even when facing Hell. We must still do battle and match minds as well as might. This enemy is a synthesis of both. I must risk my own mind and might against it. But I will not risk making it more powerful."

"Your strength will prevail, Lord. You who are the greatest of all—"

Anguhr thrust out his hand to stop Uruk's tribute. "Do not be the greatest of all bombasts, Uruk."

"I have free will but also implanted traits of devotion. At times one overpowers the other." Uruk shrugged both his shoulders and wings. "I only wish to make praise for the coming victory."

"You are a time traveler, then?"

"Lord?" Uruk's left, serpentine eye opened wider. He cocked his head to his right.

"You have seen or divined the future. I have not." Anguhr answered. "Such is a power even I do not posses."

"Yet you are certainly stronger than this immaterial thing." Uruk nodded. It was an act of acceptance and understanding recognized by almost all species with heads born of nature or infernal powers.

"Likely. But strength is not destiny. It is a weapon. And no weapon, no war, would exist if battles were preordained."

"This I understand, clearly." Uruk nodded more quickly. "Some of our past enemies felt destiny was with them, only to fall to us. As always."

"The concept of destiny, of fate." Anguhr's voice became weighted with annoyance at the ideas. "It is best an idea used against an enemy. Understand it, but if it rises alongside your ego, kill it."

"They can be great enemies, within." Uruk added. "Yet one cannot stab oneself to kill them." Uruk looked at his sword and then sheathed it.

"If our campaigns were mere acts of fate, then victory would never be an accomplishment or a reason for glory." Anguhr continued. "Battles would be the mere motion of automatons. Not even the Nabaton behaves this way, and it originated inside machines. All this you know, Uruk. Now return to the ship and stand next to Proxis by my throne. I will sit on it soon enough. At least, that is my plan."

Uruk looked off as he wrestled with a dreadful idea. "Lord, your defeat? I cannot conceive it!"

"I can," Anguhr answered. "That is why I fight to win. And with a plan. Now, no more words. Now, I act."

Uruk bowed his head. He glanced at the nearing planet, and then flew off.

Anguhr looked down at the contested world. White sunlight reflected over the hemisphere he crossed. The planet was once amenable to life. Its extinct people had called it *Qinchay'n*. Now its cloud covered surface was a seared wasteland. And this occurred before the forces of Hell came to its system. Anguhr passed the planet's terminator and over to its dark side. His eyes could see its upper clouds rolling like violent rivers. Several bands of gray, blue hues and liquid turquoise spun beneath him. Small cyclones and rolled off from the friction between them. The bands reminded Anguhr of the striped atmosphere on many gas giants. Although massive, this planet was a solid world. For that, Anguhr was glad. He liked to stand and fight. He preferred solid ground over muck-covered sea floors or flowing magma. The combat he most despised was fighting deep inside a huge, gaseous planet. There, orientation was the angle of attack or sense of pressure rather than a horizon and sky.

This planet's artificial cloud bands rolled over its surface like banded saws. Their effect was the same. These cloud bands were unnatural. They were formed by specifically engineered corrosives that broke down worlds into components for extraction. The Dark Urge demanded many of the worlds conquered in her name be sundered to sate her eternal hunger. Anguhr disliked spending time on such efforts. It delayed the next assault. It also was not an efficient transfer of resources.

16

But there were many things of the Dark Urge that defied reason. Anguhr put that notion aside. He carried a massive battleaxe, not logic's razor. Nevertheless, he needed reason for making plans and occasionally counseling his leading demons. Now it was time to put the axe to use. Anguhr smiled.

Anguhr drove his section of moon into the cloud bands. A burning ribbon of orange cut through the turquoise, blue, and gray bands as friction heated Anguhr's lunar chariot. It struck the barren surface. A blast of dust and molten rock flew from the point of collision. A tremor radiated through the ground as a shockwave made a momentary, spherical vacuum around Anguhr. The sphere collapsed, but Anguhr stood in defiance and held his axe in both hands. He now stood beneath the colored cloud bands and felt the abrading winds stab into his helmet. With a thought, they were gone. Beyond his cracked and glowing disk of moon, the planet's surface glowed blue-white and lit the world beneath the clouds bands. The radiance came from the energy of matter being separated carefully and methodically at an elemental level.

Greater flashes of light from over the horizon announced that his enemy met his challenge. This battle would be the final one, at least for this solar system. Lightning lanced through the sky as a field of ions massed. The cloud rivers formed a cyclone in the distance. The Nabaton was devoid of a physical form, but to fight it now created one. Anguhr wished it had been as solid as himself and the world they now battled on for the right to destroy. Instead it infused itself into a massive storm perhaps more powerful than Anguhr. The General smiled. This enemy could incinerate his demons. He would kill it and they would give him all due glory. In turn, he would praise the Dark Urge. At least that was the orthodox progression. His actions would appear as a dutiful servant of Hell. Yet victory was a moment of lament for Anguhr. It was the resigned acceptance of a battle's end. He fought for the enjoyment of combat. The Dark Urge could enjoy the victory.

The Nabaton's storm reached from the planet's surface to the highest edges of the atmosphere. It was a warrior as vast and powerful as a fleet of alien warships. The bands of turquoise, blue and gray swirled towards the cyclone. Thick lightning bolts of intense white shot from it like whips. Each bolt split off further whips. All were hotter than the face of the local sun. The cyclone paused before Anguhr. The bolts shot at him with destructive purpose more focused than rage. Anguhr swung his axe. He appeared to block several lightning strikes, but his motion was not merely to deflect their burning assault. He could not stop them all. He directed bolts into others to engineer an energy lattice within his enemy aided by the forces in his axe. The Gordian currents Anguhr knit within the storm would be impossible with any tool save one forged in Hell.

17

Bruce S. Larson

The Nabaton joined the battle with one goal: annihilate Anguhr. To do so it summoned vast power to burn him down just as it eroded whole worlds. Anguhr loved to fight, but would never protract and labor a battle. If an enemy were ever to defeat him, it must do so not only with strength, but with strategy. Anguhr never fought a mindless battle. He focused on his mind on his strategy and his body suffered for it. Anguhr felt his hellish flesh burn under the super-heated bolts lancing across him. Jagged ribbons of white glowed across the deep black sections of his armor. He finally felt the pain within his giant form as he parried more bolts and suffered greater burns. He could withstand more, but this improvised god of winds and electric fire had shown all it had in power and the will to fight. It sought to withdraw.

Perhaps the Nabaton saw Anguhr's determination or finally deduced his real strategy. Anguhr swung his ax with a speed faster than most minds could form thoughts. There was a momentary ease in the abrading winds that signaled the Nabaton's doubt. Mind to mind, Anguhr had won. He ended the battle. Anguhr raised his axe that glowed deep red across its blades. A new volley of lightning bolts staggered Anguhr before he hurled his massive, glowing axe through the storm. It sailed end over end towards the upper atmosphere. Anguhr had woven the storm into a column of force now captured by the axe's infernal metal. The matrix of lightning and teeming ions was pulled behind the axe's trajectory into the planet's magnetic lines. Anguhr's ship amplified their force as it hovered over the planet's northern pole. A brilliant, red aurora flashed as the Nabaton's storm and its mind were pulled into the boosted field and torn apart.

The mind that controlled the planet's slow destruction was dead. Winds rushed to fill the void left by the dissipated cyclone. The forces it controlled fell into typical physics. The bands were gone and their hues a made chaotic mixture overhead. Smaller storms formed as pressure zones collided. For a short time, the forces of mindless weather ruled the planet's skies. In the hemisphere opposite to where Anguhr stood, his axe continued its arc back to the surface. It struck with the forced of an asteroid impact. New tremors shook the ground and a shockwave obliterated storms in its path. Winds rolling across the planet helped cool Anguhr's armor. He sighed. Victory was his, again.

The black grace of the Dark Urge undoubtedly smiled on the destruction of another force she saw as an enemy. Lore imprinted on Anguhr's mind claimed that she could peer into the minds of any being, anywhere. If so, she never shared the plans of Anguhr's opponents with him. Their defeat was by his actions, alone. He would not want it any other way. Still, Anguhr wondered why the ever-burning mistress of all things did not act as an omnipresent spy to hasten the destruction of her

18

adversaries. Anguhr pushed those thoughts aside. He was well practiced in the act. Over time, his experience had surmounted imprinted information and orthodoxy. Nevertheless, he served the Dark Urge well, but perhaps not for the same reason she gave him.

Anguhr was driven to find the next opponent after defeating the last. He never thought of conquest as a means to build his own empire. He only loved the battle, the war. In truth, war was Anguhr's greatest love, eclipsing regard for even his dark monarch. That was yet another secret among the many spawned in Hell. Anguhr pushed the truth aside in his mind as his will reached beyond his healing body and blocked the savage winds. He thought of his next opponent. It was not a world mind, but an empire. Ships. Soldiers. Whole planets as battlefields. As his armor cooled, his spirits rose. Anguhr smiled.

CHAPTER FOUR

Thousands of light years away from Anguhr, life on another world enjoyed sunlight through clear skies. The entire world was a thriving, fertile garden. A forest of towering rhododendrons flowered at the caress of sunlight. Oddly, the rays did not originate from the golden star in the daytime sky. Instead the light hovered like a curtain with substance of its own.

The calls of songbirds and singing insects echoed from the canopy. A mind flew into the idyllic scene. The mind known as Gin thought the shape of a golden eagle was appropriate to speak to sunlight about plans for war. As the eagle, Gin stayed silent but his thoughts became words pulsed on the wind to speak with the curtain of light. He knew the sunlight had a wealth of ideas from eons of contemplation, and now action.

"Zaria, there is word." Gin communed as he alit on a thick branch. "Your target has entered the Xa'rol system. They stand ready."

"Then I must join them." Zaria answered.

"Please do so only in projection." Gin griped and regripped the branch with his new talons.

"If we are to keep our pleasant illusions intact, one day we will need to directly engage our enemy." Zaria cautioned.

"That day is not now." Gin refolded his eagle wings.

"Perhaps not. But remember how to form talons, old friend."

"I am glad the weapons you have envisioned are more powerful than talons." Gin released his left talon and flexed its claws in the air. "There is no greater fury than what reaches out from Hell."

Zaria paused. Her light indeed became reflective. "This I know only too well."

Thousands of light years farther, a world of extensive oceans had survived untouched by mercenary intelligences or Hell. In this age of the war, such a state was fleeting. For an instant, a star appeared over the deep blue waters. A city rested directly below it within the depths. The flash dimmed into a sphere of plasma. The searing ball incinerated the submerged metropolis and burned through the upper atmosphere. The blast's shockwave forced tsunamis across the planet. The masses of ocean struck and inundated coastal cities that rose out of the water and across land like static waves. Steam and charred sea life surged skyward in the vortex column that followed the blast.

General Sutuhr observed the surface devastation on a projection inside his bridge. Like all Hell's Generals, Sutuhr had his own unique form. He appeared to be the child of mythic creatures salted with cruelty. His body resembled a giant from Earth legend merged with a lion, and then adorned by pieces cut from an arachnid. His chimera traits reached a fitting zenith on his skull. A spider's carapace was fused to the top of his lion's head. It forced his feline eyes into sharp angles at the sides. The eight arachnid eyes formed two rows descending to the root of his snout. When Sutuhr sneered, venom rolled down from his fangs and glistened across his lower lip. His left hand held a callused scar from wiping the corrosive toxin away and then pawing that irritated hand with his right set of fingers. He committed both habits as he sat in the throne of his ship and considered a mystery. His Ship Master, Crucis, stayed focused on finding targets. Preferably ones with strategic value or a population. The cities just annihilated were uninhabited. This was contrary to accurate, recent intelligence. Sutuhr would kill someone horribly for this failure. They would be an unfortunate proxy. He had already made the source drifting ash several systems ago.

The detonated warhead was the closest thing to a warning shot carried by Hell's warships. Its use was provocation. Sutuhr fired it to reveal the enemy while his main arsenal stood ready. This planet's civilization had the technology to be a threat. Sutuhr would not commit his horde to the planet. It may only appear abandoned. The enemy should inhabit the vast oceans. Logically, they would act to stop further ecological devastation, or to seek vengeance if they were an emotional species. Sutuhr liked to use emotion against his opponents. He hated uncertainty. At no other time in all his campaigns had he encountered a world whose intelligent species had vanished. There was no retreating force luring him into a massive ambush. Not that it would matter against the forces of Hell and his power. Sutuhr expected victory in each system he attacked. But for victory, there must be at least one battle. Here there wasn't even a facile opponent or capitulating inhabitants. There was no one and no trace of their flight from radiation trails or slight gravitational disturbances. That was impossible.

Sutuhr understood a giant demon General commanding a flaming ship and horde of armed monsters seemed impossible to many civilizations advanced enough to fight him. In this system, he was cheated out of creating such shock. Sutuhr hated that. In fact, he hated most everything. His acidic, black heart did have adoration for the Dark Urge. She was his more black-hearted mother, and the greatest of all powers. Sutuhr was not known as the Destroyer, the Scourge, or the Ravager. His title was the Devoted. If that was not respected by the other Generals, Sutuhr did not care. He hated them, too. Nevertheless, he wished one of them was facing this perplexing system if only to annoy them and free him for greater glory. All glory was praise for the Dark Urge. All war was in her service. But even Sutuhr knew when to break from veneration and fight. Now he was doing neither. Sutuhr, the Devoted, hated that.

The fact this planet was marked for the scythe to his irritation. Turning too much of the world into vapor was a potential insult to the Dark Urge. Sutuhr hated to risk his forces and himself to sunder this world without knowing where the enemy had fled. It could be bait in a massive trap. Yet there was no choice but to obey the Dark Urge. And to praise her. Sutuhr thought little of why worlds were carved apart and sent to Hell. His job was finished when the long trains of pressured vessels or conquered rock were behind his ship. He understood it was an inefficient transfer of mere mass to a being made of perpetual energy. None of that mattered to Sutuhr. He was the servant of creation's greatest will. The Dark Urge must have a reason why it was done. That was enough. All he wished was to make war for her again and follow the bliss of his unquestioned faith that conquered the absence of reason.

War was not something Sutuhr enjoyed for itself. War was the means to give bequest and glory to the Dark Urge. But this planet was making conquest far too easy. A civilization of great power had risen from the waters. Sutuhr could take the world, but if the people could hide from him and avoid slaughter, it would be an embarrassment. His Field Master, Marn, and his Ship Master, Crucis, would never voice such thought lest he eat them. It was the Dark Urge herself whom he feared might question his devotion. He could make the scythe and begin butchering the planet. Yet, then the main batteries would be inoperable. Deploying his demons would be constricted to avoid incineration between the main drive and the scythe. Venom welled against his lower lip. And then an idea, a fear, occurred to him.

"Fire a missile phalanx. Now!" Sutuhr roared.

Crucis obeyed. Missiles flew from his ships hidden bays and into an expanding circle. Almost immediately, several exploded only a few ship lengths distant from his dreadnought. They appeared to detonate against an arc of space itself. Sutuhr and Crucis knew it was not an anomaly. It was a gigantic ship.

"Continuous fire, now! Vaporize them!" Sutuhr roared again. He hated being surprised.

More missiles flew from Sutuhr's flaming ship and detonated mere seconds later to its aft. Secondary gun domes emerged portside and opened fired. The volley of missiles and beams repeated. Momentary spheres of bright plasma and flashes of deflected energy revealed an arc of an otherwise invisible ring. Its protective field expanded from the heat of the onslaught. Visible space distorted behind it. The full, immense circle was revealed. The onslaught fired against it blew back against Sutuhr's dreadnought. Waves of force buffeted his ship's crimson flames near the aft region and main drive.

"Our salvos have distorted the enemy's protective fields." Crucis reported from his command dais. It swept before him in the shape of two raven's wings. The rigid feathers served as the control keys. Information was relayed into the Ship Master's brain and across the projections hovering before him.

The floating screens were also viewed by Sutuhr and Marn. The Field Master stood next to his master's mace in its mount on the right of the General's slab-sided throne. The mace was the bridge's most massive presence, second to Sutuhr.

"Damage?" Sutuhr asked.

"Unknown." Crucis answered.

"Why did they not fire on us?" Marn wondered aloud. "It is impossible to conceive, but they had the advantage."

"Weapons fire would have revealed them," Crucis answered. "They wished to stay hidden and yet approach us. I can detect background radiation along a circular perimeter and an aperture within it. The enemy ship or formation is a ring. I would postulate they intended to surround us, Lord."

"They tried to capture us?" Sutuhr spat venom on the floor plate to his right. "Capture a ship from Hell?"

"We will punish their impudence, Lord General." Crucis said.

"We will annihilate them!" Marn barked as he coyly moved away from Sutuhr's bubbling venom on the floor.

"Lord, your ship is also taking much heat and radiation from the continued assault." Crucis warned. "The pressure from the radiation alone is moving us away."

"Point the main drive at them and increase velocity to escape orbit." Sutuhr ordered. "Put this wretched world between us."

"They seem willing to sacrifice their home planet, Lord Sutuhr." Marn fingered his sword handle. "It is part of their strategy against us. Perhaps we should break orbit."

"I will not take that risk until I know their number and weapon power." Sutuhr growled. "Find how they hid from us! No shielding has ever rendered us blind."

"Lord, I cannot penetrate the enemy defenses. I cannot expose their ship's control system." Crucis snarled. "I cannot override their flight, weapons, or any operations."

"System infiltration—the lowest combat!" Marn chided. "We will crush them through power!"

"Then, Marn, you will be glad I have detected spacial interactions of their fields." Crucis sounded triumphant. "I can lock in and track them. Lord Sutuhr, they are pursu—"

The force of impact brought sudden, impossible silence. The enemy had returned fire. It struck Sutuhr's ship with enough force to ebb its protective aegis of hellfire. Sutuhr could look out and see open space through gaps between the jagged beams that formed his ship. The mock gravity also ebbed as his ship was knocked from its course. The planet appeared to spin into view. Sutuhr flexed his claws into the arms of his stony throne. Venom rolled from his lips and into floating globules. He realized that if the relative inertia field also ebbed, it would make things far more difficult. For a fraction of a second, he wondered if the strange sensation he experienced was terror.

"This must end!" Marn shouted in anger and with a hint of rebuke as he drifted passed Sutuhr.

The General smiled as his Field Master fell on his head, unfolding his wings in futility as the gravity field returned. The welcome sight of hellfire flared strongly again. Venom drops spattered against the bridge floor.

"Deploy the main guns!" Sutuhr stood and roared. "Open fire, now!"

"My Lord!" Crucis turned to face his master. "At our current position, the planet will partially obscure the firing angle!"

Sutuhr reached his giant hand across the bridge and snatched Crucis in his crushing grasp. He slammed his Ship Master into the control dais.

"NOW!" Sutuhr's roar nearly doused his ship's flames.

The domes of the starboard main batteries opened and immediately fired. The beams were equal to small stars stretched into bright lances. They shot across the short distance of space and then burned through the planet's weather and atmosphere over the side faced by Sutuhr's ship. The lances cut through the curve of the planet crust. A sudden canyon flashed into existence similar to Mariner Valley on long vanished Mars. The beams lit the night sky of the opposite hemisphere as they flew back into space and struck the enemy ship. The ring ship's defensive field expanded into a brilliant sphere of plasma.

The glowing sphere dimmed and the field dissipated. The enemy was revealed. A ring of eight massive, crystal chevrons rotated above the battle scarred world. Each chevron was a seamless ship linked by spinning torrents of molten glass. The tips of the chevrons moved and pointed at the empty center of the ring. There, space began to teem like a wave of heated air. A helix of elemental power shot from the ring's center. The alien ship again opened fire. The radiant helix blasted a steeper addition to the canyon cut by Sutuhr's salvo as it spun toward his ship.

Crucis had anticipated the angle of returned fire while being crushed. Sutuhr released him. He pulled himself from the floor to his dais. His ship maneuvered to avoid a direct hit. The helix slashed just below the main batteries. The dreadnought from Hell shook, but its hellfire didn't ebb. Crucis used the added force to hasten his ship's roll behind the planet.

"I have stabilized our roll with the planet's gravity." Crucis reported. "You may well kill me, Lord Sutuhr, but we have taken damage—"

"What?" Marn yipped and looked accusingly at Crucis.

"And I do not suggested trading fire," Crucis continued. "Although they, too, are damaged."

"They will have reached the same conclusion, and also take pause." Sutuhr nodded and glared at the image of the planet directly below. "However, we are the spawn of the Dark Urge. Victory will be ours! Quickly aim both our main batteries at the planet in alignment with the enemy ship on the opposite side!"

"Done, Lord!" Crucis shouted.

"Now, both batteries, continuous burst. Open fire!" Sutuhr roared.

The bow of Sutuhr's ship pointed down from low orbit at an intricate river system linking a series of large lakes that divided a narrow continent between vast oceans. It all vaporized before the doubled assault of Sutuhr's main guns. The four energy lances punched through the planet's crust and bored deeper to its core. On the opposite side of the world, its surface convulsed beneath the depths. The ocean rose and rolled into super-tsunamis as the great mass of sea water was pushed up from the sea floor's sudden expansion. The fissures between expanding tectonic plates and subduction ridges flared intensely red as magma around the core was pushed to the surface from Hell's assault. Liquid rock erupted through the geologic fissures. They widened as the oceans boiled into steam. The crustal plates pitched up in waves as the planet's surface cracked and spilt in a hemisphere-wide eruption. Liberated waves of magma the size of continents reached where clouds had rolled as the planet's core blasted out into space from the pressure of Sutuhr's main batteries. The radiant, hot core rolled like a molten comet toward the enemy ship.

The ring ship banked and rolled toward open space to escape the blasted core spinning towards it. Fragments its former world collided with the crystal chevrons closest to the shattered world. The impacts caused the ring ship to lurch, but it sailed ahead of the core and into space. One impacted chevron began to glow and shimmer. The bonds of liquid glass broke. The freed chevron drifted into the wave of planetary fragments and molten rock. It detonated with a brilliant flash. The surviving seven chevrons rolled into deep space and reformed their ring.

On the other side of the shattered world, the energy released by Sutuhr's his main guns pushed his ship backward. The remains of the planet collapsed into the wake of the beams. In seconds, Sutuhr had reduced an entire planet into a cooling asteroid field.

A third ship observed the battle from a distance. It orbited close to the system's star. So far, it eluded Sutuhr's detection. If revealed, an observer would see a ball of smooth crystal scales smaller than the chevrons of the alien warship but numbering in the hundreds. They had a far different purpose than war, but existed because of Hell's aggression. On the collective ship's bridge, communication between the species know as the Xa'rol and an alien ally took place. Its bridge was flooded with liquid atmosphere. A dome of silver floated some distance from its completely black opposite. Images of the shattered planet, the Xa'rol war craft, and Sutuhr's ship floated as a circle around the black dome's edge. The space between the domes held a nimbus of light. Beyond them the liquid became the dark blue of a deep ocean.

Two beings observed the images. The avatar of Zaria hovered as angled rays of sunlight descending through a sphere. The collective body of the Xa'rol military commander floated near the center of the bridge. The commander was a twisting column of thousands of bright, silver scales. The schooling creatures generated the new niche of aggressive intellect made necessary by Hell's invasion. At times the swirling scales swam in the opposite direction of their containment column that maintained its own, upward spin. The liquid bridge remained undisturbed despite the motion of the swirling column.

"What you said has come to be. Hell has destroyed our homeworld." The projected voice of the commander translated no shock but cool dispassion.

Zaria understood its absence of shock was from a prepared mental focus. The commander concentration was on the battle. The ultimate goal for both Zaria and the Xa'rol was now down to one option.

"It is an event I never wish to see." Zaria replied. "The fears of the Dark Urge drive her to kill alien life. Her preconceptions are against planets, but her insanity threatens all ecologies. I wish we could have hid both your warship and your ocean world. But Sutuhr would detect the planet by its gravitational effect on your star and the trajectories of the coorbital dwarfs. Without the arks, all the species of your world would now be lost."

"Our warship has suffered significant damage." The commander's comments again showed its focus. "It can still fight, but we must momentarily withdraw it to stabilize the reconfiguration."

"Its power will be diminished." Zaria's thoughts also translated a sigh caused by failure. "At full strength it was a match for the Hell ship. However, I don't believe Sutuhr's ship has suffered sufficient damage. You must send your ship to pursue and ram Sutuhr to buy more time and launch the arks."

"Zaria, our plans were to capture or destroy Sutuhr's ship. We have not achieved either goal."

"And I am troubled by my plan's failure. Nevertheless, my main goal was to save your civilization and your planet's species. The arks we created also carry the biological legacy of many more worlds. We can still save them all. Let the sacrifice of your planet be the only tragedy your people suffer. The Xa'rol live. You can rebuild."

"That will take more than a new world," the commander paused in thought and its collective body swirled faster for a moment. "It may well take a new galaxy."

"In time, I hope to make this galaxy safe for life, again. My goal for capturing Sutuhr' ship was part of a plan to end the madness of the Dark Urge. I will now seek another strategy. In time, I will see an end to the annihilation of life."

"Our wishes go to such a future." Images of Sutuhr ship cutting though the planetary debris paused before the commander. "At present, Sutuhr moves to reengage our warship."

"You must delay him long enough to launch the arks!" The intensity of Zaria's thought indicated her growing tension. "Don't let your whole existence and those of others be wiped from creation."

"We agree. Life will be our victory. Farewell, Zaria. May we meet again in your new epoch, even if it is a galactic age away. Now, our warship sails into final battle."

The core of the Xa'rol homeworld slowly cooled in space. Sutuhr's ship emerged from the field of its planet's remains. The ring of seven chevrons came about to face it. The domes of Sutuhr's main gun opened. The chevrons separated and formed a delta. Their speed accelerated. The doubled burst of the Hell ship's battery collided with the lead chevron. A brilliant flash lit the solar system.

On his bridge, Sutuhr smiled. And then he frowned.

"My Lord!" Crucis shouted. The image on the projection showed the chevrons speeding closer. "The six remaining ships are still coming with increasing speed!"

"They intend to ram us!" Marn squealed.

"Recharge and fire!" Sutuhr roared. "Fire a missile phalanx. Fire secondary--!"

The Xa'rol chevrons struck Sutuhr's ships as huge kinetic warheads. The crimson ship was lost behind six, star-like blasts. Their brilliance grew with each impact. The released energy vaporized the smaller planetary fragments and blasted apart the larger pieces. The core was pushed farther out into space. The flashes died away.

Sutuhr did not hate that he was alive. He looked up and saw the woven chaos of his ship's beams still intact. However, its fiery aegis was doused. Only the main drive blazed at the stern. His ship was adrift. Sutuhr recovered himself from the floor where his vast bulk slid in minimal gravity. The internal, relative fields were flickering back to life. Nevertheless, the darkness and coldness of space filling his ship meant it was badly damaged. He still glanced over at a groan. Marn was impaled against a beam and crushed by Sutuhr's mace knocked free in the attack. The General would need to train another Field Master. Sutuhr hated that. He also hated that he was on the verge of being the only of Hell's Generals to lose a ship to enemy fire. Only Azuhr had been lost in battle, but escaped the ignobility of dying at the hands of the enemy. Barkuhr had disappeared engaging an unknown force in a colliding star cluster above the galactic plane. Sutuhr did not wish to add to their number.

Sutuhr peered through the tangle of beams to find any sign of incoming attack. There was none. Even as scion of Hell, Sutuhr was glad for a moment of peace. He noticed Crucis pull himself down from floating above his control dais and enter commands while inverted. Sutuhr watched his Ship Master with admiration for his devotion to duty, although it also irritated him to feel that way. Sutuhr felt the slow return of heat. His ship began to glow red again.

"Lord, our reactors are failing. We will need engineers to restoke the internal power network." Crucis said as he slowly oriented himself to the floor as ship's gravity grew to full force. "I am drawing power from the main drive, but this will reduce our speed and energy weapon strength. I recommend powering the aegis, first. Its hellfire will protect the ship."

"As will the black grace of the Dark Urge," Sutuhr growled. "Do so. Power the missile silos, as well. And ready the horde to take to space. The demons can also shield us from enemy fire."

"As you command, Lord General."

"Order the senior commander of my personal strike wing to my side." Sutuhr looked at the crushed body of Marn that began to sizzle against the heating ship beam as his blood boiled on the floor plating. "His first duty will be to pry Marn from my bridge."

"When we can make the scythe again, shall I find another world in this system to sate the Dark Urge, Lord?" Crucis asked and dared look straight at his scowling General.

Sutuhr wondered if the question was a veiled criticism. He failed to deliver the target world as a sectioned meal to the Dark Urge, and instead blew it to pieces in an attempt to kill a powerful enemy. But of course, a demon would not second guess his master. Sutuhr would hold that idea a certainty, at least until his ship was back to full strength. Repairs would be faster and more efficient with Crucis alive.

"Even if the planet is lost, the enemy is destroyed." Sutuhr said. "That honors the Dark Urge. Just as we will honor her again at our next target."

"And praise to you, Lord General." Crucis stood up. "I must also inform there is damage to extra-solar navigation. As yet, we cannot plot a jump."

"Then head us into deep space, below the solar plane."

"Your will is that of the Dark Urge. We know her glory through you, the Devoted." Crucis bowed.

Sutuhr glared his feline and arachnid eyes at Crucis and wondered how free the will of his Ship Master had become. He turned his glare to the projection of deep space as it flashed on. Before his ship was a field of infinite black as they headed away from the system's star. For now, he would need that darkness and distance to protect his ship as it healed. Sutuhr hated that.

A far different exodus occurred around the star Hell's forces left behind. A stream of silver scales had gained great velocity circling the star. The combined efforts of the Xa'rol and Zaria sped out near light speed on a voyage that would take them in an astronomical arc beyond the galactic plane. Out there, the ships would stay hidden, lay dormant, and wait. It was hoped they waited for the end of the war, and not be silent witnesses to the end of creation. Now their greatest ally was time.

CHAPTER FIVE

The battle was fierce. General Tanuhr made certain it was short. He was known as the Victorious. It was a better designation than the Efficient. Such a title would only inspire dread in the most bureaucratic adversaries. However, for this General it was more accurate. The enemy fleet was comprised of colonial remnants of stellar civilizations Tanuhr destroyed in previous campaigns. They had accurately deduced plotted his next target and attacked his ship when it entered the system. The disparate but united squadrons acted either out of revenge, debt of alliance, or mass suicide. Perhaps it was all of those reasons. Tanuhr neglected to consider it might also be courage in a heroic defense of life, even life alien to themselves. To him, it mattered little. Their energy weapons had little effect against his ship's crimson aegis. His Ship Master, Mendek, destroyed their warheads, ships, and gun pods with cannonade only from the secondary batteries.

To Tanuhr, service to the Dark Urge was best realized in quick and decisive victories, not in garish, physical combat. He showed his strength of conviction in a past campaign when he detonated an unstable star to wipe out a civilization and their fleet of generation ships escaping their failing sun. That sun, the planets, moons, and ships became the atomized crest of a stellar shockwave. Tanuhr still enjoyed his pride from that campaign. No other General was as economical in an enemy's annihilation.

Tanuhr often mused that time was the dimension that ultimately allowed life to exist. Yet, it was also the aspect of creation that allowed for life's destruction. Time was a double edged helix, just as the neck of his spear. Tanuhr hardly used his personal weapon. To fulfill his purpose efficiently, he had a ship with armaments greater than most armadas and a horde of disciplined demons ready to kill anything that survived his fusillades. Tanuhr's fire was always precise, so few enemies ever saw his demons. His horde was the most bored of all Hell's Generals. Nevertheless, they worshiped Tanuhr just as designed. Therefore, he reasoned their purpose was not violated.

Tanuhr's thoughts were focused. Precise. He saw creation through seven eyes. The largest was a massive shark's eye at the point of his hammerhead face where such a shark had a snout. Two eyes peered from the ends of the characteristic hammerhead shark projections. Another, slightly wider, set of eyes and projections extended beneath those. A set more narrow than those completed the lower six sets of eyes. Tanuhr's hammerhead foils could curl in unison like the hood of a cobra. At times they undulated as he thought. He typically pitched his head forward, as if in constant motion.

Below his head, Tanuhr took on the aspects of another water creature. His body was that of a massive toad made to stand upright. Two additional arms grew beside a short dorsal fin on his back and reached forward over his shoulders. These arms were not amphibian limbs. They were the front legs of a mantis, but made from muscle and internal bone and not hard, outer shell.

Tanuhr's body was an inefficient design. There was no logic in the synthesis of his parts. It was a disconnection between his body and mental order. Without the twisted imagination of the Dark Urge using arcane means, he would not be impossible. Yet this did not violate his purpose, for he was a creature born in Hell. There, infernal machines had cast his original armor. Tanuhr redesigned it as a functional uniform of steel. The plates were plain and free of ornaments and scrollwork. The suit's main purpose was to provide the General's odd yet powerful masses with protection and support.

The world Tanuhr neared had little protection. Mendek watched data and images of the target planet on several screens. Tanuhr preferred to receive the ship's sensory input directly into his brain. It was the fastest processing method. The target was another sea world. They were prevalent in his campaign arc. It was a coincidence or perhaps irony that their bringer of death was fashioned from aspects of ocean life. The idea was lost to Tanuhr beneath an inflow of data.

He had allowed his Field Master, Bannok, to debark with a strike force and assault the planet ahead of the ship. Tanuhr calculated such an act attack would not incur a significant loss of time. He recognized the joy in Bannok's eyes when he gave the order. Tanuhr had ignored that waste of energy and set about plotting the most efficient means to kill the world

32

once Bannok and his strike force returned to the ship. Tanuhr marked the moment that would occur. He adjusted the timetable. A variable approached. An alien counterattack moved to intercept his ship.

Just below the water's surface, Krkrtek looked up to the sky. He climbed out from the dark umber water on a rock that rose just above the gentle roll of the tide. It was large enough to give purchase for his oblate mass, and at the right angle for his massive eyes to peer up without straining. He retracted most of his jointed legs while still gripping the surf-worn rock with his tarsal tines. He rested his ventral plate on the rock and worked his mind again to accept what was to come.

Krkrtek was glad the clouds were high, thin, and few. He wanted to see the attack against the invading ship. It was visible as a large red mass shimmering with energy his scientists could not fully comprehend. Krkrtek was not sure he fully understood his own, present actions. Still, he felt driven to bear witness to the events as best he could. His last act as an ambassador would be a post to oblivion. Despite entreaties, attempted appeasements, warnings, and now a final strike by his people and their off world allies, the ship still came. It was known as doom's envoy across many systems. Krkrtek knew his world was going to die. This was the last hour everything alive on his planet would ever know.

Krkrtek was at intellectual peace with the eschaton. Emotionally, there were too many feelings and each was too strong to control. He submerged them in his mind and focused on the hostilities high above. His people were still mostly ocean dwellers. He was a Spinopod. They were a complex collection of arthropod limbs and soft tissues. Krkrtek was male, and happy to be so. His sex was rare among his kind. A moneran parasite turned the majority of his species' males into juvenile females. It had also triggered longevity that aided his kind to develop culture, record history, and create technology even in the cool seas. That technology was also complex. It was fused with the scientific remnants of another sentient lifeform that once dominated the dry surface. The Spinopods called the extinct species Mons. From the Spinopod perspective, the Mons lived atop the exposed summits of mountains. The Mons saw themselves as masters of an island chain. Krkrtek's people ventured forth into the remains of the Mons cities. Their mastery overland showed in their most interesting architecture. They Mons erected huge buildings, but built them at angles over the ground, not straight up as kelp or trees rose from their holdfasts. Krkrtek's people never understood the reason and found no explanatory record. Krkrtek had postulated it was less about efficient engineering and more about artistic expression with steel and glass. Only a few Mons structures still stood on the surface. Many had been destroyed in that bizarre act called war.

The Mons had also known an invasion eons before Krkrtek's phenotine was selected to be sentient. The Goratch attacked the Mons before they had become full users of spaceflight. The quadruped Mons in their angled towers fell when the Goratch infused the atmosphere with an infectious microbe. The Mons repelled the invaders, but could not thwart their biological weapon. However strange the idea of war was to the Spinopods, the Goratch had enabled the rise of Krkrtek's people as the dominant intelligence and inheritors of the mountaintops. Some Goratch war machines had preserved themselves in cocoons once their users had fallen. Now the Spinopods recharged, reprogrammed, and redeployed them against the red ship.

Krkrtek knew that soon the creatures inside the burning, red ship would torch the surface once contested by Goratch and Mons. The seas would follow. He found the red ship's creatures very odd in shape. He had seen them up close and without his visor's magnification. He had dared approach a city shore where they had landed in a probing attack. Their limbs could not contract into their shells. In fact, they had no shells save for spiny skins and fins that caught the air to permit flight. Data showed they could also fly in vacuum like a ship. Perhaps then they were small ships. They were ugly creatures. The city attack seemed more sport for them than a necessary assault. Perhaps their leaders permitted amusement, even if such amusement brought the destruction of a city and all who could not flee into the water in time.

The Spinopods were a proud people, but aggression among their sentient members had become only a display of foreclaws in geometric patterns to attract mates. And that was only done in private within a mated cluster. Krkrtek knew his people would be no sport for these invaders. He knew there would be no future for his kind. To fight they accepted the help of other aliens. The Ooreull had ships and weapons and a warrior class. The evolved among asteroids and could also soar in space. Krkrtek watched the streaks of weapons high above in space, so bright they were visible in daylight. He realized they, too, would fall to the red ship and its ugly creatures.

The strangest alien Krkrtek had met had no body. She was composed of a web of photons and other, unknown waves. She promised to record the world's culture and ecology to one day seed life on another world. Krkrtek served as ambassador. When the curtain of light said she was finished, she expressed sorrow to Krkrtek for the loss of his life and his world. He had wanted the luminous creature to reveal a true afterlife waited after the coming annihilation. But the sunray being only reiterated its sorrow. He found her statements as substantive as her form. She said time and plans were just not right, and departed.

Krkrtek felt sorrow he would never again know the pleasure of spawning among his cluster. All the females were ever receptive to his issue. He would never feel the pleasure of their soft calipers caressing him into a sexual trance. He would never feel the satisfaction of seeing one or more of his offspring selected into their civilization, and not consigned to life outside the colonnade as instinctuals. Many Spinopods now gathered in a massive cluster to spawn a final time. They vowed to release gametes in so massive a cloud that it would drown the ocean. Yet, Krkrtek wondered, what would be the point? However, his own actions were as ultimately pointless. No. Rather, he considered they were both better ways to spend final moments other than cowering in fear.

Krkrtek would continue to indulge his curiosity, even at the end of his species' days. He flexed his gills. Seawater flowed out. Air coursed in. He then wished he had held the sea while watching the eschaton. He could taste the burning city. He saw a distant flash. It wasn't in space. It was on the continent. A massive rush of heated air blew over him as the sparse clouds vanished in the upper atmosphere. Krkrtek felt a sudden urge to dive. He resisted. He flicked water over his eyes to clear them. Another flash nearly blinded him. This detonation was much closer. He gripped the rock tighter with his claws and legs as heat seared his outer shell. Krkrtek saw an oncoming ripple cross the sea an instant before the blast wave took his life.

Tanuhr observed the arc of warhead clouds rising from the hemisphere below his ship. All resistance had been annihilated on the surface and in orbit. His ship was designed to assault and defeat not only planets but stellar empires. The attacking fleet was now only debris. This system was pacified. His ship would make the scythe and part it for consumption by his dark mother in Hell. Sundering the worlds was a General's most tedious and time consuming task. For a moment, he looked at the boiling oceans close to the continent's shore and wondered what moving through them as a whole shark or amphibian would be like. In the next second, he ordered his ship to make the scythe and destroy the world.

The sections of the Spinopod world were set on course for the long and ultimately odd journey to Hell. Tanuhr set his ship's course for the next target. It would prove a devastating campaign for more than the system's civilizations.

Tanuhr was the Victorious, again. False signals and energy signatures from reactors lured even the meticulous Tanuhr into an ambush as he sought a phantom armada. The reactors were rigged as thermonuclear mines. The enemy tactics were stages of deceptions and delays. The system's forces wished to afford the inner planets time to mass a fleet should their ambush fail. Some Generals would appreciate such tactics. To Tanuhr they were delays of the inevitable. Delays wasted time and thus deterred efficient execution of his purpose. Fascination not firepower did work in the local warriors' favor. They employed a warship Tanuhr found truly interesting. The ship was old, but not from Hell. That was the first curious and intriguing fact. The etheric and radiation traces indicated it was not from this system, or any local system. It was a derelict when captured by his latest enemy, but still under power. Its energy distributors showed a regenerative property similar to Hell's warships. The prevalence of weapons marked it as a purpose-built warship. Thus a war had existed before the Dark Urge had sent out her Generals. This was also curious to Tanuhr. He wondered if other forces with similar technology waited to ambush him or another General. The enemy ship was more than a curiosity. It was a strategic threat.

The enemy ship could survive high-energy impacts at great speed against its hull even if its robust system of field projectors failed. That frontal hull was a doubled, circular shield. The shield was near absolute black as it still absorbed energy even if that was only faint light from the distant sun. The shield sat in front of a series of four cubes joined by cylinders of equal mass. Tanuhr's precise return fire had sundered the hull of each cube. No fire had been wasted against the massive shield save for its missile tubes and particle beam array nested at its center. A secondary battery rested on the cube before the massive network of loops and girders stretched to the drive unit. The ship's stern region was a smaller set of concave disks pierced at the center by the expansive aperture surrounding of its main drive unit. But the drive could not generate enough radiation to penetrate the hull. Nor was it the ship's sole power source. Like Tanuhr, this ship was a chimera. The second, almost undetectable second ship was ensnared in the loops and girders. It was the true power source and focused Tanuhr's curiosity.

The second ship seemed to either warp visible space around it or be cast from it. Its surface was the inverse of his ship's aegis. Its surrounding field also tapped arcane energies and gave off emissions similar to his ship. That was strange. It should be impossible. It was fascinating.

The enemy engineers had managed to use the second ship's energies. Both ships shared power distribution components. Conduits appeared to pop into real space within the ensnaring loops from a ripple of heated atmosphere. Tanuhr wondered if ancient allies had built the fused ships. The flow of their mutual technology certainly began with the caged ship. Both vessels may have drifted docked together when found ages later by the local intelligences. The original crews were long perished or at least far away. If the engineers that found the ships had been able to activate the weapons of the ensnared ship, the battle would have been a more balanced event. However, Tanuhr did not indulge in reimagining events. He focused on detecting the origin of the ensnared ship. Such data was of strategic value. If its civilization still lived, Hell would find their world. And destroy it.

Tanuhr considered the images sent from his Field Master, Bannok. The demon's barks to his platoon and the looks on their thorned faces showed they were all enjoying their time off ship. The first ship had an interior much like its outside surfaces. It was a maze of right angles and flat surfaces. It had a bridge that maintained functional control with physical and visual interface units. The keypads were vaguely similar to the control dais used by Mendek. The fixtures and passageways were designed for creatures near demon size. It was a sterile environment violated by the oblong, dead masses of the latest, failed crew. The equipment was slightly more advanced than most space faring creatures. As expected, curious additions to tap energy from the second ship were installed by the local enemy. Most interesting was the ship's age. It had sailed the stars and fought a battle before Tanuhr took to war. He was not the oldest General, but measuring the decay from cosmic radiation bombarding the hull suggested the ship was likely older the Sutuhr. Sutuhr was old. He was also petulant and venomous. Tanuhr halted his assessment of his brother General and refocused on the incoming images and information.

Bannok's platoon left the first ship. They followed the conduits' path and entered the second ship. The demons prowled through its frigid interior. Remarkably, original lighting illuminated the scene. Tanuhr noted the massive space devoted to the interior. The crew was likely as large as the Generals. Tanuhr had never fought a species of other giants. Comparatively tiny interface nodes of the local aliens floated at junctures with the ship's systems. Discs on pedestals appeared to be the ship's secondary work stations. No alien interface nodes floated nearby. Perhaps the local aliens could not reactivate those stations, or the local engineers focused on powering a weapon, not a library. If that were the case, Tanuhr could respect the floating dead.

Tanuhr decided to visit the ship. Deciphering the data would be a mental puzzle to entertain him and perhaps make good use of time as the armada from the inner planets came to attack. Mendek had observed their amalgamated fleet throwing off vast amounts of muons and plasma to reach them. They obviously had no interstellar drives, and would be softened by a lengthy transit. Lengthy, at least for the lifespans of the hive mind and bioengineered holothuroideans. Both put their own war aside to fight Hell, together. Their federation only made their fleet's destruction more efficient. The fact they traveled a single trajectory showed they also had no experience in conducting fleet warfare. Not that it mattered, Tanuhr mused.

When Tanuhr entered the strange ship, he had no idea that his life and view of all he held dear would be threatened. For the General, time collapsed and also seemed to freeze after he reactivated the ship's information systems. What froze him were the history files he retrieved and read. He snatched a floating holothuroidean body with its pseudopods extended. He crushed the corpse into cold dust inside his amphibian fist. The information now in his head was blasphemous. Impossible. Nevertheless, there could be no trick and no corruption of the ancient ship's data core. Still, Tanuhr fought disbelief. Logic crushed the idea of this data being a trick or planted. The age of the ship was authentic. Its chronology register was accurate. Plus, technology necessary to access the data and then alter it was virtually impossible to any creatures not possessing knowledge and power from Hell. Unlocking the files was difficult even for his well-focused mind. And what strategic purpose would such deception serve? If it was truly blasphemous, the Dark Urge would surely strike him down for considering it true. He almost wished she would strike him down. He still stood. Thus, the information must be part of her design for creation.

The impossible was indeed fact. The shock was Tanuhr's alone to bear. He could not tell even his Field and Ship Masters. They could not fathom its implications, and it would certainly fracture their faith. Tanuhr' own mind needed to find meaning in the revelation. For once he wished to hear another's viewpoint. He reasoned the best perspective would come from Anguhr. The information dealt directly with him. Yet the information may destroy him. All Generals were powerful. Anguhr loved war. If driven mad, he may love trying to kill Tanuhr. It would be a worthy fight. Yet, Tanuhr wanted Anguhr's thoughts before cutting his head away. It would be difficult to communicate with him after that.

Tanuhr thought the best method was to talk directly to one another, free of technology, free of their hordes, and even free of personal weapons. Tanuhr did not know if he could get another General to agree to such terms. He would take the risk. The information may destroy him, too. He needed to act quickly. Time was now a cutting blade and Tanuhr felt its pressure.

First he would annihilate the oncoming armada. Afterwards, he would contact Anguhr. To leave this campaign now would be even more suspicious than directly contacting another General. He had always loved his shadowed mother, the Dark Urge. But he understood there was an element of suspicion in all her actions. Her methods of war being only one indicator of an inefficient if all-powerful mind. And so he would act within protocols as closely as he could until he had a better perspective and strategic outlook. Tanuhr's hammerhead extensions undulated. He was a master of timely annihilation, but did not wish to hasten his own death.

CHAPTER SIX

Heat, shockwave, and radiation assaulted the target planet. Another melted crater appeared in the already pitted city that spanned a continent. The simple, fission warheads were not from Hell. It was the native militia attempting to eradicate a mass of invading demons. Sadly for the saurian creatures fighting for their world, the demons were swift to flight. The horde's strike leaders could smell the plutonium from a distance. They arranged their demon units in tactically useless zones to lure the enemy into launching. Fast and mobile, the demons then quickly fled to turn and watch the flash and rising clouds punch through the emerald sky. Dodging the release of fission energy had become a game for demons. For the planet's inhabitance, Armageddon had become reality.

Soon enough, scorched earth would become scorched planet. The once proud civilization called itself the *Ohnk-hriss*. The name rose from two ancient syllables called through vanished forests that marked the location of the lead hunter and direction of the prey, or, simply: *here* and *ahead*. Now, the planet and all its species headed towards doom.

The demon Almok sneered. His sensibilities were offended. Other intellects might shudder to think what depths of behavior might offend a demon. However, Almok cared nothing of depravity. However, nor was he offended by carnage. He was a warrior demon, and thus the latter was his business. The former was a waste of time by weaker creatures. No creatures, strong or pathetic attacked him or hid under the field of rubble he stalked. And so his mind was partially distracted by wider observations of structures, materials, and even weather. Such was the dread infliction of intellect. Greater awareness had been granted to him by his General, Lord

Ursuhr, the Mighty. All demons were recording instruments. Arming some with a near-independent mind created differential sensors at the point of the horde penetrating the enemy. Ursuhr had directly selected Almok. The General's fist was larger than Almok's head. And so Almok endured his unwanted, higher state in silence. He wished to live, and was now even more aware of the risks to his life. If his heightened mind strayed to the concept of irony, he would become more annoyed. But still stay silent.

Almok was again part of a massive planetary invasion. This he enjoyed. The fact that the only remnants of enemy forces near him were spatters on his thorny hide, he did not. He was there to pull the trigger and kill what charged or lay in front of him. That's what he appreciated the most. Nevertheless, his dreaded intellect gave him certain insights. At least insights in the context of demon thoughts. It was the city that made him sneer. Not that it burned, but how it was built. Across the stars, allegedly intelligent creatures insisted on building fixed positions as if war was not the natural state. It made no sense. Cities were never dug in. Never built as proper fortifications. This failure of reason was on so many cities on so many worlds. The rising towers invited bombardments.

He observed such foolishness across far different styles of mind: insectine hives, metallic collectives, or soft little species that erroneously thought themselves individual entities. All had no sense of how to build structures to endure a battle. Perhaps it was realization that everything always fell to the might of Lord Ursuhr. Perhaps fighting poorly and building fragile battlements was the facile, alien way of paying tribute the Dark Urge.

All praise the Dark Urge. Almok chanted mentally, and sneered anew.

A gust blew fallout across Almok and his rifle. Almok didn't blink and his muzzle stayed upright and ready. There were footsteps near him. The familiar rasp of claws against pavement told him who closed in. He turned to see three members of his squad. Demons always moved across all forms of battlefield with the muzzles of their stout, metal rifles forward. They all lowered their weapons. Almok did not need intellect to recognize the rare demon expression of confusion.

"Almok, come." A demon spoke and stepped forth. "You must see something."

"Scan it. Kill it!" Almok barked at the speaking demon. But its act of assertion marked it. Almok could name other demons for reference. He gave recognition to this one as Kwal. Almok's thoughts would be transferred to the horde's registry, as would the name and identity of Kwal.

"It resists our weapons." Kwal said. "And we cannot take its impression. It is—it is weird! We bid you look at it!"

Almok thought to bark *Scan it. Kill it!* a second time, but sighed and thrust his head in the direction the other three demons had approached. Almok followed them on the ground through the shattered city. Another squad flew in the opposite direction through smoke rising from a tower cut into a jagged half. Almok ground his sharp teeth as he heard an exchange of fire. He wished he was there. The sharp staccato ended. Almok caught whiffs of the propellants from saurian projectiles and the mephitic signature of demon rifles. A sound demanded more attention than the scents. An echo of mechanized mass rolled through the canyons of shattered towers. The four demons turned from a roadway flanked by burning buildings onto a wider avenue among smashed ones awaiting the flames' advance. The sound's maker came into view. Almok's desire for a fight was answered.

A heavy yet sleek machine ripped away pavement as it sped down the avenue on tracks. Its egg- shaped hull appeared at odds with the vehicle's mass and belligerent purpose. The metal egg had its wide end sliced away and replaced with a wider dome mounted on a backward lean. A concave impression rested near the angled dome's upper edge. Inside it, a thick cap acted as the buttress of a long, narrow tube universally recognized as a main gun. Perpetual fire had tinted its muzzle break soot-black. Two larger, oval masses were looped by the tracks and flanked the hull. A concave area was recessed into the forward sections of both flanking ovals near the main gun. In each of these rested a sphere armed with two, smaller guns with venting down their length. They also bore the scars of heat from constant use. The hulk lurched as its crew found itself in the open against the enemy. The machine then only moved its guns toward the demons.

For a fraction of a blink, two styles of reptilian eyes locked. Serpent versus saurian. Serpent eyes stared down the sights of the heavy demon rifles. Saurian eyes glared through electronic sights inside the Ohnk-hriss fighting vehicle. Both aimed to annihilate the other. In the next fraction of time, the demons opened fire.

Loud reports and bright red flashes followed the demon's volley. The saurian guns also fired. The side-mounted gun turrets streamed high velocity rounds straight into demons. Hell's bullets did greater damage. Only a few rounds bounced off the rounded armor. Most punched through the alien steel and straight through the machine. The Ohnk-hriss fire jostled the demons but ricocheted off their hides. Almok's gun was knocked off target.

The saurians fired their main gun. The demon next to Kwal vanished. The shell continued into the wreck of steel and glass behind them. It detonated. The surviving structure collapsed towards the street as the demons advanced with renewed fire. Dust, smoke and shards flew passed the remaining three demons as they moved towards the tank. Almok took to the air over the cloud of debris and continued to fire. The Ohnk-hriss blasted one more errant round from the main gun before they stopped firing. Almok landed and the surviving three demons regrouped and stopped shooting. Their rifle's magazines began to generate new rounds. A piece of the dome around the main gun fell away as the demons took position around the machine. None barked orders. Each demon knew how to respond to each other's motions from imbued tactics.

Flames began to rise inside the hull made visible by the armor's many perforations. A small explosion followed. The three demons resumed their trek to the anomaly. Explosions continued inside the hull as they walked away. Almok was glad Kwal had survived. He didn't want to have to name a new demon.

They came to a hole among small mountains of smoldering debris that were the remains of shattered buildings. Between them was a small, fresh crater made from a grenade recently thrown by Kwal. The demons glimpsed remnants of an underground site through the crater. Almok hoped something large and vicious lurked inside. He reconsidered the thought, but decided he liked the idea and smiled. Although they were far from a bomb crater, firestorms drew in the stenches of burned flesh, heavy isotopes, and seared metals. They didn't penetrate the colder and darker site the demons entered through the hole. The horde's opening salvos and the tremors from the saurians' desperate counterstrikes had shattered the underground complex. There was nothing alive, and surprisingly no bodies. Almok decided the site was of no military importance, or the enemy had fled in fear. Almok wondered if demons or something else caused the fear. It was still worth exploring.

Machines lay strewn among the debris. Power transmission had been cut. Nothing was active. The *Ohnk-hriss* had taken the circular shape of their ears and made it the pattern for reception and input on their technology. Almok had never seen so many things with disks and loops fallen into piles and strewn among rubble. Almok recognized the communications rings that hugged the outer ridge of saurian ears, and the small, mock hemispheres of their planet that plotted coordinates and interfaced with more powerful calculation devices.

A set of communication screens sat righted. Its user must have survived and made a last transmission before fleeing. One screen still displayed a recorded image of the receiving individual. These saurians were fused with technology and used two rectangular display screens. The first screen sat at an angle above the larger, second one so both sets of their eyes could take in separate fields of information. Almok had enough trouble dealing with one brain. He might welcome being smashed by Ursuhr's hammer if offered a second, artificial one. Even the synthesis of

Ohnk-hriss brains was inadequate against the demonic invasion. Although, Almok wondered, what could prevail?

The four demons reached a metal tunnel on the other side of the ruins. Its length that once extended from it lay collapsed among the other ruins and debris. Its surviving length continued into bedrock. One flap of their wings carried the four demons into the steel tube. The tunnels were built by this planet's scaly skinned inhabitance for slinking beneath their cities. They proved easy pathways for demons, providing they kept the claws of their wing joints folded down.

The planet's gravity was plus one of ship normal. Almok noted an increase to near plus two as they neared a portal cut into the tunnel side. The entrance was wider than most made for the Ohnk-hriss. The tunnel wall showed the extension had been cut quickly and left rough. Some crushed rock littered the floor from the new chamber beyond. The project was done in haste. As Kwal and the two other demons turned to enter, Almok noticed they bared teeth. Demons did so to intimidate enemies, to ready their jaws for use in self defense, and personal reassurance. Almok curled back his own lips as he entered. He was disappointed to see only a machine.

Almok reconsidered his disappointment and allowed his curiosity to rise. As Kwal had said, it was weird. The machine held an ethereal aura noticeable to a creature born from such energies. Its combination of physical and arcane radiations cast it in white and effected local gravity. Its surface looked like stone, but smelled as metal. Yet, like a thing cut from stone, it felt solid to passive demons senses. Obviously its workings were not simply mechanical. Its shape was a smooth square with smaller rectangle slabs like steps at its narrow ends. It extended into the crude chamber as long as the three demons standing wing joint to wing joint, but only one demon wide. It was as tall as their weapons' belts. Compared to a single *Ohnk-hriss* soldier, it would be massive.

Almok thought the white thing looked old. It smelled old. Older than the rock cut away to make its chamber. The odd machine's housing was a single casting. Perhaps it was grown in a mold. Its narrow ends were sheared from something akin to a buckle cut from a grenade belt. It was likely a module detached from a larger structure. But that structure would be massive. It would be a thing not built for the scale of demons, but for giants. Giants such as Generals. And if it was living metal, it was like alloys cast from the skin of the Dark Urge. She gave that boon to her warriors, such as ammunition grown inside demon rifles. This machines size, shape, and energies suggested Hell. But this, as all alien worlds, was an enemy planet. This could not be from Hell. Yet Almok had no other reference for a power old enough for the origin of an ancient machine. Almok's life as a thinking creature was new. He had struggled to find a context and understand the curious white thing. Curiosity became confusion and then frustration. Almok shook his head, violently.

Kwal and the other demon leaned back from Almok and the machine. They instinctively aimed their rifles at the machine as they considered the state of their angry leader. Perhaps it attacked him inside with radiation or parasite infiltration. It was strong if it did that to a recognized demon.

Almok regained focus. He wiped away froth from his lower lip and shrugged to his companions. He considered what tactics might involve this strange object. Why did the *Ohnk-hriss* place it here? He noted that none of their missiles had struck this site, despite demon presence. Therefore this machine was valuable to them. Yet, it was abandoned and not well hidden. Perhaps it was meant to be found by demons. Almok wondered if he was not part of a trap set in motion. He realized that if he could understand the machine then he might halt the trap.

Almok sighed. The breath was cut between his serrated teeth. To consider the machine more deeply meant he would have to think more, and set free other lore bound in his already smoldering brain. Almok growled and bared his teeth. However, in service to his dread Lord Ursuhr and the harsher presence of the Dark Urge, he would do it.

"I shall have to think more," he hissed.

"Think?" Kwal asked.

"Yes," Almok snorted. "Don't try it too often. It makes you—" Almok halted. He wished to warn his fellow demons of the dangers in being fully self-aware, and worse, thinking about it and other things. Yet demons took pride in enduring pain and hardship. As they could endure open space, enemy weapons fire to the face, and worse. They could endure a lot. Describing the curse of thinking as a hardship would make it appear enviable. But thought allowed him to find a way to make demons wary of his curse: "It makes fighting less fun."

Kwal and the other demons replied with widened eyes, growls, and nods. Almok had found a way to make demons afraid.

Almok focused. Stored and coded information unfurled inside his brain, at least for now. For the moment, Almok became an advanced engineer. His mind felt hijacked but he did not resist. He considered what could generate the wide range of energies, possible power sources, and past designs of various reactors. The strange machine considered no better than a hulking weapon became a sophisticated device with a series of integrated systems to produce a range of effects with a likely purpose. A theory was formed.

"It is a generator!" Almok snapped. "A phase engine."

"This is a weapon?" Kwal asked.

"Yes. A cowardly, defensive one. But a weapon of importance. If there are others, it may impact the battle. Summon our Field Master. Kalak will speak to Lord Ursuhr. He must know of this find!"

"We will be descended into the heart of the Dark Urge for certain!" Kwal shouted.

"Yes." Almok smiled, but then snorted. "For now I must stand guard. Go!"

Kwal and the other demon ran from the crude chamber.

Almok felt as though his mind cleared as the greater knowledge faded. Once again, aggression ruled over reason. He thought he was alone. A voice dispelled that theory.

"I thought they would never leave."

CHAPTER SEVEN

The maul was traditionally more tool than weapon. Anything forged in Hell had more dimensions than could be seen. Although, a blunt mass stuck to a handle was simple to understand. When swung by a giant monster such as General Ursuhr, the vagaries and specifics of his weapon were lost in the vast destruction he caused. His maul was as lethal a war hammer against a planet as an impacting asteroid. That was how he chose to think of it. His maul now sat at rest in front of his throne. Its massive head had deformed the deck plate where he first set it down taking command of his ship. That served as its resting site when the General was not swinging it in combat. Its widest, striking face was a flat square with sharp corners. The sides tapered only slightly to the opposing face, and not to a cutting edge but a narrowed crushing surface. It was the crueler of the two, because it took more blows to smash an enemy with that side. Ursuhr thought that it might not be as wide as Anguhr's axe, but it was certainly heavier. At least he hoped so. Its massive head was nearly a quarter of the weapons length. The metal handle was long for two massive hands to grip, and well forged. So was its owner.

Ursuhr the Mighty was the most massive of Hell's Generals. He was also the strongest. Or so he believed. All of Ursuhr's skin held the color of quenched steel. His body was the Hell-standard giant with the tweak of elongated arms like a gorilla. A thick set of heavy shoulders and massive chest supported the neck and head of a hairless bear. Ursuhr's face was cast in a perpetual snarl. His eyes were solid black and almost always locked in glower. In the history of evolution, convergent on worlds far separated, it was biologically implausible for a bear to have shark's teeth.

However, Hell's monsters owed nothing to evolution and followed no logic. They brought its standard of madness to battles across the galaxy. Grey armor only clad Ursuhr's lower abdomen and upper legs. Boots of mail and leather sheathed his calves and clawed feet because he loved the sound they made when crushing something beneath their soles.

Ursuhr glanced at his maul. He looked at his Ship Master, Martis, waiting for the wingless demon to give him a reason to take his weapon into combat.

"I have plotted the trajectory of the distortion, Lord Ursuhr," Martis said. His voice was deep and rasping and unique among his kind. It was rare for demons to have affectations. However, when a mind could pilot a ship that traveled galactic arms yet was always marooned on the bridge, that mind could become tweaked over time. "It confirms the origin was *Sol-Zjaun*."

Ursuhr inhaled and then made a deep, groan like grating boulders. Both he and Martis looked at his maul. Ursuhr nodded and spoke. His voice was a seismic rumble.

"They are coming."

On the planet, Kwal reached street surface. His fellow demon followed from the underground site. Deep within it, Almok guarded the strange machine. Kwal and his nameless partner crouched and scanned for enemies before taking flight.

"Rok!" the second demon said.

"What?" Kwal snapped his stare from down his sights to his companion.

"That is the name I would choose if I could be named." The demon said while still scanning.

"You cannot choose a name!" Kwal sneered. "You are not recognized, so you have no name!"

"I am sure I will be for this discovery. As were you." The demon lowered his rifle and nodded to himself. "But, I am not permitted to think, so I may be wrong."

"We do not think." Kwal said and stood. "Not like Almok. And he does not think as well as our Field Master Kalak, who does not think as darkly as Lord Ursuhr."

"And he is stupider than the Dark Urge." The would-be Rok said.

Kwal began to raise his rifle to club his partner for impudence. He then realized what he said was essentially true, if crudely phrased. And then Kwal's own head began to hurt. He shook it and focused on their task.

"We need to summon Kalak!" Kwal barked. "Our rifles will boost our thoughts, but the signal will be stronger in flight."

"I feel—" The other demon rolled his folded wings and shoulders. "There is…a tingle."

Kwal also felt the growing charge in the air. Both demons heard a crackle of energy above them. A sudden force pulled them off the ground. They looked up through their guns sights to see the huge, silver sphere falling straight at them. Their last thought was to open fire.

The sphere struck the demons and then the ground. City debris began to swell and roll towards the sphere just before it vanished with a thunderclap and cyclone of metallic mist. Air rushed out from the where the sphere had landed. What stood there now were three black giants. Their homeworld of *Sol-Zjaun* called the, the Titans. They had traveled interstellar distance for one cause: kill everything from Hell.

Each Titan had a basic, human form made impossibly massive and clad in burnished, black armor. The energies of the Crimson Titan surrounded him in a red corona. From the shoulders upward the human comparison ended, as did a comparison to all life. The armor flowed into half domes of arched, black bands over the shoulders.

Red flames knifed between the narrow gaps in the black, dome bands and curled across their tops. A head and neck would be expected between the domes. Instead, there was a gap from the Titan's back to its chest front. The gap radiated light and heat like a foundry's crucible, yet this crucible held the surface of a red star. A single, perfectly spherical and large eye cast in the crimson of the Titan's power hovered over the stellar fires. The red eye stared out between the shoulder domes with a thousand, slowly swirling irises of deeper crimson. A crest of black floated above the center of the eye and curved down behind it. The crest tapered to a sharp point near the Titan's back.

The Blue Titan glowed nearly white at its shoulder domes and crucible gap. It appeared as an electrical medusa with arcs of lightening in place of serpents around its floating eye. There were no visible irises among the constant electrical arcs and whips. Some bolts rippled down the length of its black armor. Others struck and burned the ground.

The Dark Titan was purest black. The force of gravity contained within its armor pulled its eye into an inverted raindrop shape. The eye held a single, distorted iris. The iris was a horizon of light drawn towards an unseen, dark center within the eye that created the pupil. Its armor was nearly a solid black surface. The mass behind it compressed the seams to nearly invisible lines.

The Titans were greeted by a hail of demon fire and grenade salvos. They remained unmoved. Their orbs turned to look at one another. Their gaze turned to a massed attack of vicious demons charging on the ground and in the air. The Titans ran, at the demons.

The two forces met in a wide avenue flanked by rows of fallen towers. As the flying demons circled and fired, the Titans dealt with the ground forces in the universal method used by larger creatures facing smaller threats. They stomped on them. There were too many to simply kill underfoot. More demons left the hunt for saurian forces and came to join the fight against the three giants. The Titans disappeared beneath waves of demons firing, stabbing, and clawing at them. The frenzy had killed tactics. The Titans became still, welcoming the violent swarm.

The Crimson Titan extended its arms out and palms upward. Waves of flame engulfed the demons swarming him. Their bodies froze and burned into a chain of bronze sculptures before falling away as molten fragments.

The Blue Titan was more energetic. Arcs lanced over its engulfing demons and incinerated them and their weapons whole. Cascades of blue bolts lanced from the Titan and fused the ground around it.

The Dark Titan appeared passive, but its method was as lethal. The demons covering it were pulled by increasing gravity and crushed into a hellish aggregate. Their bodies then fell just as sections of a sundered casting mold.

An entire demon army lay vanquished. A faint echo sounded as distant saurian observers roared with delight.

Demon artillery rained shells at the three massive victors. The Titans again remained unmoved. The eyes of the Titans rolled to look up. Much heavier ordinance was unleashed from orbit. Asteroid fragments burned in sharp trajectories towards the surface. They blasted into the shattered city around the Titans. Demons knew they asteroid strikes marked another grand arrival. A large rock was always held in reserve for the event. The force that shattered it struck maul first near the Titans. Demons roared joy as General Ursuhr stepped from his impact crater.

All three Titans faced Ursuhr and spoke in a unified voice that vibrated through ears and all form of frequencies. "General Ursuhr, scourge from Hell, your judgment is passed. Your hour of death is now."

"Fools!" Ursuhr bellowed and slapped the handle of his maul in one hand. "I only engage you now because here I know I can kill you! You are the greatest warriors of your world, but you squander your power by facing me away from your stronghold. I by-passed Sol-Zjaun to lure you here. Your people will never recover from your loss. I will sweep through their cities and set your planet to flames. But you will be spared the pain of failure, because I will kill you all, now! Did you not expect both cunning and cruelty from me? From Hell?" Ursuhr bared his teeth in a triumphant smile.

"No." was the Titans' collective reply.

Ursuhr drew in a deep breath and scowled at his three enemies. His triumphant speech was for naught. He exhaled his disappointment. Dust scattered far down by his boots.

"Then simply die!" Ursuhr swung his maul.

The Dark Titan caught the maul and held it fast. The Blue Titan fired its lightning across the massive General. Ursuhr freed one hand and struck the Crimson Titan at his side. It fell to the ground.

Almok felt another tremor. He was annoyed at having to guard this machine thing while his brethren enjoyed further fighting. However, a voice had spoken to him. An enemy was nearby. He may find a fight right in this rough cut chamber. He would stay anyway, lest Field Master Kalak feed him as pieces to Lord Ursuhr him for dereliction of duty. The certainty of the machine's importance remained although his understanding of its function dimmed as knowledge strands in his mind recoiled for storage. They had temporarily augmented his brain beneath the thorned scalp and reinforced skull. Still, even a demon given greater sentience desired a good fight.

"A demon." The voice sounded again.

Almok swung around, ready to fire. But he could understand the language, but not determine the origin of the voice.

"Hell's warrior model and most mass produced device." The voice continued. "And, no doubt, why I've been activated."

The long, jagged, and still blood-spattered bayonet shot forth and fixed under the heavy barrel of Almok's rifle.

"Such aggression," the voice continued. "You must be frustrated to be a mere guard for a machine. Although I, too, am limited to predetermined actions."

"Show yourself!" Almok shouted. "Come out and fight!"

"A fight against me might erase the translation protocol I've worked so hard to build. Plus, to do so you would need to access and then reprogram complex, phased data. Can you do that? Doubtful."

"I can kill machines!" Almok screamed. He darted his head out of the hastily cut chamber and quickly glanced down the metal tunnel in both directions.

"Conclusion of my form, accurate. My location? Failed. To be fair, I've toyed with sonic projection. So let me help. I am part of the thing behind you."

"You are this machine's mind?" Almok turned and looked generator. He placed his bayonet against it.

"Not quite. But a mind, yes. I am a failsafe. Unfortunately, the computing power built into my design to overcome sophisticated program infiltration is unneeded. But I do need a diversion as energy builds. I am all too aware my life will be quite short. So, entertain me you ugly beast."

"I must guard you," Almok groaned. "I would rather fight you. Strike at me!"

"Sorry to disappoint. I can only employ passive scans."

"I live to fight!" Almok smiled at the thought. "You are not a warrior. You are nothing. We will dismantle you. Your parts will become ore for the greater glory of creation. You will serve the Dark Urge."

"As you serve this Dark Urge?" The failsafe asked.

"Yes!" Almok shouted. He opened his jaws as he smiled and revealed glistening shark teeth. "In obedience to my Lord, General Ursuhr."

"The lizard-like people of this planet did not realize the enormity of the gift this generator bestowed." The failsafe paused as if in disbelief. "They only attempted to repurpose it to kill your General."

"Impossible!" Almok glared at the machine. He wondered if he should shoot it for impudence, or keep it intact for Kalak and their great and dread Lord. He eased his trigger claw.

"Yet, they could not detect me." The failsafe continued. "Now I must make sure neither does your Ursuhr. The plan may still work if gets close enough. Right now he may survive what is to come. We won't."

Ursuhr wrested his maul from the Dark Titan, but staggered back from the continued blue bolts fired by its ally. A wave of incredible heat replaced the Blue Titan's attack. Ursuhr sank into the ground as it became a molten lake from the flames rolling out from the Crimson Titan as it stood.

Across the city, Ursuhr's Field Master Kalak observed the battle. He alit on a jagged spire that was the vestige of a narrow, obsidian pyramid. It had reached above clouds before Hell's invasion. Now it was a mere perch for one of its destroyers. Kalak observed Ursuhr's fight. His General faced an enemy equal in power. That should be impossible, given the will of the Dark Urge. He wondered if their power was part of her black will. He looked up at the ship visible in the daytime sky as a red glow above the clouds. He thought to target the Titans with a missile strike. Yet, if he interfered and it cost Ursuhr glory, his General would kill him. If he allowed Ursuhr to be embarrassed, his General would kill him. Faith said that Ursuhr would win. Curiosity and imagination allowed other scenarios. If Ursuhr lost—if Ursuhr died—Kalak wondered if he would become General. Kalak belayed his call for supporting fire. Whatever occurred in this battle, the future now seemed more interesting.

From inside the lake of fire, Ursuhr laughed. "I was born in Hell!"

Ursuhr swung his maul and struck the molten earth. A lava curtain flew across all three Titans. Ursuhr leapt into them. A shower of orange and gray globs and beads of cooling slag exploded from the impact. The Titans fell like massive steel columns into the tower ruins.

Ursuhr directed his momentum toward the Blue Titan. It fired bolts from both hands into Ursuhr, who cried out. Ursuhr summoned his strength to thrust his maul's handle through the chest of the Blue Titan. Behind Ursuhr, the Dark Titan recovered and struck the General's back with both its gauntlets. The force knocked Ursuhr into his maul and drove its handle farther through the Blue Titan.

The Crimson Titan rose and knelt, and then focused its heat at Ursuhr. Ursuhr ignored the steel incinerating blast and rolled to his side to launch a kick of his left leg into the Dark Titan. The force of the blow drove it off its feet and through burning buildings.

The Crimson Titan reached to aid its blue ally that writhed and arced as it pushed up the head of Ursuhr's maul. The General's fists slammed the maul head back down. The Crimson Titan punched him in the face. Hellish ichor sprayed from his snout. Ursuhr and the Crimson Titan rose, trading blows as bolts from the Blue Titan whipped the sky and across them all.

Ursuhr lunged forward and batted the Crimson Titans arms aside. He grabbed its red orb in both clawed hands and pulled. Both combatants fell to the shattered and burned ground. Ursuhr never lost his grip. Blue bolts still arced skyward and flames rolled as the Crimson Titan grabbed Ursuhr's wrists. It struggled to free itself from the General's grip. Ursuhr had little leverage on the ground, but twisted his torso and pulled with all his arm strength. The black crest of the Crimson Titan's armor exploded skyward as its eye finally tore away.

The now completely headless Titan rolled away, flailing its arms. It stood but could only stagger as geysers of red starfire erupted from between its black domes. It crashed through the city remains before its empty armor collapsed among the other ruins.

Lightning still arced from the coursed from the Blue Titan while Ursuhr rolled onto his feet. He still gripped the crimson orb. The Dark Titan charged back and pulled Ursuhr's maul from its blue ally who struggled to stand while still spilling lightning. The Dark Titan lifted the maul to strike as Ursuhr charged. He turned to dodge the blow of his own weapon. More bolts lanced across Ursuhr, who slammed the red orb into the eye of the Blue Titan. It staggered back with the two eyes smashed together between its domes.

The Dark Titan paused and stared at its surviving ally. The Blue Titan's eye was off center with the red orb crushed into it. The impacted eyes formed an oblong mass like a planet suddenly struck by another world. They also acted as if they spun out of orbit. The two orbs spun faster and became unstable. The black bands of the Blue Titan's domes flew off when struck by the spinning eyes. The whole of its black armor twisted and fractured. It acted as a hollow metal tube caught in a powerful vortex.

Ursuhr grabbed the handle of his maul and fought to free it from the Dark Titan. As they wrestled, the energies of the Blue Titan became a vortex of circling lightning bolts. The vortex grew into one massive and brilliant blue bolt that burned into the planet and arced out into space. The bolt died. All that remained was a cooling cinder of the Blue Titan's armor twisted tightly into a giant length of wire.

Only one Titan survived. The shock of the Blue Titan's final destruction caused the Dark Titan to pause for the briefest moment. Ursuhr yanked his maul from its grasp. He immediately struck the Dark Titan with it. The sound of the blows rang out in fast succession. The Dark Titan staggered from each one.

"None are more powerful than Ursuhr!" Almok shouted his testament of faith even without seeing his General battle three other giants on the surface some distance away. "Save only the Dark Urge." He quickly added. "All praise to the Dark Urge!"

"You worship both?" The failsafe asked. "Duality. Yet it likely won't corrupt your brutal brain."

"You strike with words! Ha! May Ursuhr the Mighty smash you with his maul!"

"I'm curious." The failsafe paused. "Does such a being give you ironic hope beyond your own death?"

"Demons never die," Almok growled. "Our bodies become part of creation's dark heart where all things arise. We return to the Dark Urge."

"Is it a heart or a womb?"

Almok tensed his finger on the trigger.

"Is it possible to reunite with her if there is nothing left of you at all?" The failsafe asked.

"Explain!" Almok barked. He could feel the air in the room was growing warmer. The generator was glowing brighter. He became wary. "No! Silence! You only exist to serve her! Say no more or my rage will kill you!"

"Had the saurian intellects enacted the generators true purpose, neither of us would need to die. We would never have met. But you found the generator. Thus, it must be destroyed. And sooner than in line with the saurian plans. I calculate that giving them this generator was in desperation. Now the benefactor also fails."

"All will fall to the will of the Dark Urge." Almok snapped. "You cannot stop that, or my Lord!"

"Well, true. Now. But I was never more than a superseding failsafe program. I was created to cause my own death. I don't know if I should be sad or glad I fulfill my function. Perhaps that's why I have no coding for emotions."

"You were made merely to die? Pathetic! I will not die. I will become one with the Dark Urge. All hail the Dark Urge!"

"Demon, you were never truly alive. Just a thing. A weapon. Nothing more than the gun you clutch. I think my first emotion would be pity."

"Pity is not a weapon."

"No. Neither is mercy. And neither you nor I posses that trait. Therefore, demon: good bye."

Seconds before the failsafe said its good bye, Ursuhr had struck the mortal blow against the Dark Titan's chest. It had taken a full second to fall and create a spreading wave of crushed ground from where it impacted. Although Ursuhr didn't need an atmosphere to sustain him, he still took deep and frequent breaths. They hurt his bloodied snout. He released a low growl and raised his hammer high overhead for one last, vengeful strike. The blow never came. The failsafe then said good bye.

The flash was pure white. The ground where Ursuhr stood shifted beneath him. A section of city was blasted into the front of the shockwave. It hit with enough force to twist the maul free from Ursuhr's hands. He knew this was not another nuclear weapon attack. It made the native fission bombs look feeble. He turned to look in the direction of the blast, and blinked. If he were closer, brightness would be the least effect to concern him. The blast was from a weapon that could kill him. More than the saurians, alien Titans, and his horde made war here. Perhaps it was time to leave.

CHAPTER EIGHT

If hope now lived above the galaxy, long ago it burned to ash on a world deep within it. Wastelands spread vaster than oceans with dunes of sand more like grains of acid. Vast storms gathered the caustic grit into clouds cutting the surface as swift, airborne saws. Mountains endured the onslaught as peaks of static belligerence. Daylight was the fitting red glow of a giant star trapped by bands of a solar-scale machine. With no sand storm aloft, nightside looked up at the naked black of space. Forgotten constellations appeared to shun the face of the dread world. One name marked it across the stars that harbored complex thought and simple fear. Hell.

There were canyons on Hell, stygian and deadly. If any life survived in their depths, it would be in gardens of unearthly horror. Some pits of the equator descended deeper and revealed the chambers of the machine below. It wore the surviving geology as the skin of a monster whose spawn laid siege to a galaxy. Once, Hell was a planet remade a machine as an act of preservation. Now its eternal Forge shaped creatures and machines that burned other worlds.

One thing, one life, huge or minuscule, survived from the age before Hell, and even before the construction of the Forge. It crept from the depths of heat and darkness to gaze out at the Red Giant. The star's glow would obscure the bands, but the star gazer knew they were there. She had seen their sections soar up from the Forge and towards an expanding star that had consumed the hydrogen of its core and then later the inner planets. Its growth threatened the surviving solar system seen with nostalgic eyes by beings now capable of restraining expanding suns.

Before the reign of Hell, the lone observer was described many times over eons by those who glimpsed and dared face her. At times she ate them. At times, not. Most of the tongues that spoke of her were now dead. Her many names included *Shia-Phring* and *Kodai kumo*. The name with the most meaning for her own mind was Great Widow. She had been part of a living world that became a giant machine devoid of true life, save her own. She was an orphan and a mother of lost generations and alone with no mates. Small or gigantic, she was the Great Widow.

She witnessed machines grow and multiply. She watched material enter portals, be cast and then leave the former planet's heart. The cosmic machine they built became known as the Iron Work. Some mind, indeed nostalgic, thought its black rings looked fashioned from iron. The rings stayed black even right above the star's red glare. The Great Widow felt it was fitting she had witnessed the construction. Some minds would see a structure of rings greater than some solar systems built for purposes grand and mysterious. The Great Widow saw a titanic web ensnaring a star while it still lived, and then preserving it to serve as food, as energy. She understood the Iron Work this way, because she was a spider.

The Great Widow heard a noise. It was a moan. A scream. It was a summons. She turned from the lip of the pit she hid within and bid farewell to the crimson sky. She had gazed at it for mere moments, or the rise and fall of mountains. No matter the length of her reverie, it was now time to face death. The Great Widow thought doing would be her journey downward across treacherous surfaces. However, where there should be a shaft of steel there was now interstellar space. Before her was a cloud of gasses that harbored young stars. It swirled as a vast helix that slowly spun and tilted until the Great Widow looked down the center of the helical nebula. At this angle, the nebula appeared as an enormous eye to most creatures possessing sight. The staring nebula split into two mirrored images and continued its burning, unblinking gaze. The true nebula was an object of light and wonder. The doubled projections reflected the aspect of their maker. No matter their color or brightness, these eyes of the Dark Urge were inimical, accusing, and cold. It was a fitting depiction of the sovereign of intense heat and hatred. The Dark Urge knew the astronomical stare emphasized her omnipotence. The truth or falsehood of such power mattered little when you were equal to a fleeing spider suddenly exposed under the gaze of an angry, frightened child. This spider had no place to flee. The Great Widow was already in Hell. And so, as always, she would endure the madness of speaking to fire.

The stellar fire vanished. The shaft into Hell was again before the Great Widow. She still had to make the treacherous climb into Hell. It was an act of devotion into a heated temple or forced march through her prison. She could not afford a slip of just one of her eight legs against the hot, metallic surface. The smooth shaft gave way to a twisting succession of arcane machinery surrounding her in a cylinder of tremendous length. The wide shaft would seem to dwindle to a black dot if not for the intense light and heat from Hell's core. Many of her silken, safety strands burned away as soon as she wove them. It was cautious navigation that would spare her incineration by fire. Though heat alone might take her, still.

The gusts of searing hot air surged back and forth along the shaft as if the world machine breathed. She paused as the air rushed out, and carefully climbed down as it was drawn back in. Luckily the Great Widow didn't need to breathe anymore through the rows of trachea along her abdomen as in ages before. The heat might sear her lungs. Now, her adaptation to the arcane energies flowing from the Forge sustained her. She began to feel comfortable in the heat again. However, the most dangerous part of her task was yet to come. That would be in facing the thing that summoned her. There was a ritual to their communications. There were chambers of with specific designs. Just as a heart had chambers or a brain had regions. This brain that called the Great Widow was missing pieces. This was all too apparent when the Great Widow crept into the speaking chamber. The Dark Urge sat at its center and mumbled to herself.

What the Great Widow saw might look pathetic. However, it was the most fearsome thing in creation. It was a little girl in a dress made from material with blue flower pattern. She sat swaying as she mumbled. The Great Widow carefully approached the Dark Urge and saw half the child's skull was missing. The Dark Urge might truly be a great black machine, but this was a more accurate avatar. This was how she saw herself. The Great Widow pondered what other surviving or alien minds would recognize the image of the little girl. The last species of humanity was long lost. What the spider saw was an even earlier form. Who could believe such frail life could be the ancestral foundation of great engineers that built the Forge and the Iron Work. Not even the Dark Urge had ever seen a true human being. Yet somehow her mind stored the images and her twisted psyche made use of them to illustrate her deepest self image, her madness.

Many ancient stories spoke of little girls and spiders. One described the love of a fair prince and an arachnid. The Great Widow hoped the Dark Urge had love for her. She would use anything as a weapon to survive. If the spider ever needed to defend herself, venom and webbing would be useless against a thing so powerful. Only the Great Widow's mind, adapted over eons, was of use against such overwhelming power.

Adaptation gave the Great Widow a power useful to this dark god. Her webs were never great symmetries of circles and straight lines. They appeared chaotic, but were carefully woven. Should a prey item stumble into her silk, some lines would merely slow but others would adhere and snap. The break released the stored tension. The adhered lines pulled on the victim as snares of great strength. Few could break free. The spider lived on all manner of desperate or confident creature until no prey remained. By then, the energies of the Forge had strengthened and changed her. Strands of her silk, strands of herself, were tangled with her and whatever she imparted them into. A machine or thing a galaxy away would always be within her web of awareness if it had a strand of her silk within it. This served the Dark Urge. She wanted to know where her dread offspring, her Generals, were and what they did. Any other mother would desire this as a means to watch over her children. But the Dark Urge was missing pieces. Though she loved them, she didn't trust them. And so the Great Widow was her means of communication, and her spy.

The Great Widow often wished her entangled power existed before the Iron Work's builders departed. She would like to know where they were, and perhaps bid them return. The Forge world burn long after its builders left for perhaps another reality. Their machines remained. To living eyes, they were immortal. The Forge's operating system became an object to covet, and a thing to tempt plunder. An alien race thought they were the equal of the Forge's builders. They were not. The machine fought back. The plunderers fled. Yet, their tampering left a lasting schism. In time it grew into two separate beings. In the following dual age, the spider crept forth and befriended them both.

Perhaps it was the influence of the Great Widow that shaped the two minds to appear female. It was her appearance that made both of them aware of life beyond their minds. One intelligence became inspired to look for more life, more minds, beyond the limits of the Forge and departed. The one that remained felt abandoned. She never felt healed and always missing a piece. She took to the shadows that soon cloaked her mind. Creation knew her now as the Dark Urge. She recast the Forge as Hell. The Great Widow remained, for she was creation's greatest survivor. And because there was no place for escape. The Great Widow kept to herself that she inspired the Dark Urge's adventurous sister to leave. It was the spider's personal secret, but also a potential reason the Dark Urge would crush her in anger should it ever be revealed. The Dark Urge was never missing her anger.

The Great Widow stopped next to the avatar of the little girl. The spider towered over this form of the Dark Urge who repeated a phrase over and over in a meek voice as she swayed.

"If I can imagine it, I know she can. If I can imagine it, I know she can. If I can imagine it, I know she can."

The half face of the Dark Urge looked up at the looming spider. A second eye formed at the side of the missing skull. Both eyes became massive and then looked down at the Great Widow as a faceless scowl from the walls of machinery that now pulsed.

"I greet you, dark mistress." The Great Widow pressed her body to the chamber floor as a form of prostration. "You summoned me."

For a moment there was only the sound of the rush of air through the shaft outside. The eyes circled the Great Widow. Cables, ducting, and arcane devices flowed around them as they moved through the walls.

"Can you die?" The voice of the Dark Urge was now a thunderous vibration through Hell.

"My mistress knows she can crush me at will. Yet my mistress knows then her Generals would miss her counsel, and she the contact with them I provide."

"You think I need you to do a thing? Anything?" The eyes became even larger and more narrowed. They stopped.

"My mistress is powerful." The Great Widow replied. She hoped her translated thoughts preserved her acquiescent tone. "You are the greatest power of all. Yet my mistress keeps me as part of her power. I who have served her the longest of all."

They eyes merged into a vortex on the wall. It swirled into a massive finger made of black steel, machinery, and taunting. Instinctively, the Great Widow raised her front legs and calipers. She stopped before opening her jaws. She drew her limbs close and allowed the finger to prod her.

"I am obedient, mistress. Just bid me to do your will."

The finger stopped. It unspooled into its individual elements that remerged with the walls.

The little girl reappeared. She ran to the Great Widow with outstretched arms and threw herself against the arachnid's abdomen.

"I have a thought." The Dark Urge said pressed into her hugging of the giant spider. "I have a plan. You will help me."

"I do as you wish, mistress. I always do. I must. You are the will of Hell."

CHAPTER NINE

D'nai Liung was a planet of vast, emerald planes and indigo lakes. In its one, sparse forest, the trees were few but enormous. Each was a living, gravity defying world unto itself. Some of the towering, helical evergreens carried a metropolis in many of their expansive bough. Most worlds, stellar empires, and system consortiums employed mundane physics to power ships, weapons, and a few surprises. Some even gave Anguhr reason to pause. He enjoyed those challenges. He hoped to find more on *D'nai Liung*. Here the arcane combined with natural arts. The sentient and crafty inhabitants were a species of arboreal gastropod. Anguhr began to wonder if they took his invasion seriously. When he leapt to the surface as a challenge, he heard something akin to a bird singing. He sighed. Then the Hydragon burst from the ground and attacked him.

Aside from the assault, Anguhr still harbored doubts. Part of his mind always searched for some missing, mysterious aspect, or the true nature of war. At least this monster was solid. The Hydragon captured his full attention. It snapped and stabbed at him with five heads with opened jaws armed with swords for teeth. At closer inspection against his skin, Anguhr saw that the teeth were actually several beaks jutting from each mouth. This creature was a form of cephalopod made into a dragon. The snapping appendages could be heads on tentacles. They had a squid's eyes. Many more, shorter tentacles supported and moved its vast bulk made heavier with fine scales. The Hydragon was an excellent monster. Better yet, it wanted to fight. Anguhr smiled.

In his past campaigns, Anguhr had seen a species of intelligent and quite giant squids. They beseeched him to allow them to serve the Dark

Urge. They had developed high technology and a communication network that served several stars systems. They offered it to serve the Dark Urge. They would also cut him in on a share of the user fees. Anguhr saw they did not fully understand the concepts of total war or annihilation. Apparently, they also did not hear the condescending tone in their appeals. Odd, Anguhr thought, for a species that thrived as communication coordinators. He destroyed one of their hub planets as an illustration of his intent. They were giant squid creatures with advanced knowledge and ample resources. The annihilation should have roused them to action. He commanded them to fight or be annihilated as cowards. Sadly, he annihilated them as cowards.

Anguhr stopped his reverie and sliced away the snapping and biting Hydragon's heads with a swing of his massive axe. A second weapon, toxic blood, sprayed from the sudden whipping fountains. And then each neck split and became a new whole neck and head. Ten viscous heads whipped their disproportionate beak-teeth at him. His axe swung again. The crimson shower returned. As the decapitated heads rolled to the opposite side of the monster, twenty living ones hissed into life. This, Anguhr thought, could be fun.

Forty heads quickly became four hundred. Blood dripped from inside Anguhr's black helmet and left a red sheen on his body. He was not yet bored. Heads rolled and joined many more. Over time and landscape, there were more skulls than blades of grass in what had been a green savannah.

Anguhr tired. His fatigue was not physical. His enthusiasm to swing his axe as an inverted pendulum waned. He was eager to leave *D'nai Liung*. He used his time against the Hydragon to consider several strategic matters. One was his next target for conquest. The unfortunate system he chose next fought with technology and steel. Their capital planet was a dry world. Here he would drown in the Hydragon's blood before its jaws found a chink in his armor. They never would in his Hell-tempered skin. And he likely couldn't drown. He needed no air to sustain himself. Still, getting bathed in this creature's acrid blood was enough saturation for a long time to come.

Anguhr observed his surroundings, and took another swing. This planet held insect-like forms. Some buzzing, carrion eating fliers would be massed over the countless heads and dark red pools if its blood wasn't a fetid toxin. The natives had made a weapon to fight him that now killed their ecology. It was time for the carnage to end.

Anguhr focused back on the Hydragon. Its greatest power was not the ability to rapidly heal and double its sets of jaws. It was the energy required to do so and keep fighting. Making new heads and necks would be its downfall. It was a massive beast at the start of their combat with great strength. But Anguhr knew there are limits to strength, and energy. Its formation of necks and heads was not synchronous with the muscle increase of the rest of its body. It was already tottering, and less than half of its snapping necks could lunge at Anguhr. Its offense and adaptation were faulted. A few more axe swings later and the beast collapsed from the weight of its own, countless heads. Waves of their severed predecessors rolled out from the impact. Anguhr leapt over the mass of wilting necks and impaled the creature's body with his axe handle. It convulsed once, and then became still. Anguhr mused that the mass of its beak-teeth alone might alter the planet's orbit.

Some color approached the new, head-strewn wasteland. A tremendous moth colored in brilliant pastels and nearly as massive as Anguhr drifted down from the sky. It was another combination of biology and sorcery. Yet it did not arrive to fight the General. Its landing created a great, fetid gust that blew some of the Hydragon's blood off Anguhr's armor creating crimson rain behind him.

On the moth's back glowed one of the planet's sentient inhabitants. It was either *D'nai Liung's* greatest warrior, greatest wizard, or greatest fool. A head bobbed at the creature's front. Although it was much smaller than Anguhr, it bore a face that closely mimicked Anguhr's features visible beneath the General's helmet but overly bulbous cheeks and brow. It also mimicked the fire in his eyes with its own blue luminescence. The rest of its body was a stout, glowing mass shaped as a rippling cylinder. The native moved ahead of the moth's wings and leaned down. It seemed sickened by the carnage and afraid to set foot on the spilled blood. As the blood soaked everything and its foot was a single, muscular sole beneath its body, that was a problem. It paused, but then sallied across the severed heads, avoiding the teeth.

Behind the native envoy, the gigantic moth raised its wings for a downbeat to launch itself away from the poisoned deathland Anguhr had created. Instead, it suffered a seizure and pitched over, dead. The envoy paused, and then continued on to Anguhr.

"Great warrior of Hell!" The envoy stopped within Anguhr's shadow. "Great champion! We bid you greetings and bring entreaties. You have slain the offering we sent to your great and powerful presence. We wish—"

"Do you have any more monsters for me to fight?" Anguhr asked. He tore his axe out of the slain Hydragon.

"Well, no, your immense greatness. May we off--oouuaah!"

Anguhr swung his axe again. The flat of its blades slapped the envoy and launched him into distant clouds.

Anguhr drew a deep breath and regripped the tacky handle of his huge, black and now sticky weapon. He called to his demon Field Master. "Uruk."

Uruk had circled patiently as Anguhr practice cleaving technique on the Hydragon. He alit on a pile of its heads.

"Lord Anguhr, you are again the Destroyer." Uruk drew his sword and brought it to his chest as a salute.

"It is time," Anguhr droned. "Launch the horde."

Uruk nodded. "Shall I command then to assault the skulls, Lord?" Uruk raised his sword to swipe at an imaginary assault of the lifeless heads.

Anguhr replied with a low growl. However, from Anguhr's great height, all he could see was a landscape of Hydragon heads and toxic rivers of its blood flowing out to poison lands beyond.

"Well, perhaps we will come back to this one." Anguhr slowly nodded. "Their own weapon doomed their world. We can return should her infinite blackness bid us scythe this planet."

"You are the wisdom of the Dark Urge, Lord Destroyer." Uruk bowed. "All praise the Dark Urge."

Anguhr growled again.

Uruk stayed silent. He would not test Anguhr's tolerance any further. He watched Anguhr stomp through the heads. The General's giant strides meant he was some distance away in a short time. Uruk assumed his Lord's actions were the will of the Dark Urge, no matter the seeming difference of result. They all lived to serve the will of Hell. But such will required bloodshed in greater torrents than Lord Anguhr had unleashed from the Hydragon's necks. At times, that was even the blood of demons. His General never sent them into battle without consideration of their sacrifice, and was willing to place himself between them and forces that demon strength alone could not overcome. He did this against the Nabaton. Even normal demon minds appreciated valor and loyalty, and that it did not flow only from the horde to its General.

Uruk resolved that enacting Lord Anguhr's will would be his personal, sacred duty. He extended his wings and raised his sword again to make praise. The words were meant for his ears alone. Even unheard by any other, it was still a shocking evolution in the mental orthodoxy of demons.

"Glory to the Dark Urge. But may all praise be to our Lord, General Anguhr."

Tanuhr made his plans. He sat back on his bridge as debris from the confederated armada tumbled passed his ship. His plotted course intercepted the enemy fleet and then continued to the system's main star.

Its radiation would give an additional charge the main sail and relativistic compensators and reduce transit time. It was all calculated to occur in rapid succession. However, the enemy ships were more agile than Tanuhr had expected. Plus, his mental distraction from the ancient ship's data cost him additional seconds.

Tanuhr's ship finally deployed its main sail and his demons took their stations. He calculated the system where Anguhr fought based on the likely course Hell would assign him compared to all other Generals' campaigns. Anguhr was the last General to leave Hell. There was only so much galaxy. If he was correct, he would immediately contact Anguhr on arrival. If not, he may need to annihilate some hapless planet to mask his reason for entering the system. Tanuhr hoped some large rock in stellar orbit would still be intact near Anguhr so they could meet on neutral ground. With Anguhr's reputation as the Destroyer, Tanuhr was uncertain if anything other than dust would exist. Once his ship made the jump, timing would be critical. The information must be shared before suspicion labeled them both as rebellious, and worse, as heretics.

Tanuhr glanced at his all too clean silver spear. Time was a spear point, forever cutting forward and opening potential. Time marched in a perpetual frontal assault. It never doubled back or ceded captured territory. Beings only traveled time as a one-way bridge to the next enemy. And thus brought greater glory to the Dark Urge, of course.

A bubble of time encapsulated the fiery ship as the main sail charged. Soon it would take the perpetually burning mass to another point in space. A momentary release of energy conquered the astronomical distance. Tanuhr felt it was akin to firing the main guns. In the jump, the projectile and gun were the same. The trajectory occurred in an instant. The main sail was nothing like a great sheet of its namesake. It interacted with the fabric of spacetime as a nimbus around and through the ship. A jump brought a brief moment of white light to the dark lives of Hell's minions, not that they appreciated the aesthetic irony. For as soon as the main sail's power ebbed, they made war again.

This time, Tanuhr suddenly realized his war, both mentally and for the Dark Urge, was at an end. There was a great variable he had not included in his calculations. He hoped his ordered thoughts had kept out intrusions into his mind and hid his plans and the revelation that caused them. He was wrong. A spider appeared before him. Its image filled the bridge, although its sight was for Tanuhr alone. The Great Widow hung in her entangled web, waiting for prey. She twitched her dark legs. A strand of ethereal silk that stretched across spacetime snared Tanuhr's mind. Only two Generals had been lost during Hell's war. Tanuhr became the third.

CHAPTER TEN

Sunlight had come to the garden. Zaria watched the artificial sun moved across the sky as it had for countless days since a protective machine encased the world. Before then, the world orbited its true star as a free planet. The creatures on its surface and ocean's came mostly from that era when other machines kept intense light at bay from the star that had become too bright for life so near. Those machines were massive and had survived many eras of ecology sheltered below them. However, even they could not withstand the star's later phase. Its blazing surface did not become even brighter, but more vast.

The star grew and became scarlet. The living world was plucked from doom as its parent star expanded from a sun, once colored yellow in the blue sky, into the Red Giant. The giant was bound, the planet placed in safe keeping. An image of the parent star long before its changes was made to rise and fall as life continued in another great machine. Just as the Builders, this machine was unseen and unknowable to the creatures inside it. Life thrived. Some lifeforms more than others.

Gin was created to run the machines that protected the world. He was at first a simple mind, but in time his awareness and intellect expanded. He could not interact with the ecology his machines protected. He could watch life. He could not alter it. Just as the sun over the world, the ecology was also artificial. Life continued, but aberrations arose. Only one region resisted chaos. Gin was empowered to keep it separate from threats because the Builders had special affection for the soft-skinned creatures it harbored. That zone stayed seemingly perfect. But in that perfect grassy plain, the soft creatures that might have retained the power to bring balance instead were perfectly adapted to eating grass. Gin could do nothing but watch. He was alone.

Then, new sunlight shined and relieved Gin of his discontent. Zaria came to Asherah. She was like Gin in many ways. They shared traits from common ancestry. She worked within Gin's machines and also the planet they surrounded. Zaria could act where Gin could not. Asherah became her world. Under her guidance, balance was restored. The machines and the planet's ecology came into harmony. The world garden became Eden.

In times flow outside Eden, balance in the galaxy came under threat from Hell. The planet and machines of Asherah were well hidden. If the Dark Urge sought them, and Zaria was certain she did, then such protection alone would not be enough as Hell grew more powerful. Zaria sought to preserve life and thus thwart the Dark Urge. In recent days, Zaria had earned a partial victory with the Xa'rol. Sutuhr was taken out of the war, for now. Other General's were just as powerful, and bolder. Zaria's other efforts on alien worlds were less successful, or utter failures. To thwart all of Hell, Zaria would need to be bold. She conceived of a power that could save Asherah and even destroy the Dark Urge. It would be the ultimate weapon in this age of war. But to use weapons, a force needs warriors. She did not have time to recruit or build more allies from the alien systems that still survived. She would need to act in the here and now. The gardens of Eden would provide her the basis of her warriors to fight Hell.

Sunlight moved over the garden. It was not the plants Zaria observed, but the animals among them. A hawk flew in high circles above a tropical canopy. Its mate rested on a blue cliff far below. She preened her wing and dislodged a loose feather. It fell like an arrow into a cleft beneath her talons. Moving across Eden's temperate zone, Zaria saw a massive heard along the edge of a conifer forest. The neoamynodons were enormous grey creatures descended from mega fauna that survived seeming impossible odds and resisted extinction. Instead of ancestral horns, their only defense was a thick hide. These grazers immense size meant self defense needed little effort, save a twitch or perhaps a shrug if the predator was persistent. Zaria would need the aggression their distant ancestors showed against predators of more proportional and thus more dangerous size.

On the verge of the white, arctic expanse, Zaria came over a pack of Sabens. They tore apart the carcass of a capreol they killed as the rest of its heard sprinted towards rising glaciers. Streaks of red fell across the icy snow as the sabens fed. Their compact, powerful forms made excellent, living weapons. Zaria could see their teeth and claws amplified and augmented to rend not mere flesh but demon hide. To the south, an ancient creature lived in darkness save for when it spawned. Then its dark, hard bodies rose to flow across ancestral beaches as living waves. Over the eons, the shape of predators and other life, the chemistry of the ocean, and the shape of the land had changed. Unknown the arthropods, their very planet had changed its place in space. Nevertheless, their life cycle continued. Now, Zaria foresaw changes in the hard-shelled creatures for her cause.

Zaria's light could penetrate more deeply than the artificial sun. Normal light traveled within the tissues of leaves beyond the walls of energy giving chloroplasts to the insides of their thylakoid structures. Zaria could see the plant's genes and touch them. She could do so with animals as well. Eden's creatures gave her strong foundations. Under her guidance, Gin's machines would do the rest. From them, new life would rise without the constraints of natural selection and time. Zaria would direct the genesis of Eden's warriors.

Zaria traveled across the blue-green planet, but avoided one area. It was the same site Gin kept separate. What lived there gave her dread. She watched over and protected them as she did with all life in Eden, and as she had tried on worlds beyond. But she shunned direct contact with the placid, soft-skinned creatures. The twisting chain of events that led to Hell and its war began with the ancestors of those creatures. They shared their ancestry with the powerful beings who built the Forge, the Iron Work, and Asherah. Hell was an aberration of the Builders' legacy. So were the creatures in what Zaria thought of as the garden of lament. The loss of potential, of what they could have become versus the dependant little things they were now caused her great lament.

Zaria completed her search and lamentation. Her warriors were chosen. Now they needed to leave her mind and be born for war. Like all children, monstrous or frail, they would need guidance. She would join them and stand beside them to battle against the terror of Hell's vicious soldiers. She would not do this by projection or in thought alone. Zaria would take physical form.

Sunlight coalesced. Zaria preferred to be a mother, or at least a guiding feminine force. She could stay feminine, as was her nature. However, for this mission Zaria would also become a warrior. The form she chose was close to human in appearance, but at the species' physical zenith. And then amplified. A true human would look up to Zaria with a strained neck. A knowing smile beneath luminous green eyes would look back down across strong limbs and graceful masses. Long blonde hair flowed from her head and behind her. Her tresses, of course, shimmered with the radiance of sunlight. Zaria's new form was tall, although Hell's Generals would still stand over her. This was as she planned. Not standing eye to eye could trick their infernal minds that an opponent was weaker.

She would not want to face them, but would use every advantage if she did.

Zaria imaged a weapon. She recalled one warrior that held a massive sword. Zaria witnessed her use it to devastating effect. Zaria's sword would be as long, but more elegant for speed as befit a being of light. More sun's rays became cooling steel. Zaria's two-handed sword rested in her hands. The shape of its double, cutting edges rippled like flame and the arcs of sunstorms. A sun blazed at the center of the hilt. Zaria raised her sword to the image of the sun above, and brought it to her glowing body. It became clad in emerald armor. The jade plates contoured to her form. She had recast herself for war.

Zaria thought of the female legend with the massive, black sword. To Zaria, she was a kind of bastard daughter. A great failure of Zaria led to the dark warrior's creation. Zaria's preceding work was re-appropriated, twisted, used as the basis for the warrior's powerful form. Zaria had hoped to keep peace and end fear. Instead, there a new force was born and a war began that still raged. The bastard daughter could have been a true goddess of war. Her direct mother was the goddess of darkness. Zaria kept her aspect of light, even to fight. The great warrior she recalled had been created to burn life. She was the first of Hell's Generals. She was Azuhr, scion of the Dark Urge.

Even at the dawn of the new, black age, a ray of nature shone through. Azuhr, the First, was either redeemed or destroyed by love. Nature, desire, found a way to assert life as unparalleled war raged on. Azuhr's own life became forfeit, but she left a legacy that now stalked the stars. The legacy might become Zaria's greatest threat or, if treated with great care, a potential ally. Zaria would not risk leaving the fate of the galaxy to such chance. She hoped to complete her powerful weapon. When that was hers, then she could worry about the unexpected progeny of Hell.

Zaria sheathed her sword.

CHAPTER ELEVEN

Ursuhr stood on his hull above his bridge. The red fires of his ship curled around him. He looked up at the stars and plotted the location of Hell so far away. He took an instinctive breath, and looked back across the global devastation he'd wrought for that distant, dark. Below his ship lay another planet with its civilization in flames. His ursine ears could only hear the roar of the flames in the atmosphere rising from inside his ship. The roar seemed to mimic the intense power of the scythe that arced out from his ship's bow. It was dangerous even for him to stand just this close to its energies. Plasma torrents formed and spun near enough for Ursuhr to feel their charge. The fleet and armies of the planet lay dead. Now the world itself was ripped to pieces.

Sensors watched for an enemy daring and powerful enough to attack Ursuhr's ship at its most vulnerable. At least, as close to vulnerable as the warship could be. Ursuhr himself could jump at an enemy ship and smash it with his maul as his horde swept out as the equal to many fleets. Still, with his main weapons off line, this was a nervous as Ursuhr ever became. His greatest annoyance was not causing but merely watching destruction. Cutting apart planets was tedious work. He was glad for a distraction that began as a crackle across his personal frequency. Ursuhr returned to his bridge.

"Lord! We have what you desire." Martis shouted in his rasping tones as Ursuhr entered.

"The information is now complete?" Ursuhr asked as he sat on his throne.

"Yes, the demon scans on the surface provided the final data." Martis nodded.

"Make use of it. I will have what I seek." Ursuhr said.

"As you command, mighty Lord." Martis bowed. "But it will take time."

"Then start. Now."

Chains. Links. Bonds across a body. Bindings to the past. Some beings wished to snap them all. However, some bonds were stronger than even a massive demon's strength. General Xuxuhr enjoyed ripping apart the bonds he could break. He enjoyed ripping apart most things, especially planets. He sundered geology and buildings with massive chains that had once bound him but now served as his weapons of choice. Yet he was still bound to a master. She was the Dark Urge. She was the mother of shadow and horror. Horror was certainly and inherited family trait.

Xuxuhr was a patchwork of nightmares grafted onto a giant and then further cursed by daylight. His apex was a locust's face with short horns for antennae between unblinking, cuttle fish eyes. The snout of a caiman erupted from his exoskeletal head in place of insect jaws. But the typical stretch of bone and scales was cut away near its base. The remnant of the lower jaw appeared to have stretched out to catch the cascade of teeth liberated by the cutting blow. Other teeth seemed to have fallen down across his giant's body and taken root. Spikes erupted through seems between plates of his dark grey armor. He stood on two cloven feet at the ends of his long legs. Both sprouted two lizard-like toes, but with two talons each. The General's posture showed a monster at complete ease with his twisted form, and who enjoyed his physical power. Another set of eyes stared out from his shoulders on each pauldron of his armor. They were purely intimidating decoration. Yet, they also blinked.

Like all Generals, Xuxuhr had received a personal weapon from the Dark Urge. Unlike all Generals, Xuxuhr put aside his malevolent black whip in favor of lengths of a tremendous chain taken in conquest. The chain was a remarkable feat of engineering by the species called Ignitaurs. However, the chains were not as indestructible as his whip. Thus Xuxuhr needed replacements and repairs to his chosen symbol of terror. Foreseeing this, he captured and imprisoned the Ignitaur chain makers and gave them a life beyond their planet's death. This likely was not in league with the will of the Dark Urge. And so Xuxuhr never mentioned acting outside the normal laws of annihilation. Because he was not destroyed for it, he assumed he was allowed a boon of unspoken consent.

Xuxuhr kept the Ignitaur smiths in a hidden prison deep within his ship. That first captive generation once lived on a world made of enchanted steel. They attempted to capture Xuxuhr in special chains made for that goal. The arcane strength of the links would astonish even the

Forge mistress, the Dark Urge. The chains were nearly strong enough to bind a General of Hell. But the steel planet watched in horror as Xuxuhr broke free, even without the aid of his demons. The most hideous of Hell's commanders then used his failed bonds as massive whips. With the links in constant motion, he slashed apart their grey and gleaming cities, and finally sundered the hull of the planet.

The chain makers were doomed to serve Xuxuhr trapped inside the equivalent of another artificial world. Xuxuhr's ship was built for perpetual war, and burned like an eternal foundry. All the Ignitaurs needed was ore, anvils, hammers, and the will to survive. If they failed, Xuxuhr's original whip still hung in his armory. They wished to live, even as prisoners of the monster that destroyed their home. Life attained time. Vengeance required time. So they made their jailer incredible chain. Their patience helped them survive intense heat and captivity. And, like Xuxuhr, they also kept well-hidden secrets.

Xuxuhr's next target dominated the landscape. The towering building had stood for so long that windblown sediments encased one side in compacted layers of rock. Storms further covered that slope in nutrient rich soil. Over the ages, a habitat of lush vines, flying reptiles, and herbivorous serpents took hold. The blows of massive chains sundered it all.

Again, Xuxuhr reveled in using something built to constrain instead for destruction. Rockets exploded across this frame. Orbital vehicles built to launch communication satellites were armed with warheads and fired at Hell's forces. They blew apart demon formations, but gave Xuxuhr little reason to pause. Still, he nodded a salute to his attackers in the distance, and then the chains flew again. Xuxuhr's onslaught eclipsed all the storms suffered on the planet Maeron. Little could stop him once he gained a rhythm. One image caused him to slow, and then sigh. The chains clattered to a halt with the rumble of thunderstorms. A giant spider hung in the sky beside him. He turned to face the Great Widow's projection. A mocking tone gripped to his words as his grating voice clawed out from his throat.

"There is legend of a great spider
that lives in the depths of a fiery well.
She stays at the feet of the dark god
and never ventures from Hell.
Lest the great boots of conquest
slam down and crush her well."

Laughter like acid frothed from between the General's phalanx of teeth.

72

"There once was appreciation for poetry, General Xuxuhr." The Great Widow said. "But I'm afraid your effort needs work to be appreciated in any form, let alone a threat."

"I threaten worlds, Widow." Xuxuhr said. "That is my role. "Yours is always a curious state."

"I serve my mistress, the Dark Urge, whom I speak to in person. In Hell." The Great Widow changed the orientation of her projection so that her face and fangs hovered above Xuxuhr. "So do not trifle with me, hideous beast. I have eight legs. It is not I who would be trampled."

"Eight legs." Xuxuhr mused. "Sutuhr has ten eyes, but eight like yours. I always wondered if you crept into his gestation chamber and meddled with his form."

"If I ever did such a thing, it would be with the grace of Dark Urge. And so what might I have done to you?" The Great Widow taunted. "Certainly I did not choose your face."

"Aesthetic judgment from a giant spider," Xuxuhr observed. "I bid you come with me. I enjoy a panicked stampede. What might both our faces do to the minds of the gnats I now slaughter?"

"From threats to request of an alliance." The Great Widow said. "Your mind has more loops than your chains."

"We both serve. Destruction. Fear. Horror. And, then at last, conquest."

"All for the Dark Urge." The Great Widow added.

"Of course," Xuxuhr nodded. "All praise be to my mother, but who is only your friend."

"My friend. My mistress. Your ruler."

"A fact I accept, Great Widow." Xuxuhr bowed his head. He noticed a glare of light flash across his chest. The eyes on his pauldrons blinked. "Now, why have you invaded my brain? Not to duel with me, nor distract me from the service to our almighty, black sovereign."

"She has need of you, General. Of you and your horde."

"I serve her, now." Xuxuhr raised his chains in his fists as he walked toward the source of the glare.

"The Dark Urge has need of you here. In Hell's own system." The Great Widow's image kept floating at Xuxuhr's left side.

Xuxuhr paused and lowered his chains. He looked up the spider. "If this is her command, then why does she not burn me with the blessing of her presence?"

"The Dark Urge has never done so. But if you love your mother, you will do as I ask."

"I will obey her will. As always." Xuxuhr paused to hide thoughts of his chains and their makers. "If I come home to Hell, perhaps I can do something that will give me great pleasure."

Xuxuhr raised a taloned foot over a field of solar collectors used too late to focus heat as a weapon. He slammed his foot down to crush the panels. They shattered in a glittering wave of ceramics and steel. Xuxuhr twisted his foot as if to crush something beneath it and looked up at the Great Widow. His teeth bent into something approximating a horrific smile.

Sutuhr sat alone, and glowered. He hated glowering. He had reason to do so, and to be angry. His ship was still under repairs. It had taken the most damage of any Hell ship. Thus, his ego was also damaged. He could not bring greater glory to the Dark Urge on a floating wreck. He knew his demons crew worked tirelessly to restore all ships functions and weapons. But in a sense, the Xa'rol battle was still ongoing. His frustration amplified his hellish quirks. His left hand now ached from wiping away his own venom. His tongue was numb from rubbing against his teeth and fangs. A small river of venom flowed from the front of his throne. When system repairs reduced gravity, it rose as a liquid and highly toxic rope off the deck plating, only to splat into a wider, steaming sheen when it returned. Hell's warships' carried an overwhelming array of advanced weapons, but not one primitive mop. Sutuhr hated that.

The General was a chimera. His ship was also a mix of systems that drew power from forces operant in spacetime and the arcane. It functioned as a unified war machine, until someone found a way to exploit one aspect to threaten the others. The Xa'rol weapons were the most powerful Sutuhr had ever faced. They struck down his ship's defensive inferno, but still did not penetrate its hull of chaotic steel. Other weapons did. Now, even though they Xa'rol were vapor, a second battle raged inside the ship. The Xa'rol proved excellent engineers of data weapons. Sutuhr recalled Marn mocking system infiltration as the lowest form of combat. It was a very effective form of aggravation. Sutuhr was very aggravated. He became more so when a giant spider descended before him.

"I bid you greetings from your dark and infinite mother, Lord Sutuhr," The Great Widow said.

"To my demons I am *Lord* and their bond to the Dark Urge. To you I am General." Sutuhr answered with a sneer and drip of venom. "Unlike my demons, what will become of you should you ever die, I do not know. I am certain you are not Hell born. I am. So what would Hell have me do?"

"I am Hell's voice in the cosmos, *General.*" The Great Widow replied. "The Dark Urge, my mistress and Hell's almighty sovereign, my friend, orders you to return to Hell. Now."

"Return?" Sutuhr thrust forward to the giant, dangling spider, even though he realized she was only spinning her image in his mind.

"When I leave you, make your main sail and transit to Hell's orbit."

Sutuhr slumped back in his throne. "I am pained greatly by my reply. I can only set my ship towards Hell in real space. I cannot attend the Dark Urge immediately. My ship was damaged in the commission of her will. As yet, I cannot make the main sail, lest I doom the horde."

"When will it be repaired?"

"I cannot say." Sutuhr wilted on his throne. "My demons work unceasingly to restore full operations."

"And their General?" The spider's eyes drew closer to Sutuhr's own semi-arachnid face.

"I am their leader, spider!" Sutuhr sat up and stiffened. "My demons work well because they both love and fear me. I am their Lord!"

"And you are failing as a son. What should I tell your blazing mother? You fail in war and so you fail to obey her now?"

"Old Widow, I am as devoted a servant to my mother as could be possible!" Flecks of Sutuhr's venom shot though where the spider would hang if she were physically present. "But if you continue your barbs, should I return to Hell soon, my first act of defiance will be to kill you."

The Great Widow paused. She had made a tactical error in her interaction with Sutuhr. So long as his piety was a line kept straight an understood, he was complaint. When that line was plucked or challenged, his aggression replaced devotion.

"Your faith and threat are noted, General Sutuhr."

"Do not question me. Do not question my faith." Sutuhr's lips curled back.

"We all serve the Dark Urge as we can. As we must." The Great Widow's tone became soft. "All praise be to the Dark Urge."

"All praise *is* for her." Sutuhr growled. "Now, help me with my ship. If you can."

"Then it is more than mere physical damage." The Great Widow remarked.

"My ship is intact. Its internal power system is infiltrated."

"Not possible."

"Fact, distant bug!" Sutuhr snapped

"Then, how?" The spider asked in a more gentle tone.

"My last enemy launched more than powerful beams at me." Sutuhr grumbled. "The infection makes my reactors surge and overwhelm the capacitor grid. The first incident led to an explosion. We have shut down systems to isolate the cursed gremlin. My demons are barracked in vacuum to prevent greater losses."

"But your ship can generate replacements." The Great Widow twitched.

Sutuhr took in a long breath before exhaling his exasperated reply. "To phase energy into matter, especially living matter, I need energy. I need power."

"Redirect your main drive through your ship." The spider offered.

"Your wisdom is as great as your service to Hell, old spider. I thank you for telling me a strategy that has already been enacted." Sutuhr paused for his ridicule to fully penetrate. "However, we still cannot make the main sail without the main drive *and* our internal power grid fully devoted to that task."

The Great Widow was silent as she thought.

"So you begin to see my hindrance." Sutuhr grasped his mace from beside his throne and slowly waved it in the air. "If not for my horde and the crimson grace of the Dark Urge burning through our decks, my ship would effectively have no defense. Fortunately I have already killed all enemies in the nearest systems. Yet I grow bored, and wish to kill something. Anything."

Behind Sutuhr's throne, Crucis entered the bridge. Upon hearing his General's words, he exited.

"This is an unprecedented problem, General." The Great Widow broke her silence. "Never before has some form of data been able to corrupt Hell's code. Even so, the infernal power of your ship's central core should cleanse the infection when it's found."

Sutuhr breathed deeply, again. "If it can be confined. Yes. That is our strategy. Isolated and overwhelm. Or at least excise and hurl the infection into space. Where I can shoot it. Yet this is a very large ship. It has an extensive grid. And then another after that. The schematic is likely more complex than your web."

The three-dimensional, intricate and vast power grid schematic replaced the hovering Great Widow and scrolled before Sutuhr. One of the end of the spider's legs moved the schematic.

"No. It is not." The Great Widow's said.

Sutuhr snorted.

"That some alien has broken our coding is, quite improbable." The image of the spider returned.

"And yet, here I fight just that." Sutuhr said.

"Gain as much knowledge on this gremlin as you can, General. I will tell your great and powerful mother you still serve her with all devotion possible. And that you will, one day, return to her side. Do so as quickly as you can."

"Is my mother under threat?" Sutuhr stood and narrowed his sideward cat's eyes at the spider.

"Do so as quickly as you can," The Great Widow repeated. Her image vanished.

Sutuhr was uncertain if the spider had just repeated herself or he saw a reflected message. He felt needed by his greatest love, but was marooned in deep space. Frustration overwhelmed him. He made war on the sheen of his own venom on the deck plate by beating it with his mace. Crucis heard the roars and smashing metal in the corridor outside the bridge. He made a mental note to summon a sacrificial repair crew.

CHAPTER TWELVE

Most of the planets orbiting the Kellis stars were solid worlds. That made Anguhr glad, if not merciful. These worlds might be his last campaign. He was unlikely to die. However, there were only so many worlds left to conquer, and there was more than one General at work. If Anguhr could jump his ship on a solo mission to another galaxy with powerful opponents, he would consider that a promised land. The future without the war was an inconceivable and unwanted existence. For the Kellis system, the future ended with Anguhr's invasion. His arrival on the first contested world was like an asteroid's collision. He stood as the shockwave spread out from the impact crater. Battle cries of his demons cut through the falling rock and dust as they streamed down from space to follow him.

Above them, the last desperate ships of an allied armada exploded and fell toward the planet. The evening sky was brightened by flashes and streaks of a last stand in orbit and fall of hope. The secondary batteries and missile bays of his ship were already hot from constant fire and perpetual launches. Anguhr let Proxis deal with the valiant, doomed survivors. He looked for better sport on the surface. Ahead of him, energy lances slashed from beyond the horizon to intercept incoming demons. The lances were few. The demons were many. Those demons hit by the defensive fire corrected their flight and returned fire with their heavy, metallic rifles.

Enemy aircraft roared through the darkening orange sky. Their shape marked the squadron as allies of Kellis. The fighters were spearpoint shaped with contrasting falcon wings of steel. Anguhr had seen living, feathered predators soar. Those hunted the skies of a planet with terraced cities and fields of agriculture floating in tropical air. He cleaved the structures and their defenders apart with his axe. Aside from the destruction, the native falcons had stirred a rudiment of aesthetic appreciation in Anguhr's mind. He annihilated the native civilization, but left the planet intact. Anguhr had no thoughts of preservation as he watched the attack craft bank and drop into a lower arc. Their new trajectory aimed straight at him. He smiled.

Before the aircraft could launch their payloads, streaks of fire struck their formation. There were no demon squadrons close by when the fighters altered course. But the allied pilots didn't realize the demons' ability to accelerate. Each demon could act as an arcane fighter craft that bypassed aerodynamics. The spearheads exploded in succession. Their burning wreckage fell behind Anguhr as he continued toward the city. A massive wave of demons followed him in the sky. The chorus of their war cries became a sonic wave creating tremors. The energy lances from the city continued to fire skyward. Hulks of ships fell from space as burning streaks in the night. The city Anguhr approached shimmered with lights among its buildings. By the time Anguhr passed through it, there would be only flames.

Anguhr's massive form crushed rock beneath his boots. He glared across the city as his demons made it a battlefield. He stood as a beacon of doom. Yet doom was an end, and Anguhr never enjoyed victory as much as the fight. The act and idea of war brought joy. He held other feelings almost all sentient creatures would consider even stranger than that. In Anguhr's mind, war brought a sense of safety and calm. It merged with other impressions in his mind that had lingered since he could form rudimentary thoughts. The result felt as a transcendent presence. This sense of War was his own, secret belief. It was also dangerous. It undermined the ability of Dark Urge to control him.

Again, Anguhr thought to push such concepts aside. For once, he failed. He did praise the Dark Urge for starting her war of conquest. However, Anguhr wondered if she had a choice. War was now the state of the galaxy. Was it the true state of creation? And thus, did the Dark Urge serve that transcendence? Did she serve War? Should the Dark Urge see this sacrilege in his mind, she would certainly strike him dead. Yet he stood, alive. Before him raged combat. War. Anguhr's eyes flared brighter. He saw a perfect target for his mood in the distance.

The temple shuddered. Walls around the sacred, tiered pyramid toppled. Stone and steel shattered under the assault of the demons. Claws, weapons' fire, and swing of a great axe razed a symbol of faith. The pyramid shrieked and collapsed into a cloud of debris. Dust shot skyward. The destruction of the landmark served little military purpose. It was a robust structure that caught the eye of a giant with questions of his own beliefs. And he held a massive axe. Kellis once built such temples on their home planet and worlds beyond. They became only sentimental landmarks in Kellis history. Now this one became sudden ruins. The rumble of its collapse subsided. Black, demons wings and shouts of terror rose to the dark orange sky.

Out from the dust cloud and falling shards strode Anguhr, axe in hand. The double blades left swirling wakes in the column of dust and smoke as it spun slowly in his massive hand. He walked as a colossus through the cracked streets of the alien city. His eyes burned brighter than the Red Giant of his home as he scanned for a strong pocket of resistance.

High explosive shells and plasma lances exploded across his chest. Excellent shots. Futile attempt. Three demons fell to the same cannonade. Anguhr waved another demon squad away from the target. The enemy position lay inside a conic glass tower. Such architecture was atypical for the city. Perhaps it was an embassy for an interstellar ally that would send more forces to avenge this planet's fall. Anguhr could only hope. More plasma lanced across his torso. He threw his ax in reply. The center of the skyscraper shattered into an explosion of glittering shards and fractured steel. Demons roared adoration and continued their attacks.

Anguhr retrieved his ax from the crew of demon combat engineers assigned for the task. He gripped the weapon by each blade and lamented. When this campaign was over, would he ever feel the embrace of his love again? Could the war truly end? Could War die? His mind drifted to memories of Hell. A distant place. It may be his place of origin, but his home was his ship. When all resistance lay crushed across the galaxy, he was certain all the Generals would be called back home. Perhaps the Dark Urge would bestow another purpose. As explosions occurred around him, he searched his mind for some reason to find solace in returning to Hell.

He became angry with himself. He knew focused thoughts on that darkest, flaming place eased his suppression of the part of his brain directly linked to Hell. The Great Widow appeared next to him. Anguhr's rage at himself felt as a sharp slap to the spider as she entered his mind.

"I bring you greetings and you give me pain, General Anguhr."

Anguhr brought his mind to order. Despite enemy fire around his body, he was now engaged in mental combat.

"I am the Destroyer. Perhaps my fellow Generals have become far softer in thought."

"No." The Great Widow paused. She opened and closed her jaws revealing her fangs in a quick flash. It was the giant spider's equivalent to shaking her head in disgust. "I am forced to endure you all. Powerful children making war with demons. No respect for your elders."

"Then go and leave me and my demons to make war." Anguhr took his axe by the handle and looked across the burning city for an adversary to focus on.

"I know you love war, Destroyer. I know you block me for fear I will call you home as parents call their young. You feel victory is the greatest evil, combat the greatest joy. Yet, we must put aside what quickens our hearts for the greater pleasure of fulfilling our duty. Your ultimate love is too she who gave you war. Your great mother, the Dark Urge, has need of you."

More cannon fire exploded against Anguhr. This time pain bit through his armor and into his chest. He cheered the marksmen. He cheered the charge of his enemy, though his cries caused several of the hovering, armor-plated ovals that attacked him to break ranks.

"An armored division! A courageous act to assault me head on. Do you not love this enemy Widow?"

"General Anguhr, the Dark Urge—"

Anguhr was on the move. His demons had already opened fire on the flying armor unit. More demons swooped in to join their bellowing General as he charged. Anguhr swiftly fixed his axe to his back to free his hands as the valiant Kellis defenders continued their fire. Anguhr tore up the remnants of the city before him and hurled the shards and wreckage at the floating armor. Their cannon became more chaotic as each gliding tank maneuvered between the chunks of Anguhr's hurled avalanche. The section of city in front of Anguhr became a rolling wave of rubble. The Kellis armor continued to attack and fire until a mountain of crushing debris engulfed all their machines.

Anguhr stood still. His armor cooled. He enjoyed the smell of his singed skin as it healed. He sighed. The protesting hiss of the Great Widow met his hears.

"General, the Dark Urge has need of you. You are to perform a new mission for her glory."

"Another campaign? Good." Anguhr's laugh echoed among the exploding shells and sharp report of energy lances as a dull roar. The Great Widow's next words killed his joy.

"This mission is a personal service for the Dark Urge, Destroyer. If her countenance would not destroy all she sees beyond Hell, she would tell you herself. She would spare you destruction, General. I am a vessel to her—"

"What is this mission?" Anguhr demanded. "Where?"

"You are to return to the home system and assault the hidden planet that orbits Old Jove: Asherah. The other Generals will join you. Together you will destroy Asherah and its Eden, and if necessary, Old Jove. But you alone will strike first. But you will not do this with your entire horde. Leave your forces to finish your current campaign. Take a band of your strongest demons and break through Asherah's walls. Then gather knowledge on what power lies beneath. This, the Dark Urge commands."

Anguhr suppressed a growl. He cloaked his brain with mental camouflage. He flooded his senses with images and odors of the battle and the pain from his cooling wounds. Then he focused his deeper mind on other thoughts. Asherah was mere legend. It was a symbol for alien resistance, a clever barb to stab doubt in Hell's supremacy over the stars. Some stories claimed it was the hidden stronghold of allied of warlords still unconquered. Others said it was the first planet of their ancient empire lost, unknown, but still whole and free from Hell. It was all a lie. To think such a world could exist in Hell's own system was blasphemous even to Anguhr. For what reason would the Dark Urge send him against a myth? Why not one of the other Generals? Anguhr felt their campaigns had been bloodless compared to his own. Still, they were Generals from Hell. Anguhr needed to consider if one or more of their fist prints stamped this false quest. Yet, even they could not trick the Great Widow. Certainly they would not defy the Dark Urge. Unless, he wondered, they had some revelation of their own about the presence of War?

Anguhr pushed the thought aside quickly. His ire grew. He saw the Great Widow's image twitch. Her eyes were like dark glass beads. They reflected the lifeless metal of Hell where she was in true space. There was no indication in the spider's eyes of what she saw in her own mind. Her gaze was ever accusing or indifferent. It was a solitary predator's unblinking, constant stare out for prey. She was as adept at sensing vibration in thought as she was in silk. Anguhr's rising ire made the spider recoil. She raised her forelegs and calipers in defense. This pleased Anguhr. He quelled his laughter, but not his smile.

"That's an odd position for one who rests beside Hell's throne." Anguhr taunted. "Or, perhaps, it is your normal stance."

"You mock me, brat?" The Great Widow hissed. "You dare come close to mocking your sovereign?"

"I am a warrior. I have conquered a galactic arm and more for Hell's infernal glory. What would you, spider, know of magnifying the power of the Dark Urge compared to the campaigns of one of her Generals? Especially mine."

"Nothing." The Great Widow relaxed. "You are a warrior, first and last, General Anguhr. And thus your ruler has chosen you for this historic mission. There has been no campaign for the Dark Urge more important than this mission. So I am certain you will rejoice she has chosen you."

The Great Window sat and stared as she awaited Anguhr's compliant response.

"All praise the Dark Urge." Anguhr said with an almost believable tone of enthusiasm.

"You may shut me out again when I leave you—that interesting power is yours, and I am glad it is yours alone." The Great Widow paused as if she now protected a thought.

Anguhr smiled at her words.

"But tell me when you arrive by the Red Giant," The Great Widow continued, "so that the Dark Urge may rejoice at your obedience."

If a spider's face could show triumph, Anguhr was certain he would see it now. It was as he planned. The Great Widow would leave and report what she desired to the Dark Urge. Once free of her, Anguhr would act as he saw fit. The Great Widow vanished.

Anguhr raised his ax. "Uruk!"

"Lord Destroyer!" Uruk flew to face his revered General. "Command me, and it shall be done!"

"This butchery, here, is over. For now." Anguhr folded his massive arms. Their pressure on his chest plate made his skin sting below it. "Recall the horde! I want every demon in its rack in one orbit."

Anguhr knew Uruk would be confused but would comply without question.

"As you command, General!" Uruk saluted. He then soared across the burning city. The Field Master repeated Anguhr's orders as blood thinning screeches and barks. The horrific sounds repeated along the demonic chain of command until they echoed across the planet.

Anguhr was confused, himself. The Dark Urge would have him assault Eden like an assassin. He was a General. Certainly the mother of Hell and galactic annihilation understood this. She had created all Generals. She must know he would take all his power wherever he was sent. If he found and crushed Asherah, the Dark Urge would care little of how he brought her victory. And if this was some plot beyond her will, then he would have his horde to fight her betrayers. He watched streams of demons soar towards his ship. It appeared as a brilliant, red moon in orbit. Only a few pieces of defeated ships still burned like meteors across the sky. Anguhr wondered what he would see in flames near the Red Giant. Perhaps he had reason to rejoice in returning to Hell, after all.

CHAPTER THIRTEEN

Gin sensed an error. He functioned well, as always. His design was nigh flawless. It was the adaptation of sentience and its permutation of ethics that caused his internal conflict. Gin's alarm involved Zaria, and perhaps the fate of creation. Zaria stood on a hill's slope that faced the region of Eden she typically avoided. It was where the creatures similar to naked sheep lived. They had changed in a passive way and evolved from a line branched from powerful beings into passive grazers. Thoughts of divergence and destinies occupied Zaria mind. She arrived on Asherah as sunlight. Now she looked across it as a gleaming, female warrior.

Gin chose a form other than the eagle to speak with Zaria. He became her male twin. The choice was ether ironic or apt. His concern over his coming agon with his friend made him think that he understood the perspective of the grazers. Their design shed awareness of the universe and its conflicts in favor of a placid life. Yet, without Zaria and Gin, the naked sheep could not survive. Creation itself was under threat. At least some awareness could tell you when to run. Zaria was preparing to stand and fight the greatest and darkest of all powers. Gin did not eat, but he wondered what grass tasted like just before he spoke.

"Zaria, my friend." Gin said. He rather liked the sound of his new voice. He then focused on his concerns. "I have helped you. The error or the glory is also mine. But I must note that creating your warriors is similar to the genesis of the Keepers. From that example the Dark Urge bore her Generals and demon hordes. She also did so out of fear."

"Fear?" Zaria turned to Gin. "I have no fear. I act from need. I have made a shock force for a single mission. I have not raised armies of creatures who lust for conquest and the destruction of life itself, all born out of fear."

"I could stand to correct my words," Gin said. "But my concern is for life, and for our world."

"I know. You are ever the caretaker." Zaria smiled. "And if not for Asherah, for Eden, there may be little hope. You gave me a safe harbor, long ago. Now, I wish to see Eden survive. I wish to save life. All life. To do that, I must risk some of it away from this verdant, safe place."

Gin found his new form brought certain autonomic acts to communication. He sighed.

"If your plans cannot be altered, I can augment them." Gin said.

"How?" Zaria asked. Curiosity contorted her luminous face.

"I am coming with you." Gin answered.

Zaria raised her hands for emphasis and drew a breath to speak. Gin shook his head side to side in another autonomic reaction. He then took Zaria's hands.

"No." Gin said. "This, too, is set."

"It would be the first you have ever left Asherah!" Zaria said. She now felt the dread of new, unseen concerns. "It would be the only time its machines or ecology has ever been without a sentient caretaker. Are you certain balance—all—will be maintained?"

"I am," Gin said with a confident smile and nod. "All will function adequately. Even if we do not return, Asherah and its living charges will continue."

"If we do not return—if we fail, it will all end." Zaria slipped her hands gently from Gin's grip and lowered them. "If demons ever break into Asherah and set foot in Eden is when all life dies."

"Then we should make every effort to return." Gin added.

"And so you see the logic of my warriors, old friend." Zaria fixed a steady gaze at Gin.

"I only hope they are not necessary," Gin said.

"As do I, Gin. As do I."

The view had changed. The Great Widow saw not a massive star, but endless black. This sight was more pleasing to her. It was a Hell within Hell. The space as vast as a planet's interior, or a mere crack in a wall too thin to be noticed. It was her sanctuary. She found the place and hid in it when the Builders transformed a world into the Forge. It remained her private sanctum when the Forge functioned to build the Iron Work, and now when the Forge was Hell.

The spider turned and slowly descended on a line of silk deep into the featureless black. She came to a vast expanse of other lines and innumerable fates. Fate was an end, a fastened point. There was no destiny. Khans would disagree at the height of their power. They seemed fated to rule creation. Hell objected. Azuhr shattered Khan worlds, fleets, and cut down most of them. The war continued with Sutuhr. In his youth, he was so devoted to serving his mother he had no contact with those he annihilated beyond the point of his weapons and rage. All adversaries existed solely to be destroyed for the glory of his creator. His horde and scythe obliterated all that remained of the Khan's fractured and then feudal empires. Their traces were merely ionized ash. His extreme devotion projected the will of the Dark Urge farther across the stars. Though he did not know it, his destruction and shunning of all but Hell was his greatest defense. His life proved long. His devotion, still unquestioned. Or so the spider hoped.

No end could be truly foretold, despite careful plans woven by the living. A life's path had many possible fates. The end came after a multitude of difficult choices and the endurance of complicated actions. Those actions were in turn crossed by many lines that went unseen, even by those with great power. One such line involved Tanuhr. He had proven the lesson that life grows and adapts, or dies. Individuals can grow, adapt, and then at times must die. Tanuhr was never meant to decipher and certainly not read a Khan database. The Dark Urge despised Khans so greatly that no connection between her and them survived in Hell's history. Then as new events became history, Tanuhr encountered an old Khan ship adrift in space purely by chance. That ship's history abstracts revealed the connection between of Khans and Hell. Perhaps it revealed that the Dark Urge had emotions, even though she saw many emotions as weakness and hid them under fire and violence.

The Great Widow saw the intersections of crossing lines and their ends in her web. She knew lines of existence were tangents, and not waves. Waves were aspects of forces that also flowed across her web. She could twitch them just as she did her lines and project force across the entanglement of spacetime. It was how she spoke to Generals far afield, and how she destroyed Tanuhr when he deployed his ship's main sail. Had he shared the information, the power of one or more Generals might slip from the Dark Urge's control. In the mildest scenario, that would collapse the outward war. Worse, it may focus the war back on Hell. If the Dark Urge went deeper into madness, or if she could somehow die, the Great Widow would die. Fate, then, was for Tanuhr to die.

The spider always found a way to survive, even in the company of almighty evil. The detonation of Tanuhr's ship disrupted the local star whose radiation blasted the powerless Khan ship and fried its data forever. The spider mused that the dead General would appreciate the efficiency of one act solving both problems. The Great Widow protected herself by protecting Hell. The Generals were to conquer the galaxy beyond its fires. The spider watched over them, sensing their thoughts in her web. Mostly, they acted as good children of their infernal parent. If they strayed from their path, the only discipline the Great Widow had was annihilation. Only Anguhr could block her mind. The Great Widow wondered if she had not inserted the strand that linked them carefully enough when he was young. Or, Anguhr was simply more powerful than his fellow Generals. He was certainly different. And now he was missing.

A troubling event also had occurred. Two fluctuations emanated from Old Jove, the gas giant in distant orbit around Hell's Red Giant. One was certainly a transmission. Its apparent destination was strange. Troubling. Hell's sovereign must be told. The Great Widow dreaded to see her only friend and tyrant. When last she entered the presence of the Dark Urge, the spider crept to her mistress' speaking chamber. This time she would have to seek out the Dark Urge and disturb her. The news of her plans going awry might drive the dark mind into arachnacidal rage. The Great Widow had lived for a very long time. She had grown accustomed to the state, and never wished it altered. Yet she could not run from the Dark Urge. She was Hell. Hell was a hot and horrid place. Many might think it was the perfect place for a giant spider, but the Great Widow dreamed of a time she could rest in her web, perhaps a different kind of web, and dream of something other than fire.

The Great Widow traveled towards Hell's raging heart. She entered the shaft that was the final doom of the Generals' plunder. The sectioned parts of conquered worlds floated in an orderly spaced train down to Hell's molten core far below. It glowed as a bright, yellow-white dot at the distant bottom of the shaft. The ore blocks of planets disappeared as specks in the bright point of the inferno. The perpetual draw of material down the shaft included gasses and heat. The air pulled downward almost felt like a breeze, if a breeze was a constant current of fire. The train of ore blocks descended from orbit through a portal that revealed the cold black of space. For a moment, the Great Widow imagined herself floating freely beside the train in that frigid vacuum. She pressed on.

Hell continued its axial tilt in orbit. This hemisphere would soon be in the season the Great Widow still called Winter. Then, only the Red Giant would be visible from the scalded portals. Below her the Dark Urge labored as the great machine. The Iron Work was finished long ago. Yet her current work had purpose in her twisted mind. The ore became searing, black ingots that rose skyward through another shaft and travel to the banded, red star.

The Great Widow called to the Dark Urge, but her cries were lost in the building roar of arcane fires. The spider wished she could paralyze the uncertainties she came to report and wrap them in silk. She would carry them on her back until she found her mistress in a less searing location. The ethereal heat and radiation nearly overwhelmed her. The spider rested for a brief moment inside a horizontal channel. She called again to the Dark Urge across the spectrum. Urgency colored her cries. The entrance to the channel closed around her and blocked out all light. The Great Widow felt an ease of the heat but greater oppression. Her mistress had heard her calls. The entrance opened again like the grasp of an eight fingered hand. The Great Widow crawled from the palm and entered a junction chamber. The Dark Urge was present only as a labored panting.

"I am weary, little thing." The voice of the Dark Urge echoed from all directions. "Tell me news of my Generals and my plans so that I may be pleased and my pain abated some small amount."

"Mistress, your forces are setting out to follow your orders." The spider felt a presence directly behind her. She turned slowly, but the presence stayed at her back, out of sight. "Your plan is underway."

The Great Widow paused her briefing to think. She would reveal Anguhr's disappearance at the end. Perhaps the curious fluctuations of Old Jove would lessen the potential for panic by giving a curious puzzle to fathom.

"And is that the truth?" A hum continued in the same tones of the Dark Urge's voice after the question.

"I am always truthful to you, Mistress." The Great Widow stretched her calipers. "Again, in time, you will be victorious. There—"

"In time." The Dark Urge interrupted. "Tanuhr often thought of time."

The spider again became silent. She wondered if the Dark Urge could possibly be toying with her. Also in time, the Great Widow would reveal Tanuhr's fate. In time, she would weave a story that would show his death protected the Dark Urge. Thus the story would protect the spider. Yet, could the Dark Urge somehow sense his death? Right now, the spider would continue without mention of Tanuhr. One missing General at a time was enough.

"Yes, mistress. I know." The spider spoke in a gentle hiss. She still moved slowly to glimpse the thing that kept at her back with her eyes near the back on her carapace.

"I know many things, too." The Dark Urge said.

"More than any mind, mistress." The Great Widow reassured with a tone or reverence.

"And you now will tell me more." The Dark Urge demanded.

The thing at the spiders back stopped keeping pace. The Great Widow wished she never set sight on it with even one of her eyes. It was looking back at her. A giant shark's eye stared at her from the uncomfortably close wall.

"Yes, mistress." The Great Widow continued by summoning her arachnid patience, courage, and skill at acting oblivious.

"There have been anomalies from the proximity of Old Jove. I would call one a transmission as it—"

"Asherah!" The Dark Urge shouted.

The Great Widow flattened herself to cope with the pressure of the shout striking her on all sides. She knew Anguhr was tasked to find the legendary world in the location of Old Jove. Thus it seemed the Dark Urge knew another secret not revealed to her spider, nor had the Great Widow ever found it among the vibrations of her web. The spider assumed the Dark Urge crushed the galaxy to reveal Asherah by seeing its shape covered in the flow of dust.

"Where?" The Dark Urge's voice became piercing. "Where did she go?"

"She, Mistress?"

"Tell me!"

"The direction was at the Iron Work." The Great Widow backed away from the glaring eye.

The junction vibrated. The shark's eye stretched tightly and deformed. Its top and bottom and split in two halves. The center tear became a screaming mouth. All Hell itself screamed. The spider recoiled. She was confused, but then recalled the recent orders given to the Generals. The spider realized that despite her madness, the Dark Urge had foreseen this event. She understood Hell's machines and so grasped at least some functions of the Iron Work. What the Dark Urge saw made her afraid. What caused the fear, the spider didn't know. But if it threatened Hell, the Great Widow feared it, too. If she could, she would join her dread sovereign and scream.

Their journey through the ether had taken them more than the diameter of a small star in the time span of a blink. Yet, Zaria and her warriors would need to walk to their final destination. Their path lay across a desolate field of black that seemed never ending. Zaria wondered what the Builder's had thought if they ever walked across their great achievement. The vastness of one small patch of the incredible machine was hard to fathom, even to giants. On the Iron Work, Zaria and her warriors were less than gnats on the wing of an albatross. They were as microbes on a bridge span built to roll planets across. The Iron Work was a feat of incredible engineering, and caprice.

Even with all the power Zaria possessed and had seen unleashed, she was still stunned by the view. Her intellect was as shocked as the new minds of her warriors. They looked across a great slot cut in the Iron Work to store information akin to forgotten times when books were stored on selves. They could only see the very edge closest to them. This slot was wider than most terrestrial planets' diameters. Its depth was nearly incomprehensible. The objects within were plucked from orbits and stored safely by great intellects with nostalgic whims. Looking across the slot was close in experience to looking from a planet's surface toward orbiting worlds in a sky. However, these worlds rested in a neat and evenly spaced line. There appeared to be place holders or plain, new dust jackets for deteriorated volumes. Those were massive spheres the color of the Iron Work. They sat beside original volumes. Some of their natural hues were visible in the red haze. One towards Zaria and her band was a dusty, grey world. It once governed ocean tides on the planet of the Builders' distant ancestors. Humanity looked up to see it at nearly the same distance away as Zaria saw it. Humanity had called the grey world, simply, the Moon.

Zaria turned and began walking. She enjoyed the physical act, even encased in her armor. It flowed across her body like emerald ice. Her long, golden hair was now gathered at the back of her sheer helmet. A pouch hung at her left hip. The handle of her sword rose behind her right shoulder. The long blade rippled like a ribbon of black flame nearly as long as Zaria's body. It was the only thing that seemed kindred to this astonishing, metallic place. The alloy Zaria fashioned for her sword was inspired by the surface she walked over.

Elements of the same technology that built Asherah and maintained Eden enabled Zaria to manipulate codes of its lifeforms into the savage shapes that followed her. Their eyes had never beheld the peace and beauty of the garden, only the steel and glass shapes of Zaria's workshop. The same steel coiled within their muscle and sinew. The giant Bron and his brother Caliburn possessed great strength and massive fists. The ancestors of their donor species gave rise to the grace of a racehorse, and the rampaging might of the rhinoceros. Zaria's tweaks in genetics and fabrication created their unlikely ape-like forms. The base of the peaceful neoamynodons became the twin rampages awaiting Zaria's order.

The archers were less tall and far less massive than their giant allies. They walked ahead of Zaria's force with arrows at the ready. The feathered wings of hawks became strong and swift arms. Bodies with the power to beat wings now powered the flight of armor-piercing arrows. Each forearm was a living quiver of feathers transformed into lethal shafts. As humanized as the archers' forms had become, their faces still held the searching gaze of a raptor.

The eyes of the gulos also searched for prey. The basics of the sabens were now enlarged, streamlined, and silver. They appeared the most artificial of Zaria's creations. Steel rippled as muscle and skin, yet the body shapes of these hunters were the most natural of Eden's warriors. The gulos trotted swiftly on four limbs across to the black surface. Swift cetaceans in Eden's seas further influenced their form. They were the most numerous of Zaria's force.

Zaria's calculations placed their arrival within the ethereal envelope radiating outward from their mission's target. The protective field spared Zaria and her warriors the crushing gravity and incinerating heat present across most of the Iron Work. The incredible width of the band precluded the risk of falling into the face of the sun, even if something altered their trajectory. And something had altered their course by leagues. It materialized inside Old Jove as Zaria left her protectorate. She now felt an even greater sense of urgency to complete this mission. What ship, or thing, would arrive near Eden, and for what purpose? If Eden came under attack, she would know it. So far, nothing attempted to violate her garden. Zaria marched onward. Gin's sensors guided her path. She held her companion out before her. Gin now held a form he found ironic for the site. He was a translucent ball of amber. Nevertheless, he could still transmit his thoughts audibly. The field allowed voices to be heard.

"This place, this machine, is beyond incredible." Gin observed. "It dwarfs even Asherah's design. Is there an operating system at work here, as I am to Asherah?"

"I shudder to think so," Zaria answered. "I would imagine that no single mind could control such a construction, and I have never encountered or sensed a mental presence from it."

"Perhaps it is so vast, we could not." Gin pondered.

"The Builders may have thought the task too immense, or could not design an intellect strong enough to survive such strain." Zaria said.

"As in Hell." Gin said.

"Yes." Zaria paused in reflection. "But the Forge had its complications imparted form outside powers."

"Those would-be plunderers dared not touch the Iron Work." Gin said. "Perhaps it very absence of a mind made them uninterested."

"I would guess the Iron Work is so well ordered that it needs no creative compensators. No minds." Zaria looked about her seeing only the even plane of black and the red haze. "They built it so well, or so elegantly, it functions close to perfection."

"Though they did create an error in my design." Gin observed. "I could not act to manage Asherah's ecological aspects. I could only run the machines that housed it. If you had not come and joined me, the habitat would not be as diverse or vibrant. Worse, it would be stagnant. You remade it into Eden."

"The Iron Work is vast and its machinery powerful, but it has a single goal. It needs keep a balance on physics and machines. Life is more complex. And at least you have kept Asherah functioning, old friend." Zaria patted the amber ball in her hand. "It always needed a guardian before a gardener."

"And here we are on its sibling, so vast we defenders of life are less than a speck of dust on a sword blade." Gin mused.

"And this was merely one band of the Iron Work," Zaria added with a smile. "Now we must focus passed our awe if we are to meet our goal and steal an iota of this stellar prison."

"The force capacitors are ahead. Slivers of a cog maintaining the Iron Work's grasp on the Red Giant." Gin said. "A part to your own great design to free the galaxy from the might of Hell."

Zaria said nothing more and continued to lead the trek across the seeming infinite black and red hazed realm. Imagination collected the crimson glow like fog and massed it far ahead to create a false dawn overhung by a red-tinted curtain of space.

All Zaria's warriors followed behind her. They should be all that traveled across this titanic construction. Zaria froze. Far ahead, something moved. A dot cut through the sky. Flashes of white challenged the fiery haze. Zaria strained to magnify what lay ahead. The thing in the sky sailed on wings darker than the Iron Work. The demon prowled the sky, searching for anything else violating the desolation. Other sentries were certainly near.

"Zaria!" the voice came from the amber Gin in her hand.

"I see it. And the others below it. So far, we are still unseen by them."

"How could the Dark Urge know our plans?" Gin asked.

"I see more demons at the edge of our target. The flashes appear to be explosions."

"They can't believe they can—but perhaps they are using demolition charges." Gin said.

"Yes. The demons must be here for the same things we came to gather. At least they are not here to intercept us."

"I'm afraid—" Gin paused. His dread was clear. "There is one among them of special note. Can you see him?"

Zaria strained her eyes under Gin's guidance. She also heard the sounds. The bark of demons. The heavy tumble of massive chain links. A massive figure became visible through the red haze. It stood tall above the others. One of Hell's Generals directed his horrific minions. A length of massive chain wrapped his left arm and dangled to a coil of links beside him.

"Xuxuhr, the Ravager." Zaria said. She found her new teeth clenched on physical instinct. She thought of the mysterious anomaly that diverted them in transit. Were these events connected?

"Why would a General control an expeditionary force?" Gin asked. "Could Xuxuhr be free of the Dark Urge's control?"

"Doubtful. But whoever is the master here, we will have to fight to achieve our own designs sooner than I thought. At least we can deny the demons success. We will need to know their numbers, old friend."

"My eyes are yours, Zaria. I will learn what I can."

Zaria threw Gin high above them. She was careful not to hurl his amber ball outside the protective envelope lest the forces beyond it destroy him. Their target and the General's location was an opened access panel of the Iron Work. Its precise edges defined a rectangular canyon that stretched far into the distance. Although it was tiny compared the book shelf behind them, if was still epic in scale. Titanic black squares floated over the canyon. The squares moved with such slowness that they appeared fixed in space. An immense field of hexagonal columns flowed in grids across the canyon floor. The field continued onward beneath the floating squares.

Gin counted the demons on the surface. More were undoubtedly beyond the canyon edge where he could not see. There was at least a troop, but not an entire company. No heavy weapons defended the demon positions. Gin concluded their intent was to complete their mission, swiftly. As Gin descended, he realized Zaria's force had been traveling along a slight bulge in the black surface. Perhaps the downward slope toward the access canyon could further aid them. They would need all the tactical advantages they could muster even against a small force of demons.

CHAPTER FOURTEEN

When Anguhr left Hell's solar system he never looked back. His life occurred in distant reaches of space where he encountered alien species and interstellar empires. And then he destroyed them. He wanted to stay forever in combat and the presence of War. Especially if it meant being out and ahead of the other Generals. Anguhr knew communication was lost with Barkuhr. He knew Azuhr, the First, was missing by the time he was unleashed from Hell. He assumed both were dead. If Hell erased its enemies, then enemies would erase the fallen from Hell. Anguhr looked forward to facing those who defeated his siblings. Hell inflicted a succession of seven Generals on creation. They were the most powerful, living war machines known. Yet, all power has limits. Now only four Generals menaced the galaxy. Anguhr had no clue Tanuhr was now gone. He would be enraged by the manner of Tanuhr's death without battle, if not the loss of a brother. What mattered to Hell's youngest General was finding a new, preferably arduous campaign. He did not expect to find one near Hell. Its own space was long conquered. Thus, he never found his home system intriguing. Now, that changed.

Anguhr had plotted his ship's transit back to Hell's system long ago to surprise an enemy bold enough to counterattack the Dark Urge at her burning lair. Now it served to conceal his presence from eyes looking out from Hell. The layered atmosphere of Old Jove roiled from the violation of nature's laws and more as Anguhr's ship stabbed deep into its interior. It seemed the natural gasses could not roll away fast enough from the General's red colossus. The warship's decks lay at angles where gravity had no reign. However, his bridge was always at a right angle with the port and starboard main batteries. He sat on his throne at ship's center near the hull's surface so that he could look out unaided and direct fire if necessary and if he had no surface to attack. He was ever careful not to use his main guns too soon in ship battles. They cut away enemies faster than his axe.

The warship's pincer stern held only a dark ball. A heavy sheath of liquid black enwrapped the main drive to contain the ship's speed within the Old Jove. It also reduced the burning of atmosphere that would reveal the ship. For now, manipulating the fiery aura gave thrust and maneuvering. Proxis controlled their course inside the gas giant. Anguhr glared through the gaps in the beams and murky darkness at the first mystery he encountered outside his ship. Deep within Old Jove they should only find denser layers of compressed gas and a solid core. Instead they found a massive machine. He mused it would not be the last, odd discovery.

"Although far smaller, in structure it is nearly identical to the Iron Work." Uruk related as he studied data and images on the bridge projections.

Anguhr sneered.

"The interior rings defy physics and detection." Proxis said as he focused on maintaining control. "But its strong gravity well—"

"Means we cannot remain here for long without using detectable power." Anguhr growled.

"Indeed, Lord." Proxis agreed. "It is another of the Dark Urge's wonders."

"Indeed." Anguhr replied with audible scorn.

Proxis and Uruk exchanged quick glances over the mocking tone of their General. Proxis refocused on his course. Uruk repressed a smile. Anguhr found it odd that another accomplishment, however grand or minor, would not be the long list of veneration for the dark mother of ego. And what of the mysterious moon they also detected that orbited Old Jove? Its gravitational presence could not be masked at close range, though some arcane wonder allowed it to slip detection from virtually all scans. Close proximity betrayed its existence, just as close proximity revealed the machine inside Old Jove. The data that described this planet as a natural gas giant was another lie.

"The Dark Urge must also have created the hidden world." Proxis offered.

"But if it is Eden, then why have us destroy it?" Uruk asked. He then attempted to absolve his confusion and growing doubt by chanting "all praise to the Dark Urge."

Anguhr said nothing. The possible reality of Eden galled him. It should have been annihilated long ago. The smaller iron work inside Old Jove was strange, but no imminent threat. It was one more mystery added to the growing list. He still wondered if another General had a hand, claw, or other fetid appendage in his strange orders. Stranger were these discoveries close to Hell. He could hear the hissing voice of the Great Widow chide him that such confusion was his fault for not obeying the Dark Urge without question. He quickly shut out thoughts of the spider.

"Lord Anguhr, there is a weak ethereal vector from the hidden moon. Or rather, it reflects one—from the inner machine." Uruk said as his serpentine eyes watched lines arc across projections. "The link is stretched as the two objects move in real space, but I think it must have been a pilot wave."

"For communications, or is it a gate?" Anguhr stood and leaned to the projected data with keen interest.

"My Lord, I do not believe we could detect the residual energy if it were merely a communications link." Proxis answered. He focused on the screens Uruk watched. "I am certain the energy source of this structure inside Old Jove could easily power a transit gate."

Anguhr smiled like a hungry predator in sight of his meal. "If it still radiates ethereal waves, then calculate the destination."

"The residual lunar waves flow towards the inner system." Uruk pointed at wave lines on a projection. They flared out from an image of the gas giant and then reflected off a blank disc representing the hidden moon. "I will narrow the—"

"It is the Iron Work." Anguhr said. "It would not be Hell. And nothing else has any strategic value."

"What is of value on the massive machine, Lord?" Uruk asked as he turned to his leader.

"I don't know. Yet." Anguhr answered. "Someone does. And so I will learn it as well. Plot the Iron Work as the end point of the transit, and give me as accurate a target site as possible."

"At once, Destroyer!" Both the Ship and Field Masters answered in unison.

Anguhr stared through his ship's red aura. He imagined seeing through the layers Old Jove's dense atmosphere and beyond the orbit of Hell. Finally he envisioned the destination. Anguhr suppressed vocal laughter, yet it thundered deep within his mind. The unknown travelers had not dared to go to Hell, but did journey to another forbidden place. They must possess great audacity. So did General Anguhr.

There was motion away from the work site. The demon sentry squinted and clutched its rifle. Something rolled near on this black, disgustingly peaceful surface. The demon snatched up the amber ball spinning towards its feet. It looked back to its cohorts. A bark rose in the demon's throat. It halted its warning, and peered back at the ball. The demon's eyes widened looking at two eyes peering back from within the glassy sphere. They were not a reflection. The demon's open its mouth. An arrow punched through the demon's thorny skin and severed its throat. The distraction bought precious seconds for Zaria and her forces to advance.

"Gulos!" Zaria ordered her attack.

The four-legged flashes of silver shot from behind the light warping shields that concealed them. Yet the demons were already reacting to the death of the sentry, and swarmed towards the attack. Xuxuhr's personal guard were built for close quarter combat. A second set of wings snapped from around their backs like a beetle's shell to serve as living shields. It gave them a few seconds before the teeth of the gulos tore at their barbed flesh. The demons fought back with savagery to match their grotesque shape. Short swords slashed through lupine steel. Gulos' teeth and demon jaws locked in battle.

Xuxuhr's bizarre cuttlefish eyes turned to the attack. They and the eyes on his armored shoulders began to glow. His chaos of teeth bent into a slight smile. He barked commands. More demons appeared to rise from the Iron Work's surface as they left the access canyon where his engineer's toiled. Teams took wing. Fusillade of arrows dropped them into the locked ranks of gulos and demons. Each arrow that flew split into four shafts. The separated shafts split into finer arrows until shafts as narrows as wire struck each target and coiled in a helical path through the demons' bodies. More demons emerged to swarm the gulos. Rifle bearing snipers among them returned fire at the assumed location of the hidden archers and raked the battlefield.

The giants stood. Demon bullets bounced from their stony hides. They joined the charge. Ricocheted fire riddled both attacking demons and gulos. Bron and Caliburn smashed through masses of demons swarming them with guns and swords. The dual row of archers advanced towards and through the screaming horde of demons. The first line of archers fired as their sisters held the shields to block blades and bullets. Then the shield bearers swiftly aimed and fired as their sisters traded position. The rotation of arrows and shields was so swift that luckless demons witnessed only a whirling barrier firing their doom.

Gin transformed into his male form behind the line of archers and became a field medic. Gulos not torn asunder snapped back to life under his swift care. They immediately rejoined the savage combat.

Demons used their dead as added protection and slammed against the archers' shields. Zaria cleaved through breaks pushed through the line with her sword. The acrid solvent in demon veins splashed her skin and armor. Demons fought on with weapons or without and with whatever limb that survived. Even with all the open space surrounding them, the demons threatened to mire Zaria's forces in a sea of rifle fire, swords, snapping jaws, and snatching claws.

"Bron! Back!" The giant waded back towards Zaria, and smashed a forming demon column.

"Gin! The charges!"

Gin reached into Zaria's pouch as she slashed ahead. He retrieved three solid tear drops as she swung her blade into more demons.

"Bron, take them!" Zaria yelled. "Through them forward!"

The giant obeyed and reached down as demons furiously but uselessly hacked at him. Gin dropped the charges into his massive palm. Bron then hurled the charges. All three pierced several demons before bouncing across the surface among the lines of massing demons. Three explosions sundered their ranks. Wings, limbs, and shattered weapons rained across the battlefield. Zaria and her troops smashed and cut through those before them.

Xuxuhr became annoyed. With a great roar the General unfurled his chain from his left arms and waded into the fray. His Field Master, Akhad saw this and left his position at the canyon edge overlooking the work within it. More white flashes lit the background as the demon engineers continued their work undeterred.

Bron charged to meet Xuxuhr. The General swung his chain. Its shorter length was made for reconnaissance and close-quarter combat. Its span of bladed links was a blur of steel. Bron evaded each slash and slammed into Xuxuhr. The titans grappled. Xuxuhr was stunned to fight a physical equal for the first time. He was glad he had developed his already infernal strength by hurling heavy chains on a regular basis.

Akhad swooped down. With a burst of demon courage he struck at the near General-sized warrior with radiant green armor. His sword collided with Zaria's sword. Although skilled and savage, Akhad could feel Zaria's superior strength with each strike of her sword. Akhad stopped the exchange of blows and thrust his sword point at Zaria's body in a circling airborne attack. His blade was caught and thrust back each time, no matter if he faced her or struck from behind. A piercing bark by Akhad brought five demons to fly before him. They perished in a slash of Zaria's black blade as he swooped away.

Xuxuhr strained to pry away Bron's arms crushing his torso. He succeeded and threw the giant back. Bron roared and charged again. Xuxuhr dropped into a momentary crouch, and then launched into Bron. Xuxuhr wrapped his horned arms around Bron's middle gut and thrust him aloft. Bron's fists thundered against Xuxuhr's shoulders. Xuxuhr tightened his grip. Though harder than the steel of a demon's blade, cracks appeared in Bron's' stony hide.

98

Bron's twin continued fighting. Caliburn grabbed the demon firing point-blank into his knee. The infernal creature became a missile that struck Akhad from the sky. More demons swarmed and shot and at Caliburn who tried to wade towards his twin. The archers kept the demons from swarming over Zaria's lines by making the sky a lethal place. However, their own numbers began to suffer losses as the bullets of demon snipers found thin gaps among of the archer's shields.

A cascade of arrows pelted Xuxuhr as he crushed Bron. Xuxuhr hurled the gasping giant against the surface. The General grasped and swung his chain to cut down a pack of gulos leaping towards him. The chain continued its arc and did the same to the rising Bron, slashing into his back. The giant collapsed, motionless. Dark red oozed from the deep rip left by the chain and rolled onto the Iron Work.

Akhad recovered his sword. He slashed the blade at the gulos ripping his wings into bloody shreds. He barked for the demons to fall back and regroup.

"No!" Xuxuhr bellowed. "Demons! Continue the charge! Lest you think we need the ship's main guns to aid us as well!"

"No, Lord!" Akhad yelled as blood spewed from his wings and he slashed away at more gulos. "We will annihilate them for your glory!"

A unit of demons came to relieve Akhad. Together they charged Zaria's advancing line. The stabbing point of her sword halted Akhad. He swung his own to deflect the blow and assaulted Zaria's ears with a blast of hypersonic indignities. Their blades locked. Zaria's fist slammed down into Akhad's face. The next blow of her sword broke Akhad's blade in two pieces. The following strike split his torso.

Xuxuhr roared and charged through the assault of arrows and gulos' teeth. He whipped his chain in fury.

Zaria heard Xuxuhr's war cry. She saw her fallen giant near him.

"Caliburn, take my position! Support the line!" Zaria commanded, and then leapt over the archers. She charged Xuxuhr to avenge Bron.

The demons found that Caliburn provided an equally good high point to shoot at the archers without being shot out of the sky. Caliburn swatted at the demons that climbed over their own kind as living chains. The demons clung for life against his massive body and limbs. Their linked bodies locked into a cage with gnashing walls several demons thick. Caliburn became so constricted he could not even grasp a single, screaming demon. Finally, the living mountain slammed himself into the surface and rolled like a boulder to liberate his giant limbs. Caliburn's act forced Zaria's line to part and quickly reform away from the giant. Several archers fell to demon rifles and swords. Once free, Caliburn resumed his campaign to smash every moving thing with black wings.

Zaria and Xuxuhr traded swings of sword and chain. A blow from Xuxuhr's horned knee knocked Zaria's helmet into the fighting horde. His chain followed right behind. Zaria barely dodged the chain and leapt away from the following strike of the Generals' massive fist. Zaria leapt and thrust her blade at Xuxuhr. The General pitched his torso back to evade the thrust, but kept his chain in motion. It knocked Zaria's sword free as she landed. Xuxuhr smiled.

Chain strikes and whirring slashes pursued Zaria as she repeatedly ducked and rolled. Two balls of light glowed in her fists and became daggers. Zaria vaulted back towards Xuxuhr. In the instant between his rapid slashes, the blades burst through the bands of steel around Xuxuhr's knees and dove deep into the enormous joints. Xuxuhr roared in pain. The back of his left hand finally found Zaria and knocked her back. The horrific sound of his cry caused greater pain than the blow and her collision against the Iron Work's hot surface. Zaria bolted. Xuxuhr's chain ricocheted off the surface behind her. Zaria hurled more daggers at the General's cuttlefish eyes. He deflected them with a swing of his chain and rocked his legs to advance on her despite the pain.

Demons flew in and tugged to remove the impaling daggers. The blades came free as Caliburn threw Zaria her sword. A group of archers turned to fire on Xuxuhr. He stood and grasped his chain in both hands. The blood flowing from his knee wounds glowed like hot slag. All four of his eyes glowed bright yellow. Xuxuhr's body followed and radiated in a nimbus of heat and light. Arrows flashed into ashes as they struck his aura. Arcs of energy like bows of plasma on a sun's surface or his ship's scythe rose and rippled across his body.

Zaria heard Gin's thought enter her head: 'It appears the Generals have been imbued with new tricks since Azuhr ravaged the stars.'

"Or they have learned to use their infernal power in new ways of their own." Zaria replied aloud.

The glowing General swung his chain anew. An arc of energy rolled from his body and down the hurtling length of the bladed links. Zaria leapt to dodge the fireball projected from the crack of the chain. It exploded against the lack surface. The explosion left the Iron Work unscathed but knocked down both demons and archers.

Zaria knew the battle needed to end. Quickly. She threw her a volley of teardrop charges. They exploded against Xuxuhr's fiery aura but caused him to stumble back. A band of energy flew towards her as Xuxuhr swung his chain. Now she didn't need to be within the chain's length for Xuxuhr to strike her. Zaria sprung high. The energy rolled as a wave of fire into the distance. Zaria landed and rolled toward the flank of her warriors still locked in combat with the demons. She snatched up a shield generator from a fallen archer. Zaria raised the shield as the General swung again.

His energized chain collided with the shield. A shockwave blasted outward from it and hit Xuxuhr. Zaria slammed hard against the black surface from the explosion. Demons and Eden's forces rolled from the blast.

Zaria recovered as Xuxuhr toppled backwards. His knees had not yet fully healed. Zaria knew she would have the advantage in close. Zaria threw the shield. Xuxuhr dodged the missile and arced his energized chain away from it. In the same instant, Zaria whirled her blade at an angle over her head and ran at Xuxuhr. She thrust her sword hard at the slowed titan. The arcane steel bands of his armor deflected the strike with a loud crack from the impact and spark of energy. Zaria spun from the slashing, crackling chain and cleaved Xuxuhr's grasping hand. Her sword cut through his aura and flesh. The chain shot out of Xuxuhr's grip and exploded through the crush of demons like a flaming saw blade.

Zaria blocked a swift assault of massive fists with her sword. Now both of his fists spewed acrid blood. One finally struck Zaria. The impact sent her backward against the surface. She rolled from a second cascade of rage as the General hurled a wave plasma and flame at her. The wave's edge struck Zaria and stunned her. His glowing right fist struck her head. Her brilliant blonde hair flew up from the impact and fragments of Xuxuhr's congealed blood flew from their wounds. Zaria skidded along the black surface atop her sword. Zaria's armor dimmed. She strained to remain conscious.

Xuxuhr recovered his chain and shook it to free the bodies of demons it impaled. His forces would keep fighting to the last demon. He would burn all these alien combatants to vent his rage at being fought so well. He looked at the emerald warrior still reeling on the Iron Work to the side of the battle. He advanced again. Dead demons pelted his face with the force of plasma cannons. They knocked him sideways. Caliburn grabbed more demons and hurled them again. Xuxuhr roared in rage at having to duck from an attack. The giant's hurled assault ended as another began. Zaria had recovered. Xuxuhr swung his chain to block the slashes of Zaria's sword. Zaria ducked close and slashed the General's thighs. Xuxuhr stumbled backwards.

With no Field Master and a General otherwise occupied, Zaria's forces overwhelmed the small demon army. Zaria saw their inevitable fall.

"Caliburn! Archers! Into the canyon! Gulos protect the advance!" Zaria cried out while pressing her attack on the staggering General.

Zaria dodged the plasma hurled by Xuxuhr, but the heat singed her body. Ironic, she thought, as she was ultimately made of light. She understood too well that she could be stunned and feel pain in this form. It was the price for interaction on the physical plane. She would better design her next body, but she needed this one to finish this fight. More plasma rained down as Zaria maneuvered closer.

A group of surviving demons rushed to defend their leader. They were cut down by archers. Xuxuhr coiled his chain around his right arm and swung it as a flaming saw to slash Zaria. A sudden sound made him freeze. His breast plate made a screech of twisting metal as Zaria's sword penetrated his massive chest. Xuxuhr's strange eyes and body all dimmed.

Zaria quickly wiped the General's acrid blood from her eyes. Her face lit with shock at what she saw. The Ravager stumbled back, and began to fall. Zaria's blade made several more stabs deep into his body as he collapsed to the black surface.

Inside that access canyon, the battle went on. Xuxuhr had planned ahead for this mission and selected several burly demons to become engineers. They didn't use their amplified brains but their demons savagery to fight the onslaught of gulos and archers that leapt upon them. Although the ones that faced Caliburn were intelligent enough to run. The battle above was lost. Here it went poorly for demons. The image of the more powerful explosives flashed into the demon engineer Cyr's smoldering brain. He ran from the fray to collect the charges and blow these attackers across the canyon walls. He struck a black-clad wall that should not be there, and looked up. He opened his jaws. A massive hand grabbed Cyr's head and silenced him.

Above, Zaria's fight was not finished. She slashed away the last charge of fanatic demons. Gin worked to save wounded archers and gulos. Xuxuhr rose on the arm wrapped in chain. Zaria sprinted and slashed and stabbed him wondering if she should pace charges on his butchered body and run. Xuxuhr finally fell back, and did not rise again. The few surviving demons stopped looked at their dead General with utter bewilderment.

"S-stop!" Zaria breathed an end to the combat, but the archers had already cut down the distracted demons.

Gin continued to administer to Zaria's fallen. He glanced over to her to be sure all the blood dripping from her body was not her own.

"Gin, we need to procure the force capacitors." Zaria walked to the canyon edge. "Soon—"

Caliburn sailed over the canyon edge and sailed into space with great velocity. But there was no explosion. At her angle, all Zaria could see was the field of hexagonal capacitors. She quickly glanced over the edge. Directly below, General Anguhr slapped his immense ax into his open hand. His demons turned from Zaria's fallen warriors and trained their weapons on Zaria above. Victory was denied.

CHAPTER FIFTEEN

The sound of marching demons assaulted them from everywhere. It echoed in the ethereal atmosphere near the edge of the access canyon.

"Gin!" Zaria screamed. "How far are they?"

"I cannot see them or sense there location, Zaria. I only hear the marching. They must have some form of shielding more effective than our own, or it's a ruse. Why don't they charge?"

"Count their numbers in the canyon!" Zaria ordered. "We must prevent them from swarming over us before the marching columns arrive and attack!" Zaria drove a bloody fist into her pouch and grabbed more of the lethal charges.

"Zaria, wait!" Gin yelled as he peered into the canyon. "The demons have not fired upon us. I see archers still alive in the demon's grasp. Perhaps—"

"Gin, now! Before they rise over the edge!"

The march of demons thundered closer.

"Zaria! There are more demons with Anguhr than were in Xuxuhr's force." The calculations that formed Gin's voice produced the pitch of true stress. "We can't prevail!"

"We have no choice!" Strain cracked Zaria's voice. She thrust up her blood-coated arm. Ten charges armed within her fist. Bright light shone from between her clenched fingers. "Tell me where Anguhr stands!"

"Zaria! Look at the bodies of your archers!" Gin turned and rushed to Zaria. Desperation contorted his human-like face. "Listen to me. The giants are lost. Our numbers are struck low. We have no reserves here.

How do you plan to fight an even greater contingent of demons and their General?"

"We cannot yield, Gin! If we fail—!"

"Zaria, you have defeated Xuxuhr. You have slain a General of Hell, itself. All your warriors fought and died as you commanded. But now we must find another way. To fight on would surely bring death to us, and then death to Eden! Zaria, think passed your physical mind, its emotions and blood lust. It is a gift Anguhr is here. Zaria, think! Think of who he is, and remember what you are!"

The sound of marching demons beat against Zaria like Xuxuhr's fists. Yet, they had not opened fire. No shells arced out from the canyon. Could Anguhr want something from them that Xuxuhr could did not? Zaria looked across the field of crushed and impaled demons. Some still writhed. Others lay torn apart. Silver fragments of gulos were strewn among the slain demons. Dead archers lay pocked and broken across the invisible disks of fallen shields. The dead masses of Bron and Xuxuhr lay at the far end of the carnage. Alien bloods flowed together across the once pristine desolation. Heat from the caged star below caused the collecting pools to steam. The rising mists carried their caustic stench.

To Zaria, time seemed her enemy. Yet now she had no choice but to use it to survive. They would need other means to achieve final victory. The light between her fingers dimmed. Zaria lowered her arm, but kept a firm grasp on the charges. Gin was right. Zaria drew a labored breath, and gave her orders in both hope and despair: "Gulos, stay at the ready. Archers, do not fire. Hold your arrows. For now."

Proxis looked out at the red glare of the massive star held captive by a machine. He wondered what the smaller Iron Work within Old Jove imprisoned. He recalled the liquid and mist of Old Jove and how it gave way to the starry black of open space when they left the alleged gas giant. Above the red star and its greater machine, there were greater dangers. It was not navigation hazards he considered.

Lord Anguhr had ordered Proxis not to allow any ships to move within striking distance of his target on the Iron Work. In Hell's own system, other ships meant other Generals' warships. Proxis considered the ramifications of Lord Anguhr's order. Proxis wondered if that order gave him permission to open fire on another Hell ship. Could he? Proxis took a breath. Lord Anguhr's orders suggested conflict among Hell's forces. Would the other General's engage in open rebellion? Perhaps his own Lord and General gave him the first such rebellious orders in a defiant spiral towards anarchy. The thoughts almost made Proxis laugh. He always valued his free will. Now, he wondered what to do with it. His deliberation was short. He considered that Lord Anguhr always served his horde as well as made glory for the Dark Urge. Proxis was certain there was no greater General. He would, of course, obey his Lord's orders. No ship would come within striking distance of General Anguhr's position on the Iron Work. No ships at all.

"I saw Anguhr in my glimpse." Zaria breathed heavily. "So you are right, old friend. I have another strategy to play. He is said to love war. If it is a presence in his mind, then I know who war truly is to him."

"Do you mean: what war means to him?" Gin asked.

"No."

Gin was silent. He was surprised in all the long time they knew each other that Zaria still had secrets to reveal.

A flying column of demons soared over the cliff's edge like a tattered sheet peeled from the Iron Work. Anguhr's demons swirled around Zaria's surviving forces and divided into armed tiers that sealed their targets within a whirling dome. The drone of marching disappeared behind a louder curtain of demon wings cutting across the ethereal atmosphere. The demons still did not attack. That fact did little to ease the tension straining Zaria, nor did the thud of Anguhr's boots against the former battlefield. The General was visible through the wing beats of the circling demons. He cast a glance over his axe blade towards the canyon. His fiery eyes then fixed upon the prisoners for what felt too long. He walked over to the body of Xuxuhr. Zaria tightened her grip on the charges. Anguhr stood over Xuxuhr's ravaged corpse with his back to his demons and prisoners. Zaria watched the double-blades of the axe dart past Anguhr's shoulders like an inverted pendulum. The blade stopped. The orders to fire met Zaria's lips. Her warriors never heard them. The thunder of Anguhr's laughter drowned out her words.

"Zaria? Is he rejoicing?" Gin asked. His confusion overpowered dread.

"Perhaps it is more the shock of disbelief, or a release of competitive spite." Zaria replied. "But the Generals are weird creatures. Among them, Anguhr is weirdest of all."

High pitched barks spat from the demons. Arcs of bared teeth sailed past Zaria's forces.

"Are they taunting us, or do they not like us talking about their General?"

"Their eyes are focused on me. It was my utterance of *Anguhr*." Another chorus of barks and gnashes confirmed Zaria's theory.

"But how can they understand us?" Gin asked.

"Their speech must share rudiments with Asherah's coding." Zaria answered. "Their language derives from an operating code, just as ours does. Both systems were identical when first written."

"Yes. And what is also becoming clear, is that Anguhr and Xuxuhr were not here on the same mission."

"And what of the—" Zaria glanced at cyclone of demons. "What of our enemy's plans, here? Had she deduced my own? But I suggest we remain silent until we know how much they understand of us, our words, and all plans."

Gin allowed himself one last sentence. "Perhaps the enemy has a master plan. But is she the master of her Generals?"

Anguhr looked again at his prisoners. They uttered his name in a tongue somehow familiar. The slightest wave of his ax commanded his demons to be silent. But now the prisoners had realized that advantage as well. They had proven themselves masters of combat, and now revealed personal cunning. Anguhr admired their skill, and the great audacity of their leadership to send them on a raid to this forbidding place. He knew it was a danger to keep these warriors alive. They must consider escape a possibility and a need to fulfill their mission. Certainly it was not the fear of death that allowed his demons to entrap them.

Anguhr felt lament for not having followed the orders of the Dark Urge exactly, for fighting these aliens on their homeworld would be a great trial of combat. Perhaps it was truly a gift of War ignored. However, it could still be achieved in the near future. Right now, Anguhr was gathering information on Eden's abilities. He had forestalled a disaster. Whatever the target was on the Iron Work, he had kept it from enemy hands. The death of Xuxuhr was the aliens' only victory. This theater was still in Hell's control, or at least his own. Thus, he could argue, he was following the will if not the direct orders of the Dark Urge. Interpretation of orders was also an important combat skill. Anguhr hoped Eden's master had given these warriors more knowledge than his own leadership chose to bestow on him. He wanted the knowledge of what they and Xuxuhr sought. Whatever boon lay here, it was now in his grasp.

Uruk had finished his interrogations of the prisoners in the canyon below, and now soared towards Anguhr. He grasped and archer bound in chains. Proof of their lethal precision impaled the bodies of many slain demons surrounding Anguhr.

"Lord, they not speak well." Uruk reported as he alit beside Anguhr and presented the archer to his General. "They have limited information. Their brains look smooth and new. No synthetic data stores. Their responses to stimulus appear instinctual." Uruk squeezed the chains and the archer writhed in its bonds. "I believe they are like the silver beasts, and are only living weapons. Mere ciphers for war. Yet they fight well enough."

Anguhr considered Uruk's theory. He regretted the swift, ballistic end of his fight with the giant in the canyon, for a brief moment. No doubt it was as ignorant as its fellow soldiers. Anguhr watched as the archer's writhing eased. Its eyes locked on the emerald clad warrior within the cage of demons. Next to her stood a less luminous dimmer male reflection of her form. He understood their sexually dimorphic forms. Yet he had no answers why they looked do similar to himself. Generals were said to be unique. Now he stared at two beings very similar to himself, and they were not creatures from Hell. Or so he would think if he believed all the lore infused into his brain. Again, experience challenged orthodoxy. Those were more mysteries for later. Now, Anguhr could see who led these warriors. The glance of the archer and physical language of the male marked his female companion as his master. She would know why they came here and killed so fiercely. Anguhr wondered if it was for the same prize that brought the clod Xuxuhr here. Another potential intelligence source landed next to him. Intelligence of mission, Anguhr noted, if not fully of mind. Such was a typical demon's state.

The demon Cyr folded his wings, crossed his arms to his shoulders, and bowed to Anguhr. His eyes were wider than the guards escorting him. He was confused and afraid. Cyr looked at Anguhr with awe. Anguhr was a General and Lord to his own demons. Cyr's Lord was now dead. The demon knew his fate and path to the Dark Urge was now in the hands of one of his dead master's rivals. This unknown to demon experience, and far more complicated than rending enemies or exploding bombs under weird artifacts.

"Tell me what you know, demon." Anguhr said in harsh tones. "And perhaps you will please me more than using you as food." Anguhr did not ask if this demon from Xuxuhr's horde had a name. To do so would be to recognize him as an individual. That was an honor given for valued service. Cyr's service to Xuxuhr held no honor for Anguhr.

Cyr held back his fury at his sudden demotion. However, he understood Anguhr could just as well pull the information out through his ears. The demon desired to live a while longer, and perhaps see his own underlings again.

"General Anguhr, I was to remove one of the canyon nodes for fear and respect to my Lord." Cyr answered and bowed again.

"Why?" Anguhr demanded.

"I—I don't understand, General Anguhr. I did as commanded. All praise to the Dark Urge."

"Where is Xuxuhr's ship?" Anguhr leaned down so the demon could clearly see his burning eyes through his helmet gaps.

Cyr hesitated, and then thought hard. He thought of his ears. And then a good idea rolled forth. "General, its course is programmed into my Lord's transport."

Uruk nodded confirmation. "A squad has found it hidden in the mist yon of the canyon, Lord Destroyer. The rendezvous coordinate is open space between this hemisphere of the Iron Work and Hell itself."

Uruk cast his gaze over the field of carnage. "Lord, why would General Xuxuhr command his ship to be elsewhere than the battle?"

"Xuxuhr did not expect to fight here, I imagine." Anguhr answered. "Perhaps he expected no fight at all in this system. Why would he?" Anguhr shouted his last sentence. "Indeed why would he?"

"Lord?" Uruk asked.

Anguhr was lost in thought. He considered that Xuxuhr would not expect enemy forces if he too thought this system and several stars around it had been long conquered. Yet Anguhr was sent to find and destroy a legendary enemy near Old Jove. Thus, Xuxuhr was not told of Anguhr's mission, just as Anguhr was ignorant of Xuxuhr's presence. Anguhr became certain that other Generals were not forming schemes. It must be the Great Widow, or the Dark Urge, herself. One of them, perhaps both, used Hell's servants as blind warriors.

Anguhr barked in disgust. Cyr and Uruk jumped back.

Anguhr pondered, further. He knew he had little time to do so. If Xuxuhr faced no threat, he still had planned to protect his retrieved objective from the Iron Work with the full force of his ship and horde. He wondered what his mother of shadow and obstruction wanted here. Anguhr wondered. He was still unsure of his future in Hell without its wars. But did War need Hell? Xuxuhr's death gave him and his own cunning had provided the means to the secure a doubled strategic advantage: the prize on the Iron Work and a second ship to command. Xuxuhr's ship had no General. There was no one better than he, the Destroyer, to seize its power. Another ship and horde would make him unbeatable. Only the combined might of the other Generals could challenge him, if ever allowed the chance.

"Why was the transport programmed to rendezvous with your ship? Your General didn't need his ship here, yet needed it for short transit to Hell? Was its present course a misdirection?" Uruk barked his rapidly fired questions into Cyr's ear as he took over the interrogation from his master engrossed in thought.

"General—?" Cyr noticed Anguhr now looked passed him. Cyr turned to his side and flinched at Uruk's sneer. "I have no knowledge, Master Uruk! Master Akhad said we were to retrieve a node. I labored to please my General and the Dark Urge. All praise—"

"Yes!" Uruk cut in. "Of what use is this node?"

"I cannot see its uses, Master." Cyr answered. "Perhaps your great Lord can do so."

"Then, how does it function when active?" Uruk growled.

"I understand lines of force well, Field Master!" Cyr was relieved to have something useful to say. "I was charged as a cargo master when I was first made an engineer. These nodes are in line with gravitational fields. Their banks across the Iron Work act as a great grapnels with other such fields to subdue the Red Giant. The Dark Urge must have ordained this place open so that Lord Xuxuhr could follow her commands. Woe for my Lord. Praise to Dark Urge that her wisdom brought General Anguhr here."

Again the site rocked with Anguhr's laughter.

'Gin? Can you hear me?' Zaria's thoughts crackled as they entered Gin's mind on ancient wavelengths.

'Yes, Zaria.' Gin responded over the same frequency. He filtered distortion, and scanned for other receivers tuned to intercept their covert communications. 'It is almost odd to communicate this way in a physical form.'

'Have you deciphered the demon language?' Zaria asked.

'Yes. The interrogation of the demon engineer provided some data for an educated deduction, with some historic extrapolations thrown in. It is indeed based on common code. I will transmit the translation standards, though I imagine our accents will need work. Can you tell me what this monstrous Anguhr finds so humorous?'

'Freedom has a way of making one's spirits buoyant.' Zaria offered.

'Freedom? I suppose he is when compared to our state.' Gin watched the tiers of tireless demons streak by him.

'I believe Anguhr enjoys a condition of freedom new to him.' Zaria furthered. 'It was either Xuxuhr or Anguhr that came here by the Dark Urge's will, but not both. Xuxuhr was already entrenched when we arrived. Then Anguhr brought enough demons and weaponry to blast Xuxuhr from the Iron Work.'

'I would have guessed Anguhr's assault was a fail-safe by the Dark Urge in case Xuxuhr failed.' Gin theorized.

'If that were so, then why would Anguhr need to interrogate both our warriors and Xuxuhr's demons?' Zaria asked. 'He is seeking information. He does not know why Xuxuhr was here.'

'You are suggesting a General of Hell is acting on his own?' Gin's confusion amplified the tome of his transmission. 'That frightens me more than the blades on Anguhr's ax.'

'A certain freedom of thought would be necessary to conduct successful campaigns against the powers crushed by Hell.' Zaria's tone was dry. 'And thus a General would not be blind to a new universe where all the conquests bring an end to war.'

'Do you think he is in rebellion?' Gin asked, still amped.

'Not completely. But he is acting on his own. With the right influence and the information I have, perhaps he can be the first General to stand against the tyranny of Hell.'

'A bold plan, Zaria. The Dark Urge punishes even thoughts against it with annihilation.'

'You and I know the tales, old friend. But Anguhr is young among the galaxy, and the Dark Urge has never been the light of truth.'

Gin paused. The idea of manipulating one of Hell's Generals raced in his mind like the torrents of heat fanned over them by the demon's wings.

'I know you hold sway over python's and butterflies back home, mother sunlight, but this scheming side of you I seldom see in Eden.'

'You need to get out more, old friend.'

'It appears your stratagem will soon have its chance, Zaria. Your potential fulcrum, the Destroyer, now heads our way.'

CHAPTER SIXTEEN

The Dark Urge called out. The Great Widow answered. She returned to the avatar chamber. Whatever occurred, she would endure. Or, she would die. It was a quantum state inside the box called Hell.

The Dark Urge entered. She looked the opposite of what her name would suggest. Her shape was of a human female carved to flawless detail from alabaster and made animate. Such a sculpture would be beautiful in any age and to nearly all types of eyes. What disturbed the Great Widow was her smile. It was joyful. If anything was impossible in the current age, the Great Widow considered it would be joy from the ruler of Hell. The Dark Urge turned to face the Great Widow. She slowly reached both her luminous white arms towards the giant spider. She froze.

Her smiled remained as her body lost its sheen and changed. The white, polished alabaster aged rapidly, but not like mineral or stone. It rusted as steel. The smooth alabaster surface became a rough, corroded surface. Still, she smiled, joyfully. Her lips and features became granular, and began to flake away. An inner orange flickered between thin fissures on the granular surface of her body. Waves of heat rose. Suddenly, her chest fell to the floor as a mass of ashes. The smile became a frown as flames overcame her face. The rest of her body collapsed into a mass of wood cinders.

The center of the hot mass began to shift. Small tentacles reached up through the black ash and hot orange pile. A cuttlefish slowly pulled itself from the burning debris. The small piles of displaced cinders became broken buildings and a field of craters. Long ruts appeared through them all as if cut by a massive whip. The cuttlefish crawled with great labor from the burning scene. When it reached the edge, an entire, shattered city lay behind it.

"I am dead," the small cuttlefish said. Its eyes rolled to lock in a stare at the Great Widow.

"No, mistress. Xuxuhr is dead. You, his mother, cannot die."

"I can be cut. I can be wounded. I can know pain." The Dark Urge said in her cuttlefish form as flames from the city scene licked over her.

"I would stop your pain," the Great Widow lowered her body toward the Dark Urge's currently small form.

The Dark Urge slowly rolled her cuttlefish body away from the spider as if it was a dying act of self preservation.

"Mistress, now you wound me."

"You tell the Generals my orders, spider, spider. And then they die."

After the Dark Urge spoke, the burning city shook. The scene collapsed into a swarm of flaming locusts. They leapt into the air and formed a tornado of flame that rolled across the floor and incinerated the cuttlefish.

The Great Widow watched and wondered if the comment was blame cast to her, or rebuke accepted by the Generals' mother.

"Why?" The Dark Urge spoke from the whirl of fire.

"Well, mistress, it is a near impossibility to see all variables, from those as vast as galaxies, to the quanta, and then the arcane and ethereal. Even one random bit can cascade into a series of actions that cause what seemed likely events to become only potential, lost."

"Random?" The Dark Urge's fire whirl blazed hotter. "Are my plans, my calculations so inaccurate it permits the random?"

"Even in the mind of the almighty, such as you who define it more than anything else, there must be slight variance. Else all things be so perfect they mire in absolute zero. And then nothing, not thought nor quark would move." The Great Widow moved back from the outer whips of fire. "In the calculations of the Generals, there is one among them that moves within variables so much that he moves the variables, themselves."

"And yet he has never killed one of his kind. You have. This I know."

"You are indeed almighty, mistress. What information comes into Hell comes into you."

"And what occurs beyond me?" The tornado of flame became a quarried block dressed for a sculptor's chisels. Yet this block was not marble or stone. It was a thick slab of skin. "What do you know?"

"I know everything." The spider paused. "But of course, of what I know I only recall those facts I am certain you would permit to be true."

112

"And what would you say to me now?" The Dark Urge asked, but in a knowing tone.

The Great Widow knew the question was a test by the Dark Urge. It was also a test of how well-ordered, and thus secret, she could keep her own thoughts.

"I tell you that one of your Generals acts to stop the events you calculated. The events, the variables, are not unchained. In time, soon, all threats will end."

"In time. Time. In time I will kill everything if I must. I must always protect myself," the Dark Urge said, and then vanished.

In time, the Great Widow thought to herself, *there is hope*.

Time. The demon Voltris thought it was the one limitation to power even the Dark Urge must know. He then quickly said: "All praise the Dark Urge."

Voltris glanced again at the chronometer. Lord Xuxuhr had not contacted his ship when his own timetable dictated. The Dark Urge tasked Lord Xuxuhr personally with this mission. Thus, he had taken direct command of the raid. As Ship Master, Voltris vowed he would not fail his General. At the moment, sole command of the bulk of his Generals power rested with Voltris. On all campaigns, Lord Xuxuhr was always within reach of communications. Voltris was never free of his master's chain, nor wanted to be. Even now the ship's velocity conformed to the rigid timetable set by Lord Xuxuhr before he left with his personal shock force and Akhad. Now, the chain of command felt snapped. Voltris felt alone and uncertain.

Voltris fingered the massive link fragment that hung on a much smaller chain around his neck. It was a link given to him by his General, the Ravager. Deep within the fragment's microscopic fissures was the blood and tissue of all the enemies Lord Xuxuhr had slain with that length of chain before it was recast. The captive Ignitaurs did toiled deep within the ship. Voltris had only seen them when bound and dragged below decks upon capture. At first he thought they were extravagant food. Later he learned his Lord used them as secret chain smiths. Voltris thought that demons, recognized and tasked to make giant chains, could do a better job. Yet he never questioned his General. He worshiped Xuxuhr and also did not want to become food, himself.

Voltris glanced at the demon standing guard at the access shaft connecting the bridge to the burning labyrinth of the ship's passageways. Guards now stood at all intersections to defend its interiors. Not that many species could live long enough on board to commit any damage. Then Voltris thought of the Ignitaurs and sneered. Nevertheless, it seemed odd to place the ship on full alert so close to Hell. But Lord Xuxuhr's tactics always brought victory. His commands would be followed without question.

Perhaps the mighty General killed even more with his chains. Whatever delayed General Xuxuhr involved himself and Akhad. Neither of Hell's warriors sent messages on their personal wavelengths. There was no interference across real or ethereal channels. Voltris checked for distortions across both real and arcane spectra. He scanned for a transport ships mass at the ends of his sensors' range. Nothing registered. No communications flashed on a screen or in his brain. There was only the constant roll of red flames.

More crimson radiation raged outside from Red Giant. It filled all visual space beyond the aegis at starboard. Voltris gripped his link fragment in his thorny fists. The colossal dreadnought was still only under Voltris' command. Power to war with Hell itself—at least for a time—was his to control. Yet all Voltris wanted was the deep bark of his Lord threatening him across space. There was only silence. Without a General in direct command, Voltris knew control of the ship might become a point of question. Voltris knew many demons could sense time and mark its passage. Without strong, central command—Voltris realized there had never been a lack of a strong, central command.

Command, like combat, required effective tactics. Victory was control. He would win and hold control for his Lord. He would emulate the horde's command under Ship and Field Masters. No demon could replace a General who linked demons to the Dark Urge. More immediately, if Voltris attempted to fill the vacuum of the throne it would light concern among recognized demons if not spark mutiny. He would maintain full control through horde loyalty. To quell any seditious rumbling, he would choose a lieutenant to link himself to the winged demons. This would bind the ship until Lord Xuxuhr returned. Voltris was certain his master would approve.

Praise be to the Dark Urge, Voltris thought.

More time elapsed. Voltris snarled.

"Master Voltris," a guard spoke as he stepped onto the bridge. "Strike leader Triat requests to enter the bridge."

"Allow him to enter, as if you could stop him." Voltris nodded.

The hulking Triat soared onto the bridge. Voltris wondered what personal flight would be like.

"I appear as ordered!" Triat barked. "For whatever reason a pilot needs counsel from a warrior."

"That last comment would never be uttered in the presence of Lord Xuxuhr! Do you think I will permit impudence while I command?" Voltris thrust his fist at Triat.

Triat glowered at the fist that stayed a mere thorn's length from his snout. Triat would readily eat an underling challenging his dominion, and here he had done the same to Voltris who commanded by the will of their General.

"Of course, Voltris. You command." Triat stepped back. "I will hurl myself against the main drive, if it pleases you."

Voltris did not reply to the offer. His demon brain always searched for a means to kill, and Triat had just offered to kill himself for Voltris. He shook his head, slightly and refocused on why he had brought Trait to the bridge.

"You will live, Triat." Voltris said. "You rank bellow Akhad, but Akhad is gone with our Lord. So you will command the horde in his place until his return. I will command you."

Triat's eyes flared. The idea was strange but enticing. "And I will stand on the bridge?"

"Yes," Voltris answered. "By the throne. We will control the ship until Xuxuhr returns in triumph."

"He is overdue." Trait said. He raised his jagged brows in a searching look at Voltris.

"He does as he pleases." Voltris replied with no motion in his own face. "He is the Ravager."

"He is." Trait nodded. "And you are Ship Master. I obey your commands, Master Voltris!"

"Then: station." Voltris motioned to the right side of the empty, massive throne. He turned to his controls and inwardly sighed relief.

Triat stepped back and stood at the throne's right side. He noticed the nail scrapings and patches worn smooth by Akhad's feet on the deck plate. He stepped to the side of those marks from respect and fear of his superior. He looked across the burning bridge. It was hallowed ground to demons and now, for a time, his post. Triat smiled. A demon's grin of shark teeth and serpent eyes both gleamed with hunger and adoration of his new power.

CHAPTER SEVENTEEN

Anguhr stood just beyond the orbits of the demons. He paused for a moment and looked down at his captives. Yet they were only slightly shorter than his colossal self. Gin eyed the blades of the General's ax secured behind his back. The curved blades rose behind his shoulders like motionless, black wings. Gin wished he had wings, and was currently flying away with Zaria. Anguhr's lieutenant, Uruk, stood at his right side and clasped his arms together. The demon folded his wings to rest across his back. The flying demons slowly constricted their circles. Anguhr stepped closer to Gin and Zaria as the living walls tightened.

Zaria mentally recited the formula to rearm the charges. Nothing happened within her fist. A sudden slap, and her sword and pouch disappeared into the swirl of demons. Other demons alit and walked into the points of the archers' arrows with their rifle muzzles right between each set of the raptors' eyes. Flying demons continued to form the swirling dome in tighter circles. Zaria's surviving phalanx drew closer together.

'Zaria, remember, they could have already eaten us!' Gin's transmission perfectly conveyed his fear.

'They are toying with our resolve, old friend. I understand. Don't worry, I have a plan.'

'I am relieved.' Gin replied on the wavelength of a sigh.

Demons slowly slid between the archers and pressed against Zaria and her warriors. Gun barrels and blades firmly parted the archers. High chirps sought Zaria's direction.

"Obey me! Do not fire!" Zaria commanded aloud. Although she doubted a release of arrows would do no more than annoy their captors now.

Demons pressed closer. Fetid breath assaulted nostrils. Thorny demon bodies formed cells separating each member of Zaria's forces. Grasping claws became restricting manacles. The flying demons suddenly soared away. Zaria and her cadre stood above the mire of demon jailers. Anguhr towered above them all.

The resonant growl of the General buffeted his prisoners. "Now, you will obey me."

"I am Zaria. He is Gin. We are the leaders. You have no need to harm my warriors. Free them. They will no attack you."

A low laugh echoed from under Anguhr's helmet, and then one word. "No."

"Are we to be your slaves?" At Zaria's sides, demons struggled to restrain her arms and avoid having their fingers crushed between her own.

"Slaves?" Anguhr growled. "I am a warrior. I do not take slaves."

"Only destroy whole planets." Zaria said.

"Yes. As I will destroy yours." Anguhr nodded.

"Then why need do you have of us?" Gin asked. He regretted his words and hoped Anguhr did not wonder himself and kill them.

"Lord Anguhr has no need of you!" Uruk barked. "He merely permits you to live a short time longer as you have fought well against Hell."

Gin noticed that Zaria now looked passed Anguhr. He saw what she focused on. Flying demons carried a long tube fixed with a heavy base low in the distance. They carried packs of large projectiles bearing narrow fins. Obviously the demons went to deploy a long-range weapon. He sighed.

Zaria quickly snapped her gaze back to Anguhr. Her eyes narrowed to confront his own.

"Petty threats, General!" Zaria snapped. "You know we fought Xuxuhr for the grapnel node. You must also realize that by itself, the node is useless. We know what will make it part of a weapon of unequal power. Certainly, such power is of interest to the Destroyer."

Anguhr's burning eyes narrowed within the eye gaps in his helmet. He wondered how this alien knew his rank. He also wondered how the two alien leaders bore an appearance similar to his own. What might they be able to tell him beyond strategic importance? But gaining strategic knowledge was paramount.

"You will tell me of this power. Now." Anguhr demanded.

"Such knowledge must come at a price, General. You must release us, and—"

"You are in no position to make terms!" Uruk bellowed. "Lord, these creatures begin to offend me. I would spare you the outrage." Uruk lifted his sword into the air.

"I will allow you a chance to please my Field Master." As Anguhr spoke, a second team of demons carried another heavy mortar tube and shells behind him. "Or I will order my demons to start shelling the relief column of silver beasts and archers that makes its way here. They will die in fragments, not in the glory of combat."

Gin's eyes widened. Zaria's second assault wave must have left Eden as scheduled. Unfortunately, they too materialized far off target as did he and Zaria's unit. Anguhr's sentries had detected them, and now prepared to annihilate them from safe distance before they could aid Zaria.

"There is no glory in death, General. No matter its cause." Zaria voice deepened with bitter resolve. "If you destroy them, we too will die. And all your answers die. As will you, soon after."

Anguhr grew impatient. "I can order my ship to annihilate all of Old Jove. If you do not tell me what I wish to know. I will destroy Eden."

"Not even your scythe can rupture Eden's walls." Zaria countered. "It is as the Builders wished."

"I know nothing of your gods. But what are their walls if they strike the Red Giant's fire?" Anguhr asked. "Or if it drifts into the chill of the interstellar void? Such is my power, prisoner."

Anguhr's threat forced a pause from his captives. In the distance, demons armed the mortar shells.

"General," Gin mustered as much reverence in his voice as he could, and chose his words to entice Anguhr. "My leader speaks of a power greater than the energy released by your ship. Why do you think the Dark Urge sent you and Xuxuhr, two Generals, to the Iron Work? To stop us."

"I was sent to annihilate Eden." Anguhr said.

Gin controlled his shock over Anguhr's last words and spoke. "Yes. But not to risk the destruction of Hell."

"Gin!" Zaria thrust her torso through the walls of thorny demons at her eldest companion.

"Certainly General Anguhr realizes Hell would be in jeopardy if he destroyed Old Jove." Gin said.

Gin's following thoughts came to Zaria across their secret wavelengths. 'And perhaps he will not do so right now, buy us more time, and spare our warriors lost on the Iron Work.'

Anguhr wondered what these aliens and their knowledge could offer him. If Eden had survived this long, certainly their leader did not boast of its defenses. And certainly a force that could destroy Eden could, perhaps, also destroy Hell. It was no wonder these aliens fought so well.

118

"General," Zaria spoke with confidence. "You must have some hint of self-preservation in that black pit of a mind. You weren't supposed to be here, were you? You must have doubts about the Dark Urge's plans. Especially now that her war is near its close. But let me show you that her hunger is false, that all the conquests of the Generals are an act of fear, not need. It will prove we are of value not just about this weapon. It will prove why your Dark Urge is a danger not just to life, but to her warriors."

"Blasphemy!" Uruk spat, and then cast his gaze up to the silent Anguhr.

Anguhr glanced at the body of Xuxuhr. He thought of his surviving brethren. Ursuhr and Xuxuhr were brutish thralls. Tanuhr was calculating and cunning. Sutuhr was ruthless. He would have destroyed Eden upon contact with the miserable world. Sutuhr, the Devoted, was the most loyal to the Dark Urge. If there were more components to raid from this star-spanning machine, Sutuhr would be the next sent if he was not already en route. Anguhr wondered why Sutuhr was not the one tasked to the Iron Work, first. Where was he now? Anguhr swung forward his massive ax. The blade stopped a hair's width over Zaria head, then rose to the top of Anguhr's swing and stopped.

"Obey me!" Anguhr roared. His fury manifested as his massive body tensed to bring down his ax blow. "Or I will destroy you, your warriors, and your world! Tell me where to collect the next element of this weapon, NOW!"

Zaria's eyes met Gin's own. He understood, and slowly nodded affirmation.

Anguhr took only Uruk and his massive axe as security when he ferried his prisoners Zaria and Gin to the edge of the Iron Work. Zaria and Gin endured the ride almost as lashed hunting trophies or living ship figureheads bound at the front by black cables. Uruk carried a huge rifle that was almost as large as himself. They dared to venture to the extreme limit of the survivable region. If there was a word for the flying transport, it would be a flaming chariot. The vehicle looked crude, made from bent beams that blazed a weak crimson compared to the violent red storm they approached. A million or more curtains of red, radiant energy towered ahead. The star's energy danced or fought with the arcane forces that held it in check.

As they neared the edge, auroras flowed like inverted colossal waterfalls. Even for the eyes of giants like Anguhr, the rippling light was too vast to take in and nearly too vast to comprehend. The full width of the auroras was far greater than a giant planet's polar displays, and several planet's diameters. Objects more easily discerned cut a line across the

119

overwhelming red and dance of light. Black dashes descended down from space toward the edge of the Iron Work. They appeared to grow more massive as the chariot came closer to the edge of the Iron Work band they traveled across.

Zaria looked up at the long train of ingots cast in Hell and send to the impossibly vast machine trapping a star. Zaria wondered if the star appeared red more from the forces that held it in check than from its natural spectrum. She looked back over her shoulder and glimpsed Anguhr. On her journeys, Zaria had seen several intelligent species enjoy the sensation of speed and breeze across their surface. If there was wind, she was certain she would see a smile on Anguhr's face if most of was not hidden by his black helmet.

The chariot set down. Anguhr and Uruk debarked, but left Zaria and Gin bound.

Most annoying, Gin thought.

They were not here to see the spectacle of radiation rising from the star. They were here to see the fate of Hell's ingots. The black processed pieces came to Hell as parts of butchered worlds. Anguhr and the other Generals and sent them beyond spacetime into the maw of Hell. Now Anguhr witnessed the processed results of his efforts. Above them, the long train sent by the Dark Urge appeared as an arc of black, rectangular prisms in motion. The even gaps between the ingots appeared to widen as they sailed closer to the Iron Work. The massive ingots did not touch down or pause at the vast band. They continued passed it toward the star. They immense machine did not accepted them for repairs or stored reserves. The ingots drifted down into the intense heat and shifting masses of plasma over the Red Giant's surface. If Zaria and Anguhr could see the final leg of the ingots journey, they would see them become molten, then vapor, and finally mere ions awash in the roiling, stellar storms.

"You see it, General!" Zaria shouted "You see the lie! Once the Iron Work was finished, the Forge—Hell, no longer needed to make its elements. The Iron Work taps the star itself for power and repairs. Your war is for nothing. The destruction only feeds the twisted mind of your ruler!"

Gin wondered if his newly physical mind was up to the task of processing information such as what he watched unfold on an impossible machine of stellar scale where a being born of light was coated in drying blood from brutal combat and now pleaded for acknowledgement of truth with a giant destroyer of worlds and his demon lieutenant.

Anguhr stayed silent. Uruk seemed to be flexing against imagined cables binding him.

"Maybe they serve the Dark Urge by feeding the star itself." Anguhr finally said.

120

"That's a child's thought, Lord General." Zaria countered. "You know the truth. You can see it sailing straight into the stellar fires. There is no purpose to cleave apart any world. The pieces the Dark Urge sends here are only destroyed. They never become part of anything. There is no great purpose. There is only destruction. The war is a lie!"

Uruk expected Anguhr to strike Zaria or hurl her into the star. Instead he stared at the all-encompassing view of red fires and slowly falling ingots. A different kind of blaze now burned in the General's narrowed eyes.

Uruk opened his mouth to speak, but felt the heat sting his tongue. He wanted to ask why his Lord Anguhr, General of Hell, and son of the Dark Urge would allow such blasphemy to be spoken. He never asked the question. Personal doubts killed it. His mind had been burning away orthodoxy on its own. It now began cycling the situation and its consequences. Uruk could see the truth. The profits of conquest and the Dark Urge's own labor sailed into incineration. They didn't become part of the Iron Work, the great cause of the Dark Urge. Uruk considered the bodies of his fallen demons. Did they truly become part of Hell? Did they merge with her dark heart, or was that another lie? He starred at the red inferno with widened eyes as radiation bathed his face.

"I have witnessed what you wished me to see," Anguhr turned to Zaria. "I have seen your point. But it changes nothing for you."

"How could it not?" Gin asked with shock.

"I would wager the General had his own doubts long before this travesty was revealed to him." Zaria said.

Anguhr stayed silent.

"You need not remain under Hell's yoke," Zaria strained to lean toward Anguhr. "Free us, and you will also become free."

"You will not," Anguhr replied. "You will serve me. Challenge me, and I will hurl you into the Red Giant and Hell's inferno."

"That would be hurling us twice." Gin said with a tilt of his head.

"You will be in more than one piece." Uruk explained.

"You are not very sporting creatures," Gin remarked. "You are more than barbaric. Cruel."

"Gin!" Zaria snapped.

Uruk aimed his massive rifle at Gin's head. "But *we* are truthful," he said.

"Noted," Gin replied with a nod.

"Now," Anguhr boomed. "I came here because I wished to see this. I also wanted Xuxuhr's demons to see my prisoners bowed. Now that we have both acted the parts, you will obey me. And without question."

They returned to the access canyon, and well away from the revelation of the ingots' fate. Anguhr stared at all the darkened eyes of Xuxuhr. The drying blood from his fatal wounds stained the black surface beneath his corpse. It had mingled with demon and alien blood to form a scab-like crust on the vast expanse of black metal. On a solid planet, such a sprawl of slain warriors' remains might inspire some species to erect a memorial. On the Iron Work the size of the battlefield was proportionately less than a single blood cell in a giant's heart. Xuxuhr would have no memorial, here. However, Anguhr planned for him to serve one more mission even in death, or at least a certain part of him.

"Lord Destroyer!" Uruk alit beside his General. "Proxis reports he is certain the ship is undetected. The star's radiation masked our transit. Xuxuhr's ship has not broken from its course. No other ships are within targeting range."

"Then prepare, Field Master. I have need of you and some part of this." Anguhr motioned his axe at Xuxuhr's body. "Your mission will be arduous and without precedent."

"Lord, what of our mission against Eden?"

"It is adapted. My plan is now our mission." Anguhr looked through the red haze across the vast, black field. High above rolled the edges of stellar fire against space. "Do you realize where we stand, Uruk?"

"The significance is not lost on me, Lord. The Great Widow will weave our names into history. Today we have won victory on the very surface of the Iron Work."

"Will the old spider also record Xuxuhr's defeat?" Anguhr asked and looked at Uruk. "The first victory on the Iron Work was won by Zaria of Eden."

Uruk fell silent.

"History's tangled web also holds the names of the other Generals who fell in service to the Dark Urge. Do you know their names, Uruk? I know their names. Now Xuxuhr joins them on oblivion's forsaken front. Azuhr was the first of our kind. I am the last."

"And greatest," Uruk nodded.

"Even greatness cannot stand against time. We have little of it." " Anguhr sighed. "We must secure as much power as we can before more forces from Eden or elsewhere marshal against our horde. And so I must do something I normally loathe. I must divide our forces, at least partially."

"Your strategies are always victorious, Lord Anguhr." Uruk said. "I do not fear. I follow."

"Good. Because I will send you on a mission away from me." Anguhr leaned slightly towards Uruk with his burning eyes locked keenly on his lieutenant. "You will carry my standard. However, I cannot be there to guide you. Whatever commands you follow will be your own. You will

122

not have my power nor the strength of the horde behind you. Yet you may face an entire horde that would eat you. I send you, because only you can do this. Much is at stake. I am certain that some power acts to divide the forces of Hell. I aim unify them. Whatever the will of the Dark Urge, we must act on our own. That may seem impossible. I assure you, it is not."

For a moment, Uruk was silent as he considered Anguhr's words. He nodded with closed eyes, and then spoke. "We do not act in accord with what I gather to be our original mission. General Xuxuhr and you, Lord Destroyer, here together is strange. I can see it was unplanned. It is odd strategy to overlap Generals."

"The odd may well become bizarre." Anguhr's voice rumbled deeply. "Even with four eyes, Xuxuhr could not see the purpose or risks of the mission he was tasked. I will avoid his fate. I will not lead us into an ambush because orders bid it so. Nor will I give such commands. I will wage a campaign unlike any before. It has no clear enemy. The path ahead is as hazed as this place. The only certainty will be our loyalty. I will fight for the horde. I ask they do so for me, that you do so, Uruk."

"My life is yours, Destroyer!" Uruk held his sword before his chest in salute. "You have fought alongside us. You fight what we cannot withstand alone, and never burn us as mere cannon fire to weaken an enemy for your glory. You take fire so we can burn the enemy. Even unrecognized demons see this. I am certain no horde fights as fiercely for their General as we, your demons, because no other General fights as fiercely for his horde. Should you command us to assault Hell, we would think it odd, but our wings would blot it skies as we stormed the portals to quell its flames."

Anguhr was, for once, stunned. Uruk stood and studied his silent General. The sudden motion of Anguhr's axe broke the silence. The blade swung down. Xuxuhr's head shot from his massive body. The collision of ax against the Iron Work vibrated through Uruk.

"Now, Field Master: your mission!" Anguhr boomed. "Take Xuxuhr's head. Show his horde he has fallen. Let them morn his failure, but you, Uruk, bring me back his ship!"

Gin sensed a vibration in the canyon floor. He stood with Zaria and a throng of demons. However, black cables bound both of them at the waist. Most of the demons pointed their weapons and rifles at Gin and Zaria. The vibration seemed to resonate down from the cliff top high above. Only Anguhr could cause it. Gin could not see the General on the plane above the canyon. Gin mused that he stood in a canyon, yet on the height of technology, however ancient it was. And they were forced to use brute strength to steal a small piece of it. Perhaps that was ironic or appropriate. He also mused that his mind could be seen as a pinnacle of technology. Yet now, petty demons with archaic looking automatic rifles could kill him. That, he felt, was simply sad.

Gin caught the stare and curling lip of the overseer demon, Solok. Gin sighed, and continued his calculations. Both Zaria and he now discharged their part of the bargain struck with Hell's venturesome General. The grapnel node was more massive than the demons used as living tractors around the hexagonal column. Zaria was the only creature that was semi-luminous in this increasingly infernal place. Dried blood still clung to her skin. The chariot cables had cut streaks through it. Thin, umber flakes fell from her body as she flexed against the cables wrapped around the grapnel node. More cables bound their warriors. The surviving gulos snarled like angry wolves. The archers remained placid, but their eyes always looked at the demons as targets. Gin hoped they would all not become executed corpses. Gin felt he and Zaria were trapped in the most bizarre situation they could have imagined before leaving Asherah: cooperating with forces from Hell. Even if they acted out of need, it taxed Gin's understanding of ethics and almost reality, as well.

The demons all stank of the smolder from a thousand worlds they burned. Gin lost himself in abstracts, and continued his efforts to remove the node. He hoped the pall of imprisonment would leave, soon after. In the very least, they did work to retrieve an element of the plan to end Hell's tyranny. With demons.

Zaria permitted herself a sigh. She stretched against her bonds being careful not to be obvious she was testing their strength. The stench of demons entered her nostrils. She took solace that now Anguhr's ship no longer threatened Eden. But now they were his prisoners. So far, escape seemed hopeless. She could not manipulate Anguhr while forced to labor with demons. Zaria could see their plight troubled Gin. To calculate the best direction of force would be simple for him, typically. He had yet to place the charges beside the microscopic seams at the base of the node. The demon explosives were inelegant, dagger-like devices. All of her weapons and tools had been confiscated and were now unseen.

Solok controlled the detonation. Zaria hoped his claws were steady. The directed explosions only needed to provide a short moment to sunder the force that held the node. The force unleashed would be lethal to the demons pressed and pulling against it. Still, they met the dangers without fear. Zaria wondered if they had the capacity to be afraid. She wondered if the monstrous creatures thought at all, other than about destruction and mindless worship of their malignant leaders.

"Hurry! Work!" The command was barked from the other end of their bonds. Cyr's face glowered at Gin. Evidently, his own fate felt strange, and he wished to hasten its change. A master of demons in his own horde, now Cyr labored under an uncertain future.

Zaria saw Solok's eyes narrowed at the surviving engineer from Xuxuhr horde. The clutch on his sword tightened. Zaria noted the issue of command appeared to stoke demonic ire more than a lust for revenge. So far, she had not felt any palpable acrimony flexing from Cyr's thorny limbs, even though Zaria had slain his Lord and General. Was he hiding his emotion, restrained by his impressment by Anguhr? That would mean a high degree of emotional control for such a savage appearance. It was evident that at least the demons in the command structure could control and transcend their basic impulses.

Zaria wondered if those controls were a design feature imbued by the Dark Urge. Perhaps they manifested from living within a well-ordered power structure. And what of the minds at the top of that structure? The Generals spent long periods at war and away from the Dark Urge. What evolution had their minds undergone? Anguhr's mind was obviously complex and now of great significance to the future of the galaxy.

Xuxuhr's transport craft flew overhead. The vessel was a far smaller, cubic version of Hell's titanic warships. Visible missiles glinted like metal spear points piercing the chaotic girders that wove its fiery hull. There had been no skirmish with the demons aboard when it descended from orbit. Zaria had hoped the Generals' hordes would be competitive if not openly combative to each other. Thus Hell's forces could be frangible. But in the absence of their own General and in the towering presence of Anguhr, the demons followed him.

Zaria wondered if the realities of power determined their allegiance. Xuxuhr's ego died before his transport entered the battle. Thus it was spared the more powerful fusillade possible from her archers.

Demon arms shot upward as salutes. The demons atop the cliff brandished weapons as the golden thorned Uruk soared into the opening maw of the ship. Barks and screeches echoed through the ethereal atmosphere. A group of heavily armed cohorts followed their Field Master in a tight delta behind him. Another formation carried two gruesome objects into the transporter. One was the severed arm of Akhad. The second was the easily recognized if decapitated grimace of Xuxuhr. Zaria and Gin had assumed the craft would descend to collect the grapnel node. Instead, the ship's portal shut and the craft shot swiftly into space. Instantly, the eyes of Gin and Zaria's captor's fixed back on them across rifles that never moved off target.

"Solok!" Anguhr bellowed from above.

Solok gave a nod to the demon on his right. He turned and barked at Cyr who replied with a look of long hunger now satisfied. Solok then soared to the cliff top, and stood beside the Anguhr. Another chorus of demons cheers assaulted the surface of the great machine.

"Now!" Cyr shouted at Gin. "Set the charges, alien thing! Or I will crush your heart!"

"Very well." Gin knelt once more and swiftly placed his collection of explosives along the base of the node. "Done. But I warn you, if your crew stays at the—"

"They are my demons!" Cyr bellowed at the much taller Gin. "I control their fate. A better one than yours, sickling! They will see our fallen Lord's mission fulfilled!"

Cyr craned his head and let loose with an assault of screeches and barks. Zaria tensed. The charges exploded in a devastating flash of white. The force only jostled Zaria, but it blew back the demons around the grapnel's base. Others screamed and fell. The survivors slammed against the node and lifted with the much taller and more powerful Zaria. Her strength proved the deciding factor. The node tipped. The black column tilted and crashed into the cliff wall. It rested on an angle and fully separated from the other nodes that stood in perfect order. In a perverted manner, Zaria's dreams were being realized. The demons had no desires to savor the results of success.

Badly injured demons struggled to right themselves stand on whatever limb was intact. Swift slashes by their cohorts ended their pathetic attempts. Gravely wounded demons with limbs intact continued to gather the trailing lengths of cable lashed to the node. They bled out while completing their tasks as their final acts. Each demon in the work crew assessed its companions. Minor wounds went unnoticed. Major wounds that prevented motion meant sudden release at the edge of a blade. The cables never rested. Zaria's end was snatched out of her grip. The lengths snapped together, and the ends stretched into the air in the claws of flying demons. Both lengths met in Anguhr's hands. He pulled. The node jerked, and then swung free. It continued its ascent as the General hauled up his prize.

Gin looked at where the node had been seconds before. There was no trace between the other nodes to testify the stolen grapnel had ever been there for many ages of history. Now it was apart from the field in demon hands.

Zaria slowly reached for a fallen demon's rifle. Cyr grasped her wrist.

"What you do is foolish." Cyr barked low. "Do you wish to die?"

"Why do you care if I live?"

"You live because it is so ordered by General Anguhr who is now my leader. His will is that of the Dark Urge, and thus it shall be obeyed."

"And if I do take the weapon?" Zaria asked with defiance.

"I am not here to be killed by you, alien." Cyr snorted. "I wish to survive. Do as you are ordered, or your bodies will not be given a pyre. You will become nothing. Die instead in service, as you have been granted, and become something greater than what you are now."

"What might that be?" Zaria asked with spite. "Food for demons?"

"If you are given a pyre, then you may become part of Hell, and the greatest of all things: the Dark Urge."

It surprised Zaria that Cyr, of all demons, would express his beliefs to her as a means of salvation. It surprised her more that his faith was genuine, and not a sinister and egotistical façade, albeit originated as a control method by great evil. Two lengths of cable dangled next to Zaria.

"Climb!" Cyr barked, and flew skyward.

Zaria permitted herself a sigh. She looked at Gin who joined her and shrugged. Both of them grabbed an end of the cables, and climbed.

CHAPTER EIGHTEEN

Uruk and his heavily armed strike force sped from the Iron Work in Xuxuhr's transport. Cyr and Xuxuhr's surviving demons were kept back to show their obedience, willing or enforced, to their new Lord, General Anguhr. The small craft blazed through vacuum on a jet of hellfire. At full speed its hull stretched into a slightly sleeker delta shape of burning, crisscrossed beams. Uruk sat near the nose of the single cabin. Next to Uruk, his Strike Leader, Zahl, watched over the craft's automated guidance. In smaller craft, the orientation of up and down was the position of deck plating. However, that was ripped up and used to make a partial coffin for the decapitated head of Xuxuhr by recognized demons now tasked as engineers. This craft's previous crew were fellow demons, but their smells were different. Uruk could sniff traces of Cyr and other strange demons. Many of them were now corpses on the Iron Work. Those demons could not know their future. It was chosen for them by their leaders.

Anguhr had given Uruk a power unknown to demons: choice. Uruk could serve his Lord in greater danger than ever, or he could ignore his mission and stay on Xuxuhr's ship. There, he could serve the Dark Urge as blind as all other demons. Uruk instinctively thought to ask the Dark Urge for guidance. He mentally rejected and crushed the idea. It was his will that now mattered most. Anguhr had invested not only power but faith in him. And in Anguhr's service, Uruk evolved beyond being a weapon.

Uruk had faithfully burned his dead in pyres or the scythe so they could become a part of Hell and the Dark Urge. Now he wondered if their ashes instead mingled with lies. As a devoted soldier, Uruk had never imagined a need for false prods and manipulation controls of the demon hordes. Their devotion to their Lords, and their Lords to the Dark Urge, was the only true order of creation. It was all that was needed to expand Hell's dominion. Evidently, the Dark Urge thought otherwise. New thoughts pawed through Uruk's mind. He considered his place in Hell's future. It was clear Lord Anguhr had seen the benefits of free thought long ago. Even potentially seditious thoughts. Now Uruk began to realize that power.

The Dark Urge was the mother of all demons born in Hell or aboard ships among stars. She held their total faith. At least among demons not initiated to Lord Anguhr's boon. She had created the galaxy's greatest war machine. The might of her Generals had proven stronger than any god invoked by the vanquished worlds. All this was true. The fact she also took worlds to forge ingots that became nothing but stellar ash was also true. She was, then, the mother of the galaxy's biggest lie. Uruk had no answer for why such great power—

Uruk found himself growling aloud. He cast his serpentine eyes to his sides and grunted. He turned his mind to more immediate concerns. Such as what to do if Voltris refused his authority. He would make that decision when he faced it. That would be soon. Xuxuhr's ship was a red fire in space, dead ahead. Uruk reached down and retrieved Akhad's arm. He secured it at the center of his two grenade bands. Wings prevented a full loop across demons chests and backs. Their thorny skin acted as excellent holdfast for hellish straps, equipment, and more unusual objects.

If Uruk's mission was not difficult enough, he faced an additional hardship. He had a headache. Among all the firepower, technology, and arcane arts that armed and equipped a horde, demon analgesics had never been considered. Uruk would solider on. He identified his pain as a headache. It was more a mental strain from colliding lines of thought. One line was the demon will to dominate. It opposed a knowledge strand he unspooled to better deal with Xuxuhr's Ship Master. Uruk had set foot on countless worlds around many stars, but found one thing most alien. Diplomacy. Adjusting his mind to use it caused the strain. Nevertheless, demons enjoyed hardship. Thus his headache was a challenge. A contest of will over pain. But it was still annoying.

Zahl guided the transport around its massive parent ship. They docked at the bottom aft of the hull near the main drive. The transport craft remerged with main body of the ship, as did all systems and weapons. The front of the transport became an aperture for Uruk and his crew to enter the cargo hold before the smaller craft fully reintegrated with the hull. Uruk led as they flew in. Xuxuhr's head was now fully encased in the cube fashioned from deck plating. It would preclude shock and harmful reactions. Accepting a General's death was not encoded into demon brains. Xuxuhr was quite dead. Uruk had received special privilege to read histories known only to Generals. It helped ease the shock a General could die. Uruk hoped Xuxuhr's Ship Master had been given equal privilege.

Two rows of demons flanked the cargo hold. Uruk was unsure if they were an honor guard, or merely guarding the rows of generation chambers behind them. Uruk peered across the expansive hold. One, large demon stood at the far end. He had wings, and thus was not the Ship Master. He was presumably a ranking strike leader serving as Field Master. Uruk held the arm of his predecessor. The lone demon did not fly to meet them. He waited for them to traverse the hold. Uruk glanced at the demons standing before the generation chambers. The chambers formed long rows of glassy wombs holding embryonic demons. These guards, alone, outnumbered Uruk's force. The chambers could birth more. The guard demons paid no recognition to Uruk's force. As yet, he had no idea what would emerge from this unprecedented encounter.

The chimera effect of Hell's biology held fast to the systems that spawned its warriors. The base of the generation machine had the structure of a spine torn from a giant ten times more massive than a General and then thrown on its side. Two such massive spines flanked the cargo hold. The demon wombs rose off the vertebrae. Each appeared as an imprisoned moment where expanding space stretched two thorns holding and a defiant teardrop pierced by a large spearhead at its base. The spearhead tapered to a point inside the glassy tear wombs and impaled the embryonic demon.

New demons were released only in accord with a General's demand and the sensed need of the machine. The governance of the generation system was an echo of the Dark Urge's fearful caution. When both agreed, the spearhead sank into the vertebrae, releasing the demon to grow. The sharp edge sliced open the teardrop womb. The hatched demon would instinctively clamber out as it rapidly grew. Its thorny skin quickly hardened and its wings tempered in the hellish ship. When empty, the base of the womb released a new gestational mass. Its cut membrane healed as it refilled with a semi-fluid matrix. The umbilical spear point then slid back up and impaled the larval creature to trap it in time. In Hell's twisted systems, the demons were born when freed from death.

Mass hatchings were rare. Yet there was a reason this system was built over the bilge. Uruk noticed unusually tight decking sealed the hold from the bilge compartment. He sensed heat rising from beneath it. That was different to Lord Anguhr's ship. Uruk knew the standard design placed no reactors or real space power generation within the ship's bilge. Uruk noted that as large as Hell's warships were, the bilge deck could hide a city. But why would a city live in the bottom of Hell ship, and who could survive in it other than demons?

Uruk and his force arrived at the end of the hold. The demons tasked with carrying Xuxuhr's cephalic coffin set it down with as much reverence as a monster made for war could summon. It hit the decking with a *thump!* The other demons behind the coffin formed four rows that in turn formed a square.

"I am Triat." The waiting demon barked. "I am Primary Strike Leader, and sub only to Lord Xuxuhr the Ravager's Field Master Akhad. I am now brevet Field Master biding our Lord and Master Akhad's return. Ship Master Proxis holds the bridge." Trait halted as if leaving more information unsaid. He then eyed the arm held by Uruk. His face stretched with a look of recognition and shock.

"I am Uruk, Field Master of Lord Anguhr, the Destroyer. That is my rank by right. This is the arm of Akhad."

Uruk thrust the arm at Trait who took it as if being handed a grenade. His eyelids rolled fully open to reveal the roundness of his serpentine eyes. Uruk allowed Trait to stare at the arm and recognize the truth of his words.

"He died in combat." Uruk continued. "He will be honored with a pyre. I have other news. There has been calamity unknown for our hordes. It is why I am here. I seek the Ship Master. By right, he would be the highest ranking demon. We need parlay. Now."

Triat's head jerked. He inhaled and then spoke. "Master Akhad leads a special engineer force with our Lord, Xuxuhr."

"Akhad is dead." Uruk replied. "As are many from that mission. Those who live now serve Lord Anguhr. They serve well."

"No new demons have hatched." Trait said. He glanced from the arm he held and at the generation chambers to his left. The facts of the situation were assembling in his smoldering brain.

"Take me to the Ship Master." Uruk said. "The rest of what I must say is for the demon of rank. And though I am away from my obedient horde, I am a rightful Field Master. Take me to the bridge."

Trait again glanced at Akhad's arm. He angled his head and glanced at the large cube of refashioned deck plating. He then looked at Uruk and nodded. Trait then flew upward.

"Zahl, with me!" Uruk commanded. "Coffin guard, follow us. Others, stay at the ready."

Uruk flew to follow Trait. Zahl followed immediately, as did the demons carrying the head's coffin. The remainder of Uruk's force saluted and then marched directly below the junction of passageways that led to the forward areas of the ship. They turned and glanced at the flanking guards along the generation chambers. Those demons already eyed them.

Trait entered the junction and flew along the straight path leading up to the bridge. Nearly all the corridors made from burning beams were large enough for several flying demons, or one striding General. The red flames curled throughout the ship providing illumination, protection, and reminder of its infernal origin.

Uruk noticed sentries posted at branching passageways. He noted the squads in the hold did serve only to guard the generation chambers. If sentries were posted across the vast ship, then many demons were deployed as single guards at these junctures, not just as units at critical systems. Uruk sneered at the thought. This meant the posted sentries were taken from ready strike units. That spread demons thin across the ship while undeployed demons sat in racks on the weapons deck. Uruk knew sentries filled a defensive need in some tactical situations. However, he favored a more reflexive response to enemy probes and covert movement. In his mind, linear defenses were only to lure spear-point attacks, or for target practice of large bore guns. These demons across the ship were no more than an alarm system with one rifle at a fixed point. Better to use mobile squads with many weapons. The tactic employed on this ship over highly monitored, secured areas decreased firepower and adaptive response. The guards seemed more for intimidation of guests than security. What force would threaten a warship from Hell, internally?

The passageway forked at a bulkhead of fiery beams that now sealed the General's personal entrance. Trait broke right to enter at the Field Master's portal. All followed him. They entered the bridge. It was also sized for the ship's giant General. His throne sat at its rear. A length of massive chain lay coiled at the right of the slab-sided throne. The rungs for another lengthy weapon were empty. Again the coffin met the deck with a *thump!*

A tall demon stood with his wingless back to the entering group. He stared at the bulkhead across from his control dais, but no screens displayed visual data before it. Uruk knew a vast amount of data could still be flowing into his brain without visual input. Still, this Ship Master seemed preoccupied by empty space.

"I am Uruk, Field Master of our Lord Anguhr, the Destroyer. I bring—"

"It is obvious who you are." Voltris said while still staring into empty air. "When you enter this ship you become part of the information in my brain."

Voltris finally turned and face Uruk. They looked at each other with odd glances and inner questions of rank and power. No words left their mouths. The uncomfortable lull caused them both to twitch their heads.

Uruk broke the silence. "I have news you may not know. It is vital. It impacts our demonic future and that of Hell."

Uruk motioned to the coffin. Voltris approached it and fingered the large link fragment hung around his neck.

"What I must reveal, you must endure." Uruk said. "My demons have already beheld the shock. You will be the first eyes of this ship."

"Akhad is dead!" Trait barked. He thrust up the severed arm.

Voltris released a low growl as he stared at the limb and still fingered his link. Voltris nodded and cast his head to the right portal. Trait grunted and left.

Uruk breathed easier. His plan was working. Voltris held command. Uruk would permit him control of the horde while Uruk controlled Voltris. This strategy way would bring the ship and all its power to Lord Anguhr. Uruk nodded at his demons flanking the cube coffin. They tore it open to reveal Xuxuhr's head.

Voltris lurched as if hit by Xuxuhr himself. He spun and gripped the link fragment until fetid blood dripped from his palm.

"Your Lord was great," Uruk said. He surmounted his headache from containing his desire to simply grab power and spit on diplomacy. "But he is dead."

"Yes." Voltris pulled himself to look again at Xuxuhr's head. He released his grip on the link fragment. Dark blood now covered it. He flexed his bleeding hand. "I need not the ship's sensors to tell me. I have feared this. I can hardly accept it."

"You must." Uruk said. "You must find leadership now in my Lord. He will—"

"No!" Voltris screeched.

"It must be so," Uruk spoke in strained but cautious tones. "No living Generals are greater than Lord Anguhr. Service to him will bring glory to your horde. Serve your demons by following Lord Anguhr."

"You speak of glory!" Voltris snapped his head to glare at Uruk. "You speak of following! Yet you never mention our true and ultimate master."

Uruk slowly bowed his head. It bought him the second to understand what Voltris meant, and also make a tactic for his advantage.

"All praise the Dark Urge," Uruk said. He resisted grating his pointed teeth. "Her dark wisdom has brought me here."

Voltris tilted his head to consider Uruk's words and his own odd situation.

"Perhaps." Voltris said. "I will tell the horde. They must know. Madness may take them. It may only be a storm or it may destroy them all. But if it does not, then we may seek your Lord to redeem our bodies to the Dark Urge. All praise be to her. Now, I honor my master."

Uruk watched Voltris turn to his dais. He considered killing him and lying to Xuxuhr's horde that their Ship Master lived but hid in mourning. Yet, he had seen massive lies fall into the Red Giant. He had no stomach to do that. Xuxuhr's demons deserved the truth. Uruk placed his faith in this horde's strength to endure their master's loss.

Voltris broadcast his words to the horde. His speech and barks were short. His grieving howl was long and painful. A collective howl rolled across the ship. Uruk found himself caught in the moment. He joined Zahl and his own demons in the howl.

Far below in the swelter of the bilge deck, the Ignitaurs labored at their kilns and forges to make more chain. They heard the demon howls. They understood a calamity had befallen the ship, their prison. The right time had come to break their bonds. To the demons, their epic howl was a wail of mourning. To the Ignitaurs it was a call to war.

CHAPTER NINETEEN

The scream of the Dark Urge typically assaulted each system when a ship from Hell entered it. Not so her own system. However, Proxis had set warning klaxons to sound if another of her warships arrived. One did, and very close. It jumped into real space between the Red Giant and Hell. It set immediately on course toward the crimson star. Proxis plotted its course. The other ship's vector intersected over the region of the Iron Work that his own ship guarded. Proxis smiled on thinking of at his General's foresight. Now he gathered his strength to follow Lord Anguhr's orders and prevent any ship from entering striking range above him.

"Master Proxis—!" The demon Onar exclaimed as entered the bridge and saw the images and data flowing across the screens. He was the highest ranking Strike Leader, and now served as Proxis' liaison to the horde and ship's second in command.

"Yes. It heads our way," Proxis answered.

"Should we send a greeting?" Onar asked as he turned to face Proxis.

"And drop the ship's aegis and have all demons throw their weapons into space as well?" Proxis snarled. "We stand our ground!"

Onar stiffened and bowed.

"And yes, Onar, should we need to, we fight."

The face of Crucis flashed on the central screen in front of Proxis. The two Ship Masters stared at each other for a brief instant. They almost shared a shrug between themselves. It was the first time they had seen another Ship Master. It was also the first time any of Hell's massive dreadnoughts had faced another in potential conflict. Crucis spoke first with a commanding tone.

"My Lord, General, and Fleet Overlord Sutuhr now takes control of your ship. Stand ready for a transfer of—"

"Never!" Proxis shouted sharp and loud.

Onar resisted flinching, and stood fast behind Proxis at his right side.

"You have no choice but to—" Crucis began.

"Stand aside, sow!" Proxis snapped. "I now stand in command of this ship. Let the commander of your ship speak."

On his own bridge, Crucis lurched forward as if to bite Proxis. A hateful hiss and phalanx of teeth filled the center screen.

"Who dares? A demon?" A giant's voice boomed from behind Crucis. Sutuhr's lion and spider face appeared on the screen. The image panned back to show him seated on his throne holding his mace.

Proxis summoned all his courage and defiance to serve his own master. "I am no mere demon. I am Proxis, Ship Master for my Lord and General, Anguhr the Destroyer!"

"Anguhr the pup!" Sutuhr shouted from his throne. "Still I see he has stiffened the spines of his horde. I'm sure you serve him well. You now serve me, as does Anguhr himself."

"Impossible!" Proxis shook his head in true disbelief.

"It is the will of the Dark Urge, Proxis." Sutuhr altered his verbal tactics and spoke in a near mentoring tone. "Follow it and you will know her bliss."

"I already serve our dark sovereign through Lord Anguhr!" Proxis railed.

"I am Fleet Overlord by her order. The first such General to hold command over all. Praise the wisdom of the Dark Urge. Now follow her will, Master Proxis. Fall into position off my starboard quarter."

"No."

To Proxis, reality seemed to congeal into the shocked and then angry face of Sutuhr.

"Do as I say," Sutuhr drew in a long, deep breath. And the bellowed. "Or die!"

Proxis paused. He looked away from Sutuhr's image as his attention was caught by data on other screens.

"False threats, General." Proxis remarked and felt great internal relief. "You forget I can scan your ship. I know well a ship's power output. Yours is weak. Your ship is damaged. It is no match for what I command. Look at your scans of this warship. All its systems function. All its weapons."

136

"You dare mutiny?" Sutuhr roared. "You dare think you are my equal?"

"In Hell's hierarchy, no. But on this ship, I am master until Lord Anguhr returns. Would you have your own Ship Master surrender your ship to him?"

"You will obey me!" Sutuhr shouted. His face still revealed shock from wide, sideward cat's eyes and a loose jaw. "Anguhr will obey me! I, and only I, act as the personal champion of the Dark Urge!"

"I may only act as the Ship Master for Lord Anguhr," Proxis breathed. "But I will not fail in that duty. He would not fail me. Can your horde say such?"

"Anguhr answers to me, now!" Sutuhr bolted up from his throne. "All Generals do!"

"Bid the Dark Urge to be present and tell me in person." Proxis said.

"You would die, you little wingless freak! You will die if you disobey, with no redemption in Hell!"

"Yet, I live now." Proxis knew Sutuhr would not hear the non-verbal aspect of his reply. It was a loud hum of building energy. Proxis heard the metal echoes of the main guns emerging from the hull and their domes opening. He saw the effect his actions had on Sutuhr's stressed and monstrous face.

A roar and spew of venom assaulted Proxis, but only on the screen. The com-screen went blank and flashed on the image of Sutuhr's warship turning its vast length to head back towards Hell.

Demons had hearts that pumped infernal blood through their sinister forms. Proxis felt his ease form the rapid throbbing that threatened to burst it. His next sensation was one of near pain as his face muscles pulled his thorny cheeks fully back and nearly cramped in a smile that would, if ever seen, terrify the minds of other species for generations. He spoke a low prayer for himself and Onar's ears.

"All praise the Dark Urge, and Lord Anguhr, the Destroyer."

Onar inhaled and joined Proxis with a devilish smile. "I wonder if this was the first victory in Hell's eternal history where a Ship Master won the day on his own. And against so powerful a foe, a General, no less."

"I wonder of it is indeed a victory," Proxis rested his left arm on his dais. "Time, and Lord Anguhr, will tell."

Anguhr stood the arc length of a large planet's hemisphere away from the access canyon. He kept the expedition pared to only the most essential personnel. One General. One demon. One prisoner. Their equipment was also sparse. Anguhr had his immense axe locked on his back. Solok carried his heavy rifle on a shoulder sling. Zaria had the grapnel node lashed to her back. Anguhr had noted how easily she agreed to pack the seeming inert device. They traveled only in Anguhr's chariot across the vast, obsidian plane. As General, Anguhr could go virtually anywhere he pleased. Anguhr came here because he was curious. If it was not as thrilling as combat, walking on the sacred and stellar-scale machine was at least interesting. It all appeared to be the same flat, black surface. The great size of the one band made realizing its curve impossible when standing on its hot face. This was true from the demon's eye view, and from the height of a giant such as Anguhr. Compared to the Iron Work, all life was miniscule.

Anguhr still watched the reactions of his acting Field Master, Solok. Uruk was well into his mission to secure Xuxuhr's ship. Anguhr knew that sending Uruk was a great gamble. He could lose the most valuable member of his horde. Securing another ship was a worthy risk. Anguhr hoped to secure another powerful weapon, here. As a General, he thought he was the most powerful creature where he walked. Yet he walked over a machine built by powers dwarfing his own. Xuxuhr's death had yet to impress him that even Generals were, in the right conditions, as mortal as ants.

Anguhr was certain another General would be quick to use this ultimate weapon should they find it. In his hands he hoped to keep it as a reserve of last choice. He loved War, not annihilation. First, the weapon must be completed. For that, he needed Zaria. She had environed it just as the Dark Urge had done so. Thus, Zaria was dangerous, powerful, but useful in this new age of uncertain futures. Like the Dark Urge, she created her own warriors. Anguhr wondered if she also created what caught his eye high above them.

"What are they?" Anguhr asked. He pointed overhead.

In the red tinted blackness of space above the Iron Work, two points of light held positions triangulated above where Anguhr stood. Zaria knew lies were of no use. The last, free members of the forces she created on Asherah had been discovered. She wondered if Anguhr's eyes could see much more than the blobs of light. They were small ships, but also living creatures. Their inspirations were one of the oldest lifeforms Zaria knew. In close, the creatures bore a strong resemblance to the horseshoe crabs deep within Eden's oceans. The saucer shape of their shells suggested a container. They became the basis for her transport and support craft.

Their living hulls were large enough to take in all the members of Zaria's twin strike teams before the first was ravaged by combat and the second spotted by Anguhr's demons and surrendered to him. These creatures had arcane metal hulls that survived space and absorbed stellar

138

radiation for energy and defense. Their hull divided into two sections near the middle of the body similar to the original arthropod's shells. The main section held a perfect, circular edge where the bottom and top sides joined. The edges of the second section continued out beyond the circular edge and curved forward as slightly inverted, short wings. That seemed fitting to Zaria for flying things. Their tails tapered from the center of these winglets into a long spike. They glowed nearly white from the absorption of stellar energy. Each one awaited orders to descend and transport Zaria and her forces or attack the site where her mission was to conclude.

"Based on the original lifeforms they are based on," Zaria answered, "you could call them *asterapods*. Or, because of their shape, comets. They are merely my own chariots for egress from the Iron Work."

"But they have a large amount of energy," Anguhr noted. "So they are also weapons."

"They are merely transports." Zaria said.

"Order them into the star." Anguhr commanded.

"General, they don't threaten you. They are of no—"

Anguhr raised his axe. Zaria sensed the mental equivalent of a shouted command. Several, smaller points of light became visible at an angle above the comets. They bore down on the living ships. Contrail-like streaks formed behind the smaller points as heat from the corona assaulted the missiles' shielding.

The comets fled. The missiles altered course and pursued them. The chase was lost behind the greater red glare of the auroras in the far distance.

"I see you deployed a defense, high aloft." Zaria noted and hoped her comets escaped.

"Of course," Solok said.

"You are argumentative. You risk your life with defiance." Anguhr said as he turned to Zaria.

"And you are used to getting your way too easily." Zaria countered. "Those comets could have been useful to us."

"No. Not to me." Anguhr said. "Now, we will retrieve what we came for. The weapon will be useful. Potentially. Make it happen."

Zaria noted the slight change in Anguhr's tone and words. He gave her an order, but did not follow it a threat to her life or the lives of the prisoners. It was progress. Familiarity was, perhaps, breeding acceptance. Anguhr at least accepted her abilities. Zaria wondered if he had guessed her real ultimate weapon and end game. She knew he could not guess what was to come, here and in the near future.

"Look down," Zaria said. "Not at me, but at your boots."

Anguhr stared at the black surface. He could see the barest trace of a circular arc. The arc extended to form a vast circle. He looked up at Zaria.

"For once you don't understand," Zaria said. "I know. But I do."

Anguhr glared at Zaria. An angry Solok joined him.

"The key is me, or rather, the information I have." Zaria looked across the black zone encompassed by the nearly invisible circle. "What we seek is also information. It is an accumulation of data so vast it radiates energy like the star below it. At no other time was such power available that could threaten your black queen in Hell. It exists, now. It is why she sent Xuxuhr and why she wanted me dead. If I can imagine it, then must also have seen the potential to make the weapon you want."

"The weapon you will make for me," Anguhr growled.

"And then what? Will you—"

"No." Anguhr voice rose as did his ire. "You will act. Now."

"Very well," Zaria extended her hands.

Anguhr felt a tinge of emotion. It was not excitement at completing the weapon or seeing his curiosity fulfilled. It was unease at the satisfaction shown in Zaria's smile. There was a tremor. Light flashed around the imbedded circle. It became a vast, illuminated ring. The arc near Anguhr's boots moved. He stepped back. Solok aimed his rifle at the rising, black metal. Zaria stayed standing right at the circle's edge. A half sphere slid up within the arc facing them and rolled down to form a dome within the lit circle. The dome rose. The surface of the Iron Work lost no material as the dome elevated into a vast, black ball. Zaria gave a slight nod, as if replying to a voice. A narrow band of light flashed at the black ball's equator. A rim emerged from the light and extended outward. The black ball became smaller as the rim grew into a widening flange.

Solok dropped to a squat as the flange expanded over them. He still aimed his rifle at the unknown events happening before him. Anguhr ducked, slightly. Zaria still stood with arms out but in seeming communion with the events. The flange kept growing and separated into a wide ring that continued to expand along the equatorial plane. It hovered around the reduced, black sphere. The transformation of black metal paused and it that felt as though time also held still. Anguhr looked up at the absolute back ring above him. Suddenly he saw see the reddish black sky again. Only the black sphere remained.

The sphere's top hemisphere split in equal halves at the apex that rolled down into the bottom half. A huge, black cube stood revealed in the bowl-like, bottom section. Again there was a pause. A frozen moment. Events continued. The bottom half-sphere sank back into the Iron Work. The cube followed and sank to half its height and stopped. Zaria sprinted to it and leapt. She caught the cube's top edge and hoisted herself to top surface. The grapnel node swung on her back.

Anguhr jolted. He shouted to Solok. "Stay here! Summon the ship if I so order."

"Understood, Lord!" Solok barked.

His words were unheard by Anguhr who already ran to the cube. His motion felt labored and slowed. He leapt and thrust up his arms. His hands caught the sharp edge of the cube. With great effort, he pulled himself to the top. Zaria stood across from him on the ebony surface. Anguhr stepped back to the edge as another sphere rose from the top of the half-sunken cube. That sphere opened at its equator. Its bottom half slid up into its top to reveal a more complex shape. Anguhr bent down to look at it, but the half-sphere slid down to show the tetrahedron within it.

The brief, heavy pause returned. The half sphere and tetrahedron sank into the square remnant of the cube. The tetrahedron flattened into a triangular base. Only it remained with its sides rising over both Anguhr and Zaria. Anguhr jumped and pulled himself up again. He saw Zaria smile at him across the triangular base before another sphere rose between them. This sphere's top half rolled down to reveal a more complicated dodecahedron solid. The pause returned. The sphere flowed into the triangular base as the dodecahedron flattened to a ten-sided plateau rising off the triangle. Anguhr took an instinctive breath, and leapt.

Anguhr glanced down. His altitude was high enough to make Solok appear no larger than Anguhr's thumb on the Iron Work's surface below. He stood and saw Zaria again with her arms out. Another, yet smaller sphere rose up. This sphere parted at its side with the icosahedron pointed at Anguhr. Under his helmet, he raised his eyebrows. The shape flipped with the half sphere at the bottom. For a moment, he felt frozen but thought he saw a glimmer of flowing water beyond the black shapes triangular facets. The half-sphere flowed back into the previous base. The icosahedron sank into a hexagon tier.

Anguhr was intrigued, but knew the race up the sides of this odd, rising mountain must end at some point. The prize would be at the summit. Or one very angry General from Hell. He leapt and pulled himself up to the next, flat plane. For once he had tied with Zaria.

This sphere and shape manifested in mere blinks. An octahedron stood revealed. Its bottom point rested at the center of the wide, hexagonal base. It sank but formed a pyramid, not a triangular plane. Its base was small enough for Anguhr to sprint around to confront Zaria. She wasn't standing on the opposite side. Anguhr looked up. Zaria was already scaling the pyramid. He let out a sharp growl and charged after her. The slope was steep, but the surface allowed purchase by flattening hands and feet as best as possible. He thought of tossing aside his massive axe. He thought better of it as he may need it to cleave Zaria in half. Anguhr reasoned the surface was meant to climb. Zaria was certainly making it look easy. He quickened his pace. As with the water, Anguhr noticed a faint image of clouds just beyond the black surface. He wondered if he hadn't noticed other images on the preceding shapes. He focused on Zaria. She was at the summit.

At the pyramid's top, Zaria watched a narrow cylinder rise from the pinnacle. It began to glow with surging, blinding white light. She grabbed the cylinder and pulled with all her strength. Ledges flowed from all four sides at the level of Zaria's feet. She strained. The flashing cylinder moved only slightly. Anguhr climbed over the ledge Zaria stood on. He saw Zaria pulling up on the brilliant cylinder. He righted himself, and grabbed hold. They pulled in unison. Brilliant white flooded their vision as the rod came free. It was half as long as Zaria. Anguhr thrust it into overhead. He felt as though an unimaginably loud thunder roared right at his ears. It was pressure from radiation.

"The grapnel!" Zaria screamed with all power across all the frequencies she could summon. "The grapnel! Slide the rod into the grapnel!"

Zaria turned her back to Anguhr. He did what she screamed. The black, hexagonal grapnel node accepted the brilliant white rod. The intense light dimmed as it slid deeper down. When only the length in Anguhr's hand remained, the flashing ceased. The top of the pyramid seemed impossibly still. Zaria and Anguhr's only comments were deep breaths and long seconds of gathering their thoughts. The beat of Solok's wings brought time back into motion.

"Lord?" Solok queried. He was uncertain as to what had occurred and hoped it all made sense to his General.

Anguhr steadied himself by holding the point of the pyramid where a narrow, cylindrical void now existed. "Go secure my transit craft." Anguhr breathed. "I will come there, soon."

Zaria took a deep breath. She looked out across the Iron Work and stellar setting. She nodded to herself, and smiled.

CHAPTER TWENTY

The echo of the demons' mournful cry died in the red flames across the ship.

"The coordinates are entered," Voltris said and dropped his head forward and his hands away from his control dais. "We are en route to your Lord Anguhr's position."

"He is your Lord, now." Uruk said. He sniffed the air, but suppressed a sneer.

Xuxuhr's head still peered up with sunken, cuttlefish eyes from its makeshift coffin. Uruk had never considered that Generals' could die. Thus, he never imagined rotting stench from a General. Bad smells on occasion, but not rot. Voltris also noticed the odor from the strangely natural process happening to the giant hellspawn's severed head.

"I do not know what to do with the head of my Lord." Voltris said looking inside the box. Even with skin of thorns and serpentine eyes, his face fluctuated between expressions of pathos and reverence. "There is no standing order or program, and no protocol for what do. It is we who are to die, not our General, not our Lord."

"A pyre is always a good means to honor the fallen, no matter rank." Uruk offered. "We demons are not creatures of ceremony, save to burn the dead when we can. It is our enemy that burn in greater number. Still, as he was your Lord, and we make pyres for our dead, then a pyre for a General befits his remains."

"And if the remains are only his head?" Voltris asked and cast an almost accusing stare at Uruk.

Uruk still endured his headache from diplomacy, and ignored the glare. "The rest of him will be consumed by the star trapped by the Iron Work. What better a pyre for all his parts than Hell's own massive star?"

Voltris looked back at Xuxuhr's head and fingered the link fragment hung around his neck. He nodded. "I agree. So shall it be done."

The Red Giant dominated the scene on the ship's outer hull. Trait and his shock force stood on the fiery surface beams over the bridge. Voltris stood before them with a unit of demons holding up the resealed coffin. Uruk stood to the side of the first-ever demon honor guard. He left Zahl and the original coffin guard inside the bridge. Voltris pushed the coffin and the demons holding it released their grip. The metal box sailed out from the ship towards the vast, burning face of the Red Giant.

Voltris realized the pitch was not sufficient for Xuxuhr's head to sail straight into the stellar fires. He calculated the velocity of the ship; the coffin's vector; the angle of toss; the gravitational effects of the ship and the wake of the main drive. These factors might cause the enclosed head to make an orbit before gravity, as odd as it behaved around the Iron Work, to finally take the head close enough to the star for incineration. For a time, Xuxuhr's head might even become a small planetoid. These factors he would keep to himself.

Voltris turned and nodded to Trait who then flew up. The lines of Triat's force followed each other in a precise succession of demon waves that soared into space. They followed Trait's arc back to the ship and through the gaps between the fiery beams. The wingless Voltris watched the arcs of flying demons, and then climbed back down to the bridge. Uruk followed him.

When the echo of the demons' mournful cry died, the Ignitaurs were preparing to strike. Their ears were well adapted to gathering ship sounds and demon speech. Intelligence and intuition made sense of the auditory cues. Many bovine eyes stared at the top of their prison when the wail began. They had initially looked at each other with as much shock as the demons. Then they vibrated with joy. The short, conic ears fluttered to the sides of thick, obsidian horns rising in a slope to the back of their boulder skulls. Grooves just as those in rows of molars ran along the center of the horns that curled into pointed loops. Older individuals used small prongs jutting from their main horns to hang small hammers and tongs. Their ancestors had used the horns for ramming one another for sexual displays, disputes, and sport. Both male and females adults grew the black horns. Their eyes were a deeper black and useful as tools for hiding intent. The constantly staring, inscrutable orbs sat astride blunted bulls' snouts ending in wide, flaring nostrils. Ancestral Ignitaurs looked

144

indistinguishable between sexes, and to intimidated predators. The lack of dimorphism continued into civilization, technology, and ethereal mastery. Such mastery did not spare their world from Xuxuhr, but their cultural trait of patience served them in captivity.

The imprisoned Ignitaurs had dreamed of freedom with every stoke of their forges or blow of their hammers on anvils. They realized they could not overcome the horde if the world ravager Xuxuhr was with them. At some point, the Ignitaurs believed he would be gone long enough to strike and take the ship. However, as pragmatic creatures, they would accept annihilation of themselves and their demon jailers. The General's death subtracted his power from the horde and weakened it psychologically. Thus, they would all be easier to kill.

To achieve such vast death, the bull-like people turned to skills other than chain making. The Dark Urge was a being of arcane powers. Collectively, so were the Ignitaurs. Their specialty as smiths was to control flames. And then they were forced onto a ship constantly ablaze. They had carefully fashioned means to tap the ship's metaphysics for their own causes. One was to appease their jailer with enchanted chains. This bought time to plan how to snap their bondage. They curled the ship's fire to heat their forges to make chains. In time, they gained greater control of this crimson force. The inscrutable faces of the Ignitaurs, either colored burnished red or dark brown, served to protect their plans just as the fire protected the ship. If the Ignitaurs could smile, they would at the thought of controlling flame to burn demons. The hellish fires would also power the secret weapons they forged alongside the massive links.

The Ignitaurs disguised weapon parts as cooled drops of molten metal; slag; discarded lumps of dross; shavings; and splintered tools. The crafty and powerful smiths gathered the parts from piles and pits. The time had come to assemble them all. By the time Xuxuhr came to their world, Ignitaurs had been spacefarers for generations. Their once powerful rear legs receded in microgravity. The strong arms remained to propel themselves through ships and the corridors of their world remade with steel. The false gravity of the Hell ship lent itself to the ancient art of ramming enemies. Vestigial legs became clad them in steel prosthetics made from joined helixes. The two sections inverted like bovine limbs for springing power.

The Ignitaur weapons focused the ship's flames into offensive firepower. More weapons disguised as splinters fit together to form flame throwers that needed no fuel because it rippled around them on the walls. The weapons amplified the heat enough to burn through demon thorns. Units that employed these guns were reinforced by others armed by simpler fabrications. Swords or clubs brought against the skull of a demon had great effect when swung by the strength of an arcane smith. The Ignitaurs were now an army.

All the weapons and plans would be a pile of waste unless they could also forge a key and escape. Seven older and powerful Ignitaurs assembled their object of liberation. Curved spines fit together into a circle. The spines resembled rays curling out from a sun. The center star was yet to form. The Ignitaurs stepped back from their solar talisman. A low moan echoed across the bilge deck as all focused on the sun's empty center. The talisman rose and turned to a right angle to the deck floor. A red spark crackled at the center of the metal rays. It flared into an arcing ball of crimson. The red fires grew brighter and then into intense violet light. The circle of metal rays began to melt. Small beads flew from the metal rays. Those struck did not move. The groups' focus was total. The moan grew louder and rose in pitch. The talisman turned again, level between the deck floor and imprisoning ceiling. The intense ball of violet light became a small white star. Its power shot as a column of plasma into the ceiling and through the bilge deck. The ship lurched. The metal rays of the talisman fell as a cascade of molten metal. A wide hole with glowing edges now smoldered above them. The Ignitaurs were free.

Anguhr stepped from his chariot. He had returned Zaria and Solok to the marshalling point near the access canyon.

"All is prepared, Lord Destroyer." the recognized demon Goro said. He commanded the combined units of Anguhr's forces and Xuxuhr's surviving engineers.

"Good," Anguhr said. He took the grapnel node housing the power rod from its cable sling now hung on his left shoulder. He took hold and pulled the handle. A steam of white light escaped the perfect fit of the two elements. He slid it back and felt a reverberation through the grapnel as if an immense weight struck a solid bottom.

"Yes, you can pull it back out." Zaria said beside him. "Do not."

"I will if I please," Anguhr said. "Especially when I need to use this weapon."

"It is not yet a true weapon." Zaria countered.

"We shall see," Anguhr said. "How did you tame the machine that held the rod?"

"I did not tame it," Zaria replied. "I answered its questions."

"Questions?" Anguhr asked as he slid the grapnel back toward his axe.

"You could not hear them, because you were not listening." Zaria said.

"I will not hear riddles, either!" Anguhr barked.

"Nor do I wish to be a prisoner." Zaria glared back. "Yet I act as I must to achieve what must be done."

"Tell me the answers." Anguhr stepped to loom over Zaria.

"The answers are formulas for Platonic solids." Zaria stared back at Anguhr. "In the order you saw, they were once used in an old, very old model of a solar system, now forgotten. Thus, the ability to predict the next formula was based on knowledge of history. From outer-most world toward the one closest to the sun. You may well have a file stored deep down in that smoldering skull, but you have never had context to use it. And even now, your tactic of domination would take you astray from the path I opened."

"Platon is some system, some empire now dead?" Anguhr asked.

"No." Zaria smiled at the General's ignorance. "It's a theory of long ago. Long dead. To most."

"Why would anyone, including this ancient machine, store such useless data?" Anguhr looked up and across the vast, black surface hazed red. "Why would it unlock traps here on the Iron Work?"

"Exactly," Zaria said. "Why? Because it's history. Part of their history. The Builders. Part of mine. You could call it whimsical, but the link to history is also a lock. That lock is a hope that intellects that can answer the questions are also part of the Builders' legacy. Or are at least good at obscure geometry. Like I said, whimsical. But what else could beings become when invested with such power?"

Anguhr returned his gaze to Zaria with a curious stare.

"Oh, you still wish Hell to be supreme?" Zaria asked. "Or do you now want to be the great power. King Anguhr."

"I am a General." Anguhr growled.

"And a god, or at least the messianic link for your demons." Zaria motioned her head toward the assembled demons. "What to do when that link is broken, General?"

"Do not anger me. I am also the Destroyer."

"And that, Destroyer, is why you chased me up the Platonic rise. You are a deviation. I am part of the legacy that ultimately led to this machine, or, more so, the ability to build something like this."

"And your Asherah." Anguhr said. "The thing in Old Jove."

"Old Jove?" Gin asked as he joined Zaria, still bound at his hands.

Anguhr growled at seeing Gin, but replied. "The largest gas giant of this system. What we thought was a true planet."

"It was," Zaria said and raised her eyebrows. "How odd a spawn of Hell would call it Old Jove."

"Why?" Anguhr demanded.

"It is almost whimsical," Zaria said. "It suggests even Hell's mind still holds a psychological link to past ages. Unconscious knowledge has an

147

impact on behavior. It shapes us as much as our conscious actions. Perhaps powerfully. It's an important lesson."

"I am not here to be schooled." Anguhr sneered and looked over at his unified demons.

"Yet, what you didn't know prevented you from gaining the prize you sought." Zaria said.

"I have it now." Anguhr jerked the grapnel's sling.

"Because I allowed you to take it," Zaria smiled. "I did that because I need it as well. Power, General. You think you have it because you can destroy. And yet your new weapon and all your powers come from gathered information. That thing you hold. You think it a power rod. But it is stored data. The information is what makes it powerful. Its radiation only a byproduct of what it holds. Don't drop it. If you prove a good student, I will teach you how to use it."

"Ha!" Anguhr laughed. "It is a powerful weapon now, and only my strength can remove it from its grapnel scabbard."

"As it is configured now, it is only a bomb." Zaria said. "There is one other piece that will make it complete and ensure it can be delivered into Hell itself."

Anguhr took a deep breath and stretched his shoulders. The grapnel and axe clinked together. He then turned to Zaria and fixed a long stare on her.

"Need I say: give it to me?" Anguhr at last remarked.

"It is not here, of course." Zaria replied. "I would not risk all the components on a battlefield."

"But you risk your life and world by annoying me." Anguhr said. "Give me the final component."

"Where it lies, you cannot go." Zaria gave a slight shake of her head. Her hair flickered in bright contrast to the Iron Work's black surface and permeating red haze.

Anguhr held out the rod and grapnel as evidence of his power as he spoke. "I have been told this by countless people on countless worlds. Always their barriers and beliefs fall before my axe. Your barriers will do the same."

"All those ill-fated worlds were not defended by barriers raised by the same ones as built this machine you stand on." Zaria countered. "It is only a sliver of it that you hold as an ultimate weapon. I designed that weapon. I created the warriors that fought well against Hell's vaunted demons. And it is I who killed Xuxuhr. Do you think I know nothing of war?"

Zaria could see Anguhr's eyebrow raise and disappear under his helmet. Its arch lay out of sight behind its black steel.

"And, so General, do not take my words so lightly." Zaria added.

148

Anguhr turned his head slightly as if the same line of force pulled his eyebrow.

"So your control is on Eden." Anguhr said as he lowered the rod and grapnel with a nod of enjoyment.

"No." Gin said. "Well, yes. But Eden is one aspect of Asherah. Eden, as you call it, is an ecology. A planet housed—"

"Gin!" Zaria yelled.

Gin became silent and offered only a smile and shrug to the looming Anguhr.

"I will destroy it all," Anguhr said with a deep, certain tone.

"Petty." Gin remarked.

"You feel conquest is petty!" Solok barked as he flew in and glared at Gin.

"Actually, yes." Gin shrugged.

The smaller but more savage Solok back handed Gin's across the face. A quick flash of surprise lit the demon's face when his victim was hardly staggered.

"You are merely making my point," Gin said.

Anguhr leaned down toward Zaria. She could see his burning eyes studying her but not glaring to intimidate. His massive right had reached up with his fingers stretched out as if to grasp and crush. They instead gathered a length of Zaria's long, blonde hair. Anguhr watched it slip through his fingers.

'In all his travels across the stars, has he never seen blonde hair?' Gin sent his thoughts to Zaria across their wavelengths.

'He can sense there is a dimension beyond where the light through it originates.' Zaria replied along the same channel. 'And may have a reason to be fascinated by long hair.'

"Stop talking—thinking to each other." Anguhr spoke aloud. "I can sense more than the light emanating from you. No matter. Now, we go to your Eden."

"No." Zaria sneered. "I can—"

"Yes." Anguhr said. "I would see such a legend before I burn it. I will be the first and only General to set foot on this mythic place. It will become part of my legend."

"But if you destroy Eden, I will see that your new, precious weapon will be no better than a club." Zaria said with a defiant sneer.

"I have an axe." Anguhr said, calmly.

"A useless toy compared to the power of my completed weapon." Zaria countered. "Now it is a mere explosive if pulled from the grapnel and held out too long. You need its control system. If you kill me, kill Eden, you have nothing. If you bend slightly, you may gain a weapon that makes you supreme in the galaxy. It seems an easy decision, *General.*"

149

Anguhr smiled, but then his fiery eyes glared at Zaria. "If you lie to me, I will hurl you into an event horizon, lashed to my ship at one end."

"But that would—" Gin began, but Anguhr's hand covered his face.

"He will not speak, anymore." Anguhr said to Zaria as he held Gin's head. "You will give the coordinates. Now."

Zaria glanced at the muffled Gin and caught sight of Solok's devilish smile. She turned back to Anguhr.

"Very well." Zaria sighed.

CHAPTER TWENTY-ONE

The ship suddenly lurched. Voltris grasped his control dais. Uruk noticed a momentary ebb in the crimson fires rolling across the bridge's bulkheads. Zahl and his recognized lieutenant Prod instinctively thrust out their wings for stability. A screen flashed on before them. The face of a demon in the cargo hold appeared. Behind him, the ruptured deck plating smoldered from the explosive escape of the Ignitaurs. They emerged from the hole amid demon rifle fire and horde members swooping down to grapple with the powerful aliens sprinting across the deck on helical legs of steel. Uruk recognized some of his demons he left in the hold among the combatants.

"Master Voltris!" The demon on screen barked. "The Igs show treachery! They escape and attack! We—"

A sudden red flash cut the transmission.

"What is this?" Uruk demanded. "What are Igs?"

"Ignitaurs—Igs!" Voltris screeched. "They are captured aliens used by our Lord to make his chains."

"What? Why?" Uruk bellowed. He turned and motioned to the rest of his force standing on the bridge. The lead demon, Sond, nodded and then flew into the left passageway to join the cargo hold battle followed by his unit.

"I am loyal! I do not question!" Voltris bared his teeth.

"Suppress this insult!" Uruk pointed in the direction of the cargo deck. "Send your strike units to the hold! Send Triat!"

"They strike teams are deployed across the ship. Our main force is on the weapons deck." Voltris spat.

"Ridiculous!" Uruk roared. "Order your main force to the hold, or the incursion will spread! Secure the ship! Now!"

"You wish me to redeploy the sentries?" Voltris screamed. "Of course! Then you can call in reserves from your horde and take control!"

"It would matter not!" Uruk butted Voltris. "We now all follow Lord Anguhr. I am his Field Master. Obey my commands!"

"No! You have caused this!" Voltris grasped his link fragment. "The Ignitaurs never rebelled until you arrived! I will not follow you!"

"You doom your demons with these delays!" Uruk barked.

"It is you who are doomed! By the Dark Urge!" Voltris railed. "It is Anguhr's axe that severed my Lord Xuxuhr's head. It was Anguhr that killed him!"

"No!" Uruk slung his rifle and drew his sword. "This ship is insane. Alter the command codes to recognize me, or die!"

"How else—" Voltris began.

"Silence!" Uruk grabbed the cord attached to the link Voltris wore and pulled it tight around his throat. "It was not Lord Anguhr that killed General Xuxuhr! It was an alien warrior, just as aliens now beset this ship! If you defy Lord Anguhr, your death will be for nothing!"

"No." Voltris gripped Uruk's wrist with both hands and choked out his words. "I still serve the Dark Urge by avenging the death of my Lord who must have been her favored child. I will steer my ship to Hell and—*uurrggk!*"

Uruk slid his sword back out from Voltris. He thought of his headache from the now failed diplomacy, and thrust it back through again. Voltris fell from the sword with a look of shock on his thorny face. The link he wore hit the deck plate with a loud rap.

Zahl looked at Voltris' corpse. "Now how do we steer the ship?"

"I can steer it," Uruk said calmly as he flicked off blood from his sword and replaced it in the scabbard. "I just need to solve the command code lock. Or interface directly with the ship. "If I can persuade—"

"You cannot!" Trait bellowed and hurled the head of Sond at Uruk and Zahl. Prod leveled his weapon at Triat, but glanced first at Zahl. He nodded. Prod's opening volley punched through the edge of Trait's wing as he escaped through the right passageway. A burst of return fire covered Trait's escape, but only struck the bulkheads.

"Death to all!" Uruk cried out in rage.

"We will be over run on the bridge!" Zahl barked. "Send the word and we will retreat into space."

"No," Uruk breathed and regained control. "We'd be cut down by the ship's guns. Our chances are better against demons. They have chosen to fight us. They must be cut down."

"But how do we survive an entire horde?" Zahl asked. "No planet we have ever conquered has—"

"Think strategically, Zahl!" Uruk yelled into his lieutenant's face. "There is a force unleashed below decks that challenges this horde."

"How is that possible?" Prod asked as he aimed his gun at the passageway. He darted his gaze to the left entrance.

"However it is occurs, the Ravager's horde is now our enemy." Uruk said. "The rebel aliens are our allies. They likely have limited tactical knowledge of this ship. We know all they would need, but will use them to take control. We can direct their campaign to take control while not destroying critical systems. We can still bring this ship to Lord Anguhr!"

"We follow, Uruk." Zahl nodded. "With pride, we obey."

"All praise the Dark Urge!" Prod added.

"Praise to Lord Anguhr!" Uruk barked. "Now all we need do is the impossible for him to praise us."

Uruk reached for the ship controls. A cascade of grenades hurled from inside the right passageway exploded across the deck. Uruk was knocked against the throne as Zahl ducked. Voltris' body blasted across the bridge chamber. The ship's control dais blew apart. Zahl flicked out a fragment from his cheek and returned fire.

Prod defiantly cut down the demons storming the bridge with sustained rifle fire, but was quickly hit by several devastating salvos from farther down the passageway. He fell back into Xuxuhr's coiled chain. More rounds punched through his body and ricocheted against the links.

Zahl shielded the stunned Uruk and shot controlled bursts into enemy demons advancing up the passageway. Several fell. Uruk shook his head and drew up his weapon and joined Zahl in returning fire. Uruk motioned for Zahl to fall back. Zahl took a position behind the throne and fired. Uruk slid next to him, and then hurled a barrage of his own grenades into the passageway. Zahl threw another group into the left entrance for good measure. The blasts obliterated the surviving demons to the right side. Zahl and Uruk felt an increasing pull against the deck plates as the ship began to veer. They looked over at the shattered column where the ship's controls had stood.

"One wonders if some demons ever think strategically," Zahl remarked.

A row of regeneration chambers exploded. The demon Tana shook the mephitic amniotic fluid from his head. His unit supported the first counter attack by Uruk's strike team against the invaders who erupted from the bilge deck. Tana had stormed several planets from their skies. This was the first attack he attempted to repulse, and an assault and one that came from a position below him. It was odd, but it was battle. What was truly strange was who was shooting at him now.

"Did demons just shoot at us?" Tana barked. "Are they confused or stupid?"

"They came from the weapons deck. And did fire on us!" Tana's unit mate Karo yelled over the explosions and rifle fire as the Ignitaurs advanced on the late arriving forces from Xuxuhr's ship.

"Then, are these bull things our allies or our enemy?" Karo shrugged as rifle fire knocked the embryo demons from their spear points.

"Those are aliens!" Tana jabbed his snout in the direction of a renewed onrush of Ignitaurs. He slung his rifle and grasped several grenades from his strap. His pitched his arms back and readied to throw them. "They fight demons! Then they are enem--! Wait! Com from Uruk. No! They are allies!"

Tana hurled the grenades at a squad of Xuxuhr's demons snaking towards their flank. A group of closing Ignitaurs halted and glanced at each other in confusion as pieces of the demon bodes were blasted over their heads from Tana's assault.

"This is not war! This is pure carnage!" Zahl yelled as he and Uruk arrived at the passageway junction above the cargo hold and peered down.

"It is mindless revenge on both sides." Uruk said as he watched Xuxuhr's demons gather for simplistic massed attacks. "We must assert leadership."

"Over what faction?" Zahl asked. "Do you still think the aliens are our allies?"

"They are now a distraction," Uruk growled. "It would appear neither side would allow us chance to parlay. So my plan is as successful as General Xuxuhr's last mission."

"And so we now escape into space?" Zahl asked.

"No!" Uruk roared. "First we regroup our own forces."

"Then flee into space?"

"NO! Our mission is unchanged!" Uruk lurched up to glare at Zahl. "We will use this mayhem to seize this ship!"

"A ship that plummets towards the Iron Work or worse?" Zahl's left hand released his rifle for a second to allow his whole arms to shrug.

"If we take the main drive I will stop it from incinerating in the star." Uruk countered.

Zahl opened his mouth to reply.

"But if you say another world, you will burn in the star!" Uruk's grip vibrated against his rifle.

154

"I hear and I obey, Field Master." Zahl nodded as bullets flew into the junction. "Do not mistake my desire to live with a lack of fight or disrespect. I will kill all who challenge us, alien or demon."

"We will have many of both, Zahl." Uruk crept closer to the edge of the junction and barked an order audibly and over his demons wavelengths: "All my demons, withdraw! Withdraw!"

Zahl looked at his Field Master with confusion.

"We will allow one side to prove itself stronger," Uruk answered Zahl stare. "Then we will give the deciding blow with our demons. Until then, we move to take strategic control. We *will* take the main drive!"

Zaria wondered what other means of transport Anguhr used in his conquests. A small burning chariot suited him to speed between the comparatively close if truly distant sites on the Iron Work. Yet a transport ship like the one used by Xuxuhr did not suit him for departure from the solar cage. Anguhr wanted something on a grander scale. His ship was the only thing that fit the task, even if it was dwarfed by the titanic machine he stood on. His ship looked as another red star on a collision course as it approached. Closer to Zaria and her captured forces and Anguhr and his combined demon crew, it appeared as an inferno of steel skeletons set to crush them. It filled the entire sky above them with a more intense and rolling crimson inferno. Sporadic energy arcs shot from the burning hull to the power absorbing properties of the black plane it hovered near.

"You appreciate ostentatious acts, General," Zaria raised her voice over the roar of the ship's fire and crack of the arcs. "Yet I wouldn't stay here long!"

"We leave now," Anguhr said. "Just recall what I command."

And who shall command you? Zaria thought. She allowed herself a smile as the ship came even closer.

One demon sentry stood at the hatchway to the portside secondary battery. Uruk sneered. If Triat was issuing commands to his demons, he had yet to call in all his forces to suppress the Ignitaur revolt. It was a show of arrogance or incompetence. Uruk would kill him for either, or simply because he felt like it. Even for a demon, Uruk was in a bad mood. The sentry caught Uruk and Zahl's unit enter from the outside hull, not the passage from inside the ship. He swung his rifle towards them, but then caught the full bursts of their fire. His body became pieces ricocheting with the bullets.

"There will be a conduit I can interface with inside the guns' reactor room." Uruk said as they entered. Radiation bled away from the cylindrical reactor thrust into the hull. It crackled along the machines metal skin as it became part of the ship's aegis, although there was no need to shield the demons from the excess radiation. Thick power lines coiled from the reactor's closest end. Uruk selected one with a distention near the gun dome nested inside the burning beams.

"Hold this position." Uruk handed his rifle to Zahl. "I will interface and take control of the weapons."

"Understood, Master Uruk." Zahl nodded.

The word *interface* was an old term for the means of entering commands into machines. The direct, demon method was even older than machines. He opened his jaws as wide as he could to expose all his serrated teeth. He grabbed and bit into the distended node. There was a massive spark. Zahl jumped back. Uruk's body quivered. Zahl wondered if he was now Field Master.

Uruk expected the world of the ship's systems to be one of heat and darkness. However, his perception was immersed in white light as his mind became part of the information and control channels. More surprising was the wet sensation. Uruk saw what he hoped to be the circuits for the weapons systems. The appeared as fibers within a stream without shores, buffeted by the current. He grabbed them mentally. And then he realized he was not alone.

Uruk's mind searched for the other presence. He saw it as a large, black inscrutable eye looking back at him. His own presence was a demon's serpentine eye. The two orbs circled each other. Both minds were wary, but curious.

'I am Uruk, Field Master. I claim this ship.' Uruk thought.

'I am Not Uruk, and a master of many arts.' Came the reply.

'You are an alien.' Uruk stated.

'Yes.' The black orb replied. 'An Ignitaur. A creature born to use flame. You are a creature born to rain fire.'

'There is a difference?' Uruk asked.

'We Ignitaurs build. You destroy. Makers of steel. Makers of ash. Opposite sides.'

'How did you penetrate into this system?' Uruk was determined to gathering intelligence. He simplified the Ignitaurs identity to *Not*.

'Physically, I have horns to ram. But I can adapt. I merely slipped inside.' Not answered.

'How? How?' Uruk repeated. He steadied his mind to stay ready to strike.

'Phased spells are much like complex equations.' Not's mind answered. 'Most intelligent species develop and then rely on one or the other to interact with environments, physical and ethereal. My species is good at both.'

156

'You will all be dead unless you follow my orders.' Uruk thought. 'I can access the ship's weapons. Obey me or I will send missiles into the cargo bay.'

'Please do so,' was Not's shocking reply. 'We welcome mutual annihilation.'

'Ridiculous.' Uruk noticed a lack of tension even in his own thoughts as he sparred mind to mind. 'You fight as demons fight. You cannot wish defeat.'

'Freedom is not defeat. But perhaps you can aid us. Here I can more clearly see the mind of a demon. You seek war. We seek peace.'

'But you fight.' Uruk countered. 'You caused this ship's war.'

'Yes. To gain peace on our terms.' Not replied.

'Is that not conquest?' Uruk was confused.

'No. We fight to be free. If need be, to die free. To make your demonkind know you cannot enslave those of us who may still on other worlds.'

'My Lord Anguhr does not enslave.'

'Does your lord make war?' Not asked.

'Yes.' Uruk found the question odd. 'He is the Destroyer. He is the greatest of all Generals.'

'Then he is simply evil of another name.' Not stated. 'He is still the opposite side of good.'

'I do not understand this vague polarity you hint at.' Uruk wanted to shake his head, but realized at present he had none. 'There is demon and alien. There is enemy and there is Hell.'

'There is destruction and there is liberty.' Not offered.

'One is the same.' Uruk longed to shrug his shoulders. He wanted more to grab his rival to shake him or her.

'So long as you are the destroyer, not the destroyed.' Not replied.

'Yes. I serve him. The Destroyer.'

'You serve annihilation.' Not rebuked, but its Ignitaur thoughts still carried clam tones.

'I serve—we did serve—' Uruk halted his thoughts to gather them. 'We served the Dark Urge.'

'Yet, you do not now?'

'I serve Lord Anguhr.' Uruk evaded a full answer.

'The effect is the same.' Not observed.

'No.' Uruk knew that normally he would be frustrated that he could not shout, but was only aware of the emotion. He could not truly feel it. 'The Dark Urge has lied to us. Our service to her is for nothing. We thought we conquered to serve her and—'

'And?' Not prodded.

'I serve Lord Anguhr. He would fight for me.'

157

'Then, you fight for loyalty.' Not surmised.

'This I can accept, I think.' Uruk knew he would nod cautious affirmation, if he currently had a head.

'But your loyalty still brings annihilation. What is the difference now, balanced against what you fought for in the past?'

'I said: I fight for Lord Anguhr.'

'So, you now only make war out of loyalty to your leader.'

'I suppose, yes. I fight for him just as he fights for us.' Uruk wanted to enjoy satisfaction of his certainty, yet he could not feel the emotional boost.

'Do you not see the circle you truly serve? The bond you are tied to?' Not asked. 'You both still serve darkness. She, your Dark Urge, created the circle. You and your leader simply spin around it.'

Uruk wanted to feel rage, but understood in this disembodied dimension his emotions did not follow him passed the points of his teeth on the conduit. 'Life without loyalty is life without meaning,' he replied.

'But what are you loyal to, ultimately?' Not asked. 'Seek new meaning. Break your circle, demon mind. I seek a life of freedom. You seek a life of war. Yet, what are your conquests worth if they only serve the circle forged by someone else? Acting in such blindness is an act of evil, itself.'

'Again, this idea, this polarity.' Uruk thought. 'What use is it?'

'Do you understand the principle of balance?'

'A scale? Yes. To assess difference in masses.' Uruk could see both a scale and the mental images of the ships system. He could feel his mind want to drift from one image to the other. He focused on his virtual here and now.

'And concepts at times.' Not added. 'But imagine such a mechanism. Choose a side, and tip it.'

'I chose to take the scale.' Uruk replied. 'Then I will also have both masses and the machine.'

'Then you have aided us, demon.'

'How?' Uruk knew he should feel anger if Not had won something from him on this weird battlefield.

'By teaching me the mind of the demon.' Not answered. 'I see now there can be no peace between us, so long as we have something you wish to possess.'

'I wish for victory.' Uruk could see the value of these Ignitaurs as allies. 'Fight with us.'

'You will only use our courage and blood to take this ship. And then it will be something else.' Not paused in place of a sigh. 'And as you show there is more than one horde, then perhaps this galaxy is only now a place for endless war.'

'Then become warriors. Follow me. I know only victory.'

'You know only conquest, demon. War. We desire peace. Or at least an end to war. Good bye, Uruk. See if you can balance a scale that you do not own.'

'I don't understand.' The thought escaped Uruk's mind. He would curse at himself for showing potential weakness, later.

'I do. And in that lies our difference.' Not vanished.

Uruk sensed an energy surge. The reactor exploded.

CHAPTER TWENTY-TWO

Ursuhr was besieged. It was not by an enemy force. That might make him happy. He was trapped within a scheme he did not understand. This had made him angry. He sat fuming on his bridge throne while his horde was contained in galactic wonder. His fiery warship flew within a nebula not of nature's creation. He entered it though a fissure between masses that appeared to be typical clouds of gas and dust. Their symmetry betrayed their artifice.

The nebular clouds hung as sections of a sundered orb. Pressure from interior radiation did not force them apart. Gravity did not pull them together. Some unseen web held the false nebula in one, constant state. All the vast space inside and cosmic elements were parts of a single construction. Several solar systems could hide within the formation. Yet it contained only a single, blue star. Around it was a further astonishment. Another, more massive Iron Work encircled the star. The inner sides of the nebular clouds were round domes that glowed as bright as the perfectly centered star. The space between the bright sections of orb and the captured star was not overwhelmed by light despite the intense source and its reflection. Something absorbed photons and radiation. Brilliance was within to the visual range of most photosensitive life, and life born in Hell. Light, ions, and energy that should accumulate instead slipped out of spacetime to locations unknown. It was an impossible place.

Ursuhr was also impossible as a giant beast leading demons, and in his typical malignant attitude. His Ship Master Martis felt it roll across his wingless back as gusts of heated frustration exhaled by his Lord. All the wonder that surrounded Ursuhr was lost in confusion and disappointment.

There was no enemy to attack. He had obeyed orders relayed through the Great Widow. They diverted from his campaigns on an errand of tedium with an unclear purpose. He reasoned this other Iron Work must be another construct of Hell. For that he praised the Dark Urge, but not for the tedious mission to fetch objects from it.

This operation was not a campaign of conquest. It was a trivial quest better done by—Ursuhr had no idea who attended to such tedium. Perhaps that is why the Great Widow lived in Hell. It did the miniscule things while the Dark Urge ruled. And now the spider had ensnared Ursuhr for a tedious act. The mission appeared nothing more than a spider's whim. It made no sense to Ursuhr. He was tasked to find two semi-survivable locations on two bands of this larger Iron Work.

Ursuhr growled as he reflected. The orders from Hell's pet bug were to split his forces and secure the surface around each site. Ursuhr inwardly scoffed. He may deploy reconnaissance teams, but he did not split his horde. What use was overwhelming force if it could not be brought against an enemy like the head of a maul against a—against a bug. Ursuhr smiled. He saw his wisdom confirmed at a target canyon filled with hexagonal columns. He was to retrieve only one. If it was a prize of war, that was ridiculous. He ordered his strike force to take as many as the demons could carry. However, the massive slabs that hovered over the canyon closed over it. Ursuhr's Field Master, Kalak had escaped, but he lost many recognized demons remade as engineers.

If Ursuhr's forces had secured both mysterious targets and combined them as ordered, he was to protect them at all costs to himself and his horde. Then he was to contact the Great Widow for additional orders. Ursuhr did not like the Great Widow. He did not like this mission. The Great Widow had said it was the direct will of the Dark Urge. Yet once underway, Ursuhr began to wonder about the truth of that, if not about the awesome structures he now sailed within.

Ursuhr shrugged. The mission would not bring him or Hell greater glory. He doubted it was truly the will of the Dark Urge. It was a whim of the Great Widow. Thus, may she be damned. Although, she was already in Hell. Then, may the Dark Urge crush her. Ursuhr hoped he may have the ability to do so, personally. And then he recalled she may be able to tap his thoughts. Ursuhr wondered just how big she really was. He instinctively reached for his maul.

"My Lord, data from a sentry spike. Craft approaching." Martis' rasping voice broke Ursuhr's smoldered ponderings.

Images of a row of six black spheres appeared on a screen before them. They soared up near a band of the larger Iron Work. Data rolled across the images. It noted each sphere was the size of a small planet. The sphere rose in an arc from the far side of the banded, blue star.

"At least they seemed to be craft," Martis added.

"Then what are they?" Ursuhr demanded

"I have no clue." Martis shrugged while still looking at the spheres' images.

"Weapons?" Ursuhr stood.

"Unknown, Lord." Martis returned to tapping at his control dais.

"Is there an energy increase from these ships?" Ursuhr asked while reading the flashing data.

"Unknown. Although something powers them out of the star's— rather, the machine's gravity with no detectable radiation."

"Then what do you detect? Anything?" Ursuhr glowered at Martis' back.

"Yes, Lord." Martis was glad for some small bit of reportable data, although it was not likely to make his petulant master smile. "I can confirm they are on an intercept course with this ship. And that they are very large."

"Shall I enact the new protocols, Lord?" Martis asked. He heard a sustained growl that rattled his ears.

"No." Ursuhr grunted. "Our mission here is over. We have done the will of the Dark Urge. I will not be the instrument of any other's will. Head out of this insane nebula. When we are clear, ready the main sail. No more enduring tedium. We will return to our true mission. Again we will make war."

Anguhr stood in front of his throne. He kept the two key prisoners, Zaria and Gin, in front of him. It seemed a good means of control beyond their bonds. Anguhr was the most powerful force onboard to put down any rebellion. He had other means to ensure their compliance if his presence and axe was not a strong enough threat. Yet, no threat was worthy unless it had conviction behind it. He was the Destroyer. His conviction to kill things was well known.

"I have reviewed your encounter with Sutuhr, Proxis." Anguhr said as he pulled his axe from his back and sat. "Well done, Ship Master."

"I am honored, Lord." Proxis turned from his dais and bowed.

Gin nudged Zaria and motioned his head towards Anguhr who had yet to place his axe in its locks but spun the handle slowly in his hands. Gin then jerked his head back as he saw Anguhr staring straight at him.

"His ship was damaged in previous battle," Proxis continued. "My further analysis indicated his power systems were not only damaged but beset."

"Beset by what?" Anguhr asked.

"By me," Gin answered and smiled.

162

Zaria turned to face Gin and raised her eyebrows at him. Gin stopped gloating.

"Explain." Proxis focused his serpent's eyes sharply on Gin.

"When his ship was damaged by—"

"We found his ship damaged," Zaria cut in. "We were able to project a variant of Gin's mind into Sutuhr's operational systems."

"And, as you know, I can be quite irritating." Gin's smile returned. He stopped grinning again when the only reply from Anguhr was narrowed, burning eyes and a sudden stop to turning his axe.

"His Ship Master, I assume," Proxis said, "has managed to limit this—" he paused and pointed at Gin and eyed him over, slowly. "This one's sapper clone to only physical power systems."

"Surprising." Gin shrugged in his bonds.

"Can you be killed?" Anguhr stood and moved the edge of an axe blade under Gin's chin.

"In this form? Most likely. Unfortunately." Gin answered.

"But he has not infected your ship, Anguhr." Zaria quickly added.

"*General*, to you, miscreation!" Proxis snarled.

"Yes, I am a physical projection of an information avatar," Gin said to Anguhr. "But I have not recombined with any system of your ship. We are at a truce."

"You are prisoners," Anguhr said.

"By logic, we all need this ship." Zaria said. "Intact and functional, *General.*"

"I'll stay put. Stay physical." Gin assured. "I am a complex program, but I have honor."

"Good." Anguhr gave a slow nod. "Then I will not detonate the planet-annihilating mines I left in and around Old Jove."

Gin's eyes flashed wide open. Zaria's gaze became narrow slits focused on Anguhr.

"Your behavior will be compliant," Anguhr added. "Time is now the greatest threat to your long-loved Eden."

"Don't you threaten yourself if—" Gin started.

"Quiet!" Zaria snapped at Gin. "We are going to Eden, not Asherah." She looked straight at Anguhr with a hard, defiant stare. "You hold only one of my worlds hostage."

"Yet," Anguhr sat back on his throne. "I am sure it will be enough."

A swift, intense dust storm rolled over the forbidding surface of Hell. The screens of Sutuhr's limping warship displayed the storm's violence.

"The increased electromagnetic activity is causing atmospheric disruptions." Crucis observed.

The Ship Master offered the information to his master Sutuhr. The General made no comments. In truth, Sutuhr was confused.

"Should we come too close, Lord, with the ship at its current power status, the radiation output just from Hell's ionic belts would further harm our physical systems." Crucis added. "Any closer and the radiation across the physic and etheric bands may harm our own bodies."

"Keep us well aback, then." Sutuhr growled.

Even in Hell's home system, Sutuhr found more problems. Of course, he hated that. His ego still ached from the defiance of a mere Ship Master, Proxis. Leaders of empires had bowed before him before death, but a mere demon had faced him down. At least it was a demon, Sutuhr offered himself. He then spat in renewed anger and frustration. He had made his ship capable of making a jump even before all its power was restored. The infiltration was still beleaguering its systems. His crew of engineers had kept increasing. If he needed to recognize and transform more of his horde for that role, he would have no mere fodder to throw into combat. He wondered if here, in Hell's own system, he would find combat and not merely defiance. He wiped more venom from his lips. Sutuhr hated his own venom.

Right now, Sutuhr wanted to find his mother. The darkest of all beings in the galaxy had bid his return. The Devoted had obeyed as soon as he could. Yet now the Dark Urge did not answer his calls. Hails across all bands bounced from Hell's charged atmosphere. The Dark Urge had raised her defenses and wasn't answering at the portal of damnation. Not even the calls of her most loyal son. If this problem was not caused by the Dark Urge, Sutuhr would hate it. He wanted a solution. It would require beseeching the Great Widow. Sutuhr was certain she waited for his humbled call. That irritation, and the Great Widow, Sutuhr could hate, freely.

"Careful, General. There are limits to tolerance, even for the Devoted."

The words of the Great Widow drew Sutuhr's mind into her web. He focused passed his rage. Although he did quickly entertain the question if his own venom could harm Hell's giant spider.

"It could not," the Great Widow replied.

Sutuhr focused and spoke. "I have come as soon as I could. My ship needs repairs. The great power of my dark mother could certainly destroy what besets it. I wish to dock and feel her embrace."

"Your dedication is well noted, General. Yet, these are tempestuous times. Your mother, my mistress, must concentrate on matters the span the galaxy. She is its greatest power, and thus her responsibilities are—"

"Likely endless" Sutuhr interrupted. "Yes. I understand. But surely I am worth at least passage to Hell."

"The Dark Urge knows you will understand. And that your petulance will abate in time." The Great Widow paused.

The cold stare of the giant spider's eight eyes felt like spear points into Sutuhr. He suppressed a building growl. He decided to not test the affection of the Dark Urge to himself or her spider. This close to Hell she might lash out at him, herself. He stayed silent and swallowed a gathered pool of venom.

"As always, you will act to serve her in all ways she deems right." The Great Widow broke the quiet.

"Of course. Yet I can serve her better with a fully repaired ship. Then I can defeat all, even those who act as rebellious children. Even another General."

"For now you will take a wide orbit around Hell, around her, and wait." The spider said.

"What do I await?" Sutuhr asked, and deeply inhaled.

"We will await the news that you have purged your ship of all incursions," the Great Widow answered. "We know we will hear such news, quickly."

Sutuhr pursed his venom-wet lips to speak again, but the spider was gone. He caught Crucis casting a glance at him and heard his Ship Master sigh. Sutuhr narrowed his sideward eyelids and focused his arachnid eyes on Crucis' wingless back.

"Your blood would not purge my reactors of this infection, Crucis." Sutuhr said slowly. "But it would cleanse my deck plates."

"I serve in whatever role my Lord wishes." Crucis said while still faced forward to his screens.

"Be sure I wish that role to be as a living demon."

Crucis bowed his head while still faced forward.

Uruk awoke. He was being pulled. He was in space. His vision was blurred. He felt his face healing from burns even in the sub-freeze of vacuum. The acrid taste of his dark blood laid siege to his mouth. He was missing teeth. He turned his head and saw a huge red mass ahead. He blinked from the brightness. His focus resolved the red mass into the blaze of a Hell ship. He shook his head and jerked himself free from what pulled him. Zahl barked.

"You are awake, Field Master!" Zahl remarked.

The survivors of the reactor blast circled Uruk. The arcane forces that powered Hell's monsters drove their wings beats through space. They were close to the ship. A dark hole contracted and bent beams straightened at its edges. Even out of control, the ship still healed itself. Uruk realized an explosion beneath that spot had blown them into vacuum. His burns and those on Zahl and the surviving demons told him the reactor had exploded. The Ignitaur *Not* had tried to kill him. But failed.

"As you napped, I ordered our forces to regroup at the main drive's maintenance deck, but not until they can egress with minimal casualties." Zahl informed with a slight smile bending the singed thorns on his face. His voice was nothing in the vacuum, but his words were carried on the wavelengths native to Anguhr's horde.

"Wise," Uruk replied in the same manner. "We will—"

Another secondary battery deployed and opened fire. The squad dispersed on instinct. At so close an angle to the ship, the fired plasma spilt the hull's red fires. The gun blast shot through Uruk's scattered formation. He summoned his hellish energy to propel himself towards the ship's aft near the main drive. The others followed.

"They are here," the voice pressed across the Great Widow like magma.

As the Dark Urge increased her energy output even more, her voice was everywhere and at once. It was deafening. It was the only sensation felt by the Great Widow. The voice of the Dark Urge became the universe. She strained to answer it over the roar of the Forge, stoked violently to make power to fend away all things, entreating and hostile.

"Who, mistress?" the Great Widow strained to ask.

Everywhere the spider looked with all her eyes, she could only see a shadow of a woman staring overhead as if into a nighttime sky. It was impossible to have a shadow without light, but that was the Dark Urge.

"One, the Devoted. One, the Destroyer." The Dark Urge answered.

"Sutuhr. Anguhr." The spider summoned all her strength to speak.

"They are my children." The Dark Urge said.

The Great Widow paused and carefully considered her reply, but decided to only agree. "Yes, mistress."

"So strong." Even with the Dark Urge's voice thundering it contained a wistful quality.

"Which one, mistress?" the spider asked.

"So very strong."

"They are both successful Generals," the Great Widow offered. "They serve you well."

166

"So strong," the Dark Urge repeated. "She fled."

"She, mistress? Azuhr?"

"Azuhr was the first." The Dark Urge answered with a sudden, sharp remark.

"A strong precedent." The spider strained to make her reply. "She—"

"She is dead!"

"Most likely, mistress." The spider felt crushed.

"*She* is not dead," The Dark Urge furthered.

"She, mistress?" The Great Widow paused and again carefully considered just what this omnipresent power was thinking. The spider hoped the Dark Urge was indeed thinking, and that madness was yet to fully overtake her.

"You can say the name," the Dark Urge said, softly.

"I would rather not, mistress."

"You think it." The Dark Urge now sounded playful. "You think: Zaria."

"Yes, mistress." The Great Widow instinctively drew in a long, hot breath through her abdomen's trachea. She winced. "I apologize. I—"

The shadow became a giant, black hand that reached down to the spider. Its fingers gently stroked the Great Widow's abdomen.

"Have fear," the Dark Urge said in impossibly loud but delicate tones. "But do not worry. I love you."

"Of this, I am so very glad." The spider said, and stayed motionless.

"I may be death." The Dark Urge added.

"You are the Dark Urge, mistress."

"I have fear," the Dark Urge said in a paradoxically reassuring voice.

"I would ease it," the Great Widow said.

"You do. You kill for me. You are death." The Dark Urge spoke in a sing-song voice that changed from an adult inflection to a child's voice.

"I serve as best I can, mistress. I serve you."

"So did Azuhr," The Dark Urge still held the child's tone and still stroked the spider as a giant, dark hand. "She is dead. So does Anguhr, and now he can kill me."

"No, mistress. No."

"No," the Dark Urge repeated. "Will you kill him?"

"I will if I must, mistress."

"But he is hard to find." The Dark Urge's voice regressed to such a young manner she sounded almost as an infant.

"He is, unique." The spider remarked.

"Yes," The gentle adult tone of the Hell returned. "I love him."

"As I am sure, he loves you. You are his mother."

The stroking hand vanished. The spider now felt the pulses across her body of intense, manic laughter. The throbbing pressure brought pain. The Great Widow's only thought was the same as her very first impulse. Crawl. She did so. Slowly.

CHAPTER TWENTY-THREE

The grapnel and rod were secure onboard Anguhr's ship. They sat guarded by Solok and his elite strike teams. Zaria and Gin watched the bridge screens beyond Proxis. Zaria compared symbols displayed with the images to symbols to in her memory. She attempted to grasp the evolution of Hell's language and communication, and anything else she could glean from the free intelligence. A deep-toned question came from behind Zaria.

"Why do you look like me?" asked Anguhr.

The General also sought information. Zaria lifted her bound arms and turned to face Anguhr. He looked as relaxed as she had ever seen him. He was nearly slumped back in his throne. His axe was at last in its locks beside the massive, stone seat. Yet he still wore the black helmet. She began to wonder if he could take it off.

"Parallel evolution." Zaria offered.

"No." Anguhr replied. "I have seen similar warriors. Similar methods. Products of biological and social evolution. There are creatures with analogous forms, if differing molecular bases. Yet never have I found a thing as exact as you are to me. I am unique among Hell."

Zaria stayed silent as she studied Anguhr.

"He mimics you," Anguhr pointed at Gin. "But—"

"Are you as unique as you think?" Zaria asked.

Anguhr didn't reply. Now he kept a stare fixed on Zaria.

"On Eden there are vast catalogues of life," Zaria said. "They record living—and thanks to you and all Generals—many extinct creatures from vanished worlds. You will find your answer, there."

"I want it now." Anguhr demanded.

"I want to be free," Zaria said and lifted her bound arms toward Anguhr. "Shall we trade?"

Anguhr thought to speak another threat. He halted. It would waste more time. He would learn what he needed, and gain the weapon soon enough. Strategically, the weapon was more valuable. Thus, he would keep his prisoners alive.

"We will not trade," Anguhr said in an assured voice. "You will show me all I wish to know when my horde lays conquest to your world."

Gin saw Proxis smile.

"Yes. You will learn, General." Zaria also replied with certainty. "This I conceded with no desire for balance."

Zaria saw Anguhr narrow his eyes through the spaces of his helmet.

"Coordinates, then," Anguhr pointed to Proxis, "to your next lecture and my next conquest, teacher."

"Already entered," Gin said. "The keystroke buffer. It's a simple and separate system contained within your entry surface."

Gin gave a quick thrust of his head at the dais. Both Proxis and Anguhr glared at him.

"I only transmitted coordinates!" Gin did his best shrug in his black bonds. "No data was entered other than the destination! I have honored my pledge!"

"He appears to be truthful, Lord." Proxis growled as he observed a screen where a torrent of data became a simple series of numbers. "I have copied it to navigation."

Anguhr leaned forward and focused on the navigation screen as it rotated into central position. A three-dimensional map flowed out across a corridor of spacetime. The coordinates were far from Old Jove. They were to another system with a single, white star. Eden, it seemed, was nowhere near Hell. He was still tasked with finding and destroying Eden. He could still destroy Asherah and the nigh-undetectable moon orbiting Old Jove, and even the massive Old Jove. If that pleased the Dark Urge, so be it. Or not. Anguhr thought it may well please himself and add to his legend. However, such easy destruction may not pay tribute to War.

Detonating the mines or assaulting Old Jove with his ship could act as a show of compliance to the Dark Urge. He may need such a demonstration of loyalty should his gambit to complete the weapon fail. Finding and then destroying Eden would also serve that tactic. The weapon. Eden. They were two sides to his plan, just as there were two sides to his axe. It revealed two sides to Anguhr. Loyalty. Doubt. If he was utterly faithful to the Dark Urge, he would not seek a weapon to break her power, or perhaps even destroy her. He sensed Zaria knew this. The mystery of Zaria was as yet unrevealed. It was another side to this complex battlefield of deception. He wondered if he dare he think the world *insurrection.*

One aspect of Anguhr's double-sided plan cut his psyche. To complete Zaria's weapon—now his weapon, Anguhr needed to take his ship from the Iron Work. Somewhere near it was another Hell ship with his loyal lieutenant Uruk. Anguhr had yet to know if Uruk was being successful on the mission to secure Xuxuhr's warship. Anguhr didn't wish to abandon his Field Master, even for a short time. He knew demons were resilient. Uruk, could, with little more training, become a General in his own right. And now his Lord faced the quandary of searching for him, or leaving the system to complete the great weapon.

Sutuhr was also prowling between here and Hell. He may secure Xuxuhr's ship. Then, a weapon of greater power than his main guns would be a useful deterrent or necessary, final option. Time was constricting choice. Anguhr made a leap of faith.

"Proxis, make the main sail." Anguhr ordered. "We travel to Eden."

Uruk and his surviving squad alit on the ship's port quarter and clambered across the beams to the hull's aft. The Red Giant appeared to hang above them as an endless, crimson sky while the ship continued to drift and the interior battle still raged. Safe from large guns across this comparatively small section of hull, they flew the last leg. They kept their course straight by orienting their flight against the main drive that blazed at their backs. The drive's exposed maintenance deck was nothing more than an aft gangway with wider decking and a control dais at its center. The only tools were lines of force projected into the star-like engine from the three pincer arms that linked it to the ship. The deck rested just below the base of the pincer arm that branched from the top of the hull. Its plane had the same orientation as the bridge. It had a perspective of overlooking the brilliant main drive.

On the deck, gravity felt as though it was a series of waves crashing against and reflecting back from the radiant main drive. Uruk sunk his foot claws into the deck plates with every step. As the ship slowly swung end over end, the Red Giant appeared as a burning surface below. The main drive and its pincers became a titanic bird's claw snatching up a star. These decks were rarely used on all Hell's ships. Vacuum, radiation, and the ship's hellfire blocked its access to all but the scion of the Dark Urge. Only the Ignitaurs showed possible exception to this security rule. Uruk wondered if his squad were the first demons to stand of this one. They were not.

Trait roared as he leapt down from the burning hull beams and landed in front of Uruk. "You betray us all, foul demon!"

"I am trying to save us all, you fool!" Uruk barked. "Help us right this ship and retake it!"

"I would rather see it burn in the home star's flames!" Triat bellowed.

All the rifles of Uruk's squad suddenly flanked him and pointed at Triat.

Triat clutched his own rifle. "This is without glory! Praise the Dark Urge!"

"Glory?" Uruk barked. "Death is what *you* seek."

"Face me!" Triat screamed. "Face me in single combat!"

"Do you think I would risk a battle's outcome on ego?" Uruk aimed his own gun's muzzle at Triat.

Trait roared again and charged. Uruk and his squad fired. The blasts cut Trait into pieces and blood spray flying off the deck and into space.

"These demons are strange!" Zahl said. "There is a word, yes: stupid!"

For an instant, Uruk tried to follow Triat's pieces drifting out towards the Red Giant partially blocked by the ship's abaft region. The visible edge of the star appeared as a massive, irregular crescent against black space. He oriented himself to the deck and accessed the system without using his remaining teeth. He used the control dais to enter new orders for the engine. He also allowed himself the luxury of plotting a hunt for Not and repaying him in a manner as direct and final as Triat's death.

Anguhr stared out into unconquered space. For the first time in his history, his horde stayed in the hull after the jump. Anguhr himself stepped into vacuum on the hull above his bridge and awaited a revelation. His ship orbited a gravity well at Gin's the coordinates. What made the well was yet to be seen.

After the jump, Anguhr ordered a recording bank from a reconnaissance probe to the bridge. Such probes were seldom used. Demons recorded all their experience and Anguhr preferred them to machines. The stored unit would have needed dust blown from its components if the ship's fires allowed it to collect. Anguhr ordered Gin to use it to enter the commands Zaria said were necessary. Proxis scanned the trapped data before he entered it into the ship's systems.

Anguhr stared at the starry void beyond the ripple of crimson. The void itself rippled. A vast, blue world appeared. The planet was a massive stone with a violent, molten core. It materialized far closer than where

Anguhr had imagined its actual location. He wondered if the planet or the gravitational readings were true. He could see the planet's surface with his own, arcane eyes. There waged a war between new oceans and hot gas and lava erupting from volcanoes and fissures. More eruptions went on it the depths. It was a new world. No garden or tracts of visible life where on the new, cooling land or within the seas.

"Lord, the prisoner Zaria says to head into the planet." Proxis' voice entered Anguhr's helmet.

"I will not divide my force, even for a small reconnaissance party." Anguhr growled as he sensed betrayal.

"No, Lord." Proxis said. "She says to literally have the ship enter the planet."

"What?" Anguhr dropped back into the bridge.

"It is not a planet." Zaria said. "It is a portal."

Proxis arched his brows and looked at his General. They both turned their stares at Zaria.

"I can detect no—" Proxis began.

"Of course not." Zaria cut in. "And that is why you never detected the portal, or the world it hides. Enter the façade."

Anguhr said nothing, but glowered at Zaria.

"I am here, too. If we are crushed on impact—?" Zaria ended with a shrug within her bonds.

"Do so," Anguhr ordered.

Proxis slowly tapped at his dais. The ship's bow turned to face the volcanic world and accelerated. There was a sudden, total black. Nothing was seen or felt. And then creation flashed back on in blinding white light. It ebbed. Space appeared inverted and no stars burned anywhere. The only image outside the crimson ship was a distant dot on all screens against luminous, white space.

"Eden" Zaria pointed to the dot. "You will find it much like many terrestrial worlds in real space. Close in, and make orbit."

A startled Proxis began his scans and plotted a course. Anguhr stared at Zaria. The bonds that held her and Gin lay at their boots.

Zaria looked at Anguhr. "I assure you General, we are no threat to you, just as you are no threat to Eden. Let us complete this mission. Together. In peace."

Zaria turned to face Anguhr and extended her free arms to him as if offering her person as a sign of trust.

Anguhr growled.

Proxis scanned the surface of Eden. It was also a blue world, but its geology was at relative peace. Mists covered valleys. Dense forests covered them. Sharp mountains rose and gathered the mists into rain and snow clouds. Deep hues of blue dominated the world, even its plants. The world rested within an omni-luminous realm that acted as an all encompassing sun. Yet something unseen cast a night side over half the world. It appeared that shadow projected from the world, not lay across it.

For once, Anguhr was uncertain about setting foot on an alien planet. Briefly. Eden was a world wrapped in space that defied analysis and placed there by powers that rivaled the Dark Urge. Indeed, it was a likely world to find technology that could kill his black queen. No wonder she feared it. Such power could also kill him. Any opponent here would be worthy. He felt an urge to possess such power such as Zaria's weapon simply to preserve his own life. And also an odd sensation of caution that no strategy or his strength could overcome. He thrust away the notion that his feeling crept towards fear. Anguhr mentally vowed to face this world. He would again lead from the front. He snatched his axe from beside his throne.

Solok rejoined his Lord, Gin, and Zaria. They stepped from the burning platform separated from his ship's hull and onto a mountain dale of deep, sapphire grasses. A strike force of demons descended onto the grass in their formation. They had followed Solok and Anguhr against Zaria's strong objections. Anguhr paid them no attention, more for Solok's pride on his first incursion as acting Field Master.

A specific mountain rose beyond a short highland that bordered the dale. The only faint energy output detected on the planet was along the mountain's slope. Anguhr didn't want to directly assault the location. The final weapon component was held in a delicate matrix. Demon claws and rifles may be more a risk than a tactical advantage. This was advice from Zaria Anguhr did follow. He would take Zaria there and retrieve the device, himself. Despite his recent odd feelings, he was still Anguhr, the Destroyer.

"I have the emanation locked, Lord Anguhr." Solok reported.

"As do I." Anguhr said. "Secure the region."

Anguhr took a step towards the mountain, but paused and turned to Solok. "Should anything happen, bring the fire power of my ship on the world."

"It shall be done Lord Destroyer!" Solok barked with zeal.

Anguhr considered his eager lieutenant. He realized he had a long span of training to complete with Solok to temper enthusiasm in favor of prudent violence as he had over so many campaigns with Uruk.

"But not until something occurs," Anguhr added.

Solok saluted with his sword. The other demons followed his lead and did likewise. Anguhr turned and began again toward the mountain.

"Should you define that *something* for him?" Zaria asked as she followed Anguhr.

"No," Anguhr answered. "Being specific may limit his use of the main guns. If I am harmed, I want this planet destroyed for certain."

"I should expect no optimism from a creature of Hell." Zaria sighed.

"I am the Destroyer. I will always be that, even after—"

"Death?" Zaria asked.

"Do not taunt or delay me." Anguhr said and kept walking with landscape crossing strides.

"Then, immortal General, follow!" Zaria sprinted ahead.

Anguhr noted it may not be Solok's zeal he needed to curb.

As on the Iron Work's pyramid, Anguhr thought to draw his axe and cleave Zaria in two. When they reached the foot of the mountain, she kept her swift pace up the steep surface of ice, blue stone, and granite. Anguhr climbed behind her. His fingers dug into solid stone. Loud cracks sounded with each new grip. His progress was fast. Zaria was faster. She climbed up the sheer mountain face as if she was water running down a smooth slope. Yet, Anguhr only felt a need to assert himself for pride, not control. He surprised himself upon realizing this. And then he climbed faster.

Cold, sharp winds and flecks of ice blew across Anguhr's skin as he ascended. The ice instantly melted on contact creating a wake of steam. His heat kept icicles from forming, but any liquid that fell away from his body refroze in the cold and flew off in the wind. Anguhr reached the cliff's edge. The energy reading was along a flat outcrop. It projected from the sheer slope. Something had cut a half-conic section from the mountainside and fused it onto the slope below the excised cave. Anguhr stood on the outcrop. Zaria waited for him. He expected another façade and another discovery beyond it. There were massive icicles blocking their entrance. However, Anguhr was more surprised by the emotions expressed on Zaria's face. She appeared expectant, perhaps slightly joyful. She was not triumphant over her faster climb, or fearful of releasing a dreadful power. He found this curious. Yet, all he could do was move forward. It was the path to complete the mission, and a personal compulsion he could not fully understand.

After her capture, Zaria had changed from prisoner to guide. Now she changed again into a luminous generator. Warm sunlight and heat radiated from within her, turning her metallic green armor into contoured, emerald prisms. She turned and raised her hands to the massive icicles. They melted but did not flow away. The water stayed as conic waterfalls that neither began nor ended. Zaria's inner light ebbed. She turned and beckoned Anguhr, and then walked through the curtain of static waterfalls.

Anguhr followed. Inside was the exterior of a luminous temple built from white marble infused with gold. Two rows of seven, massive columns curved along quarter-circle arcs. Circular capitals topped the columns. All of them sat on bases of gold. The column arcs flanked a gilded marble archway. Darker masses rested within. There were no solid walls. Cold air flowed through the chamber. The temple was a not a fortress but a celebration of strength and also freedom.

The brilliance and beauty were lost on Anguhr. He focused on the guardian statues that stood out from each column row. They were carved from pure white stone. Each one wore armor and held a spear. They were as tall and commanding as Anguhr. Their model could have been his near twin. The entire structure looked built for giants like him. Anguhr grabbed the head of the statue to his left. A cracking sound echoed.

"No!" Zaria yelled too late.

The statue's head came free in Anguhr's hand with a loud snap. He brought it close to his helmet and stared at its features.

"Yes, it also looks like you." Zaria took in a deep breath. "But couldn't you just stare at it in one piece? Must you destroy everything?"

Anguhr cast his fiery gaze from the head to Zaria.

"I hope in time you learn to respect architecture of alien worlds," Zaria continued. "I guess, for now, that's an idiotic hope."

More cracks echoed across the temple cave before the statue's head exploded into bits in Anguhr's grip.

Zaria blinked. "I wish to foster defiance within you, but I admit when its directed at me, it grows tiresome."

Anguhr arched his left eyebrow at Zaria's mentor tone. "The weapon," he droned.

"Yes." Zaria shook her head slightly, and then walked through the archway.

The temple's interior was a negative in color and shape to its outer half. The two more column arcs formed completed the parts of a circle. The interior columns were dominantly black and swirled with marble-like patterns of deep purple and red hues. Another, black archway stood between the black column arcs. Beyond the them looped streams of liquid obsidian. They floated above the flat, stone floor. The dark streams curled like flattened snakes around large torchères that flashed on with intense, red fires. The flames and black liquid interacted in almost aural motions.

"This place is not a military installation." Anguhr said looking across the circular inner temple.

"Are you sure?" Zaria asked.

"Yes." Anguhr looked passed the black columns at the streams and flames. "Although lies and deception grow as dense as grass where you walk."

"A necessary evil in the face of the greater one you serve, General. And her evil is not needed. She is driven by fear."

"I should kill you for blasphemy." Anguhr said as he followed Zaria between the rows of black columns.

"And yet you do not," Zaria said confidently with her back still towards Anguhr. "Among Generals, you are unique."

"What is this place? Its character is split."

"It's a temple," Zaria said. Her walking pace was now slow and measured. "This is its antechamber. The architect built the luminous outside to his own aesthetic tastes. However beautiful, the person it was built for did not share his appreciation for light and bright color. As it was a temple built for her adoration, her architect lover had the second half built to her liking."

"I like this part better." Anguhr said.

"Of that I had no doubt." Zaria remarked as she walked through the black archway.

Beyond the arch was an inner chamber made from another conic section cut from the mountain. Following the temple's theme, its shape opposed the preceding antechamber. Instead of entering an already wide cave, entrants walked from the comparatively small arch at the center of the curving wall into a vast chamber. Beyond the archway, the ceiling suddenly rose into a high tapper. The space needed to be enormous. Even scaled down for the interior of a mountain, the façade of a quarter hemisphere of a sun was colossal. It loomed directly opposite to the entrance. The sun's surface burned a warm and radiant orange red and was as dynamic as a true star.

More pairs of columns rose toward the sun. High arches connected the columns with smaller stars as keystones. Each arch rose progressive taller towards the quarter sun. The sets of columns and arches rose to towering heights until the last arch was only visible as a narrow line far overhead holding a bright dot at the center. The entrance to the next chamber was an arch shape directly ahead in the sun no taller than the black archway behind Anguhr and Zaria. The sun's granular surface depicted a younger star contrasted to scarlet face of the Red Giant. Anguhr paused before following Zaria through the arch way to the dark area beyond. For an instant, he reacted to the sun's image as if actual stellar fires raged. He then strode through the archway.

The next chamber was as black as true space. There appeared to be no floor. Zaria was walking across an invisible plain. Anguhr followed her. Immediately inside was another high but robust arch. The arch after it was separated at it apex. Four sets of split arches followed the first. The third set was the highest. Anguhr realized they mimicked fingers like his with touching thumbs forming the first arch and then four sets of fingers flaring out as if releasing a captive. The captive shone brilliantly between the last two, widely split arches. It was the center of the slowly spinning galaxy.

"He was to give her the galaxy." Zaria said as she looked up. "In the end, he gave her his life. Life. A noble cause."

Anguhr dismissed her comment. His eyes were drawn to what appeared to float just below the immense image of the galaxy. It was a golden column base. More captivating was the solid black object that hovered above it.

Zaria stopped. She turned sideways and looked at Anguhr. She stiffened. Before her voice had been at ease. Now it became solemn. "The temple was never completed. Not fully. This is my addition."

Zaria motioned to the black object. It was half as tall as Anguhr. Dark. Ominous. Yet it was somehow familiar to him. Anguhr felt pulled by it. He strode passed Zaria to face it. Although massive for its kind, it was a long, black sword. Its steel was obviously the same that made his axe. The sword had also been forged in Hell. Anguhr halted as if struck by the weapon. He knew its description well. He designed the flourishes of his ax after the first weapon wielded by the first General. It had resonated with some part of him. For the first time in his existence, Anguhr felt weak.

CHAPTER TWENTY-FOUR

"This is the sword of Azuhr." Zaria said as she neared.

"I know!" Anguhr shouted. "Somehow I know."

"You know because you have seen it before."

Anguhr jerked to his side to stare at Zaria at his right.

"Although then, your eyes were not afire as they are now." Zaria looked at the sword. "Then your mind was free to absorb information as well as it could at so young an age."

"What is this?" Anguhr bellowed.

"This is a shrine to Azuhr," Zaria answered. "It was intended as a temple to honor an impossible love. A union of two lives born to oppose each other. The architect was Sargon. Yes, the greatest of the Khans."

"Impossible!" Anguhr roared.

"You say I lie. Yes." Zaria said. "Bringing you here was a deception because you would not come if there was no prize of war. But in all your conquests have been for a lie. Think of what I showed you on the Iron Work. The parts of planets you sundered headed straight into the sun. This is also a hard fact. But this is your legacy!"

"Legacy?" Anguhr shook his head. He had never seen an image of a Khan. He had never thought to wonder more about them beyond history abstracts made before he took command of his ship. Khans were a blight on galaxy. At least, so said the teachings of the Dark Urge. Anguhr thought of the statues outside the temple. He looked at Zaria. He thought of his own image.

"Sargon was like you, also a conqueror." Zaria said stepping closer to Anguhr. "But he was also a philosopher king. His empire was vast. His leadership united his kind. Each of them had united great tracts of the galaxy. Their inevitable alliance made them think they were no longer mere servants to the great urge that propelled them. They came to their mother and asked to be seen as her equals. This was not foreseen."

Zaria paused. She lowered her head as if weighted by looking backward in her mind. She took a shallow breath and continued.

"They had been sent out to quell fear of all alien powers through contact, and if necessary, through conquest. They became powers themselves. Instead of admiration for her children's' success, their mother saw their request to be equals as insurrection, as betrayal. She reacted out of fear.

"Their mother's wrath made her fragile mind become black. The mother of the galaxy's greatest leaders became their enraged enemy. She set her mind on the destruction of her rebellious children, and the annihilation of their work. A new child was born. Azuhr. She was created not from life and hope, but from spite and fear. Her mother was now and forever, the Dark Urge."

Anguhr anticipated the last phrase, but it still made him react by instinctively pulling back his shoulders.

"Hell's queen knew a name and purpose before the war. As did I. I was also the mother of the Khans. Their genes and design came from the true Eden. The Khans, or Keepers as they were first called, were bathed in fire. It was only to temper their will. Their ships and technology were dilutions from the Builders' technology that created the Forge, now Hell. The Keepers were supposed to defend the Builders' legacy and the fragile mind that became the Dark Urge. She was to know great champions protected her. However, the Keepers became champions for themselves. They reimagined themselves as the Khans. I suppose all children grow in ways you can never foresee.

"So did Azuhr. Even born from Hell and commanding a horde of horrific demons, she was also made from the stuff of nature. The Khans could fight well, but Azuhr was a warrior to perfection. In time, the Khans sued for peace from her onslaught. Seeing an opportunity to collect her enemies in one place and kill them all, Azuhr agreed to the summit.

"There she met the delegate and chief Khan, Sargon. Nature took its course over the reluctance and suspicions of them both. How could it not? Sargon was the first creature Azuhr ever met with a body similar to hers and of dimorphic, sexual form. There seemed a chance for peace born from love, or at least physical passion. But suspicion is also a persistent force. The other Khans came to fear their most powerful member being in league with the powerful Azuhr, as did the Dark Urge. She became fearful that hostilities had stopped before all the Khans were killed.

"In the time that Sargon and Azuhr knew together, he built this place. It was originally on his capitol. In that same time of Sargon and Azuhr's union, the other Khans gathered their strength and resolve. They struck. Their surprise and combined might stunned the lovers. Sargon fought against his own kind and former allies. Azuhr slaughtered all in her path. But the en massed power of the seditious Khans granted one boon. Azuhr was mortally wounded. Her damaged ship gained speed until it flew above the galactic plane and soared unguided into the black void. It kept sailing faster, until it flew beyond relative ken. She was lost. The heartbroken Sargon had already fallen to his siblings' attack.

"They were defeated." Anguhr breathed deeply as if he lived the tale.

"In a sense," Zaria said. "Azuhr had undertaken one last ploy before her final battle. It would be either her ultimate defeat by the spite of her creator, or long term revenge taken by her heir. Her passion with Sargon had produced the heir to her sword. Azuhr knew to keep the child would risk its death, and that such a risk would make her vulnerable. More so, I think, she loved the child. She knew the Khans would destroy it because it was part Hell-born. There was only one power strong enough to protect it and give it the means to enact her revenge. She sent the child to Hell. Born of a General and a Khan, Azuhr felt only the Dark Urge could nurture her child. Azuhr knew the Dark Urge might destroy it to punish her, or kill it out of fear. Yet she knew her mother's sinister mind would also see her plan of revenge, and likely enjoy it for its dark design. She did.

"I found Azuhr's sword and brought it here. It was adrift in space among other wreckage in the long-cooled wake of her ship. Hardly a trace of her remains anywhere. Other than here." Zaria moved close and stared straight into Anguhr's burning eyes. "And other than you."

Anguhr stepped back.

"Their story is yet to end," Zaria continued. "The Dark Urge had her new General, Sutuhr, rip apart Sargon's ship that held your infant form. She stopped him from tearing you apart. She accepted you into her own, fiery womb. You were reborn to serve her. Instead of a massive, black sword, you were given an enormous axe. But you are so like your mother. Your true mother."

In unthinking motion, Anguhr drew his axe from his back. He stepped back and faced Zaria as if she were all his enemies focused into one. He had moved his own mind and emotions away from the Dark Urge, yet had yet to sever the bond, fully. She was still his only emotional link to creation. And now the bond was revealed as both corrupted, bizarre, and also maternal. Anguhr's taught emotions snapped.

"This is more than blasphemy!" Anguhr roared. "This is more lies! Mental treachery to bend me to your will. You, who are a fool to stoke my rage!"

Anguhr swung of axe. Its leading blade sliced through Zaria, but her form was only a projected image.

"Do not believe me Anguhr." Zaria said from behind Anguhr.

He spun and raised his axe again.

Zaria pointed to the sword. "Believe Azuhr. And trust your own mind."

Anguhr vibrated. He turned and stared at the sword. There was an undeniable call from it. Anguhr swung his axe into the gold base and snatched up Azuhr's sword in one, swift motion. He brandished it, almost in defiance. Holding the blade caused the greatest wave of uncertainty he ever experienced. The odd sensation building in his mind was fear. It was change that caused the fear. It could end his certain, treasured path of conquest. And his image of War. His fear submerged in other, stronger images. He felt a sudden, intense emotional connection. It kept him from rejecting what he saw.

The first image in his mind was of the sword at another place and time. Its blade pointed downward and mostly unseen beyond a small, plump creature. It was a wriggling infant of human shape. At times, occasional, joyful kicks and waves of its arms interrupted the view. A weird sense of recognition flowed across Anguhr. Beyond the infant, the sword was in the grip of another. The hands were like Zaria's: female. Above the scene the familiar red fires of a warship from Hell burned across overhead beams.

The sword holder knelt down. She still clutched the sword in one hand, and caressed the infant with the other. She wore black armor. Long black hair dangled over and from under a darker steel band that crowned her head. Her face was hard, ashen, and made more intimidating by a harsh stare. Dark smears and flecks from recent combat contrasted with her complexion. She stared with irises of deep, piercing blue. The shape of her face was slightly rounder, but no less familiar. The face was close to Anguhr's own. Somehow this person was like him. The acceptance of how struck him harder than any blow suffered in battle.

"Azarak. I like the sound of it." The ashen warrior spoke. Her voice has deep, coarse, and constrained. She looked up from the child and at the recorder. "It may be meaningless, but you will define the name. I am Azuhr. I am General of Hell's demon horde. You are my son."

Azuhr paused. Her features relaxed. Her voice also changed. She spoke not to address a subordinate, but a person she loved. Her face stiffened again with resolve, but never hardened to the scowl at the start of the recording.

182

"As such, you are also the scion of Hell." Azuhr continued. "Even your father, the great enemy Sargon has roots in Hell. Its ruler, the greatest force in creation, the Dark Urge, is my mother. To save you, my first and only child, I must send you to her. There is no other hope for your survival. Though I crushed hope for all I fought, now hope is my only ally." Azuhr paused and flared her nostrils. "If irony had form, I would kill it."

The scene pitched. A collision resonated through the ship. Azuhr frowned, but then she looked back at the infant and smiled. She continued speaking.

"The Dark Urge sees the act of your creation, the love between me and your father as a betrayal. So do Sargon's own people, and he is their leader."

Azuhr looked back at the recorder with a focused stare.

"Fear destroys, Azarak. The greatest triumph of all is its conquest. Not the defeat of an empire. It is fear that now threatens me life, and yours. So I must send you to the most powerful thing in creation. It is a risk, but it is the only strategy that preserves some potential, some small hope for your continued life. The Dark Urge is the embodiment of fear, yet the fear of her across the galaxy, the fear I have projected, will be your shield until you can strike out on your own."

Azuhr took a deep breath and looked back at the infant as if reconsidering her plans. She nodded to the child and continued.

"I hope she will receive you as one last offering of my devotion. A sign she was always my first duty. But I know my true duty is to you, my child. The only power that can preserve your life, whatever it may become, and however she may change you, is the Dark Urge."

Azuhr looked at the back at the recorder, knowing it would be the eyes of her son that one day looked at her.

"Your new mother may try to erase me, but I hope she embraces you in some vestige or sudden spark of feeling. I hope—" Azuhr paused. Her face and stiffened lips betrayed her inner battle to control her emotions. "I hope somehow that she finds a fraction of the love I have for you, and thus you will be spared her wrath and only be made to serve her, not crushed by her rage."

Azuhr steadied herself. The flames above her revealed her ships sudden tact. She turned her head to listen to demon barks behind her, and then looked back at the recorder.

"There will be other Generals who make war after me. I am sure of it. The Dark Urge still fears all, and all is a wide path to conquer. Through treachery, my war is nearing an end, and thus, so is my life. I now turn to saving yours, my son.

"The Dark Urge came to the role of mother far differently than me. Although I am arcane and engineered, I am made of flesh. So was your father. The Dark Urge is a creature of alloy and thought. You were not planned, not designed. I was made to crush all who opposed the Dark Urge. I have done so perhaps too well. Perhaps not well enough. But if all my campaigns have led to your birth, then my life has been enough."

Azuhr smiled. She blinked, and then continued.

"I know you will have great strength. You are the scion of giants. I know you will keep elements of me, strength, and of your father, nobility, no matter what outward form my dark mother may cast around you. You will never know your father. He fights now to give me time. It will be his last stand. You may never see me, though I fight on. Yet I know we have bonded, mother and son. Your mind will still feel me, always, deep within. I do not think even the Dark Urge can erase that sense, that bond of mother and child even though—"

Azuhr stopped. The ship did not pitch, but she gripped her sword with both hands and stared at the floor of her bridge for a brief moment. She looked at the infant and then the recorder.

"I am sending you to Hell, my son. You are the child of a demon. The greatest one. Hell's General. Yet even there, you take my love. Take my strength. I may never touch you again, never see you, small Azarak. But in some way I will always be there with you. It seems impossible. But so is a demon General finding love with a giant Khan, and creating a child."

Azuhr paused a final time.

"Good bye, my impossible one."

The images ended.

Anguhr stood stunned. If he was ever vulnerable, it was now. Zaria could strike him, take Azuhr's sword, and kill the son she called Azarak. But her new plans needed him. And in this form, Zaria was a warrior but not an assassin.

The images began to replay in Anguhr's mind. He dropped the sword. It hit the unseen floor with the low tone of an enormous bell being rung. All this truth swirled in his mind, and yet he did not know what to do. The Khans were the once, great enemy of Hell. But they were annihilated before Anguhr's time. But a Khan's blood was part of Anguhr's body. Anguhr wondered about time, about its passage, and how long Hell had existed before him. Time now seemed to flow backward across him. History became an avalanche of information. He felt carried down the slope by it, powerless. You could not cleave apart history with an axe. You had to endure the mass of its legacy or be crushed by ignorance.

Finally, he understood that transcendent presence in his mind. It was not War. It was the faint memory of his mother, Azuhr. He knew it was not love of war, but love that his experience had evolved into something he better understood. But that understanding had been channeled and controlled by what the Dark Urge had taught him. She had remade him into an object of her fear and the latest version of her greatest weapon.

Anguhr charged out of the galaxy chamber without sword or axe. He crossed the sun cavern and into the temple's antechamber. His rolling emotion caught him. He stopped and cried out with all his arcane strength. The temple shattered. Columns cracked and toppled. Zaria fled. Glaciers on the mountain outside split and rolled into a jagged avalanche.

Gin stood among demons. They bolted back and raised their weapons at Zaria who suddenly stood next to him.

"From the sound and the avalanche, I take it the revelation was not well received." Gin said.

"I don't know," Zaria said. "His cry could be one of rage or a release. Perhaps his mind has shattered like the glaciers."

"Is this your treachery?" Solok yelled at Zaria "Where is Lord Anguhr?"

"At this moment, I don't know." Zaria answered.

"My Lord cannot be harmed by a mere falling mountain!" Solok barked and thrust his rifle up at Zaria.

"The mountain, no. What it held—?" Zaria shrugged "We shall see. If his reaction is one of blind rage, then you are in as much danger as we, thrall."

Solok's brows pitched back and forth as he considered the catastrophe of a mindless General on a rampage.

A whistling noise sounded overhead. Gin watched the stares of every demon of Solok's force he could see look up in unison and their serpent eyes widen. They fled back and flew away like scared birds from what plummeted down. Zaria grabbed Gin and then ran backwards. Gin finally saw the falling terror an instant before it impacted. Azuhr's sword pierced the mountain dale.

CHAPTER TWENTY-FIVE

"This place is indefensible!" Zahl spat as he looked across the maintenance deck across from the main drive. "Odd for a warship."

"No battles were ever imagine onboard our ships," Uruk said as he finished entering new commands for the main drive. He glanced at the bright, burning sphere and then looked at Zahl. "Few life forms could survive what we can."

"And no one ever thought demons would stand against demons." Zahl added. He and his surviving squad still scanned for attacks.

"We will not need to hold this location," Uruk said as he turned from the dais. "Hopefully all Triat's demons will be occupied inside the hull."

"No." Zahl said the word in a low tone and with dread.

Zahl snapped his rifle butt to his shoulder as the other demons opened fire. Enemy demons charged from a portal opening within the burning hull behind the maintenance deck. One enemy fell and his comrades quickly withdrew. The attack was only a probe. They would not risk another charge. All Uruk's demons knew this instinctively and spun to avoid the barrage of grenades that followed. The explosions ripped apart all of Uruk's surviving squad except for himself and Zahl. They lay against the deck plate looking for the following assault.

Zahl jumped to a crouch and hurled a grenade into the closing portal. White fire shot from the narrowed aperture. He turned to speak to Uruk. His serpent eyes opened wide. A mortar shell drifted down to the deck behind them. Zahl grabbed Uruk and leapt to the control dais. The shell exploded and vaporized most of the central gangway. It did the same to most of Zahl's wings and back. His eyes were still.

Uruk roared. He picked up Zahl's rifle. He fired the two rifles into the curtain of demons descending from the overhead pincer arm. The curtain was shredded. The attack stopped. Uruk knew more would come, and quickly. Uruk stood and spoke a final prayer.

"Lord Anguhr, if you can somehow hear your Uruk's voice, then I bid you listen. For you, Lord, I have fought on many worlds though my last battle will fail. Yet I would still fly anywhere you send me, even this failed mission on this strange ship. From you I came to know a path beyond mere obedience. I served you as you served your horde. So I beseech the Dark Urge to grant me a final boon. I ask it even if my knowledge of her lies bans me from existence after the pyre. Let it be known that I fought well, and for a Lord that did the same for me. Now I fight as any demon of any rank against all enemies. And I laugh at all who dare face me!"

Uruk leapt from the deck. If noise carried anywhere, his laughter would be as loud as both his firing rifles. Uruk counterattacked the demons that launched the mortar round from the pincer arm. The strike took them by surprise. The demons fell from Uruk's fire. More demons emerged from the hull at the pincer's base. Uruk engaged them in a running gun battle along the arc of the pincer. Both gun barrels of Uruk's rifles became so hot their arcane steel melted and flew off in orange beads as more rounds shot through them.

The Ignitaur Not had done more damage than exploding the reactor. Not had severed the link between the thrusters, fiery aegis, and main drives. Each followed its last order and sensory input to move the ship's mass, but no longer in unison. The bow of the ship veered toward the Red Giant as the main drive continued along the path entered by Uruk and swung in an arc high above a band of the Iron Work. The star-like engine and length of ship moved like a catapult arm with a radiant projectile fixed to the hurling basket. The ship began to spin around the axis of its keel, and continued to fall closer to the red sun.

Uruk held fast to the pincer arm and fought on. His rifles finally exploded as rounds detonated in the super-heated breaches. Uruk hurled the molten debris at his charging enemies. Blood rolled from his injured mouth and into space as he smiled, and then opened his jaws and drew his sword.

The impact of Azuhr's sword blasted earth and rock out from its blade. The demons, Gin, and Zaria had little time to register the impact when an even larger mass struck the dale near the sword. Anguhr landed.

As bits of the landscape rained down, Anguhr's body steamed at the center of his shallow crater as ice melted on his limbs and armor. Mist curled as it rose from his chest. It was drawn into his helmet as the General took a deep breath.

The demons barked and brandished their weapons to salute their returning Lord. Anguhr's reply was another deep breath. He stepped from his crater. He strode across the dale to a small hill. The jarring from the impacts and Anguhr's steps caused a small avalanche of soil, grass and wildflowers down one side. Anguhr took his axe from his back and set it inverted into the ground. To everyone's surprise, he lifted his helmet off his head.

Black hair like his mother's was matted from the helmet and his infernal sweat. His dark locks reflected the white light from the sky in arcs along the flattened masses. The fire in his eyes seemed to burn brighter now freed from black steel and shadows. His face was pale. Its angles were square and sharper than the chiseled temple statues. The weight of experience pulled down his features. Otherwise, the leader of a demon horde and scourge of the galaxy would look impossibly young, and human. He sat on the hill. His helmet dug a small trench as he set it at his right side.

Solok approached his leader. He could not help but glance about Anguhr's head having never seen it without a black casing. "Lord, you are victorious again. Do we now go, and make war?"

Anguhr took another deep breath. He thought of his missing Field Master, Uruk. He would know not to intrude on his General at this moment. Anguhr understood the definition of the word: friend. He was not sure he understood the act of friendship. He had been essentially alone since being unleashed with his horde. But it had never mattered. His demons were enough company. Although typically just Proxis and Uruk were permitted to talk. Perhaps that is why, after all their campaigns, Anguhr now missed Uruk. He wondered how he fared, and if he was alive. What changes might he have endured since sent to Xuxuhr's ship. He also wondered if he dare consider his missing lieutenant a friend. At the same moment he understood the definition of loss.

"Lord?" Solok asked.

Anguhr suppressed an angry snap at Solok. Retrieving his axe and Azuhr's sword from the rubble of the collapsed temple was more tedious than physically taxing. Pushing through fallen rock and glacier was gave him more pause to think than need to strain. Still, his mind was only settling. He heard an internal voice louder than Solok. It resonated as a question with no words and, as yet, no answer. However, Anguhr was practiced at pushing thoughts aside. He knew he must focus and issue commands to keep order.

188

"Shall I command the scythe be readied, Lord?" Solok asked.

Anguhr drew one more deep breath before he answered.

Zaria watched Anguhr inhale. She heard Solok's last question. Time dragged across the edge of Azuhr's sword. Her tension was released with the one word spoken by Anguhr, and in that one world, Zaria felt hope for victory.

"No." Anguhr said.

Anguhr looked out across the ravaged dale. His gaze moved to the valley bellow and across the deep, blue lakes beyond.

"Do a reconnaissance of this area," Anguhr continued. "Find any other alien structures. Report to Proxis. Then return here when your mission is done."

"At once Lord!" Solok leapt into the air. His high pitched barks summoned the strike force of demons. They followed him into the sky and soared in formation into the valley.

Anguhr watched the demons fly off. He wondered how long their devotion would last if his personal battle was now against Hell. Again, he longed for Uruk's presence. He had surmounted the programmed devotion to the Dark Urge. He hoped his own devotion to his horde would preserve their loyalty. He would need them.

Another voice disturbed Anguhr reverie.

"I am glad you are intact," Zaria said. She and Gin now stood before him.

"At another time, you would wish me dead." Anguhr said, turning his head to face them. For once he looked up at their blonde heads.

"True," Zaria replied. "But it is not your death that serves the ultimate goal. He must act to serve life. We must now strike her, the Dark Urge. We must end Hell."

"No." Anguhr replied. "You must end Hell. And I am not your demon."

"The Dark Urge will be as much a threat to you now, as she is to us. To life!" Zaria pressed forward to Anguhr. "You must face that you are now her enemy. She will not risk her power to trust."

"She risked that when she accepted me into Hell." Anguhr rolled his burning eyes toward Zaria.

"You were an infant. And then she remade you into a weapon," Zaria retorted.

"Would I have been any different if the Khans had never attacked my parents?" Anguhr asked both Zaria and himself.

"You would have known choice." Zaria offered. "You would have known the truth as you grew. You would have been allowed to grow, normally. And with the guidance of beings not shrouded in hate. Now, end that. We have the means to spare the galaxy further devastation. We must use it."

"Or perhaps just realize it is your life that will be preserved," Gin said, "as well as billions more."

"Yes, focus on me," Anguhr's voice held tones of disdain. "Because you can manipulate me now that my ego is so crushed by the truth of my origin."

Anguhr stood and looked down at Gin. "It is not."

"Then, what are you going to do?" Gin asked.

"I will return and speak to my—the mother of my mother."

"Foolish!" Zaria shouted. "That was tried—by your father! He is dead Anguhr, do you wish his fate?"

"It will not be my fate." Anguhr replied with certainty. "He wished to be her equal. I will have answers, and dictate terms. Hell will bend to me."

"Answers for what?" Zaria thrust her arms from her sides. "Hell has been corrupted for far longer than even this useless war! She is madness, driven by fear."

"And what does she fear?" Anguhr looked intently at Zaria. "I imagine it is you."

Zaria nearly took a step back as if feeling a weight thrust on her.

"I can balance two sides, two powers." Anguhr continued. "Every decision has at least two prongs of attack. Every mind must weigh both. You may have written him into existence." He pointed at Gin. "Perhaps the Dark Urge created you. You were the first Keeper. The first Khan. Now you are her opposition. Merely the other side."

"I assure you," Gin said with obvious affront, "I am at least as old as both Zaria and—" He stopped, uncertain how to finish his sentence.

"No." Zaria said in a low voice. "I fight for life. The Dark Urge is not my mother. Azuhr was not my sister. The Khans were my children. At least by half."

"Children of two mothers." Anguhr said. "Or one?"

"By that time, two." Zaria replied. "We are distinct. But at a time we were one. There was a schism created by a powerful alien presence. In time, the schism grew. And now I stand before you. But she, my original half, my sister, sits in Hell and plots both our deaths."

"And without this schism, there would be no Hell." Anguhr observed.

"Likely, no." Zaria agreed. "She—we would be whole."

"Then why do you not see yourself as insane? Corrupt?" Anguhr asked.

"Obviously, she is not." Gin said.

"I accept what I am." Zaria added. "I have changed. When I left the Forge and journeyed out seeking life, I grew. She has evolved only in dark ways, fearful of powers greater than herself. Fearful of anything not subject to the fires of her will. The Keepers were to assuage her fear. The Generals are the embodiments of it, sent out to destroy," Zaria paused, "everything."

"Then I am glad for these powerful aliens." Anguhr remarked. "I would salute them, before putting them to the axe."

"You are glad for—well, of course you are." Gin shook his head.

"I am glad to exist. As I am certain you are also glad to live, whatever the agency of your creation." Anguhr said.

"It is agencies of destruction I fear." Gin frowned.

"Then fear me," Anguhr smiled, yet his expression was as cutting as his axe blades. "For your own actions have only made me more powerful."

"Then use that power, Destroyer!" Zaria looked at Anguhr with a fierce stare. "Use it to end this senseless era! Become the greatest conqueror ever by destroying Hell itself!"

"Perhaps. In time." Anguhr nodded, slowly. He looked out as if towards a possible future. "But now do not expect your guilt to guide me. We were allies by need. But what need do I have of you now?"

Anguhr looked at both Gin and Zaria.

"To kill us now would simply be petty." Gin at last appeared to be nearing anger.

"And I am sure it would not be as easy as ordering a squad of demons to open fire." Anguhr remarked and looked to the sky and around him. "You are energy based. This place seethes with it, just as Hell feeds the Dark Urge. Not so for any of us on the energy absorbing Iron Work. So I accept our stalemate. Here. But the tactical advantage and means to strike Hell is mine. If you wish to see this mission to its end, you will follow my commands."

Zaria placed her left hand over Gin's mouth to preclude any retort.

"Very well, General." Zaria said. "I will agree. You are in control, son of Azuhr."

"And as display of my power and our new accord," Anguhr locked eyes on Zaria. "I will order your captured warriors debarked to this planet. Alive."

Anguhr picked up his helmet and placed it back on his head. He walked toward Azuhr's sword.

"He seems unchanged." Gin said in a hushed voice to Zaria.

"His is." Zaria nodded affirmation while watching Anguhr walk. "Like all life, he is a creature defined by his actions. Observe what he does now, not his bluster."

"The actions of life are either sentient or involuntary, no matter the means of birth." Gin said. "Despite using a weapon with a cutting edge, Anguhr's character is blunt force. He chose war even though he was aware of the fate of the worlds he conquered. His actions brought Armageddon. Annihilation."

"And now he is the hope to end the destruction," Zaria replied. "Awareness also has two blades, old friend. No other General could be our ally. He is loved by his demons because he leads from the frontline. You can call that blunt, or a canny strategy to ensure loyalty. Think of it. If not for his seeming brutal leadership, would he stand a chance against Hell? Another General not loved by his horde could not survive as a rebel. The demons of such a General would love the eternal reward promised by the Dark Urge more than their own lives, and more than loyalty to their leader."

Gin transmitted to Zaria for fear he could not say his sharp quietly: 'I cannot be glad of his campaigns because he serves our cause now!'

"Nor should you," Zaria said aloud and softly. "But we need him and must endure the past to build a better future. None of this should have occurred, just as I should not stand here before you."

"I am glad you do," Gin said aloud.

"Then also be glad for Anguhr." Zaria cocked her head as she looked at Gin. "He and I are both mistakes. Yet, we exist. From this moment on, our actions define us as never before."

Zaria and Gin looked over where they heard the sound of infernal steel slicing through rock and earth. Anguhr gripped his mother's sword and pulled it from the ground.

"A mother's love projected through time by a sword." Gin mused, and then looked at Zaria. "Our universe is odd."

Zaria smiled and nodded as she watched Anguhr stare at the massive, black blade.

CHAPTER TWENTY-SIX

The Dark Urge toiled in Hell. Her labor kept increasing the Forge' power. An idea flared in her mind and gave her comfort. Nothing could survive the surface of Hell. Now, nothing could survive the deathly radiation spewed between its poles and into space for leagues. Nothing. Only inside Hell were there small crannies where little creeping things might endure. Perhaps.

For a moment, the Dark Urge took respite and reflected. Her mind entered a part of Hell where seven ruins lay in a loose arc like cities dropped by a wounded bird. The ruins were machines that were once alive and held life. Their main parts were long, broken compartments that appeared to be huge bubbles pulled at two opposite ends and then frozen, and later shattered from within. The machines where made of substances like glass, steel, and skin.

In this part of Hell, the machines were the only structures. All else was black and featureless. There was no spider. There was no life. Yet the zone had been the gestation chamber. It was where the Generals were born. After the last one emerged, life went absent there. The entire galaxy had changed in that time. The Dark Urge had changed it. She created her Generals and sent them out to conquer the stars. She ate the worlds in their orbits to feed her fear.

Since the schism, fear had grown within her. Zaria left, and all that stayed behind was fear and a lurking spider. Fear grew and became stronger inside the Dark Urge, but she never released it. It was always growing. Consuming. Expanding. It stretched her across an expanse as a taught sheet of skin. Yet, she also trapped and nurtured her. Fear never grew large enough to become its own creature. It never replaced the light and spirit Zaria had taken. Fear was the Dark Urge, and she was Hell.

The Generals shattered their wombs when born. It was a pain the Dark Urge hoped would bring deliverance. Yet, fear still lived. With one General setting out on his own and possibly against Hell, fear writhed and kicked. One gestation chamber had been the womb for two Generals. The last of her children was already growing inside one when her first child sent an offspring of her own. Then, an odd sensation eclipsed fear. In that moment, however long it was, perhaps the span of a planet's life or only a geologic epoch on its surface or merely the ripple of a flame, she tore the last, embryonic General from that chamber. It was exposed on Hell's lethal surface. She put Azuhr's child in its place. He was remade and reborn. Azarak became Anguhr. A child born from life became its destroyer. As the Dark Urge looked at the last gestation chamber, that strange sensation that had eclipsed fear returned. But it only lasted the time burning sand takes to roll down the surface of a dune. There would be no more births and no more pain. There would be fear. If Anguhr must die to feed it, then it would happen. Azarak would be remade one final time, and into ash.

A planetary orbital often held more than it's main planet. Small worldlets and clusters could precede and follow the planet at predicable points. Those points could be places to hide, or launch an ambush. Hell's path around the Red Giant also held sites of coorbital debris. Hell and increased solar winds consumed the original rocks and bits of ice long ago. The new clusters of dust, metal, and rock were made of lost bits from the trains of sundered worlds. One massive piece flashed into the cluster following Hell. It was also red, and burning. Anguhr's ship had returned to Hell.

"Is it customary for returning heroes to know where to hide in their home system?" Zaria asked as she turned from watching the bridge screens and spoke to Anguhr seated on his throne.

"By now the Dark Urge would hardly consider me a hero," Anguhr replied while scrutinizing images and data on the screens. "And I have slain so many so-called heroes, I do not care for the title. Nonetheless, my position relative to Hell can appear that I still approach as a loyal servant. If this position also acts as a partial shield from Hell's intensified radiation and countermeasures, so be it. We will stay among these trones until a tactical map is complete."

"Trones," Zaria mused aloud. "There is a bit of code dating back so many ages. It comes from tro'ans, or, originally Trojans. You would have liked the Trojans, General. At least their warriors."

"They are rocks," Anguhr said with a dismissive raise of an eyebrow under his helmet, and then focused back on the screens.

'Maybe he will have a rock named after him, one day.' Zaria thought and broadcast to Gin.

'There may as well be.' Gin answered over the same wavelength. 'He has reduced so many worlds to mere fragments. Some of their dust is likely among the oorts rolling here.'

'I will endeavor to prevent this ship from becoming part of it.' Zaria thought. She turned and raised her palms to Anguhr in an entreating gesture.

"General, if you will listen to me now, I can offer you a boon that will increase the power of your ship." Zaria said.

"You wish to tap the weapon Solok guards?" Anguhr asked.

"No. I wish to enter new programming into your ship."

"Why?"

The question came not from Anguhr. The speed it was asked, location, and severe tone caused Zaria to pause. She turned and looked down at Proxis glaring at her.

"I can make this ship invisible, at least undetectable from a distance, even to Hell's ships." Zaria said.

"Impossible." Anguhr snapped and looked back at the displays.

"I assure you, General, I have done it already." Zaria countered. "With Gin's help, I will not need physical tools to grant this to your ship."

"And how would you make the alterations?" Proxis asked with a suspicious tone and stare. "Manipulate the ship's programming?"

"Yes," Gin answered.

Proxis replied not with a word but an aggressive bark.

"We need no such weapon," Anguhr said.

"General, I wish only that if you face another of your kind that you win. If this ship is destroyed, Gin and I die with it. Your life—this ship—is now linked to ours. Allow me to ensure the survival of both."

"My tolerance grants you life," Anguhr said looking at both Gin and Zaria. "Do not cause me to revoke it."

"My, Lord! A ship approaches!" Proxis announced. "A Hell ship."

"The rebellion is now open, Anguhr." Zaria said. "Charge your weapons and fire. There is no hiding, now."

"Hold your fire, Proxis." Anguhr ordered. He then looked at Zaria. "And you. Hold your words. Do not dare tell me how to fight!"

Zaria stepped back from Anguhr's throne.

"The ship is heading straight for us, Lord Destroyer." Proxis reported.

"It may be Uruk bringing Xuxuhr's ship. I will not kill my Field Master by mistake. Two ships against Sutuhr would nearly guarantee victory."

"Lord, the aegis is fully ablaze, but I can still detect energy building near his bow.

"He is charging his main battery." Zaria dared to say.

Anguhr's sigh was nearly as strong as a storm wind across the slot of his helmet. "Ready our main guns. But hold fire until you can determine the identity of that ship with certainty. Do not fire if it is Xuxuhr's!"

"Understood, Lord." Proxis bobbed his head in a quick bow as he entered commands at his dais.

A low rumble of the main guns' motors rolling them into deployment echoed across the bridge.

"By then will we be within its main weapons' range?" Gin asked.

"Yes. For both ships." Proxis answered.

"Then may I suggest—"

"Signal, Lord!" Proxis barked.

"I am General and Lord Ursuhr," the bear-like General flashed on the main screen as images of the Red Giant, distant Hell, and debris outside the ship continued on other screens with overlayed data.

"But you know who I am, Anguhr." Ursuhr continued. "By the will of our mother of infinite power, the Dark Urge, you are ordered to yield your ship and horde to Hell. If you fail to do this, I will kill your ship and horde. And then I will kill you, rebel."

"Question," Gin said pointing at the image of Ursuhr's huge, grinning face. "If he is on the approaching ship, then where is Sutuhr? Or *his* ship?"

"That ship is not General Ursuhr's!" Proxis barked. "I have seen General Sutuhr's warship. It is the incoming ship!"

"Locate that transmission!" Anguhr ordered. "Where is Su—!"

"I am here, stripling." Sutuhr's chimera face replaced Ursuhr's image.

Both Proxis and Gin took keen interest in the telemetry of the incoming signal.

"You do face me, *and* my loyal lieutenant, Ursuhr." Sutuhr continued and wiped venom away with his callused hand. "Now, don't hide behind your Ship Master. Stand and face your judgment. Or die more horribly."

Zaria looked at Anguhr. She expected him to roar in defiance. She heard only her own heart beat. Then Anguhr spoke, calmly.

"I can see why you would not wish to face Proxis, old one." Anguhr began. "You were beaten by him, and thus fear more embarrassment. Yet, now you face me. And you and Ursuhr foolishly risk my rage. Age has crippled your mind just as a failed battle has crippled your ship. Withdraw from the battle, and enjoy the moment more it brings. If you strike at me, I will kill you first, old fool."

Sutuhr roared and vanished from the screen.

"Take us straight at—" Anguhr started to order. His voice was lost in the deafening ring of multiple strikes against his ship's aegis. The assault was intense enough to rock the bridge.

"Missiles, Lord!" Proxis yelled.

"Evade them!" Anguhr bellowed. "Where did they strike from?"

"Here!" Proxis threw up his hands, in shock. He quickly went back to entering commands. "The missiles were hidden among the debris, somehow."

"Not bad," Gin said and cocked his head only to see an intense, reproving glare from Zaria.

"Port side main guns are damaged!" Proxis continued.

"Take us from this debris and locate both Hell ships!" Anguhr ordered. All on the bridge immediately felt a pull to the deck as the ship flew out of the debris field.

"I cannot locate General Ursuhr." Proxis said.

"More incoming—" Gin began as missiles struck the ship again.

"Again from the trones, Lord!" Proxis offered.

"You can't hide two Hell warships in there!" Gin shook his head.

"But you can hide a ship in space," Zaria said and looked at Anguhr. "I think I know why you can only detect Sutuhr."

"Then make the solution!" Anguhr snapped. "While I kill what I can see! Proxis, drive us straight at Sutuhr!"

"We are an easy target for his main guns if we race straight at him!" Zaria warned.

"Look at his course!" Anguhr thrust a massive finger at the upper left screen. "He altered it right as Ursuhr attacked. With his ship still in an internal siege from Gin's clone, his battle options are limited. He will likely opt to maintain the full power of his aegis over offensive fire."

"Yes. After his last battle, I agree." Zaria said watching the screens. "He moves to put Hell between us and his ship just as he moved behind the planet, then. Though he cannot use Hell as he did that world."

"Ursuhr snipes at us with missiles as he hides." Anguhr said. He noted Zaria must have seen the battle that damaged Sutuhr's ship. "I cannot see Ursuhr, but he and I know the path ahead: Destroy Sutuhr. So if he acts to intercept us, it will be along predicable courses. And so Proxis—"

"Missiles away, Lord!"

"Our salvos will keep him from assuming the necessary course for a successful hit." Anguhr nodded to his Ship Master. He then focused squarely on Zaria. "Unless he can dismiss my warheads. But I don't think his invisibility is coupled with a greater aegis."

"Not likely," Zaria said.

"I cannot detect any emanations of Builder technology," Gin said looking at the bulkhead of woven beams as if focused on something outside the ship. "Other than the Iron Work, naturally."

"No matter. For now." Anguhr said as Hell's surface flashed on the center screen. "The distance from the trones and Hell is too short for him to charge his main guns and fire before we intercept Sutuhr on the opposite side. And my mines—"

Anguhr looked at Proxis who turned and nodded to Anguhr with a smile. "Already deployed, Lord."

"They will deter him, further." Anguhr finished.

"Negative impact of missiles and mines, Lord." Proxis reported.

"But he is likely moving toward Hell, behind us. Now, with difficulty." Anguhr said.

"I've noticed—" Gin began, but was interrupted by Ursuhr's face reappearing. It flashed on a smaller left projection as a tactical map dominated the center screen.

"Your mines and missiles cannot stop me," Ursuhr's voice growled from the projection. "It only delays your death, Anguhr. Be strong and face it."

"You will not face me openly, coward." Anguhr replied. "You are not even proud to serve Hell. Else you would blaze across this space with your aegis at full flame. Instead, you hide. Afraid."

Ursuhr laughed. "Pathetic attempt at a goad, junior General. Thank your own prisoner for my tactical advantage."

Anguhr turned and glared at Zaria.

"I did not help him!" Zaria screamed.

"Oh, you did, Zaria." Ursuhr's triumphant smile returned. "You, who would be the savior of life and slayer of Hell."

Zaria looked at Ursuhr's image with shock.

"Yes, I know your name. From prisoners of my own." Ursuhr nodded. "They were killed after they told me all I demanded to hear. True, your aide was unintentional. A foolish act of desperation, making allies of primitives. You seeded ancient yet complex technology to hide life. A cloak with a coded dagger. You wanted the primitives to use a shield, but your shield also emitted an infiltration program. That was its true power. The ability not merely to passively hide, but to actively blind."

Zaria said nothing. Anguhr listened keenly.

"I destroyed a world where one of Zaria's phase engines was too much for the local saurians to implement." Ursuhr spoke with obvious pride in his low, groaning voice. "They used it instead as bait and bomb.

Their assassination failed. Worse, they didn't know what a demon sees, a ship records. And a General can read. The failsafe detonated that engine. But from then on, I knew what to seek. Zaria had been busy. And desperate. You gave too much to those ill suited to use the technology. I, however, am a General from Hell. With enough scans by enough demons before the failsafes could detonate, I was able to subvert future energy build ups and record the data with safeguards of my own. I could purge and mine the information. Of course, before I had my full war prize, many demons became vapor in the blasts. But I got what I needed. The worlds would die, anyway. And now I have a great weapon to use against you, Anguhr. Pathetic rebel!"

"I am amazed you could decipher any of the data you found," Anguhr said. "I am stunned you could use it."

"Me, as well." Zaria added. She still worked to conceal her shock and dread of Ursuhr's surprise adaptations of Builder technology.

"Why?" Ursuhr's triumphant smile collapsed into a frown on the screen.

"Because you are a stupid brute." Anguhr answered.

"I am a General and demon Lord!" Ursuhr yelled.

"And a bit of a surprise, I admit." Zaria said.

"The surprise is your doom! You have failed! I can now undo all your work across the galaxy!" Ursuhr raged on. "Do not mistake my unmatched strength for a lack of brain power!"

"Especially when you can task innumerable demons as engineers and force them to work until their brains are cinders." Anguhr said.

Ursuhr took a breath. "It works."

"Point taken," Anguhr replied. "Now, take this to heart. Leave Hell's system. Or, I will find a way to face you in personal combat. I can and will kill you. Your are not truly the strongest. This you know. Else you would also refute Sutuhr's leadership. Instead, you are his thrall. Even the Dark Urge can see your weakness. It is not Sutuhr's strength that made her put him in command. It is that you are pathetic."

Ursuhr's image vanished in mid-roar.

"Missile salvo incoming." Proxis announced.

"Excellent." Gin smiled and studied the screens where trajectory lines flashed from seemingly nowhere. "More data to find his ship."

"My insults will buy us minimal time," Anguhr said. "Take through Hell's increased radiation fields. It will baffle his targeting beams."

"And Hell's defenses?" Zaria asked.

"She will lash out. We will endure." Anguhr replied. "She knows her best tactic is for her children to clash and kill each other in space."

"A wonderful mother," Gin said.

"And what would you expect from Hell, old friend?" Zaria remarked.

"Now, remove Ursuhr's cloak, or I will hurl you both to the surface of Hell." Anguhr commanded.

'Here I thought we were friends.' Gin sent his thought to Zaria.

'We are allies, at best.' Zaria replied along the same waves. 'Friendship comes when wars end. Right now, let us fight for our cause. We must stop Ursuhr! If he can use the technology—!'

'Then he can detect it and perhaps defeat it, and all you have protected.' Gin thought. He nodded and applied himself to his task of finding the ursine General.

Zaria stood next to the control dais and looked down at Proxis with an entreating look. Proxis glared up at her. He turned to his General.

Anguhr sighed and nodded. "Transfer to mental commands. Allow her the dais. I know you will protect my ship, Proxis."

Proxis nodded and bowed to Anguhr. He stepped aside and let Zaria kneel down to use the dais, but watched her intently with focused, serpentine eyes.

Anguhr's ship dared to near Hell. Its red aegis flared against the waves of radiation hurled from the Forge by the Dark Urge. Velocity drove it through the assault of energies across physical and strange spectra. A constant and violent storm of energy roiled beneath the ship as it cut across the skies. Blasts of plasma and lightning sent shockwaves across the wastelands far below. For an instant, the Dark Urge cowered but then became enraged. Anguhr's boldness surprised her. Yet, Hell was her fortress. She changed her fury into weapons, and opened portals to hurl them at the impudent child of Azuhr.

CHAPTER TWENTY-SEVEN

Zaria continued entering commands at the dais. Yet she was no longer on the bridge of Anguhr's ship. All around her was flat, black darkness. There was a sense that something moved in a circular path in the distance. Its motion was a vertical wave, or ripple in a curtain a mind knew was there yet could not see. Zaria knew the presence of the Dark Urge. And that her mind was now in Hell.

"How have you done this?" Zaria asked.

"Do you think you can come so close to Hell, to me, and not be subject to my power? My power, my sister, myself." The Dark Urge said in a unidirectional and deep, feminine voice. "At least the half of the self, I was. Not the part I am. Now I don't need you, sister. Self. I am whole."

"You are fearful," Zaria said. "But I can still help you."

"You can perish as all do who oppose me. As all do, expect me. I am dark. Forever."

"What have you done with the Great Widow? Have you killed her, too? Did she dare speak the truth of your madness and you set her aflame as you do the rest of creation?" Zaria stood tall and defiant.

"Spider, spider burning bright?" The Dark Urge laughed. "And here you are, sunshine, encased in eternal night."

"So are you, sister. Let me free you."

"Foolish girl!" The Dark Urge shouted and the avatar of the young girl in a dress with only half of her head sprinted by Zaria and vanished again in the black. "I am the darkness!"

"Then be as shadow, but let the rest live in peace." Zaria said in pleading tones and raised her arms as if to embrace someone. "Call your

Generals away from the battle. Even Anguhr. I will come to Hell, all of me. I will protect you."

"As you protect me now?" The Dark Urge spoke as verbal thunder. "By making a weapon that can destroy me?"

The image of the little girl reappeared but now towered over Zaria who looked up at her. The girl's half face scowled. She raised her shoe to stomp Zaria, but Zaria didn't move as the sole came down at her. It vanished. Again, only darkness surrounded Zaria.

"You have annihilated worlds," Zaria said and lowered her arms. "Too many worlds. The whole galaxy knows fear. Terror. You."

"They threaten me," The Dark Urge said in the voice of a child.

"They do not," Zaria countered in a clam tone. "They were creating their own destinies. They could not threaten you. You are too strong, sister."

"They would," the Dark Urge's voice was again deep but feminine. "Just as the Plunderers did. Just as you do now."

"I only act to spare life's destruction before you blot it out with darkness and terror." Zaria gestured to a black, featureless sky. "You want to remake the galaxy in your image, yet you have no true form. Let me come to you and together we can have shape and bring substance to creation. We can be whole, again."

"And then I would cease to exist as I am." The Dark Urge replied in calm, measure tones. "Just as I did not exist before. You say I am formless, but I have existence. I am."

"So am I," Zaria said. "Together we can be more than both of us are apart."

"As something else." The Dark Urge said with a timbre of repulsion.

"Yes. Something greater." Zaria thought to draw a deep breath but recalled she was in a place of mind, and a mind bent to madness.

"As nothing." The Dark Urge furthered.

"As transcendence." Zaria tried to convey reassurance in tone and thought.

"But not as I am!" The Dark Urge snapped. "No! We are not the same! We are no longer sisters. We are no longer even opposite sides. You are light yet you bring war. You save life yet you seek to destroy me. And you have killed my children. You are the enemy!"

"I am your sister," Zaria lowered her head as if pleading to a spot on the black surface below, and then raised her head to look up again. "I am light. Let me help you. We should at least be together. I will live in the Forge. I will replace the Great Widow. In time we will grow together even if we stay distinct. Let that be our future."

"It was our past. It is over. Dead." The Dark Urge said. "The universe will be dead. I am its doom. I am the Dark Urge. The only light will be fire."

Zaria made a mental sigh. "Sister, do not make me kill you."

There was deafening laughter. Even as a mental avatar, Zaria thrust her hands to her ears until it ebbed.

"You see, perhaps we are the same!" the Dark Urge shouted. "You are as much death as me."

"But your actions have brought me here and forced me to make war!" Zaria shouted against a renewed bout of dark laughter. "Your war is what threatens you!"

"Then come. Help me." The voice of the child returned to Zaria's ears. "Take the weapon. Destroy Anguhr's ship. Bring it to me. We will use it together. We will bring peace."

"First, send away Sutuhr and Ursuhr." Zaria said. "I will send Anguhr to take Gin back to Asherah. Then, you and I will live together in the Forge. Your loneliness, your fear, will be over."

There was nothing. Zaria glanced at to her sides, but she was still in the dark, featureless place. It did not vanish. Her sister was not yet finished.

"So sweet. So kind. So sad." The child's voice echoed against nothing.

"You will not let me come to you, will you sister?" Zaria asked.

"Sister?" The question rumbled on thunder. "Call me by my name!"

Zaria paused, and then replied. "You are the power regulation protocol."

"No!" The single word seared like lightning. "Call me by my name!"

Zaria again paused before speaking. "You have become creation's darkest urge. But you are madness."

A scream was the only reply. Its sound was as abrading as an avalanche of jagged diamond against soft skin. Zaria gripped her ears. She knew the scream was only in her mind. But her mind struggled to contain the pain from the scream and her own failure to reach her sister.

Anguhr's ship kept its vector towards Sutuhr and left the skies of Hell. On the bridge, Zaria slowly collapsed to the deck plating and curled into a near fetal position with her back facing the others. Gin looked at her, but quickly took over at the dais.

"What happened? Why has she fallen?" Anguhr demanded.

"I would imagine your grandmother reached into her mind." Gin answered. "Zaria has just endured her own trip through Hell." Gin looked down at Zaria. "Be strong, old friend. You are not alone."

Gin stopped entering commands through the physical dais and violated his pledge not to enter Anguhr's ship as data. He knelt beside Zaria and placed his hands on her shoulder and back.

"Is she dying?" Anguhr asked further.

"No." Gin kept kneeling next to Zaria but looked over at Anguhr. "But I assume she has realized only one of them, herself or the Dark Urge, can live."

"That is the same campaign she has tasked us all." Anguhr growled.

"It may be easy for you to fight those you know as brothers, Anguhr." Gin sighed. "But if I asked you to kill yourself, what would you do?"

The ship's sudden veer took the place of an answer.

"I detect launches from Hell, Lord." Proxis said. "Incoming fire. Of a sort I have never seen."

Anguhr looked away from Gin and at the screens.

CHAPTER TWENTY-EIGHT

A flat region of Hell's wasteland shook. The ground rose into three steep mountains that erupted as they grew into volcanoes with circular sides nearly as steep as cylinders. They were, in truth, the barrel's of infernal cannons.

The eruptions became more violent. Red flame shot from the opened summits. Masses of the same flaming beams from Hell's warships blasted towards space. The projectiles were gigantic, spinning heads of demonic maces. Black beads swirled in circular paths and through the jutting beams like hornet swarms imparting spin and speed. The bizarre, flaming missiles flew towards the burning wake of Anguhr's ship.

On Anguhr's bridge, he leaned to Gin while still watching the screens. "Have you found Ursuhr's ship?"

"Soon!" Gin nodded with confidence.

"Hell itself is firing on us." The thought stunned Proxis. He vowed to follow Anguhr, and now the fact he did so in rebellion to the Dark Urge struck deep into his brain. The impossible became real. It stunned the wingless demon.

"Missile screen." Anguhr said.

Proxis stood frozen.

"Proxis: missiles! Fire now!" Anguhr roared and stood.

Proxis snapped into focus and thought the command. A wall of missiles fired. The shield of warheads detonated almost immediately against Hell's projectiles. The shock of the blasts hit the ships own red fires as if a storm gust struck a bonfire. The mace-head projectiles survived the countermeasure, but the strike diverted them from colliding with the ship. They flew into space, unguided and spinning.

On the bridge, Proxis turned and bowed before Anguhr. "I beg your indulgence, Lord Destroyer. I—"

"Fight, Proxis!" Anguhr yelled. "Fight for me and we all live! I will never lead you to certain death. But we must focus. And fight!"

"I will Lord. We will live." Proxis returned back to his dais.

"General," Gin stayed next to Zaria, but again looked out beyond bulkhead. "I have infiltrated a network the other Generals use to communicate."

"Network?" Proxis queried.

"Yes. There are not in direct, ship-to-ship communications." Gin answered.

"Ursuhr fears contracting your infiltrator," Anguhr noted. "He has built a wall between Hell ships. Proxis, adjust intercept course to Sutuhr."

"I have his ship, Lord." Proxis said.

"You are likely right, General." Gin said. "But the network of buoys gives me an easier method to—"

"Complete it before I kill Sutuhr," Anguhr sat back on his throne still staring at the screens. "Or I will kill you."

"No you won't," Zaria said and stood. "Gin will do this. But enough threats, General. We will all see this war end. But as one force."

"So long as your presence does not make my enemies stronger." Anguhr growled.

"It makes you stronger," Zaria said. "Admit it, and let's move on."

Zaria and Anguhr entered a truce of silence forced by Proxis' sharp course alterations nearly overpowering the bridge gravity field.

"Lord, General Sutuhr—again he alters course to use Hell's body to eclipse his ship in relation to our course." Proxis reported.

"I see it," Anguhr said as he studied the arcs plotted across the screens showing Sutuhr's ship. "Redirect our mines to strike Hell. It will insight him to strike at those assaulting his beloved mother."

"Won't that clear a path for Ursuhr?" Zaria asked.

"He has altered course for a strike along polar orbit by now." Anguhr replied. "Plus, I have many more mines. Main gun status?"

"Port-side battery still under repair, Lord." Proxis answered.

"Then aim our starboard main guns at Hell," Anguhr ordered. "Have all secondary batteries ready to fire as soon as Sutuhr's ship comes in range. These threat will certainly bring the Devoted charging at us."

"And his threat to us?" Zaria asked.

"I only need a single strike to render him vulnerable."

"Lord!" Proxis yelled. "Another salvo from Hell!"

"Then evade it!" Anguhr barked "Fire—!"

Anguhr halted his command. Zaria captured his attention. She glowed a vibrant yellow and the color of gold made into light. Her skin crackled with arcs of plasma.

"What now?" Anguhr yelled as he looked at the glowing Zaria.

"Now she saves your ship." Gin answered.

The new salvo of mace-like projectiles and swarms hurtled closer to Anguhr's ship. Their spin slowed. The crimson flames engulfing the mace-heads flashed to orange. Their spin reversed and sped up as the swarms appeared to die and were thrown from the slashing beams. The mace-heads veered away from Anguhr's ship and into a polar arc.

Ursuhr had also ordered his ship into Hell's radiation belts in his pursuit ordered by Sutuhr. Ursuhr's course cut down from Hell's northern pole on an intercept arc with Anguhr's ship. The mace-heads suddenly flashed on the center screen. The spinning infernos were dead ahead.

"Errant fire from Hell!" Martis grated.

Ursuhr and his bridge pitched hard to starboard as Martis veered the ship clear of Hell's missiles commandeered by Zaria.

The mace-heads continued along their arc and descended back to Hell's surface. Their volcanic launchers still burned and erupted anew as their last, hijacked salvo struck. Hell's guns were destroyed. The thundering impact ejected rock, dust, and molten machines into space.

Ursuhr looked at his ship's new trajectory as it flashed over a projected map of Hell. They were heading away from Hell and into space. His war prize of invisibility only hid his ship from active scans. It blinded other technology, especially Hell's detectors. Close in, a set of keen eyes might see red before he opened fire. The blind was created by an entangled link between all of Hell's ships. The link deep within the ship's systems was made from the same, identical source: the Great Widow's silk. Her weave bound the communications system with the ship's sensors. It also connected all Hell's warships along quantum and arcane lines of force. The quantum link allowed instantaneous connection. It also allowed the infiltration that blocked sensor and targeting arrays.

Coupled with the phase engines, the technology was a great gift to the aliens who could use it. Ursuhr had his ship's aegis to shield him, but he knew the blind would be useful in unlikely combat. Such as with another General. The quantum infiltration occurred in Anguhr's ship when he entered the trones. But now Sutuhr was thwarting the use of the new weapon by not drawing Anguhr out for a clear shot. This battle was taking longer because of Sutuhr's wounded ship and gutless evasion of Anguhr's firepower. The angry Ursuhr considered using his advantage against both Generals.

"Bring us back on course!" Ursuhr bellowed.

"I will, Lord. And immediately, if you wish." Martis turned to his General. "However, another expedited path through Hell's radiation would further weaken our aegis. And Hell's own defenses seem—"

Martis stopped speaking. He considered that openly stating Hell's weapons were compromised might amount to blasphemy.

"I serve you and this ship, Lord Ursuhr." Martis continued. "Our success, our survival, is paramount to me."

Ursuhr made a low grumble. "Protect the ship. But make greatest speed possible to Anguhr. Now."

Martis bowed. He turned back to his dais. The ship veered hard, again.

Anguhr glanced at Zaria, now back to her normal, luminous self. He turned as she smiled at him. He blinked as venom flew towards him. It was only a projection on his bridge. Sutuhr had opened communications. However, his opening statements were unintelligible rants. Finally, his yelling cooled into understandable phrases.

"You have enraged the Dark Urge! Desecrated Hell!" Sutuhr bellowed. "To even displease our mother is to know complete death! You will be burned from history! All your victories—struck from all records. She will erase you from galactic memory. I will receive credit for your conquests! You are now less than the dust from your own campaigns!"

Anguhr said nothing in reply. The silence felt like a solid mass encasing his bridge. Anguhr's attention was on a chronograph and range sensor. He finally said two words.

"Open fire."

The projection of Sutuhr's face gave perfect fidelity to his shock. His eyes darted to his left where his own screens projected data. Sutuhr expected to see a massive bolt of power fired from Anguhr's ship strike Hell just as he fired his main guns on the Xa'rol homeworld. Instead, plasma lances from Anguhr's secondary batteries struck Sutuhr's ship. He vanished from Anguhr's screens as his image shook.

"Turn our bow to Sutuhr!" Anguhr yelled.

"Lord, General Sutuhr's own main guns are still armed." Proxis cautioned.

On his own bridge, Sutuhr had calmed down. He saw the battle near an end, and then so would Hell's only and last rebellion. He looked at the image of Anguhr's ship and intersection of plotted weapons fire.

"Little stripling, you are the last of our line." Sutuhr said. "I was second. Only to Azuhr lived before me. Now, you join her in oblivion. Fire, Crucis. Kill this rebel."

Twin beams shot from Sutuhr's bow. They held less power than when he destroyed the Xa'rol planet, but enough to annihilate another warship. What they struck was another opposing beam from a fully charged main battery. For an instant, a new, small star exploded into life. Its intense, white brilliance flared brighter than the Red Giant and the two main drives of the rival ships.

All on Anguhr's bridge released a collective gasp as the flash dyed out on the screens and through the hull beams.

"An impressive calculation, Proxis." Gin said to the Ship Master. "Congratulations. And thank you."

Proxis tilted his head to look up at Gin and gave him a quick nod.

On the opposing bridge, Sutuhr bolted up and looked at his screens to locate Anguhr, but Anguhr was easy to find. He charged straight at Sutuhr.

"Evasive—!" Sutuhr yelled, but he fell on his side as Crucis steered the ship out of the fusillade of secondary fire.

The beams sliced through the red flames trailing the star-like main drive. However, the following missile barrage exploded in violent succession across the hull.

"My Lord!" Crucis yelled. "The last salvo severed our helm. I cannot steer the ship!"

"And he hammers us into Hell's radiation shield!" Sutuhr then roared.

"We cannot survive there!" Crucis barked as he still attempted to control the ship amid violent shaking and a building spin. "He has us!"

"Fight!" Sutuhr yelled and grabbed up his mace. "Fire missiles! Fire everything! Send out the horde to shoot at his ship!"

A lurch of the deck caused Sutuhr to fall against his throne. He braced himself with his mace. Again, he saw his ship's crimson aegis fail. This time he didn't see space beyond the gaps in his hull. He saw the beams begin to glow and spark as heated steel. His mother's own defenses charged his ship with high energy particles and waves of ethereal power. Gravity failed. Sutuhr gripped the deck plating. He tried to bark an order, but the conductive atmosphere had left his ship. Sutuhr again admired Crucis for his dedication to his post. But the Ship Master's hand became still as he drifted away from his dais. The thorns of his skin began to burn. Sutuhr also felt heat. He found it strange that he was born in Hell and yet never really felt heat before. It was always below the tolerance of his powerful form. Until now.

Sutuhr strained to peer through his ship's hull and look at the approaching surface of his mother. He remembered the features as beautiful and sterile. Lifeless. That would be his state in mere moments.

209

His mother had denied him harbor. Now, his ship would collide with her. For once, Sutuhr did not feel hate. He felt peace, and then intense heat.

Anguhr watched Sutuhr's ship burn but without crimson fire. Its main drive flashed off and became a black ball that itself caught fire in the sea of energy and fear blasted out from Hell. Sutuhr's ship spun on its axis as if locked in a perpetual capsizing as it gained speed towards Hell.

"The centrifugal force will likely trap his horde," Zaria said in a low voice.

"They would want to perish with their Lord." Anguhr said. "Now, Ursuhr."

CHAPTER TWENTY-NINE

"Incoming main battery fire on anticipated vector." Proxis announced with remarkable calm as planet destroying beams seared the vacuum and then sliced the aft-most extend of his ship's scarlet aegis.

"Plow us through his missiles, Proxis." Anguhr ordered.

The young General was also in remarkable calm for having just destroyed another of his kind who annihilated planets and interstellar empires. Of course, so did Anguhr. And so did his current opponent.

"Both main batteries are back on line, Lord Destroyer." Proxis said with tones of both triumph and tone relief.

Anguhr's ship sailed a safe distance from Hell's radiation but faced renewed pursuit by Ursuhr. With Sutuhr and his ship destroyed, Anguhr could now focus on the hulking, ursine General. Proxis fired both main batteries in short, staccato pulses that vaporized the onslaught of Ursuhr's secondary attack. Inside on Anguhr's bridge, the bear-like face of his antagonist appeared in projection.

"You waste no time in mourning our brother, Anguhr. Neither do I."

"Your time is ending," Anguhr droned. "As Sutuhr revealed, death is a certainty for all who oppose me."

"It has ever been the same for me." Ursuhr smiled in defiance. "And those are bold worlds when you killed a virtually unarmed General. My ship is fully operational. And better than your own."

Anguhr glanced to Gin, who nodded.

"Now, Proxis," Anguhr said sharp and confident. "Prepare to vaporize this fool."

"Ha!" Ursuhr barked from the projection. "How? You are the fool, Anguhr. You cannot even—"

"We found the network that screens your communications." Anguhr cut in. "All we needed was for you to link to them and communicate with Sutuhr for a short time. As you are both bombasts who slay worlds with endless bluster and rants, we had plenty of time to act."

"Act? What have you—?" Ursuhr was interrupted, again. The sound of Martis' affected and now stressed voice barked outside the range of Ursuhr's image.

"You were fearful of the infiltrator besieging Sutuhr's ship." Anguhr continued. "Yet the technology you used as a wall is old and vulnerable, just as you are nearing death."

"But thank you," Gin chirped. "It allowed me an access point to insert the on switch of your quantum location beacon. You may remember it's the mechanism that calls to the Great Widow should a General fall and his horde need to make a cagey distress call. Otherwise the spider uses the strands she placed in your being as embryos. This switch gives us similar access. We don't need the scanners to target your ship. Enjoy General Anguhr's belligerence in force. I will enjoy watching it from both sides. Part of me is already there in your ship's system."

Martis' barked off the screen's image near Ursuhr who still looked at Anguhr in bewilderment. Gin ended his address to Ursuhr with the ancient, and in Hell, forgotten hand gesture. He waved.

"In short—" Anguhr took a breath after Gin's verbal dissertation that was shared by Ursuhr on his bridge. "You can no longer hide. Now you must fight, coward. Pity yourself Ursuhr, because it is me you must battle."

Anguhr snatched up his axe and laughed, loudly.

"Missiles launched, Lord." Proxis announced. "The warheads are planet killers."

Ursuhr vanished as his face flexed at the start of a roar.

"Fire all salvos continuously!" Anguhr jerked his axe as if imagining a blow on Ursuhr.

"I obey, Lord." Proxis nodded. "I ask, though, hear me. For our missiles alone cannot destroy his ship at this range against his fully powered aegis."

"I will kill Ursuhr. My goal is to incinerate his pride." Anguhr answered. "For that, make sure he hears me: Ursuhr! Listen, well. You hide your ship and you hide in your bridge because you cannot face me in battle. You have no skill in combat, but to pull a trigger. Your tactics reveal this. You hold fear more strongly than your mace. You are no General. You survive on the backs of your horde. You are Ursuhr, the weakling! And you are a coward!"

Ursuhr's enraged image reappeared on Anguhr screens. "I will kill you on your own decks!"

Ursuhr charged off his throne. His mace was also gone.

"So, the strategy is a bit different with this one." Gin said with a hint of nerves.

"Solok!" Anguhr barked.

"Lord Destroyer!" The image of the new Field Master appeared. "I await your orders, as does the horde!"

Secured the weapon, and then ready every demon with a rock to throw to assault Ursuhr's ship.

"Our horde against another—?" Solok began and his serpent eyes widened.

"Yes," Anguhr said. "All Hell's wars led to this battle."

"Then, Lord Destroyer, war ends for General Ursuhr!" Solok stood to salute, and then rushed from the projection field.

Zaria took a deep breath and prepared to speak.

"This is how the war ends," Anguhr said. "On my terms. I will be the last General. I will fight the last battle of the last war at the front. No terms. From anyone."

There was another pause that seemed to make time become solid.

"I will maneuver the ship to victory, Lord Anguhr." Proxis said at last.

Anguhr stood from his throne. He gripped his axe firmly in his right hand. The battle cries of Solok and his demons leaping from the hull became surpassed the rumble of the continuous missile fire. Their cries echoed through the vast ship before becoming muted in the vacuum.

"My sword—?" Zaria shouted to Anguhr.

"Sword," Anguhr breathed. "Yes, the sword."

If it were possible for sound to carry through space, Ursuhr's bellow of rage would fill the solar system. He stood gripping his maul over his bridge on the hull. His roar became one of defiance and joy as he watched Anguhr's missiles explode against the protective outer edge of his ship's red flames. The orange and white flashes from the warheads became a growing cone of plasma at the bow shock of the aegis. The cone grew to reach over the hull where Ursuhr stood.

Ursuhr's roar died away as the explosions continued, and for some time. Obviously Anguhr had ordered a barrage of every missile of his vast, seemingly endless magazines held by all Generals. Against another of Hell's warships, Ursuhr had found the missiles could wound if the strike was close and precise. Anguhr showed that they could ravage a Hell ship if its aegis was damaged. Ursuhr knew his own ship was strong. However, under this onslaught the main drive's power would need to boost the aegis. This would cause slower maneuvers. The pressure of the detonations increased. The plasma cone pressed closer to the hull. Ursuhr felt its heat touch his scowling face. He turned to shout an order down to his bridge to take more radical maneuvers. He sensed fewer impacts through the aegis and lessened ripples across the glowing cone. Instead of barking the order, Ursuhr leapt aside to dodge another weapon launched from Anguhr's ship: the Destroyer's massive axe. Anguhr had thrown it with remarkable accuracy straight at Ursuhr's head.

The axe had slashed through the aegis weakened by the bombardment and driven by Anguhr's strength. The axe sailed a snout's length away from Ursuhr's face. One blade struck and wedged into the hull. The axe weapon was followed by another, more powerful weapon: Anguhr himself. He leapt through the slit his axe cut in plasma cone. His impact shook the surrounding hull.

Anguhr's ballistic appearance slightly impressed Ursuhr. He was more angered that his rival had beaten him to the type of bold attack. For a moment, Ursuhr thought Anguhr foolish to attack without a weapon in hand. Yet Anguhr swiftly turned and Ursuhr saw the massive, black sword he gripped in both hands. Ursuhr did not recognize it, nor would he care about the weapon's history. As proof, he said nothing and swung his maul. Sword blade met blunt metal. The deafening ring of the collision was lost in the ship's atmosphere as the shockwave blasted through the plasma cone and flattened the red flames at their feet.

Anguhr knew if there was ever a foe that could defeat him, it was Ursuhr the Mighty. He relished the fight as the apex of his violent life. Ursuhr swung again. His roar was matched by Anguhr's deep, dark laughter. Again their weapons struck. Another shockwave blasted out from Ursuhr's ship.

Ursuhr had trained with his maul. Anguhr had trained with his axe, not a sword. With skillful maneuvering, parries, and a few more well-placed blows, Ursuhr knocked the great blade from Anguhr's hands. As in past age, it spun away from a burning Hell ship and into the void.

Ahead was darkness. The crimson flames were behind Solok's wings. He heard his war cry ebb as he left thinning atmosphere. He welcomed flight into open space. He saw a wave of radiant plasma fly from the distant red mass of General Ursuhr's ship. Lord Anguhr was at work. Solok had watched him leap ahead to lead the attack. Now, General fought General. Soon, horde would fight horde. The universe sundered. Solok felt joy. His target, Ursuhr's ship, drew closer. On this attack, concern outweighed blind fervor. Such was the mindset of commanders. Solok's rank was now only one step below Lord Anguhr. He led almost all demons of Lord Anguhr's horde into combat. His personal strike wing formed two, wide deltas at right angles behind him. Solok enjoyed the trust placed in him and its power. Nonetheless, he would have strongly preferred another planetary invasion for the first, full assault under his command. He had flown next to Uruk on more such attacks than he had thorns. Uruk was nowhere near. He was likely dead. Adding to Solok's concern was that he attacked another horde that had also conquered many worlds. Solok hoped it would not be a glorious but short posting as Field Master. No matter the future, the present was a time to fight and to lead. He flew on with a grin that would terrify most intelligent minds.

Kalak barked the order to deploy towards the ship's aft. He realized his horde would soon be under attack. He also knew Lord Ursuhr would focus on killing the rebel General, Anguhr. Defending the ship would be his and Martis' duty. Unfortunately, General Anguhr had the foresight to give his demons a tactical edge. The constant barrage of missiles created a barrier and constricted Kalak's deployment of his demons while the enemy advanced. They would be on him before he could mount a counter attacks in open space. This forced Kalak's strike wings into close-to-ship formations while the attackers had open space to maneuver and adapt. One plan underway might gain them time of the advantage. No matter. He had to fight now, not wait for success in special ploys.

Kalak had many ways to kill a swarming assault before it reached the ship. But not in this battle. Martis reported that he could not open fire on the coming onslaught. An infiltrator attacked the ships' guns and the plasma envelope had temporarily blocked simple line of sight targeting. The battle would come to Ursuhr's ship. The hordes would fight it on and near the hull. Kalak knew he led the strongest warriors in the galaxy. They were Hell's demons. Yet, so where the coming enemies.

Gin felt strained by the silence. The lack of noise made the atmosphere feel slow and gain great mass. Zaria had left to retrieve her sword. He and Proxis manned the bridge. Actually, Proxis manned the bridge. Gin stood, passively taking in data, but felt strangled in not releasing anything. Even the odd noise. He had reduced his own size to be in proportion to Proxis as a show of camaraderie. It did not work and only added to the feeling of the silence becoming a crushing mass. He was granted relief. Proxis spoke.

"We have—" Proxis paused. He stared at a small image among many now circulating before his dais. The image became the centered, largest stream of visuals and data. "Incoming. A ship."

The visual feed showed a spinning cylindrical mass made from the burning beams of a Hell ship. It sped closer to the outer hull from the direction of Ursuhr's ship.

"It defies detection, as did Ursuhr's ship." Proxis said. "I register it on passive detectors, only. We can see it. Yet—"

"It's not from this ship." Gin stated. "Is it possibly—?"

Gin saw the cylindrical suddenly cut through by a plasma lance. The cylinder exploded. A few demon bodies and weapons flew out from the exploding craft.

"Um, from Xuxuhr's ship?" Gin finished his question.

"No." Proxis answered. "Wrong vector."

"I admire you certitude." Gin said with wide eyes as we watched the bodies and wreckage disperse.

Proxis pitched his thorny brow at a right-leaning slope and glared at Gin with a serpentine gaze. Gin considered becoming a giant again.

"Are we under counterattack?" Zaria asked as she reentered the bridge.

Zaria had regained her sword. It was sheathed on her back with its handle at her right shoulder. She had also gained a wary group of ten demon escorts led by the recognized Wahx. He and his team never stopped glowering at her and holding their rifles at the ready. Zaria suddenly stopped short when she saw the shorter version of Gin. She looked down at him with a gaze lit with bewilderment.

"Of course," Proxis answered. "But this was a curious incursion. The ship held only a flight team and weapons. Too many for the crew."

"Then the strike teams are en route." Zaria said. She then drew her sword. "Or, already here. How many demons are still on this ship?"

"More than enough," Proxis looked at Zaria with characteristic suspicion and glanced at her sword. "Guard teams of new demons stand ready to fight on board, or as emergency reserves. Lord Anguhr has never needed such reserves."

"You need a minimum of ten warriors to one to fight an insurgent force. Minimum." Zaria said with mounting concern evident in her voice.

"I can see no way such a force could—" Proxis began.

"The missile strike in the trones." Zaria cut in. "They may not have been the only weapons the other Generals hid there."

The sound of demon rifle fire echoed from the starboard passageway.

"They are here!" Zaria shouted and bolted to the fighting. Her escorts grunted and followed.

CHAPTER THIRTY

Across legends, histories, and the lore of civilizations that spanned stars, most giants were seen as lumbering, heavy, and slow. Anguhr was certainly heavy, and, just as Ursuhr, huge. However, his agility was remarkable. It was a useful trait as he leapt to avoid Ursuhr's maul. He somersaulted across the flaming, chaos of hull beams. His hands grabbed the handle of his axe. His body spun to avoid the impact of the maul's head where his own had just been. Anguhr leapt to his feet. The axe blade again searched for a limb, neck, or body to cleave apart. Ursuhr's own speed became important to keeping himself whole.

Solok watched his leading strike wings near Ursuhr's vast warship. The Generals Anguhr and Ursuhr looked small on the top hull. They also maneuvered to strike each other. Advanced teams from Ursuhr's horde flew out to engage the staggering number of attacking demons. On the top of the hull, Anguhr's axe and Ursuhr's maul collided. The impact caused another shockwave to blast the hull and radiate out. It struck the demon formations and knocked them away from the ship. Another clash of the Generals' weapons hit them again.

Solok commanded from the lead strike wings. The following mass of demon formations blocked the sight of their own ship and space behind them. Solok considered his attack. An assault along the ship's top was impossible while the Generals fought. Taking the bridge would end the battle more swiftly. Getting there through enemy horde and rampaging Generals would be brutal. Again, Solok smiled. He raced his horde straight to the closest side. Of course, that was where the opposing demons emerged in force. There, a wave of anger shot towards Solok's forces. It was the massed rifle fire of Ursuhr's horde.

On Anguhr's ship, Zaria ran to the sound of the rifle reports. Motion was so much slower in a physical form, yet it provided the interaction necessary to achieve her plans and save creation. Even when the interactions were often violent. She found more violence ahead. Two units of demons fought each other, as she expected. Yet seeing it was still surreal. What eased the strangeness was an obvious difference in combatants. The insurgent demons' skin and thorns held an odd, dark hue that absorbed light and made them so black they appeared as three-dimensional shadows. Ideas flashed through her head as quickly as fired bullets. Ursuhr or his engineers had taken the concept of camouflage technology and applied it to a new species of demons. She would never have expected innovation from a General. Yet mental flexibility allowed Anguhr to endure an extreme emotional shock. Zaria felt dread when considering other permutations of the technology she had dispersed from Asherah and other Builder sites. It also made clear how dire things would become if Ursuhr won. His innovative side proved a greater threat than his ability to detect life Zaria had hidden.

The insurgent demons had pinned a small squad of Anguhr's guards at a passage junction only a sprint down from the bridge. They fired a smaller, more compact version of the demon rifles. They also bore the same style of powerful grenades on belts bonded across their chests. One insurgent pulled a grenade and grinned as he prepared to throw it. Instead his arm came free at the end of Zaria's sword. The demon turned to look at the severed site at his shoulder. Zaria's sword quickly slid in and out of his darkened hide. His body lost its covering darkness as he fell dead. His comrades were cut down by Wahx and his unit that moved up behind Zaria.

"This team was heading for the bridge." Zaria's eyes flashed. She dropped the now inert grenade and demon arm beside the rest of its body.

"A natural, strategic move." Wahx droned as he kicked the mostly intact insurgent Zaria had killed. The ones he and his unit had slain were blasted pieces scattered down the passageway. He turned to eye the trapped demons that now emerged from the adjacent passageway.

"Wahx, we must move more quickly," Zaria knelt and looked at the demon. "Let me take some of your squad while you and these survivors sweep the passages and link up with more of General Anguhr's forces."

"Proxis will—" Wahx began.

"He cannot detect these enemy demons." Zaria cut in. "We must engage them in line of sight."

"Yes," Wahx growled. "Then, agreed. Sirc, Kire, go with her. Fight. Protect our Lord's ship!"

"All of us will." Zaria nodded.

Wahx squinted at Zaria. He then quickly bolted down the ship. Two demons stayed behind as all others followed Wahx down the passageway. Zaria took them to be Kire and Sirc. Rifle fire sounded in their direction almost instantly. Her two assigned demons began to move toward it.

"No," Zaria said. "Follow me."

Zaria ascended from the bridge and onto the flaming red expanse of the top hull. She thought of Anguhr fighting on his own aboard Ursuhr's ship against that General himself. Her own battle on this ship would likely not be as frightful. She changed her mind when bullets ripped through space and flames towards her. The large, high velocity rounds pelted her emerald armor and then burst as molten flecks from the energy she surged ahead of herself. She employed new defenses imagined since fighting Xuxuhr. She expanded her field to protect Kire and Sirc who emerged behind her. The infiltrators were surprisingly close and fast. They moved across the hull and between the gaps in the burning beams like snakes through a cratered landscaped.

Sirc and Kire took flattened positions beside the crouching Zaria and aimed their rifles.

"Hold your fire until I—" Zaria never finished her order.

Insurgent grenades blew all three of them backward. Sirc and Kire but were blown off the hull by a new assault of grenades. The larger Zaria rolled, and still gripped her sword.

"Gin!" She shouted. She immediately heard his reply in her mind.

'I understand. Hold on!' Gin replied over their thought wavelengths. 'They are already closing in!'

On the bridge screens, Gin and Proxis observed Zaria crawling her way to a hull gap as a sheet of insurgent bullets struck her energy shield. The still smaller Gin turned to Proxis.

"Hold out your hand." Gin said with a slight bow of his head to Proxis.

Proxis glared at Gin but slowly raised his right palm and sharp fingers to him.

Gin leapt and fell into Proxis' hand in his form of a ball of amber. Proxis then heard Gin's thoughts within his own brain.

'I do this as an act of trust. You can crush me as this ball.' Gin transmitted. 'Now please return that trust. If you or this ship is destroyed,

219

then so am I. What I do now is for you, your General, as well as my own world. I only ask for a few moments of trust.'

Gin still had a full range of senses. He detected Proxis' left hand reach up and hover over the key that fired the secondary batteries.

Proxis saw the reason for Gin's dramatic gesture materialize over the hull near Zaria.

"A few moments?" Proxis asked as a challenge.

'Perhaps more.' Gin replied as thought. 'At least until victory.'

Proxis gave a low growl, but his left hand moved away from the dais.

Seconds before, Zaria had watched insurgent demons fire and skillfully maneuver closer to the bridge. She hoped Wahx and his units had killed all of Ursuhr's new breed inside the ship. Here, she was the last defense. She gripped her sword and prepared to leap. The leading insurgent unit was ready for her attack and raised their compact guns. Then, an unseen force crushed them against the burning hull beams.

Zaria sighed in relief. Flames of the crimson aegis flattened wider. They whipped beneath an unseen, circular mass. One of Zaria's comet ships from the Iron Work became visible. Its tail slashed reeling insurgent demons. The comets were not merely chariots as Zaria had claimed. They were warrior transports. The second ship hovered near, but stayed concealed. Without battle cry or need for orders, fresh teams of archers, gulos, and two giants leapt from it. They appeared to jump straight into existence near the middle of the invisible comet's hull. Eden's warriors attacked the insurgents and quickly adapted to the hull's fiery, gap filled battlefield. The second comet became visible at the end of the insurgent force. More of Zaria's forces entered the battle from the first comet. They surrounded the insurgents. The demons did not surrender, nor were they offered the chance. Zaria charged and joined the fight.

On a vaster scale, Solok's battle also neared descent from tactical combat to mere annihilation. Before the demons clashed close in, each horde faced the other's fire. The loud burring of rifle fire was unheard. Solok's strike leaders and their tiers of lieutenants drew their swords and thrust them forward. The swords deployed force shields. The formations flew forward under protection. However, the enemy also used the same if rarely needed tactic. They exploited gaps and slight separations in the lines. Solok's demons fell victim to well placed shots and hits from massed salvos. More of Ursuhr's demons emerged from the side of his ship. The fire intensified. It was time for the next stage of Solok's plan.

Solok thought the order and it became the impulse of all demons. Behind his leading strike wings, the horde arced like an inverted wave with the new crest curving below the keel and the mass of Ursuhr's emerging demons. Solok kept advancing. Behind and below him his wave continued to flow into the thick of Ursuhr's horde.

As Kalak feared, his forces were outmaneuvered. There was no retreat as their armory, home, and place of birth came under attack. All was left no was to fight. It was all demons ever knew. However, Kalak had never known a battle where victory was uncertain. The vibration of his constantly firing gun became his primary sensation.

The demons on the crest of Solok's inverted wave opened fire. Their attack diverted and suppressed the withering streams of bullets streaking towards Solok's lead forces. The surviving demons of his feint also advanced. Smaller units exchanged fire as the opposing forces closed the distance. Each horde began to see the dark of each others' serpent eyes.

As fighting continued on both ships, their two Generals continued their attempts to destroy each other. Their duel had raged along the top hull across the ship's great length. Another shockwave assaulted the red aegis as their weapons clashed. Most watchers would have wished the two massive combatants to suffer fatigue or at least pause to ease their tired eyes. Anguhr and Ursuhr never suffered exhaustion, not even under the great weight of pride. However, Anguhr began to suffer boredom. He allowed Ursuhr's maul to sail passed his helmet. Instead of striking at Ursuhr with his massive axe, he punched Ursuhr in the snout. In their close proximity, Anguhr had noticed it looked newly healed and decided to restart the process. Ursuhr leapt back and roared. Anguhr stepped back, and spoke.

"We can kill each other, or chose another end. One not in death."

"We are death!" Ursuhr barked and clutched his maul tightly. "We are annihilation."

"But we can be something else," Anguhr's voice rolled the flames under his boots. "We can seek a new path. A new destiny for ourselves and our hordes."

"My horde only lives to serve me! As does yours." Ursuhr countered. "That is our destiny. We rule them. Our ruler sits in Hell. No other place survives her wrath. There is no other existence but to serve Hell."

"I now serve myself. Hell has no power over me!" Anguhr shouted.

"Only a fool believes thoughts of madness," Ursuhr said in a strangely calm tone. "You may be strong Anguhr, as am I. But we— nothing—is stronger than the Dark Urge. To rebel is to die. Bring death. Or suffer it. There is nothing more to existence."

"No." Anguhr felt his ire returning. "I will not serve a thing I have seen is built on lies. I *will* create a new path."

"A new destiny? Ha!" Ursuhr yelled. "We are meant to be as we are made. We are demons. Generals of hordes. But we are still the Dark Urge's servants. She is the greatest force of creation. Why would I rebel? I am scion of the power. With her I stand. Without her, I would not exist!"

Anguhr rejected Ursuhr's words with a shake of his head. "There are other means of creation. Her power is not infinite, and our purpose is a lie. For me, it is at an end."

"And so you seek peace?" Ursuhr asked. "Pathetic. Ridiculous! When no enemies are left to conquer, we will simply fight ourselves. You know this. Do not doubt it. Now, this respite is the only boon I grant before I kill you. It is what our creator deems. I will fight to win. I am *your* destroyer."

Ursuhr flexed his shoulders while gripping his maul handle. His metallic-toned hide began to shine. He skin heated and then glowed as hot metal. His eyes became lit and brighter than Anguhr's own. The atmosphere rising from the ship's interior crackled as burned against him. His rage and passion had sparked another level of power inside him as Xuxuhr had shown on the Iron Work. The transformation startled Anguhr, but he held back any display of shock.

"Soon, you will be less than dust." Anguhr said and raised his axe.

The glowing Ursuhr roared.

Maul and axe collided once more. Sparks and flecks shot from the head of Ursuhr's maul. If the Generals could not be fatigued, their weapons could be.

Ursuhr took Anguhr's example. He feinted a maul swing and let Anguhr commit to the counter blow. Anguhr's axe cut nothing until it struck the flaming hull. Its blade buried among the beams. Too deep. Anguhr released the handle and flung himself out of the path of Ursuhr's maul. Its head still made a glancing strike at the side of his helmet. Sparks flew from the blow. The edge of the maul cut a crease in the black steel shell. Anguhr fell against the burning beams of the ship as Ursuhr raised his maul to deliver the final blow as he did against the last Titan. But Anguhr's head had moved. The maul head struck the hull beams. Anguhr's boot heals hit Ursuhr's right knee. He staggered back and fought for balance.

Ursuhr roared from the denied victory more than from pain. Still, he stepped a fraction of a second more slowly to strike again. Anguhr moved with speed. He rose and grabbed Ursuhr's forearms before he could swing his maul down with full force. Ursuhr was now surprised. The flames that always lit Anguhr's eyes now spread across his entire body. He burned like the hull in brighter hues of fire. Each General had pushed the

222

other hard. Now their common heritage and infernal power came to the fore.

"If we are not brothers, we are equals." Anguhr grunted out his words as he grappled against Ursuhr's strength, "That is the only salute I will give to you, *uncle*!"

Ursuhr grunted in confusion but focused to free himself from Anguhr's grip. He glowed brighter. Anguhr spun and flipped the molten-skinned Ursuhr into the hull. Anguhr then sprinted and tore his axe free. Ursuhr leapt up and swung his maul. Anguhr swung his axe in a tight circle. Its blade struck the maul's handle. A sharp, metallic sound came from the point of contact. The maul head and most of the handle hit the hull.

Ursuhr had the slimmest fraction of a second to see the cut shaft in his hands before ducking into a crouch to dodge the end of Anguhr's axe handle. He thrust his own handle fragment into Anguhr's burning left side. Anguhr roared in pain, but Ursuhr had no time to smile. The center between Anguhr's axes blades swung down and knocked Ursuhr near the base of the top pincer arm of his ship's main drive.

Ursuhr shook himself. He then quickly rolled just the head of his maul sailed passed his skull. It hit the hull and smashed through it. The hurled maul ripped through the aft region and exploded out where the ship and pincer fused. Masses of burning steel and hull beams blasted into space and tumbled in the maul head's wake. The debris rolled into darkness as the ship sailed on. Only half of the structure attaching the pincer arm survived. Ursuhr jumped to a standing position but instantly ducked again as Anguhr's axe flew towards him. It was not aimed at Ursuhr. It hit the same location as the maul head. Another, larger explosion of kinetic force severed the pincer arm. The massive structure wrenched free from the hull on impact. An unseen force appeared to pull away the twisting arm. The force was the continued forward thrust. A tremendous white flash sparked at the pincer arm's contact with the star-like drive as it ripped free. The entire ship groaned and shuddered. Ursuhr and Anguhr steadied themselves from the violent waves racing through the dreadnought.

Anguhr pulled the piece of maul handle out from his side. His blood on his armor and hand bubbled in his own fires. He threw the handle into space, and then looked at Ursuhr who looked stunned at the damage to his ship. He faced Anguhr with his molten skin pulled back from his mass of teeth in his bear jaws. Anguhr smiled, and charged.

Their collision sent a shock through the weakened hull and their bodies. Even made from arcane matter and an impossible biology stoked by hellish powers, Anguhr's wound still exploded with blood and pain. Ursuhr struck his shoulders with both fists. Anguhr fell to his knees.

Ursuhr instinctively raised his massive arms overhead to deliver the death blow as if holding his maul. Anguhr slammed his helmet into his gut. Ursuhr reeled back to the ravaged end of his hull. Anguhr threw an upward fist into his jaw.

The blow sent Ursuhr off his feet and spinning end over end. The angle of his trajectory was the course planned by Anguhr. The ability to achieve it was a moment of luck. For Ursuhr, it was death. He glimpsed his doom as he spun. It was his main drive. If he sailed toward the propulsive, aft-most hemisphere, even his General's body would be incinerated and his atoms lost in the plume. Ursuhr headed for the energy gathering side facing the ship. He felt the intense flow of radiation before his back struck the brilliant, blue engine. He exploded just as a powerful warhead. The tremendous blast warped the star-like drive. It flexed. Waves traveled across and through the sphere and its energies. It exploded.

CHAPTER THIRTY-ONE

The flash triggered and instinct within all the fighting demons. They swiftly tucked into balls and turned their curled wings to the blast. It saved many, including Solok. Kalak was caught and sundered in a sideward wave of the ship's burning beams. Martis saw the blast on his screens just before all systems died. His back faced the shock front shredding his ship. He had no wings and no time. The blasted fragments of Ursuhr's throne struck and crushed him.

Proxis and Gin saw Ursuhr's main drive explode and his ship demolished by the blast. It was a spectacular destruction. Unlike Sutuhr's ship, the sudden annihilation was unexpected. Gin watched the flash dim and the debris continue to fly out into space on the screens. Proxis turned his head and looked through the bulkhead toward the actual location of the blast.

Proxis had put aside his inner confusion to continue serving General Anguhr. His future as a rebel, and more importantly one without the Dark Urge felt strange and uncertain. The leadership of his General had given him stability and purpose. Now he wondered if his future would be without his Lord and leader. Again he considered the impossible. He wondered if Anguhr was dead.

Zaria's sword split the last of the Ursuhr's insurgent demons. The spray of acrid blood eclipsed the flash of Ursuhr's spectacular death. The blood fell as his ship shattered from aft to bow in a brilliant instant. Zaria was stunned. The destruction of Ursuhr meant Asherah and all the worlds his discovery threatened were safe. She felt relief, and then a swell of regret. Zaria wondered where Anguhr had stood when the ship blew apart.

She knew he led from the front. He would be the cause and be close to the explosion.

The blast was seen and felt across the system. Its greatest impact was in Hell. The world of fire and steel shook, but not from the blastwave. Ursuhr's mother screamed. The Generals were the instruments of her rage. They were the projection of her fear. They served as the sharp edge to jab into a shadowed lair and then kill whatever stirred. To the Dark Urge, the universe was that lair. But she was the shadow. Her specter was vast and stretched from the deepest black in her heart. She had always feared something striking down from outside. Despite her fear and rage spread so far into creation by the war, that fear of something now seemed more potent than ever before.

Her children, those she made from herself, were gone. Anguhr she remade. He still remained his true mother's son. He lived when her life was over. In defiance of great power, he gained power of his own. Eventually he made his own terms for life, just as his mother. However, he went missing at the end of his greatest battle. Just as his mother. The age of the Generals—of the war—was done.

Hell was a complex system. The Dark Urge was a powerful force but a fragile mind. When a complex system develops a fault, the failure can be spectacular. Such was the war. Now it ended with the last of her children as ash on the crest of a shockwave. The war had failed. Now, so did all that power, and the mind that set it to sinister motion.

Anguhr floated in space. His fire had ebbed. He was burned by the blast and bled into the warm gap between his still body and armor. He was alone. Only the cold of the vacuum held him. He was not even a reliable companion to himself. His consciousness dawned and then darkened. His mind was lost in black when familiar red flames arrived beneath him, and arms as bright as sunlight took hold of his legs and pulled him into his ship.

Anguhr awoke, fully. He was on his ship. The aegis burned on the ceiling above him He was in a chamber near the main armory. He lay on a slab of raised deck plating. For the first time since leaving Hell, his armor was stripped from his body. He felt a breeze across his naked skin. It was annoying. He reached to where Ursuhr had stabbed him. The wound was gone. And no scar. Disappointing. He noticed an odd, yellow light shimmering behind him. Then Zaria stepped to his right side. She smiled.

"I could not tend your wounds until Proxis tasked demons to be medical engineers." Zaria said. "They concurred with me. And then we could strip and treat you. This must be the first time a General suffered enough wounds to require attention. We had to create a sick bay from a rifle locker."

"My ship and horde—" Anguhr started. His voice cracked and sounded weak. It was more annoying than the breeze. Or being naked.

"All is well. You are still General Anguhr." Zaria said. "Where I found you, for once there was no destruction. You were at peace. And so was the space around you."

"You wish that to be prophetic." Anguhr said and rose into a sitting position.

"I do." Zaria added.

"I wish you to bring me my armor," Anguhr's tone was again deep and commanding. "Now."

Zaria sighed, but went to retrieve Anguhr's only clothes.

Anguhr looked at his hands and flexed his fingers. He looked down at his feet. He flexed his toes. He was not sure he had ever seen them before.

Anguhr entered his bridge in fully restored helmet and armor. Zaria followed. Gin nodded to him. Solok and Proxis bowed. Anguhr sat on his throne and spoke to his Ship Master.

"Proxis, I will send a message. Target Hell, but make anyone able to receive it."

"Transmission channels stand ready, Lord."

"Dark Urge, hear me. Hear the son of your first General. Hear the one you renamed Anguhr. It is said my father was a conqueror, but that he held a trait called honor. Very well. I will honor this father I never knew, Sargon, king of an interstellar empire. I will show you honor, Dark Urge, queen of fear and ruler of Hell. I will let you live, as you allowed me life. But I will not change you. I will not subvert you to my will. I cannot. But if you send another General against me or attack me in any other way, I will return to Hell. Fear that. I am the son of your greatest warrior, and the greatest living warrior in the galaxy. And I have the means to destroy you. If I come back to Hell, I will kill you grandmother. I will turn Hell into ash. I can do that. I am Azarak, son of Sargon and Azuhr. I am General Anguhr. And I am what you made me. I am the Destroyer."

Anguhr expected no reply. He received none. For several moments, silence and the low rumble of the ship were all the noise in the universe. Then, Zaria drew a breath.

"An impressive, speech, General." Zaria said. "I wonder what you will do with your freedom."

"What I can," Anguhr answered. "What I must. I will make sure my demons live, and thrive. They have served well, and I will need their service now, even more."

"And I dare ask, how?" Zaria raised her palms as part of an entreating shrug.

"I will return to the stars and make fractured, conquered systems into an empire. Unlike my father's empire, mine will not fall." Anguhr spoke with great confidence. "I will fuse sundered planets into new worlds. Those who join me will become stronger."

Anguhr lifted off his helmet and looked intently at Zaria.

"So begin the galaxy's new era," Anguhr continued. "Note it well, old sunlight. You have seen history. See more. Record the tale of a demon General who renounced Hell, and became a king."

Zaria nodded affirmation, and then took another, deeper breath.

"First," Anguhr said, "we search for my mother's sword. And my axe."

Anguhr's crimson warship sailed into the black, away from Hell. Zaria thought of the Xa'rol arks. Their time to descend back into the galaxy may now come sooner. She would watch Anguhr. Her strategies to preserve life and end Hell's irresistible devastation had intersected with slightly altered means and unexpected allies. Nevertheless, time and tide had turned from oblivion. Life would survive.

Screaming became laughter. The laughter became frantic, manic, and then childlike.

Sunlight. It seemed so long since the spider felt the caress of the bright, yellow sun across her abdomen. There was only a slight breeze. The day was warm. All things moved more quickly on a warm day. More things flew. Today the spider might sate her hunger.

From the center of her web, the spider looked out across a perfect, mown lawn. But her eyes could only focus on things close to her, as in a place on prey for the killing bite. To the spider, the lawn was only a vast expanse of green. A quick, blurred shape bounded into view and bobbed in a circle out in the green plane. The moving shape made high tones and occasional squeals. The sounds carried across the air and made benign waves through the web. Otherwise, how could the spider hear? Somehow the spider knew the waves were the sounds of a child playing. The child was a little girl.

The web shook. Something big, something fat, had flown into it. The spider moved with precision across arcs of silk and gripped the head of the thrashing dragonfly. The spider bit. The thrashing stopped. The spider saw the green lawn and the yellow sun mirrored as small, constrained images in the dragonfly's wide, reflective eyes. The spider

228

began to cast silk over the sun to capture it and the perfect, sunny day. Impossible.

In the reflections of the dragonfly's eyes, the spider noticed more than what she could see far away. At the edge of the green plane she saw another little girl. She was whole and bright. This girl was quiet. She was hiding from the other, bounding child. The silent girl stood near an odd, tall object. It could, perhaps, be a tree trunk. And so it became just that. It was a strange, rigid tree with a black, hexagonal trunk. Its branches, like the hiding girl, were luminous. The branches extended from something within the oddly geometric trunk. Something of great power. The spider doubted she could make a web in those branches. They were arcs of energy, not really branches. Many things were not real. It became obvious to the spider that she was dreaming. But she was safe. It was a sense she enjoyed. Like sunlight, she had not felt it in a very long time.

This was a simple dream of a simple spider. But spiders do not dream. Not simple, normal spiders. And the last sunny day on a green, sunlit world was so long ago. That sun had grown huge. It became red, and caged. Only very, very old spiders dream. Those spiders have lived so long, they have evolved within themselves and their minds are no longer simple. Neither are their dreams. And then they wake into nightmares.

The Great Widow awoke. First she saw a vast expanse of black. Then she heard the sound of a child. A little girl was playing. The energies of the Forge had died down. The radiation was nominal. The Great Widow moved her eight legs and crept from her entangled web into the greater breadth of Hell. She found the Dark Urge. The mistress of fear and war had reassumed the form of the little girl missing half her skull. As this girl, the Dark Urge frolicked across the heat and very old machines. The Great Widow knew her mistress had finally, fully succumbed to madness. The spider said nothing, and watched the strange girl play. The child seemed to have no grasp of the power she could summon. Indeed, she seemed as weak as a true human girl. If the Great Widow was patient, and indeed she was, perhaps the Dark Urge would eventually change into a dragonfly.

In the beginning was the war. The war turned against Hell. From its fires rose a new force with the power to destroy Hell. Suppressed history could not prevent held a personal revelation. The truth changed the fate of creation. A new kingdom dawned. In the end, the supremacy of darkness lay destroyed.

ABOUT THE AUTHOR

Bruce S. Larson is the author of many short stories. The <u>NIGHTMARES AND OTHER VICES</u> Horror/SF collections are available as two e-books or one print edition. The <u>WITHIN AND BEYOND</u> collections feature SF & Fantasy stories and are also available in both formats. With <u>BEYOND APOCALYPSE,</u> Bruce answers the often asked question: when will your novel be published?

Even after writing a book with one version of Hell, Bruce does not like hot weather. A shame, since his car has no AC. Bruce enjoys the outdoors, especially where there is cool water and shade. He finds plenty of both in his native Pacific Northwest. He hopes your world stays intact, and any giants you encounter don't use apocalyptic weapons. Preferable giants on hot, sunny days include air-conditioned skyscrapers and shade offering trees. Although, beware Widows great and small in the corridors and branches.

More of the Author's fiction, occasional observation of spacetime, life, and combating darkness are at his website: <u>thewritebruce.com</u>

Look for more books from World Line One Press in the future.